GRAY WOLVES
AND
WHITE DOVES

JOHN D BALIAN

ISBN: 1439267618
ISBN-13: 9781439267615
LCCN: 2009912830

Printed by CreateSpace, An Amazon.com Company
CreateSpace, Charleston, SC

DEDICATION

ACKNOWLEDGMENTS

I feel blessed and am forever grateful for the advice and wise guidance provided by Arlene S. Trust, John Benjamin Sciarra, CB Owen Hughes, William Greenleaf, Tom Topalian, and Dennis Oberhofer.

Special thanks to my wife, Sosi Balian – without her support and encouragement this book would still be only a dream.

Sweden
BALTIC SEA
Almanya
(Germany)
ISTANBU
SEA of MARMARA
N
MEDITERRANEAN
SEA
DjO

Russia
BLACK SEA
CASPIAN SEA
Georgia
Armenia
Azerbaijan
MT. ARARAT
Turkey
DIYARBEKIR
Iran
Syria
Cyprus
Iraq
BEIRUT
Lebanon
JERUSALEM
Israel
Jordan
Egypt

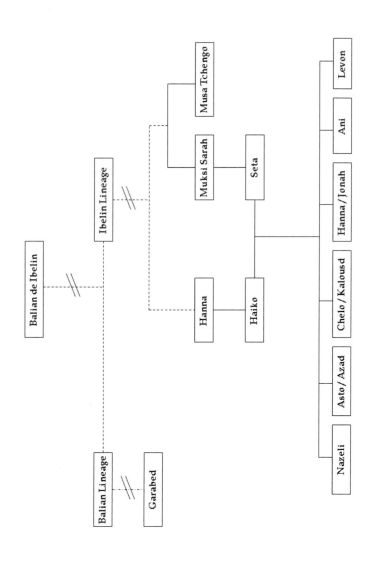

PROLOGUE

Paris-Orly International Airport
Friday, August 18, 1978

A fugitive with no home, no means of escape and no hope, sixteen-year-old Jonah Ibelinian was determined to carry out the plot entrusted to him. He was destined to end the future of so many and everything they held dear, as it had been snatched from him a decade before. An audacious plan it certainly was; and the cause was just.

He positioned himself at a safe distance from the theater where he would play his part. Leaning against a column, he took special but discreet note of a pair of Gendarmes as they strolled by, each man wearing the distinctive de Gaulle cap, one swinging his baton, the other almost comical in his pomposity as he casually rapped it against his left palm. As soon as they had disappeared around a corner, he shifted his attention to the clock visible above the line forming ahead—anything to avoid acknowledging the passengers and their companions milling around him, young and old, well groomed and unkempt, drab and colorful, all buzzing with preflight anxiety. How pitifully oblivious they all were. Anxious to board a flight--their final journey--certain to end in an inferno.

He pondered his next move and shuddered in anticipation. Shortly, Vrej, the leader of the operation, would bring him the suitcase, after which he would join the line at the Turkish Airlines ticket counter. His palms felt damp and his heartbeat was erratic.

But the cause was just—wasn't it? Well, no use doubting himself or the mission now. To gain courage or perhaps to justify the mayhem he was about to unleash, Jonah squeezed shut his eyelids and tried to recall his mother's beautiful image. All he saw, instead, was a child stranded on a rooftop, confused, scared, and vulnerable. He shook off the memories and tried to concentrate on the task.

I am committed, he reminded himself emphatically, before focusing on the queue in front of him. He studied the people lined up ahead, spotting a middle-aged man with unruly hair and bushy eyebrows who reminded him of his father and, nearby, a waif-like teenage girl, perhaps his sister's age, all legs and arms and hardly any curves. There was an attractive woman too, probably pushing forty, who, despite her weary gaze, looked elegant in a conservative pantsuit, a slim bag slung over her shoulder. Was she a professor? A businesswoman or administrator of some kind? At the head of the line, shrouded in all-enveloping Muslim-Turkic garb, stood a beleaguered mother, who was struggling to contain her rowdy brood of half a dozen young children, while desperately trying to calm the infant she carried in her arms by rocking him to sleep.

They remained blissfully unaware of what was to come, mired deep in the here and now, focused on the tiniest of details, *inconsequential* details that, in a mere flash, would cease to matter at the appointed instant when their aircraft had attained an altitude of five thousand feet. He would be responsible. He would end it all. And the irony was that they didn't even know of his existence, let alone his presence on the scene.

Once again, he closed his eyes, tried to picture his mother, and failed. No photographs of her had ever existed.

No trace whatsoever remained of her, not a single memento to remind him of the person she had been. She had simply been plucked away and only the wistful images, held tight in his soul, had survived. Usually, with some effort, he could conjure up an image of how she used to be, even if it was a mere semblance of the woman she once was. Not today. All he could see were the faces at the counter: the overweight man; the frail, lost-looking teenager; the delicate woman; the distraught mother, battling confusion and frustration to gather up her young. He searched the faces of the others in the queue, hoping to find someone he could hate enough to justify his actions. His scrutiny quickly turned inward. And looking within himself, he found only hesitation. Doubt. Fear.

He closed his eyes tightly—he was desperate to blot out their faces—but the din pressed in around him.

So many people.

He labored for breath, the way he had not so many Easters ago at the Holy Sepulcher Church back in Jerusalem, when he and hundreds of others had been swept up by the bloody fervor unleashed during the flash-of-fire ritual.

An acrid taste filled his mouth. Despite strict orders to the contrary and at the risk of endangering the whole scheme, he bolted toward the men's room, feeling more nauseous with each step. As he raced down the concourse, he caught sight of Korvat and waved off the nervous, quizzical glance coming from his backup, slowing down just enough to whisper, "I'm going to be sick!" before pressing on.

He held off his roiling stomach long enough to find a vacant stall, rush in, and slam the door shut behind him. He spent the next few seconds—agonizingly slow ones, further prolonged by a steep drop in his blood pressure as stars swirled around him—hunched over the toilet bowl. When he was done at last, he remained on his knees for another minute or so. Then he pulled himself upright with great effort and staggered out to the sink to rinse out his mouth and splash his face with cold, soothing water.

His thoughts turned to the people waiting to board the flight. Why had they been chosen? Who were they? What had they done? He wasn't sure he had the courage—or was it cowardice?—to do it.

"*It-oghlu-it!*" a gruff-voiced man cursed in Turkish, startling Jonah.

"Ouch!" a young child yelped.

Jonah turned in time to see the door of another stall fly open and a heavyset man emerge, dragging a little boy behind him. The man yanked the child by the arm and swore at him. "I told you to go to the bathroom in the hotel!"

The little boy whimpered in pain as tears flowed down his blotchy cheeks.

Jonah felt a brief flash of certainty; *I hope this child abuser is on my flight.* But he regretted the thought the moment his eyes returned to the child who, in all likelihood, shared the man's itinerary. He continued gazing at the boy and thought: *What a beautiful child!* With his curly blond hair and blue eyes, the pale little boy looked nothing like the brute's dark complexion, jet-black stubby hair, and facial features reminiscent of Central Asia.

The boy's tear-filled eyes met Jonah's. They seemed to be pleading for help.

"Stop crying!" the man snapped and crisply gave the boy's right cheek the back of his hand. The boy's already flushed face now glowed with the mark left behind.

"I will beat these wimpy *gavour* tendencies out of you!"

About to turn and splash some more water on his face, Jonah stopped short. The slur triggered a more wrenching spasm in his abdomen. "Bully," muttered Jonah in Turkish.

The man noticed Jonah and glared at him with disapproval. Brazenly defying the other man's glower, Jonah took a closer look at the boy. His heart seemed to stop in midbeat. *That gavour boy could be my...*

"Enough!" The father roughly wiped the boy's tears before grasping him by the neck and leading him out of the restroom.

Jonah hesitated briefly and then raced after them, ignoring Korvat as he passed by him. *Why did the Turk call the little boy a gavour, an infidel?* After searching the crowd for a moment, he spotted the duo joining a young woman in line at the Turkish Airlines counter.

He looks so much like me. Could it be? I have to know.

He strode with newfound purpose toward the young boy, hoping to reach him before his family got to the front of the queue, but the boy's father intercepted him.

"What do you think you're doing?" the man demanded.

Jonah pointed at the child. "He's my kidnapped—"

"*Siktir!*" the man cursed, swatting Jonah's outstretched arm away.

Jonah swore back at him, adding, "He is not yours!"

"*Siktir! Pezeveng!*" This time, the man gave him a mighty shove, sending him sprawling onto the tiled floor.

The crowd parted around them and even as Jonah lay there, he felt the curious gaze of the Turkish Airlines agent at the counter upon him.

"What's going on?" the man demanded.

His face crimson with embarrassment and the sudden fear of discovery, Jonah scrambled to his feet and turned awkwardly back the way he'd come. *This is crazy. I'm going to get caught.* He hurried off in the direction of the lockers, intent on alerting Vrej. It was time to abort.

But he'd only gone a few yards when a shout from behind stopped him in his tracks.

"Hanna! Hanna Ibelin!"

Jonah turned to face whomever it was that had addressed him by his childhood name. No one had called him by his original name in years, not since he was shipped away. *That was a lifetime ago.* Craning his neck for a good view, Jonah saw an old man deftly part the crowd with his outstretched right arm to reach him in a hurry. He scrutinized the man's wrinkled face with growing amazement.

Impossible.

CHAPTER 1

The village of Palu, Anatolia, summer 1967

"Hanna!"

His father's voice came to him, riding on an echo from beyond the vineyards, past the lush orchards and verdant watermelon patches that surrounded their village, out near the hills that marked the only horizon Hanna had ever known. But Haiko was much closer, perhaps only a hundred feet away. Hanna would have been able to see him too, had it not been for the golden sea of wheat that separated them. Only five years old, the boy was dwarfed by the towering wheat stalks, most of which grew to heights far beyond his reach.

"Coming, Papa!"

With harvest time fast approaching, Hanna had tagged along with his father to the fields for one last inspection of the crops. Although a blacksmith by trade, Haiko could grow anything, as evidenced by the watermelon patch they had walked through to get here. The patch had begun as nothing but seeds buried beneath several neatly spaced mounds of soil; now it was bursting with gargantuan melons too big for Hanna to carry, each one ripening beneath the blazing summer sun.

As for the wheat field in which they now stood, out of each other's sight, but not out of earshot, it too had begun as a vacant plot of land. Hanna, who often took lunch to his father in the fields, would invariably stay back to lend a hand, as he had that

day in early spring, when Haiko planted the field with the help
of the family ox. Despite his tender age and short stride, Hanna
had managed to keep pace with his father, who kept the ox plow-
ing forward by clicking his teeth and murmuring a steady stream
of kind, soothing words by way of encouragement. Eventually,
though, Hanna had dropped behind and endeavored to balance
himself in the straight, deep furrows dug by the plow, while his
father continued on ahead, singing stoutly as he guided the ox.
As soon as the field was readied for sowing, Haiko had slung a
bag over his shoulder and, with each measured step, rhythmically
scooped free a handful of wheat seeds and scattered them in a
wide arc. Now, with summer in full swing, a sea of flaxen wheat
swayed in the gentle afternoon breeze as far as the eye could see.

"Hanno!" his father called out again, using his favorite
term of endearment. "Where are you, lad? Sunday services will
start soon. You promised Uncle Musa you would go to church
with him."

The wheat field, which rose on a gentle incline on the outskirts of the village, was, for Hanna, a source of mystery and
adventure. Here, in the southeastern corner of Turkey, only half
a day's donkey ride to the Syrian border, but centuries away from
Istanbul, there was enough to keep any young boy busy.

One of Hanna's favorite pastimes was attending the village
school, a recent addition to an otherwise medieval setting. All
costs of improvements to the village infrastructure were borne
by the village itself. The Turkish government collected funds
and promised to bring electricity or running water to the village,
but never delivered it. The gendarmerie used to collect funds as
salary for the soldiers' "protection" of the village. The soldiers
themselves seemed to be omnipresent. They kept a watch on the
villagers, scrutinizing their every movement, but, of course, were
nowhere to be seen when marauders from neighboring Muslim

areas descended on this village and plundered it. The regional governor held a series of meetings to collect a large sum for the construction of a road. Months later, work began on paving the road, which, the villagers discovered, ran from Diyarbekir to Midyat, missing the village perimeter by a good kilometer. It was used mainly for transporting troops to areas of conflict with Kurdish guerillas.

The school, however, was a benevolent gift from the interior ministry. The decree was to educate, assimilate, and mold the non-Turkish citizens of Turkey in the image of Mustafa Kemal Ataturk and the beliefs he personified. The slogan bandied about was *Ne mutlu Turkum diyene*: what joy and triumph to declare oneself a Turk. Two Turks were dispatched to teach the village children. One taught the Turkish language and the other, Turkish history. The language teacher was a nice man, while all feared the history teacher. Students were severely punished if the history teacher overheard them speaking any language other than Turkish.

Hanna was too young for school, but he wanted to do everything his oldest brother did. So he constantly followed him to school. Haiko begged the teachers to allow him to attend. They were more than eager to accommodate the boy. A younger mind was easier to mold. Hanna enjoyed the school outings in the fields and hills near the village the most. The teachers led the children in song as they walked and picked fruits and flowers that grew along their paths. It was fun when the language teacher was there and the songs were mostly folk songs. When the history teacher was present, however, the mood was tense. They were instructed to sing martial and patriotic songs in praise of the founder of modern-day Turkey, the great leader Ataturk, and pledge to fight for the fatherland. During the outings, the history teacher focused on identifying non-Turkish ruins. His preoccupation was not to explain the historic background of the cultural remnants they came across, but rather, to order the students to use them for target practice. Particular targets singled out for obliteration were standing walls of ancient edifices, stones bearing non-Turkish inscriptions, and the elaborate carvings of Armenian stone crosses. The history teacher took special pride in teaching his students how to erase the history of nations other than his own by eradicating all evidence of the cultures that had existed previously.

To the displeasure of Uncle Musa, his one-armed great-uncle, Hanna often returned home singing the catchy tune of a particular march: *"Dagh bashini duman almish, yuruyelim arkadash-lar."* There is smoke on the mountaintop; march on, comrades, it exhorted listeners.

A more exciting activity took place in the no-man's-land between their village and the neighboring Muslim one, where rival gangs—Hanna's older brother being a member of one—traded taunts and engaged in skirmishes, armed with sticks and stones. And of course, there was this wheat field, home to rodents, rabbits, and countless nesting partridges.

With each visit to the field, Hanna felt the thrill of immense possibility in the very pores of his skin as he disappeared into the forest of wheat stalks, his only goal being a direct encounter with whatever hidden surprise lurked behind the next thicket. Invariably, he would stumble upon a nest of partridges, and the birds would squawk and sputter before taking to the air, leaving him to explore their nests. When it snowed in the winter, hunting them was as easy as walking up to one and catching it with his bare hands. Hanna would then join his mother in the kitchen and help pluck the bird's feathers in preparation for a family feast.

"Hanno!" his father's voice rang out again.

"Coming!" Hanna repeated as he trudged through the wheat, still hoping for an encounter that would send his heart racing.

"There you are!" his father said happily, as Hanna emerged from the wheat stalks. Haiko was gazing down at him with a smile on his face, the golden highlights in his bushy eyebrows and unruly hair glinting in the late afternoon sun. "How many partridges did you see?"

Hanna cast a glum eye at his surroundings. "None, this time."

"Don't worry, my son," Haiko said, playfully mussing Hanna's curly blond hair. "There is always tomorrow."

"How many did you see, Papa?"

"I saw one flutter away. It had wings longer than the span of your arms. You could have mounted that monstrous bird and it would have flown you to church."

"Drink of it, all of you," the priest droned, raising the chalice heavenward, "for this is my blood of the covenant, which is—"

The doors of the Assyrian church burst open with a loud clatter and ten gun-toting gendarmes stormed inside.

"Out!" roared the sergeant in Turkish as the confused congregants murmured fearfully to one another. "I said, everybody out!"

Standing by a wall in the middle of the church's nave, Musa Tchengo, as Uncle Musa was branded in the village, felt a piercing pain shoot through his severed left arm. He reached reflexively for his stump and then, as his skin paled and his head began to swim, grabbed hold, instead, of his young great-nephew Hanna to steady himself.

"I said, *out!*" The sergeant collared the nearest man, dragged him to the center aisle, and shoved him toward the door with a kick to the rear. "*Gavour kopek!*"

The soldiers hooted and hollered as they repeated the slur, "Infidel dog!"

The congregants remained paralyzed.

"Get out!" screamed the impatient sergeant in his haste to snap them out of their stupor. "Stupid *gavours*," he grumbled, grabbing hold of another man. Dragging him to the center, he mercilessly thrust the butt of his rifle into the man's abdomen. "March, *gavour*, march!"

Before the man could react, the sergeant sent him reeling backward into the hands of waiting soldiers, who guffawed as they dragged him to the door and flung him outside.

The villagers did not need any further encouragement and obediently filed out. Only the shuffling of feet was audible at first, but soon, a woman began to sniffle and a child nearby started crying.

Musa Tchengo clutched Hanna's hand tightly and whispered, "Don't be afraid."

Musa remembered a wintry November afternoon in 1915, when the usually bustling market in the heart of the city of Diyarbekir had become deserted. Fifteen-year-old Movses Ibelin hurried past the Armenian Cathedral of St. Garabed. He consciously averted his gaze from the vultures circling overhead, refusing to look at what hung from the bell tower: the mutilated bodies of the priest and six members of the parish council. He had been told the lynching was intended to serve as a warning to the rest of the community, lest anyone disobey the *firman* or edict posted on the church door. As instructed in telegrams received from the Turkish capital and signed by Interior Minister Talaat Pasha himself, Diyarbekir's regional governor had ordered *all* remaining Armenians of Diyarbekir to join deportation columns in three days' time. Women, children, the aged, and the infirm would soon form wretched caravans snaking through the unforgiving terrain, completely abandoned to the cruelties of a harsh climate, ravenous beasts, and marauding Turkish Army Irregulars alike.

These forced and unrelenting marches only led to a calamitous end. The able-bodied Armenian men of the Ottoman Empire had already perished. They had been rounded up to form labor battalions to "assist" in the war effort against Russia, Great Britain, and France. Musa Tchengo knew from a survivor of one of these work brigades, that the men were slaughtered en masse on the very same roads they had built by the very Turkish army for which they had labored.

Now, in a similar church courtyard, the scowling sergeant menacingly prodded the terrified villagers in the chest with the barrel of his rifle as he paced to and fro. Finally, he stopped in front of the priest. "Turn over the terrorists!" he barked.

The corpses of two soldiers had recently been discovered at a roadside not far from the village. The facts were hardly in dispute; it was common knowledge that the assailants belonged to the PKK, the Kurdish guerilla army. Nevertheless, on the pretext of carrying out a thorough investigation, the gendarmes had come to interrogate the elders of Palu, the only Christian village in the vicinity. The stupefied priest took too long to respond, which only enraged the sergeant.

"Are you deaf?" he screamed. "Turn over the assassins!"

"*Chavoush Effendi*," the priest stuttered, addressing the man as Mr. Sergeant. "We don't know—"

"Liar!" the enraged Turk hissed, striking the priest with the back of his hand.

The priest reeled from the blow and blood began to drip from his left nostril. "We don't—"

"Traitor!" The sergeant spat in his face. "You'll be sorry not to have cooperated." He barked an order to his men and they marched away as quickly as they'd come.

For Musa Tchengo the harrowing past, the crucible of his people, and the shame of victimhood were etched into his stump. Over forty years of festering silence and the tormenting memories associated with the barbaric events to which he had borne witness to, only aggravated the phantom pain. Every day, there was the gnawing sensation that the dismembered arm sprouted protrusions, tentacles, or a mangle of fingers, only to become, yet again, bullet-riddled, afflicted, and gangrenous, needing an agonizing dissection.

Movses, his Armenian name, had been supplanted with the Arabic/Turkish Musa. And though his Kurdish nickname Tchengo, "wings," had survived, it was a cruel and ironic reference to his missing arm, rather than to his swift feet, which he had once put to good use as a messenger boy for a fledgling resistance and to aid hapless deportees. Musa became a muted survivor of a genocide that had taken place during the darkest days of his people's several-millennia-long history.

"I remained silent because I was ashamed," Musa Tchengo acknowledged, later that night. "Now I am ashamed to remain silent."

It sounded more like a rebellion, an act of defiance against his own demons, than an argument with Haiko.

"Silence is not only golden," Hanna's father countered, "but a matter of survival for us."

"The children should know."

"I forbid it."

"The Turks will be back."

"No, Musa. This is a tactic. The *Chavoush* wants a *baksheesh*, a bribe. We'll slip him a few hundred liras and that will be the end of that."

"Till the next time."

The family sat around the fire and listened with growing apprehension. Once Musa Tchengo had left, the children begged their father to tell them a story, hoping to get over the day's trauma.

"Hmm. All right. I will tell you a real story."

Haiko Ibelin, an ever-flowing fountain of mesmerizing stories, was unrivaled in the region when it came to folklore. He spun tales that transported listeners to a dreamworld from which they were reluctant to return, and he often shared amusing anecdotes that left his rapt audience wondering whether the yarn was a true story, a family legend, the figment of his imagination, or a fable he had picked up during his frequent travels to surrounding villages and towns.

Five feet six inches tall, Haiko had an unruly mane of bushy light-brown hair, long eyelashes framing blue-green eyes that lit up with a mischievous gleam, and thick eyebrows that met over the arch of a prominent nose. By trade, he and his brothers were blacksmiths, but Haiko spent less time either at work or at home than at coffeehouses in the different villages and towns, recounting stories and entertaining patrons while playing cards, smoking unfiltered cigarettes, and drinking tea. Four of his children—Nazeli, his older daughter, Asto, his eldest son, Chelo, the middle son, and especially Hanna, his youngest son—longed for the nights when their father would return from the coffeehouses to reveal to them the wonders of the magical places he had visited during his travels. Ani, Haiko's younger daughter and not much more than a toddler, was too young to understand the stories, but the soothing cadence of his voice was reassuring and always lulled her to sleep.

"*Chiroke, Chirvanoke, Khajkhajoke,*" Haiko murmured playfully, beginning that night's story, as he always did, with the same three words. No one knew what the phrase meant. A Kurdish limerick, perhaps, or simple gibberish. Haiko was notorious for inventing nonsensical rhymes that sounded plausible, nonetheless. "I had a good friend named Poke," he went on. "He had land, cows, goats, and a horse. Poke was strong, handsome, and taller than my three boys put together."

"No!" Hanna exclaimed with a giggle of disbelief.

"He was so tall he could not find a suitable girl to marry. He traveled far and wide, even seeking the help of matchmakers, but his situation seemed hopeless. The sadness of his plight weighed on him heavily. One day, Poke accompanied me on a visit to a nearby village. There we stopped to see Rashid, an old acquaintance of mine. Rashid's wife was tall and very beautiful. When Poke saw her, he leaned over and quietly asked me who she was.

"I whispered in his ear, 'She is the daughter of Rashid's father-in-law.'"

Haiko's wife Seta wagged her finger in disapproval. "Now, now, that's very naughty," she admonished him and wistfully went back to rubbing her very pregnant belly.

The boys, on the other hand, laughed heartily.

"For several weeks following the visit," Haiko carried on, "Poke badgered me to mediate on his behalf. Finally, I gave in, but told him that I would not go empty-handed and he should provide me with a roasted lamb to offer Rashid when I visited him." Haiko chuckled merrily.

"What happened? What happened?" Hanna begged impatiently.

"For several weeks, Poke eagerly delivered provisions and gifts intended for Rashid. Only when I asked for a gold watch did he become suspicious and ask the *Mukhtar*, the village alderman, about the daughter of Rashid's father-in-law."

The children chortled with glee.

"Three apples fell from heaven," Haiko said, signaling the end of the story in keeping with Armenian tradition, "an apple for you, an apple for me, and an apple for our ancestors."

After some hand-wringing and polite, but inconsequential Middle-Eastern-style parley, the Turkish sergeant deigned to accept a paltry sum of three hundred liras as a goodwill gesture from the village. "I will not name your village in my report to the army and the Interior Ministry," he reassured the village elders. He then graciously thanked them for their thoughtful suggestion that he keep the money for his troubles. "I must consider the families of the slain troops," he said magnanimously. "In any case, from now on, you have my word that your village, your animals, your homes, and your lives will come under my protection."

With that promise in hand, the villagers insisted he accept two hundred liras more.

The extortion of an additional two hundred liras by the sergeant would shield the village against any punitive action by the authorities for three months, one of the longest periods marked by peace in recent memory.

Chapter 2

"Hanna! Hanna?"

Hanna was chasing chickens in the courtyard when he over-heard the muffled cries from the kitchen. He ran in and saw his mother doubled over, sweating profusely; she was grimacing in pain and clutching her belly.

"Please run and fetch that witch," she gasped in between groans.

"The witch?"

"The witch! That snarly old woman who will help with the baby."

Hanna dashed out and sprinted to the midwife's house on the outskirts of the village near the cemetery.

"Come quick. My mother is in pain!"

The gnarled old woman needed no convincing. Once they arrived at the Ibelin courtyard, the midwife and her assistants shooed Hanna away and went inside. Hanna went and fetched his friend from the neighboring house. The two boys climbed an embankment, located an opening that served as the window to the stable, and settled down to watch the developments without being discovered. Inside the stable, in the midst of piles of hay, Seta lay facing their vantage point. Sharp yelps of pain occasionally punctuated her moans. Despite the layers of clothing in which she was enveloped, her protruding belly looked enormous above her outstretched legs. Her arms were slung around the shoulders of two attendants who skillfully kept her upright.

The midwife knelt in front of Seta, murmuring constantly, and occasionally reaching up and even disappearing under the garments. Upon receiving commands from the midwife, the attendants skillfully positioned Seta on a bed of straw, lifted her heels, and pushed the knees against the swollen abdomen. Perspiring continuously, Seta appeared exhausted, grimacing with pain as she tried to suppress her whimpering. The midwife issued another set of instructions, and the attendants picked up Seta's neatly braided hair and inserted a good amount in the laboring woman's mouth. She bit hard on her hair and bore down; tears of agony streamed down her cheeks. Suddenly, the boys saw a gush of yellowish fluid, mixed with blood, running down Seta's feet and washing all over the midwife.

The old woman stepped aside and muttered a curse. "This doesn't portend well," she said. "The bag is broken and the good luck has vanished."

"Ohhhh, please," Seta begged through clenched teeth and a mouthful of hair. She was in no mood to listen to prophesies of doom.

"You must baptize it on the fortieth day," the midwife went on relentlessly. "Light a candle at church from now till the fortieth day and seek the intercession of the Virgin Mary. You must not celebrate the birth of this child until after the baptism."

Seta groaned in pain.

"Promise me that you'll do all I've told you before the child sees the light of this sinful world, or it will suffer a terrible bereavement."

"Yes! Yes! I promise," came the muffled voice before it contorted into a moan.

"May the Mother of God shed light and forgiveness. Now push as hard as you can."

Relief came with a final grunt. The smiling midwife lifted a slimy, bloody baby from under the clothing.

The midwife heard the gasps of the two boys and looked up, startled, toward the window. Before she could abuse them roundly, they had jumped down the embankment and made a run for it.

One night, gunfire shattered the tranquility of the village. The reverberating shots jolted Hanna awake and, for a brief moment, he thought it was time to celebrate the arrival of his infant brother Levon. He rubbed his eyes and realized he was outdoors. He stared up at the starry sky in bewilderment.

"Father?" he whispered.

There was no answer, but as his eyes adjusted to the darkness, Hanna remembered where he was: in his family's courtyard, where everyone had slept for the last several nights to escape the stifling heat indoors. He glanced over at the spot in the courtyard where his father had bedded down and saw that he was gone. So too was his mother. Accustomed to the noise of sporadic gunfire erupting in the distance, his brothers and sisters still lay fast asleep. He saw his great-uncle in the distance, by the door to the courtyard, sitting cross-legged and still as a statue. His right arm clutched a rifle, its barrel resting on his lap.

Hanna knew that bandits from distant villages had come to cause trouble. Turks, his father called them. Kurds. Muslims. He had met such men in the daylight when they came to Palu to trade, barter, or conduct official government business. They brought their horses to the family's blacksmith shop for shoeing, and Hanna often peered at them from behind a scrap heap, watching, studying, searching for what it was precisely that made them alien and dangerous. They seemed friendly enough and not so very different from the people he knew, barring the language they spoke. But at night, with everything shrouded in darkness, such men were to be feared. They came to the village not to buy or trade or proclaim the latest government directives, but to kidnap, rob—and even kill.

Prowling Turkish and Kurdish gangs attacked with regularity and impunity. Since the government's indifference to the plight of the villagers was tantamount to sanctioning the raids, the villagers were forced to resort to self-defense, with Hanna's father frequently at the helm. Whether day or night, the moment gunfire crackled in the distance or other signs of an assault became apparent, off he would go to join the resistance.

Hanna sat up and glanced at the stone wall towering over his great-uncle. Three feet thick and nine feet tall, it surrounded the courtyard. Atop it, piled four feet high, lay stacks of firewood, which helped deter intruders bent on a stealthy attack, even as they supplied the family with much-needed fuel for heating their home in the winter. The only way in was through the heavy, virtually impenetrable gate that Uncle Musa guarded now, maintaining his nocturnal vigil with unwavering alertness. Haiko, Hanna knew, had slipped quietly through that very gate moments ago. If he were still inside the compound, the heavy iron bar that normally sealed the door for the night would lie across the middle in the locked position, weighed down by the huge stones used every night as an additional precautionary measure.

As soon as he'd found his bearings, Hanna rose to his feet and furtively climbed up the stone stairs that led to the rooftop, where he knew he'd find his mother. He slowed down as he reached the topmost step.

There, on the roof, she stood motionless, her white nightgown draping her slender silhouette. Her arms hung limply at her sides and her long hair shimmered in the moonlight as she strained her blue eyes to follow the fighting in the distance.

Each time Hanna's father rushed to defend the village, Seta hurried to the roof. To watch. To wait. To worry. To pray.

She turned as soon as she noticed Hanna. "Come, come, my little one," she soothed.

He hurried to her, wrapping his arms around her legs for comfort. "Is Papa out there?"

She ran a hand through his blond curls. "Yes."

"Will he be home soon?"

"Of course. He always comes home."

When not obscured by clouds floating swiftly by, a full moon bathed the village in silver light. In the shadows cast by walls, Haiko moved boldly in the direction of the sputtering gunfire, maintaining his crouching stance to avoid detection. The shelling, he thought, seemed unusually close. As he turned a corner, he saw a long shadow stretch menacingly across the street and caught a glimpse of a man standing atop a wall, a rifle in his hands. *That can't be my neighbor*, he told himself. He hugged the wall and crept alongside it as quickly and quietly as he could.

Just then, a bullet ricocheted off a stone near his feet. Haiko fired back.

Flashes of light streamed in his direction, accompanied by a hail of loud, popping sounds. He ducked and ran, making no effort this time to move silently.

Several villagers raced up alongside. His brother Yusef was with them.

"How many?" Yusef asked.

"I don't know. I only saw one on the wall. The others must be close by."

After a quick huddle and a whispered discussion, Yusef led one group off. Haiko and the rest of the men headed in another direction.

Before he and his group could stake out a position for the impending encounter, Haiko heard his brother yell, "Cut them off! They're retreating!"

Men ran every which way, some barking out orders, others whispering nervously. To Haiko's immense relief, not a single shot was fired. In the darkness and confusion, there was no telling friend from foe.

"There! They're running for the lake!"

"Let's get 'em!"

Haiko spotted a pack scampering off at full speed. Then he made out a second group—his brother's forces—in pursuit of the brigands. He shouted a command to the others. "Let's go around the lake and cut off their escape route!"

Haiko's men dashed in the direction he had indicated.

But by the time he reached the lake from the other side, everyone had dispersed and clouds were once again obscuring the moonlight. Haiko was alone. He could hear shots ringing out from different directions. After quickly mulling over his options, he decided to head to the relative quiet of the nearby hills, where, having climbed up some distance, he sat down, leaned against a rock, and waited.

A few minutes passed. He thought he heard someone say, "They're gone." But he wasn't sure. He sat utterly still and continued waiting.

After a half hour or so, he emerged from his hiding place and started back toward the lake. He slowed down, approaching cautiously. Then he heard noises below. In the darkness, he could make out thin, dim trails of light and, now and then, a curling tendril of smoke. He crept closer and could just make out the silhouettes of a group standing around, smoking cigarettes. He relaxed. *We've staved off yet another attack.*

"Hey!" he called out as he bounded toward them. "Where'd the horde...? Oh!"

Haiko shrunk a few steps back into the sharp point of a dagger while someone else jabbed the barrel of a rifle into his chest. Haiko tensed and dropped his weapon.

"What have we here?" chuckled the thug holding the gun to Haiko's chest.

Haiko expected a bullet to rip through his body; instead, he heard the insult *"Gavour kopek!"* and a rough-handed, weighty slap landed across his face. A kick from behind to the crooks of his knees knocked him down, and a frenzy of beating ensued. Haiko pulled his knees up to his chest, buried his face in his thighs, and covered his head with his arms to shield himself from the kicks, punches, and rifle-butt jabs that were raining down on him.

"Please stop!" he begged as loudly as he could. "It's me— Haiko! Haiko, the blacksmith!"

"Stop!" one of the bandits hollered, struggling to rein in a big, burly man who seemed to take a perverse delight in smashing the tips of his boots into Haiko's back. "Stop! Hey, Rejep, stop!"

"Careful, Bulent. The next kick will find your behind if you stand in my way." Rejep pushed Bulent aside and kicked Haiko in the ribs.

"It's Haiko! Haiko, the blacksmith!"

"One and the same to me!" Rejep snapped, delivering another kick.

"No! Stop it!" Bulent protested, "Hasan will come after us if he hears we killed Haiko!"

"Who the hell is Hasan?"

"Hasan Gumus. Not the man to pick a fight with. I say we set Haiko free."

"The only place he goes to is hell!" Rejep snarled, raising his rifle menacingly. "And if you insist on defending him, you can go with him."

Haiko's defender refused to back down, and the gang split in an instant into two blocs and leveled their rifles at each other.

The leader of the brigands stepped between them. "Let's not settle this with bullets. We'll take him to our elders. Let them decide what to do with him."

Rejep grudgingly consented. A member of his brigands led in the horses they had kept waiting around the bend, tied the semiconscious Haiko's hands to a saddle with thick rope, and dragged him back to their village.

After a tense and rancorous debate that lasted till dawn, the village elders decided to turn Haiko over to Hasan Gumus, a Kurd from a neighboring village. An unconscious Haiko was summarily delivered to his house. When Hasan's wife, Shushe, saw Haiko's limp body, she let out a heartrending wail and buried her face in his curls.

"Shushe, Shushe-jan," Hasan murmured repeatedly, stroking his wife's long, light brown hair. "He'll be OK."

He finally pulled the sobbing woman away and with the help of his children, washed Haiko, and put him to bed.

For three days and nights, Shushe sat at Haiko's bedside and nursed him back to life.

When Haiko opened his eyes and saw her, he frowned deeply and used what little strength he could muster to curse her. "Damn you!" he said. He then averted his gaze and did not speak another word for the remaining eleven days it took him to recover.

Musa Tchengo and the *Mukhtar*, Palu's village elder, visited Haiko every day, their main task being to convince the wounded man to remain in Hasan's house until his injuries had healed and the village medicine man had decided it was safe for him to travel. When the time to leave finally came, Hasan and Shushe sent Haiko home on a donkey led by their eldest son. They also gave him a gold bracelet as a gift for Seta.

Once the beast had crossed the outskirts of the village, Haiko snatched the reins from the young boy's hands and, in a tone of utter disgust, ordered, "*Siktir ol!* Get lost!" He hurled the gold bracelet at the boy, spat in the direction of the village, and angrily spurred the animal to hurry home.

Back in Palu, the whole village helped celebrate Haiko's return. The feasting, singing, dancing, and village games lasted the whole day and well into the night. And after all the guests had departed and everyone had fallen asleep, Hanna snuggled up to his father.

"Father, tell me a story," he demanded.

"*Chiroke, Chirvanoke, Khajkhajoke,*" Haiko whispered. "In the year of the heaviest snow this region has ever seen, a blond, curly haired, blue-eyed boy came to life."

"Was that you, father?"

"Shush." Haiko gently placed his fingertips on the boy's lips. "He was a spirited child, yet his baptism was delayed because his grandfather had gone to heaven only a month after he was born."

"Oh."

Hanna suddenly understood that *he* was the boy in this tale. The fact that his father didn't know the date or even the year in which he had been born, was lost on him. In the village, births were not recorded. Instead, birthdays were remembered through their association with major local events, like an unusually bountiful harvest, a snowfall so heavy it had been marked in memory, or the passing of a family patriarch.

"This child grew into a young boy with agile feet and a sharp mind," Haiko went on. "He loved the fields and hunted partridges well. He ran like a cheetah and leaped higher than a gazelle. Overjoyed with the young boy's progress and talents, the villagers proclaimed proudly, 'You'll become a great shepherd or an accomplished blacksmith like your father and your father's father.'

"But the young boy was not content with their modest hopes for him. 'This isn't my wish,' he protested. 'This isn't my kismet. I aspire to something special—to the greatness of my ancestors and distant relatives.'

"One day, fate called and the boy left his village, crossed the seas, and reached foreign lands, joining other voyagers in the pursuit of wisdom, fame, and fortune. He gleaned knowledge from various sources, mastered languages, and learned the art of storytelling like his own father, his father's father, and his other ancestors. *My destiny is set*, thought the boy happily."

Haiko stopped a moment to caress his son's curls and then continued, his tone now tinged with apprehension. "In fact, it seemed his star shone brightly, surpassing in radiance that of his companions and even his elders. But even as his star rose, a dark cloud appeared on the horizon. Then many clouds gathered and dulled what had hitherto been a bright light. Before long, the flock, elders and friends alike, had gone through an alarming transformation. One man turned into a wolf and became intent on hunting the boy down. Soon, there wasn't just one wolf, but many. All part of a ravenous, determined pack."

Hanna burrowed deeper into his father's embrace, holding onto him as tightly as he could.

"The young boy was pursued through the fields, the forest, and the desert," Haiko went on. "He climbed mountains and hid in caves. But no matter where he fled, the wolves still kept pursuing him.

"Fear and doubt clouded his thoughts and eventually conquered his mind. The little boy was ready to give up. Just then, the sky parted and a beautiful angel appeared.

"'Why have you given up, little one?' asked the angel.

"'There is no safe place here!' the boy cried.

"'Then take my wings and fly away.'

"'But where should I fly?' he asked the angel.

"'I can only give you the wings,' replied the angel. 'You must settle the winds.'"

Haiko paused, kissed his trembling son, and whispered, "Three apples fell from heaven. I give you all the apples: one to bring you wisdom, one to bring you courage, and one to bring you good fortune."

CHAPTER 3

Grandmother Sarah arranged for a *madagh*, the traditional Armenian offering to thank the Lord for the safe return of her son-in-law. As expected, the entire village gathered in and around the Ibelin courtyard to participate in the ritual that was intended to spiritually cleanse the family and ward off potentially harmful influences.

The priest raised his palms heavenward, seeking forgiveness on behalf of the family for sins committed, knowingly or unknowingly. He prayed for the exorcism of evil and pleaded for divine intervention to protect the innocent and the repentant. He blessed the four corners of the earth, as well as salt, bread, and water, the symbols integral to life. Then he blessed Hanna's family, in need of the Lord's protection, and finally, the sacrificial lamb.

As the deacon swung a censer casually, spreading smoke and incense, a short, stout man wearing a filthy apron stepped forward and grabbed hold of the lamb, lifting it effortlessly. Laying the animal, which was bleating in protest, on its side, he produced a sharp machete, and with a sudden, almost furtive movement, slit its throat. Hanna tearfully watched the animal he had playfully chased around the courtyard only the day before. Now pinned down beneath the butcher's knee, it reflexively kicked the empty air with all four legs. The executioner held its snout and stretched the neck to allow the blood to flow freely, and a geyser of red gushed rhythmically from the lamb's severed carotid artery.

The priest blessed the coagulating puddle, dipped his right thumb in it, and imprinted the sign of the cross on the foreheads of the Ibelin family members.

A big feast followed.

Hanna's parents were not wealthy, even by village standards. Sarah, his maternal grandmother, had inherited enough money, land, and jewelry to sustain the family—that is, until her daughters and her deceased husband's nephews usurped a significant portion of the assets through a rancorous feud. Hanna's father had gambled away the rest of the fortune in the coffeehouses he frequented. When Grandma Sarah's wealth eventually dwindled to nothing, she resorted to hard labor to supplement the family income from the crops they cultivated and the Ibelin blacksmithing trade. She worked as a cook for a prominent landowner who lived just across the border, in the Syrian town of Kamishli, and had employed her to prepare meals for his migrant workers.

Seta visited her mother whenever she was in the mood to vent her disapproval of her husband's gambling and frequent absences. However, the trips to Kamishli, apart from involving illegal border crossings, could be undertaken only along a route passing through a region that had become a hotbed of activities involving the Kurdish independence movement. Starting out from the village on the backs of donkeys, the travelers rode to an isolated location near the border and then crossed over to the other side on foot. Once they were at a safe distance from the border, Arab Bedouins escorted them for the remainder of the journey. As a baby, Hanna had made several trips to Kamishli, strapped to his mother's back.

"Hanna, do you know why they call me 'Muksi' Sarah?"

Several hours had passed since the exhausting *madagh* ritual and the family had gathered on divans to rest and reflect.

"I know the answer," offered Asto.

Grandmother Sarah smiled at Asto, but her question had, in fact, been rhetorical. "In this region," she explained, "I am the only *muksi*. This is an Assyrian word, meaning 'pilgrim,' like *haji* in Arabic. A *muksi* or *haji* is a person who has made a pilgrimage to a Holy City. For Muslims, it is Mecca. For us, it is Jerusalem. This cross on my arm marks and confirms my *muksi* status." She proudly extended her right forearm to display a small but elaborately wrought tattoo of a cross. "I remember my mother taking me to Jerusalem before my wedding. As an offering, we had donated a pot of gold to the Armenian monastery to help the orphans and refugees."

"Orphans?" Hanna asked.

"Oh, my little one, so few of us survived!" Sadness filled Sarah's eyes. "My dear brother Musa knows how they all perished. Terrible deaths..." She wiped away a tear with her handkerchief. "Yes. Musa knows."

Musa Tchengo sighed and shook his head grimly, but did not comment.

More secrets, Hanna thought. There were many things he was not meant to know and countless discussions he was not supposed to overhear. But he had learned to loiter nearby, unseen and unheard, as the secrets flew back and forth between his parents and others, while they were pored over and debated at length.

While playing in the courtyard several months earlier, Hanna had overheard Musa Tchengo discussing a country called "Hayastan" with an elderly relative. The next day, the boy had asked his father about it.

"There is no such place. Never mention that word again," was Haiko's curt reply.

Hanna had pretended to leave, but remained within earshot of the argument that subsequently broke out between his parents.

"He thinks he can recreate the past," he heard his father say. "As if it was *that* glorious. That man will be our downfall."

Hanna's mother, however, stoutly supported her uncle. "His account should be passed on," she insisted.

"Tsk, tsk, tsk! You must be mad like him!"

"He should teach them about Armenia and our heritage. They need to know the truth."

"The *truth*?" Haiko spat out. "What truth? He thinks we have Frankish blood."

"That's what our grandparents and great-grandparents passed on to us!"

"Woman, get this nonsense out of your head. Forget our past and forget Hayastan," Haiko said, wagging his finger in reproof. "The Turks consider the Armenian Question a charge yet unfinished. It is best not to provoke them."

On another occasion, Hanna had asked his father why the village boys sometimes taunted him. "They mock me and call me a foreigner and the child of a sinful marriage."

"Naughty. That's all they are. Don't pay attention to them."

Dissatisfied with the answer, Hanna had asked his mother to explain the reason underlying those taunts.

"This is an Assyrian village," she explained. "Our family is Armenian and arrived here as refugees forty years ago. The village elders were kind enough to offer us shelter and land to cultivate."

"What was so sinful about your marriage?"

"Your father and I are cousins. Our parents wanted to preserve our heritage. So we intermarried."

"Mother, I don't understand any of this."

"The time will come, my son, when you will."

As he was leaving, Hanna overheard another argument break out between his parents. It initially focused on the way the Ibelin family had come to their village and veered off into a discussion of the differences between Armenians and Assyrians.

Hanna's most traumatic experience involved being the target of taunts leveled by a village boy who, angry with him for one reason or another, had jeered, "Your father's sister is a Kurdish whore!"

"Shut your filthy mouth!" Hanna had shouted back. "My father has no sisters!"

Even though Hanna had not known what "whore" meant, he sensed that it was something shameful.

He waited for a few days before reporting the incident to his parents and was shocked when his father reacted violently to his words by slapping him across the face, something he had never done before. Later, that same day, his parents had one of their worst quarrels ever.

"Why do you still deny Shushe's existence?" Seta demanded to know. "She was the victim in this case, wasn't she? Why blame her for the kidnapping?"

Hanna's father turned his anger on his wife. "I have no sister!" he yelled. "She is a Mohammedan whore!"

His parents' discussions frequently degenerated into quarrels and this one had ended with his mother arguing in favor of moving the family over the border to Kamishli.

"Nonsense," Haiko had responded. "I'll soon be moving the family to Almanya."

"Ah! The Germany dream!"

"Yes, Germany. There is plenty of work there."

"You have plenty of work here in the blacksmith shop with your brothers," Seta had retorted. "But I don't see you working."

"We'll get rich in Germany," Haiko had replied, ignoring his wife's barb. "It is safe there."

"How will we get to Almanya if you keep gambling away every lira at the coffeehouses?" was Seta's rejoinder.

Hanna darted like a cheetah and leapt like a gazelle, and the little white lamb straddling his shoulders bounced up and down, as the two fled as fast as the boy's legs would carry them. To get to Almanya, he knew he would have to be crafty and quick; otherwise, he and the lamb would be devoured.

Yet, still they came. No matter how fast he ran or how high he jumped, the pack of wolves gained on him. He could hear them growling and gnashing their teeth, and the earth shook under their massive paws as they drew within striking distance.

With his pursuers closing in from all sides, fear threatened to paralyze Hanna. His strides grew shorter and more labored and his legs weakened, as did his grip on the lamb lodged precariously on his shoulders. Just as he began to lose all hope and give in to his fate, he saw something floating out of the clouds above him—a beautiful woman with golden hair.

Hanna woke up, besieged by terror, and was deeply relieved to find his mother stroking his head. Her pale face looked ghostly in the soft light cast by an oil lamp, but the boy drew comfort from the familiar fragrance of her long, reddish-gold hair, which hung past her shoulders and tickled his face.

"There, there, my little one," Seta soothed. "It was only a bad dream. Everything will be well."

Still shaking and sweating from the nightmare, Hanna clung to his mother. *She'll make everything well*, he told himself.

CHAPTER 4

Though several days had gone by since Haiko's homecoming, the event continued to generate much debate. Some interpreted it as good karma; others saw it as a clear warning; and the most devout perceived it as nothing short of a miracle. Whether God's commission or the devil's, the incident triggered something within Musa Tchengo. After years of suppressing the traumatic memories of the past, he finally felt compelled to purge himself of the affliction and set it free. He hoped, thereby, to liberate himself as well.

"Come," he said to Hanna one day, lifting the boy onto his shoulders with his one good arm. "I have something to show you."

He carried his great-nephew from the courtyard into his modest one-room abode, which adjoined the far end of the Ibelins' L-shaped home. Once inside, Tchengo pointed at the sole painting hanging on his wall. "This is Mount Ararat," he said with equal parts longing and bitterness. "Never forget it. Forever in its core is the seed of our people."

Hanna lost himself in the oil-painted landscape, which featured the snowcapped twin peaks of a mountain rising majestically from the valley into an azure sky. An ancient church rested on a stunted hillside in the foreground and nearby, a pair of slender linden trees jutted up from the arid terrain, side by side, but forever separate, like two young lovers yearning to be close to each other.

"The trees are called *sosi* trees," Hanna's great-uncle said softly. "The church, a convent in those days, was built on top of the underground dungeon of Khor Virab, where St. Gregory the Illuminator was cast to die. He miraculously survived in that pit for thirteen years and rose to convert all of Armenia to Christianity in the year three hundred and one. We are the first Christian nation in the world."

Pride replaced the anguish in his great-uncle's voice, and Hanna felt the old man's leathery hand squeeze his own soft one. "Noah's Ark landed on this mountain," Tchengo told his great-nephew.

Hanna's eyes lit up. While everything his great-uncle had rattled off thus far was unintelligible to him, Noah's Ark he had heard of. He searched the painting again, looking for the familiar sight. "Can we see the ark? Have you ever been to Ararat, Uncle Musa?"

"Ah," Tchengo answered in a faraway voice, "it is a sight one can never forget."

"Uncle Musa," Hanna asked cautiously, "why do my friends say I'm different?"

"Because," his great-uncle replied matter-of-factly, "we're not Assyrian."

"But we *speak* Assyrian," Hanna retorted, knowing full well that Uncle Musa preferred to speak another, more mysterious language. "*Everybody* in our village is Assyrian."

"Our family is *Armenian!*"

The steel in the old man's voice startled Hanna. His great-uncle was normally soft-spoken. Tchengo paused and then added whimsically, "It is also said that our ancestors had Frankish blood."

"Frankish?"

"French. One thousand years ago, the crusaders, ferocious fighters and princes from Europe, settled in our towns and villages. Our family bears the name of one such French knight— Balian de Ibelin. When our forefathers left their ancestral lands in Armenian Cilicia four hundred years ago, the family split into two branches. Our side of the family kept the Ibelin name, while the other branch claimed the Balian name. The Ibelins moved to central Anatolia, while the Balians moved west and, eventually, to Constantinople. The Balian branch of our family produced several generations of world-renowned architects. They built some of the empire's most magnificent structures, including the Dolmabahce Saray, the Sultans' most marvelous palace. In Ottoman history, their architectural fame is second only to Mimar Sinan, another Armenian."

Hanna didn't quite understand his great-uncle's words in their entirety, but he did find the story of palaces, princes, and knights intriguing. He glanced up at Musa Tchengo and noticed that a twinkle now lit up the old man's normally sad and dejected eyes.

"Were you a fierce fighter like those princes?" the boy asked eagerly.

"What?" Uncle Musa seemed confused by the question.

"Didn't you lose your arm fighting the Turks?"

"I lost much, much more than my arm." A long silence followed the somber tone, before he continued more combatively, "One day you will pick up the struggle. Remember, words and not guns should be your weapon."

CHAPTER 5

Harvest season

Late one afternoon, just as the sun's heat was beginning to lose its edge, a motley group of women and children made their way back to the village. Among them was Seta, followed by Hanna, who ambled along lazily behind her. Earlier, while the women had been helping with the harvest, Hanna had frolicked with the other children in the wheat and hay. Soon, this would all be gone, leaving an empty field in its wake, but Hanna would draw solace from the great rituals that followed.

The memories of last year's celebration were still so vivid, it seemed as if it had taken place not so long ago. It had begun in the field with the harvest, and had ended back at the village by the shores of the lake, a body of water so small that it dried up in the summer. To Hanna, it might as well have been an ocean. To mark the opening ceremony, a priest had blessed the crop as well as the farmers, and the whole village had gathered to watch spry men armed with pitchforks encircle a towering stack of harvested wheat. Singing in unison and performing a two-step dance as they moved in concert around the stack, the men had heaved a bundle of wheat into the air. The wheat had rained down on them heavily, while the chaff drifted on the breeze. A fire had been lit and an enormous cauldron filled with water set on it. As soon as the water came to a boil, the women had added salt to it and poured a few sacks of grain into the cauldron. Several of them had taken turns to churn the mixture, singing all the while. Hanna could almost taste the briny traditional *hadig*, served steaming hot. Meanwhile, another group of women had taken the separated wheat and ground it into flour, using two large wheel-shaped stones as a rudimentary mill. While one woman rotated the top stone, another had poured the wheat that had to be ground.

Accompanying his mother back to the village now, Hanna could feel his feet drag with each step. Exhaustion overwhelmed him and hunger gnawed at his stomach. As for sleep, which often felt like a punishment when he wasn't ready for it, it was now an eagerly awaited reward after playing hard all day.

A flock of sparrows descended from the brilliant blue sky, landed nearby, and fanned out across the earth, scouring the rocky soil for worms. Hanna shifted his gaze from the sparrows to his mother and saw her long shadow stretching out across the dirt toward him. He hastened his pace, intent on tiptoeing along the shadow, but just as he reached it, the sparrows distracted him again, taking flight as swiftly as they had come and moving in concert once again.

When Hanna looked back at the path ahead, his eyes went directly to something that made him start in horror. "Look out, Mama!"

Even as the words flew from his mouth, Seta stepped inadvertently on the very object that had struck fear into her son's heart: a snake the color of dirt. With the tail caught beneath her heel, both the woman and the reptile recoiled from the contact. Hanna's mother stumbled backward and the snake slithered away in the direction of a cluster of large stones lying nearby.

"Mary, Mother of God!" Seta muttered in a voice just above a whisper, but the intensity with which she let loose those words made them seem like an uninhibited shriek. She crossed herself, her hands trembling, and Hanna ran to her side.

"A snake!" he exclaimed excitedly.

Taking their cue from the serpent, the others in their group scattered in panic, leaving Hanna and Seta to gape at the reptile which, in its desperation to escape, had wedged itself so tightly between two large stones that it could neither move ahead nor backward, whipping its exposed tail against the rocks.

"Tut, tut, tut!" An old woman now stepped forward from the group that was watching from a safe distance and approached Seta and Hanna cautiously. Hanna recognized the birthing witch. With her shoulders permanently hunched and her teeth mostly missing, she frightened the boy far more than the snake had. "A terrible, *terrible* omen," she lamented.

"Let's go," Seta whispered to her son and tried to rise to her feet, but the old woman put a determined hand on her shoulder and prevented her from moving.

"Snakes are cursed by God," she pronounced ominously, shaking her head over and over again. "To step on one…This portends evil." She bit her lower lip and shook her head again from side to side. She then glanced from the snake, which was still struggling to wriggle free, to Seta. "You must rid yourself of this curse. The snake must be slaughtered." She shook her head again.

"Let's go," Seta repeated, taking Hanna's hand firmly in hers.

But the gnarled old woman stood in their way, rooted to the spot where they had stopped.

"Like St. George, you must vanquish this serpent," she insisted. "St. George has interceded by preventing the evil from escaping your judgment. He has trapped it for you to sacrifice it. And I have just the right…" She rummaged through her large knapsack and, after a quick search, produced a pair of long knitting needles.

"No!" Seta said, backing away.

"You *must* do it! The curse may spread to the rest of the village if you don't act like St. George." The old woman forced the knitting needles into Seta's reluctant hand and coaxed her toward the snake.

The two women knelt beside the ensnared reptile as Hanna looked on.

"Like this," the old woman said, showing Seta how to stab at the creature with the two gleaming needles.

Seta's first strike was tentative, wide of the mark, and fell harmlessly in the dirt, but the next pierced through skin and flesh, as did the others that followed. Soon, the writhing stopped and Hanna stared, both fascinated and repelled, as the snake was reduced to a coil of mangled flesh in a pool of blackish-red mud. The boy grimaced, but did not look away.

Once the gruesome business had been taken care of, Seta dropped the needles and, still on her knees, retreated a few steps, appearing too drained to rise to her feet again. Tears streamed down her face.

The old woman, on the contrary, seemed invigorated by the experience. "Now the spell is broken," she muttered. She picked up the needles, glancing around her, as if searching for something. Then shrugging her shoulders, she wiped the knitting needles off on her frock. "We sent the snake back to hell," she declared with satisfaction.

A week later, Hanna was woken up before daybreak. Groggily rubbing sleep from his eyes in the stillness of early morning, he stared at his mother in confusion. "Why do we have to leave so early?" he asked as she readied him and his younger siblings in the dark courtyard.

"Because," Seta answered hurriedly, "the journey to Muksi Sarah's home in Kamishli takes at least half a day. And the farther we can travel before noon, when the sun will be at its fiercest, the better."

The eastern sky was a flaming pink now, but the sun had yet to show its face.

"Why can't I stay with Asto and the others?" Hanna asked, longing for the comfort of a soft mattress inside the house where his three oldest siblings were still sleeping.

"You're too young," Seta said. "Asto, Chelo, and Nazeli will be staying with your cousins. Uncle Musa is going to take them there later in the day."

"Papa will look after me, then," Hanna retorted.

The words rang hollow. In the days since his triumphant return from the Kurdish village, Haiko had been spending increasingly more time away from home, whiling away the hours in the coffeehouses of neighboring towns. Was he gambling away the family's money once again? Hanna didn't like to dwell on such unpleasant thoughts. Fortunately, his mother did not press the point. If his father had been more or less absent of late, Seta had been present in body only. Something was nagging at her—even little Hanna could feel it—for she vacillated between melancholy and irritation. But mostly, she was distracted. Her mind was evidently elsewhere.

At the boy's suggestion that his father would take care of him, Seta could only shake her head.

"What about Uncle Musa?" Hanna persisted.

"He is too old—and too busy."

Just then, their guide for the day, an elderly man with a scraggly beard and an easy shuffle, led a donkey through the front gate and into the courtyard. Two baskets hung down the animal's flanks on either side and on its back rested a small rug that Hanna assumed must be the saddle.

While the boy stroked the donkey's muzzle, the old guide placed Ani in one of the baskets and tiny Levon, who was still swaddled and asleep, in the other.

The donkey leaned into Hanna, giving him an affectionate nudge.

"He's friendly," the young boy said to the guide.

"That he is," the old man agreed. "He will carry you and your family."

Hanna walked around to the donkey's side, waiting to be lifted onto its back, but his mother intercepted him.

"You must wear your *boncuk*," she whispered, kneeling down beside him and fumbling nervously with the safety pin.

While still a toddler, Hanna had lost a sibling who would have been his oldest sister, had she lived. Her unparalleled beauty and uncanny resemblance to Seta were still spoken of today by the family as well as by many of the villagers. The latter were convinced that the young girl had attracted the "evil eye" and fallen victim to its malevolent powers. Not long after his sister's death, Hanna's mother had given all of her children *boncuks*—round, turquoise eye amulets designed to ward off evil and protect their owners from the adverse effects of ill will generated by envy.

As soon as his mother had attached the *boncuk* to his sweater, Hanna let his body go limp long enough for the old guide to lift him high in the air and place him on the donkey's back. The docile animal looked just as big from above, and Hanna was impressed by its wide back and rippling muscles. His eyes grew even wider as the guide handed him the reins. Then Seta climbed on behind him and took hold of the ropes that fastened the baskets and with that, they left the compound to join a small group of women and children who would be making the same dodgy journey to Kamishli, just on the other side of Turkey's border with northern Syria.

Between the two countries lay a desolate stretch of uninhabitable desert, a no-man's-land where illegal border crossings were routine but perilous, where travelers feared the ruthless Turkish border patrols more than they did the bandits that roamed the region. The slow-burning war for Kurdish independence was being fought here, as were less politically oriented battles between smugglers, drug dealers, and warring clans.

Hanna, though, was unaware of the hazards. All he knew was that this was the way to his grandmother's home. Villagers revered Sarah as a *muksi*, and they often sought her out for advice and guidance as well as for mediation in disputes. Feuding parties would invariably accept the judgment she passed as arbiter as the final word. The vast wealth her family had enjoyed in the past, their foreign origins, their legendary relations in Constantinople, and their fabled Crusader lineage commanded considerable respect.

But for Hanna, Muksi Sarah was simply his doting grandmother, and trips to her home had always been undertaken purely for the pleasure they gave his family. This time, however, there was, inexplicably, a more ominous feel to it. Hanna had begun to sense it the previous night, when his mother had explained to him the nature of their journey. "Muksi Sarah can undo the snake's spell," she had whispered to him as the others were falling asleep. "We will go to her."

By the time Seta and her children left the village after gathering with the small caravan, it was well after sunrise, and the two-hour trudge that followed brought them to the outer reaches of the dry, barren terrain that was Syria's northern desert. A narrow, well-trodden path marked their route through the arid landscape studded with fist-sized, sharp-edged pieces of gravel, rocks jutting forth from the earth, and knee-high thorny shrubs.

"This is the beginning of Der Zor," Seta said, turning to Hanna and pointing at the badlands ahead. "In this desert, Sodom and Gomorrah descended upon our people. Uncle Musa knows the secrets of this desert all too well. Every time Muksi Sarah makes this trek, she collects bones on her way while shedding tears for the fallen."

Hanna did not understand, but with noon fast approaching and the heat intense, he wasn't inclined to ask his mother any questions. His head was burning under the blazing late-morning sun and his curiosity had evaporated in the muggy heat.

Up ahead, the old guide wiped beads of sweat from his forehead. "Let's rest awhile," he suggested, sensing, perhaps, Hanna's discomfort and that of the others.

The group dismounted, quenched their thirst, watered their animals, and then sat in the rock-strewn dust, pulling any available piece of clothing—a shawl, a blouse that had been discarded hours earlier—over their heads for protection from the sun's searing rays.

Ani darted behind the donkey and Hanna gave half-hearted chase. It was too hot to play.

Levon, meanwhile, began to cry. It was time for his feed. Seta reversed her chador, draped it over her head and bosom, and nursed the baby within its shade.

Finally, after everyone had gotten a chance to rest, the guide stood up. "*Yimshi!* Let's go" he yelled in Arabic and smiled. "There are no border markings in this area, but we are close to crossing into Syria, and, out of the reach of the Turkish patrols," he said cheerfully and then began rounding up the mules and donkeys.

The convoy of women and children began moving again. Relieved that the destination was within reach and they were out of danger, Seta decided to walk alongside the donkey.

"Don't you want to be up here with me?" Hanna asked from atop the animal as they brought up the rear.

"No, little one," his mother answered. "It's good for me to stretch my legs." She sighed as she took in the parched landscape around them. "In the past, no plants grew in this desert. People say the shrubs sprouted in lieu of the lives that were swallowed by the sand. The thorns apparently represent the suffering they endured before they died, and the lush colors of the wildflowers symbolize the light in their eyes before it was extinguished forever. This time, instead of bones, we shall take flowers to Muksi Sarah. Yes, let's make a wreath for her."

"Good idea!" encouraged Hanna, grasping only the wreath concept. "I want to help, Mama!"

"Of course you can," Seta assured him warmly, "but first, I must pluck the flowers."

Hanna watched as his mother, humming her favorite lullaby, inspected and sniffed at an assortment of wildflowers and flowering bushes along the way. Each time she spotted a particularly colorful or eye-catching specimen, her pace seemed to quicken. The boy didn't begrudge her the work. Most of the flowers bloomed on thorny shrubs that Seta had to delicately pick her way through in order to reach her prize. After fifteen minutes of snapping branches and carefully plucking thorn-studded stems, she had enough of the blossoms to fashion an extravagantly ornate crown.

"Look, Mama!" Hanna squealed with excitement, pointing ahead to an array of shrubs laden with blood-red flowers.

"A burning bush!" Seta headed toward the brilliantly colored blossoms and started to hum the psalm, "I walk before the Lord in the land..."

"Halt!" a thundering command in Turkish echoed from afar.

The sudden boom spooked one of the mules, which darted ahead, and, in turn, sent the other animals, along with their human cargo, into a frenzy.

Hanna leaned down and whispered into his restive donkey's ears. "You're fine. Nothing's going to happen to you. I promise."

But the voice came again, this time, from somewhere closer. "Halt!"

Hanna swung around in the blanket-saddle and peered off into the distance but was blinded by the blazing sun. He turned his sight to his mother and a jolt of terror shot through his heart. The fabric of her dress had got caught on one of the branches of the thorny bramble. Seta was frantically tugging on it with one hand as she shielded her eyes from the sun's glare with the other that still held the bouquet of flowers. Before she could break free, several soldiers appeared between the rocks above and behind them, not more than seven hundred meters away.

"Turks!" the guide hollered. "Stay calm! As long as we bribe them, they won't hurt us."

Chaos ensued. Hanna, very alarmed, watched the screaming women and children whip and prod their pack animals to a gallop.

Hanna's gaze swung back to his mother, who was still struggling to break free from the bush that entangled her. "Mama!" he cried in panic. "Mama!"

"Mother of God, help me!" Seta cried, flinging aside the clump of flowers. She tugged desperately at her dress with both hands until it finally tore free, leaving a large section of fabric still speared on the bush. "Hanna, I'm coming!" she called out.

But she'd only run a few paces when her right foot caught a stone and she tripped, falling headlong into a thorny bush.

"Mama!"

Seta was up in a flash, but this time, her chador remained entangled in the shrub. The gold circlet ribbon that held her hair under the chador was still in place, but the shoulder of her dress was torn and dangled at her waist, exposing her white undergarment. Undeterred, she kicked off her sandals and rushed toward the children.

When she reached them, Hanna could see streaks of red on her forehead and cheeks. His gaze traveled to her hands and feet and he saw that these too were scratched and bloodied.

"Halt!" This time the order rang out with clarity. The soldiers were closing in rapidly.

"Hurry, Mama!" Hanna extended a hand to help her mount, even as he struggled to control the donkey, which, though admirably calm until now, was getting rattled by the tumult.

Seta hurled herself atop the donkey and managed to land on its back, stomach first, her head and arms dangling over one side and her legs jutting forth from the other. "Go!" she yelled, slapping the confused animal's rump.

The soldiers issued another command for them to halt. Only this time, they expressed the seriousness of their intent by following it with a warning volley of shots. The gunfire startled the donkey. It staggered and then bucked forward, throwing Seta to the ground as it scampered after the animals ahead of them.

"Stop!" Hanna shrieked. "Stop!"

The commotion, combined with the donkey's frantic movements, woke up the baby and Levon let out a furious wail. Ani, meanwhile, remained perfectly still—and quiet—in her basket.

Hanna looked back and saw his mother struggle once again to her feet, her long, bulky robe and undergarments now a tattered mess.

"Halt!" one of the soldiers hollered at them. "That's an order!"

But his mother ignored it. "Hanna," she yelled as she sprinted toward him, "don't stop! Don't look back!"

In fact, he couldn't have stopped the donkey if he had wanted to. Nor could he have stopped himself from looking back. He looked on in dismay as another volley of gunfire erupted from the soldiers' rifles, the smoke belching forth before the crack could reach his eardrums. A second later, his mother's head jerked back and her body arched violently. Propelled forward by an invisible force, she took a few slow, short steps before coming to a complete stop. Hanna saw her examine her chest and then calmly but longingly reach out in his direction. With her arms splayed, Hanna saw a dark stain blooming rapidly on the right side of her white shirt, just below her breast.

The boy tried to call out to his mother, but not a sound escaped his lips. He wanted desperately to grasp the outstretched hands and lift her to the saddle, but the agitated beast only added distance between them. As the soldiers descended like wolves from the hilltop, he could feel the pounding of their boots in his chest. He prayed that he would turn into an angel, swoop down, and carry his mother away to safety, but remained paralyzed in place on the donkey's back. He thought he heard more gunfire—or was it thunder?—but as his ears stopped ringing, he realized it was only the screeching wail of his baby brother.

CHAPTER 6

Two days later, Hanna was back home. Nothing, however, felt familiar. Even the overcast sky seemed alien. It was a dull white and hung so heavy, it hid the afternoon sun. He sat alone on the stone steps that led to the rooftop, bewildered by the occasion that had brought so many people to the courtyard.

Despite the swelling crowd, the crescent-shaped courtyard was steeped in silence, save for the occasional word, uttered in a hushed voice, or the sound of a shoe scuffing against the courtyard's stone surface. Hanna let his gaze drift from one man to the next, each one in his Sunday best, and began to wonder if every male in the village had descended upon his family's home. Some of the men leaned against the thick stone walls; others squatted. Some sat cross-legged. Most twirled and counted their prayer beads. All smoked.

Haiko stood in the center, surrounded by Uncle Musa, Hanna's other uncles, the village priest, and the deacon, the latter casually swinging the censer to and fro, just as he had the day they slaughtered the little lamb. Gray plumes billowed from the burning incense. The smoke trailed the censer as it moved back and forth, and rose heavenward before dissipating into nothingness.

Hanna's father looked diminished, a far cry from the man who could hammer a slab of iron into a plough, grow huge watermelons and the sweetest grapes, and nurture abundant wheat fields; the man whose legendary storytelling, full of myths and mirth, had brought visitors from far and wide to their village. Haiko looked utterly lost.

The sweet smell of the incense filled Hanna's nostrils as he stood up and hurried down the stone steps. He felt the sudden urge to speak to his father, although he had no idea what he would say, once he had his attention. As he made his way past the village men, Hanna could recognize pity in their gaze or at least in the expressions of those venturing to make eye contact with him. Most glanced away as soon as they saw him approach.

But before the boy could reach his father, the priest began addressing the legions not present in the courtyard and on this earth. "Into the heavenly city of Jerusalem," the priest read aloud from the scriptures, "in which the just are assembled..."

Hanna came to a halt a few feet from his father and waited for what felt like an interminable number of minutes until the priest had finally completed his supplication. He then hurried to Haiko, who was wiping the tears off his cheeks, and tugged at his hand.

"Papa," he whispered, looking up at his father.

Haiko looked down at Hanna and stroked his hair.

The boy opened his mouth to speak, but said nothing. Instead, he wrapped his arms around his father's leg.

"Come on," Haiko said gently. "Let's go inside."

He took Hanna by the hand and led him past the kitchen into the big room where all the women were gathered. There, Hanna saw his grandmother all wrapped in black, sitting in the middle of the room, and sobbing quietly to herself. It was strange to see Muksi Sarah so heartbroken and listless, she who had always been vivacious and cheerful. But Hanna was beginning to get used to this new, melancholy old woman; she had been crying ever since they arrived at her village two days earlier. Surrounding her were her five remaining daughters and several other women.

All were crying, though not as silently as Muksi Sarah. Instead, they raised their arms toward the ceiling as they chanted prayers and repeatedly made the sign of the cross.

One of them, the same old woman who had forced Seta to kill the snake, was beating her breast and wailing loudly. "Vay, vay, vay!" she cried. "Where are you, Seta? Where have you gone? Vay, vay, vay!"

Hanna slipped free from his father's grip and raced back outside, hoping to escape the weeping women whose clamorous displays of emotion he found both unsettling and incomprehensible. The courtyard, choked with hordes of faces distorted by grief, offered no respite either. Confusion and fear enveloped him for a brief moment, but he shook them off and tried convincing himself that the events of the last two days hadn't taken place at all. He spotted the stone stairs and hurried up them. He knew his mother would be where she always was when trouble came to his village: firmly rooted on the rooftop, searching the horizon to detect and fend off the approaching menace.

CHAPTER 7

Every night, as he prepared for sleep, Hanna saw an image outlined against his shut eyelids: his mother stood alone on the rooftop, her arms wrapped around herself, her white nightgown fluttering in the gentle breeze. He saw her long hair shimmering in the moonlight as her sky-blue eyes surveyed the horizon. And every night, as he clung to her memory, she receded further into the distance, an angel ascending heavenward.

Six months had passed since her death. That night, as the hour grew closer when Hanna would, yet again, try to hold on to the last thread of memory that connected them, he sensed a further fraying of the tether that would inevitably snap and cause his childhood to vanish forever. The stone walls that enclosed the courtyard outside no longer seemed so invincible after all.

"The lot is cast into the lap," Hanna's father announced cryptically one evening as the family sat quietly in the living room, "but its every decision is from the Lord."

"A man's own folly ruins his life," Uncle Musa said curtly, "yet his heart rages against the Lord." He stood up to leave.

"Am I to blame?" snapped Haiko.

"Why must our future be so uncertain?" Muksi Sarah intervened. "Is this our kismet?"

Haiko shrugged. "Fate abandoned our family—our people—long ago."

Much of what was said left Hanna confused, as confused as he had been before his mother's death, when his parents would argue about subjects quite beyond his comprehension. But that night, a decision had been made and his great-uncle seemed unhappy, as did Muksi Sarah, who had been staying with them all these months and taking care of the little ones.

"But haven't we suffered enough?" the matriarch of the family asked in a dispirited voice. "Shouldn't the Mother of God protect these children? Our prayers have fallen on deaf ears." She kissed the tattoo on her right hand and crossed herself three times, having apparently said something that she shouldn't have. "Must you drag the children along?" she now asked her son-in-law.

"I will not leave them behind," Haiko answered firmly. "I will not abandon my children. All but the two youngest will come with me. Later, when they are ready, Levon and Ani will follow."

On this last night in their village home, Haiko's response was unwavering. Hanna would later reflect on that moment and realize that his father's pronouncement had brought to an end this phase of their lives. It marked an untimely end to childhood, home, and family, all relegated now to the tangle of vague, nostalgic memories.

"You are their father," Muksi Sarah said resignedly. She turned to the children and gazed at them with tears in her eyes. "Bless you all and your journey," she whispered as she knelt down and swaddled Hanna's baby brother, who had already fallen asleep on a soft blanket.

"I'll bid you all farewell in the morning," Uncle Musa said and started for the kitchen.

Haiko nodded to him and then turned to address his three oldest sons and Nazeli, who were still gathered around him on the living-room rugs. "Tomorrow, we'll go to Diyarbekir and from there, we'll board the bus to Istanbul."

"Diyarbekir," Hanna's grandmother repeated, shaking her head wistfully. "Our Dikranagerd, the city of Dikran the Great,

King of Kings, conqueror, and challenger of the great empires of Europe. He vanquished mighty generals and signed a peace treaty with Pompeii. I wasn't much older than you, my children, when our family fled the city on the eve of the deportations and the great calamity."

Haiko's reply was terse. "The children should go to sleep now."

Muksi Sarah burst into tears and her shoulders shook with sobs. "First, I lost my Seta," she mumbled softly as she cried. "Now I must lose her children who have always been like my own." She hung her head in defeat.

A long, stifling silence followed. Hanna stole a glance at his two oldest brothers, Asto and Chelo, who, though clearly despondent, had stood up and were busy making their beds. Hanna followed suit and soon he was lying on his back, away from Haiko. He wouldn't snuggle up to his father and beg for a story tonight. Instead, he closed his eyes to conjure up the memory of his mother that had sustained him for so long.

The embers in the *tonir*, the cooking pit in the kitchen, shifted and crackled. A moment later, Hanna's nostrils caught the sweet whiff of *lavash*. Judging by the aroma that suffused their home, the bread for the next day's trip was apparently ready.

Uncles, aunts, cousins—the whole family gathered in the courtyard next morning, where they were joined by friends and neighbors, many of whom made no effort to hide their grief. But no one seemed more distraught, Hanna thought, than Muksi Sarah, whose sorrow weighed so heavily on her that she needed two of her daughters to hold her up, one on either side.

When he could stand the sight of her tears no longer, Hanna ran to his grandmother and wrapped his arms around her waist, burying his face against her ribs. "Don't cry, Grandma," he mumbled into the folds of her robe.

But Muksi Sarah continued to weep and pray.

Hanna felt someone else's arm around him and he looked up and saw it was his great-uncle.

Musa Tchengo pried the boy loose from his grandmother, hoisted him up with his right arm, and clasped his small head to his chest with the stump of his amputated left arm. "You are my wings," he whispered in Hanna's ear.

As the light faded from the sky, they drew closer to Diyarbekir in an open-bed truck. Hanna could make out the jagged silhouettes of the rooftops against the orange-purple sky. Smudges of dark smoke rose from the seemingly countless smokestacks that dotted the city. Hanna sat up on his knees to gaze at the structures that loomed ahead.

The truck entered Diyarbekir bouncing forward and lurching sideways in the jumble of automobiles, animals pulling laden carts, pedestrians, vendors pushing wagons, and packed bazaars. In this bustling city grinding engines, squeaking wagon wheels, shouts peddling wares, the store displays, smoke rising from eateries, and clanking metal mixed with the jingle of mule tackle created more voices, smells, and colors than Hanna thought possible.

Finally, they maneuvered through the old city's narrow cobblestone alleys to reach the remnants of the Armenian section, which was bound by high, dark brick walls. After rapping on the gate of the hermetic enclosure and negotiating for five minutes with the elderly sexton through the small, unwelcoming opening cut out in the gate, they were allowed inside. They had barely stepped in, when the guardian of this remaining bastion of

Armenian presence in Diyarbekir hurriedly shut the high timber gates, locking and double-latching it behind them. The sexton allowed them to camp overnight on the cold and dusty stone floor of the crumbling cathedral.

At dawn, the muezzin's call of prayer from a nearby mosque awoke them. Bleary-eyed and struggling to make sense of their whereabouts, the children, led by their father, left the Armenian enclave to board a rickety, crowded old bus. The twenty-four-hour journey to Istanbul felt never-ending to Hanna. The vehicle chugged along narrow, bumpy roads with long stretches of desolate surroundings. Hanna drifted in and out of sleep while the driver, hunched over the wheel, seemed to urge the tired jitney on through sheer will as he negotiated treacherous mountain passes.

Finally the road transitioned to smooth asphalt and the rocking and vibrations of the bus lessened. Soon after, excited chirpings from fellow passengers announcing their approach to the legendary city roused Hanna from his fitful slumber. With the rising sun at their back, he beheld a view more unimaginable than Diyarbekir; a wondrous expanse of a metropolis, bounded by seas and hills spread below them. Tall, pointy Ottoman minarets with crescents at their tips speared the orange shimmer of the sky, while round domes of Byzantine churches and Roman arches of ancient fortifications softened the horizon.

The ride through the city seemed less frenetic than in Diyarbekir despite the traffic growing thicker and noisy trucks, cars, and mopeds aggressively vying for right-of-way among the seemingly endless throngs of city dwellers. Roughly cobbled side-streets shot off at all angles from the main thoroughfare, offering Hanna the briefest of glimpses into a maze of narrow alleyways. Taut lines crisscrossed at odd intervals and angles across the narrow canyons, bearing electricity, communications signals and fluttering clothing of every description. The drying garments flashed every hue of reds, blues, purples and bright greens in sharp contrast against the dusty, sooty gray backdrop of city life.

At the bus station they were met by Father Abram Varujoghlu, a short, chubby priest whose handsome face and kind, jovial demeanor reminded Hanna of some of the angels he had seen in his dreams.

"Welcome, welcome," Father Abram said, laughing as he patted Hanna's head.

The boy tried to smile back, but threw up instead, missing the priest's leather shoes by inches.

Father Abram drove them to the Armenian patriarchate in Istanbul's Kumkapi District. "You'll have shelter in the basement of the church," he said to Haiko who sat with him in the front seat. "We'll help you find a job and an apartment. The accommodations aren't the best, but *insh-Allah*, God willing, within two weeks, you will be in a nice apartment."

Every day, Haiko went to look for work, leaving early in the morning and returning late in the evening. Nazeli tended to the meals and did the cleaning. Asto, Chelo, and Hanna enrolled in the Bezjian Armenian School located in the patriarchate compound.

"I know you are Armenian," Father Abram explained calmly, as he accompanied the anxious brothers to school on their first day. "Others, however, will be suspicious of your antecedents, because the district you originate from is now inhabited mostly by Assyrians and Kurds. If anybody...anybody in the school..." The priest paused to give them a stern look. "I mean, if *anybody* inquires about your religion or ethnicity, reply firmly that you are Armenian without the slightest hesitation."

Hanna and his siblings nodded as it seemed to be expected, but confusion was evident in their eyes as they struggled to understand the complicated new instructions that were in contradiction to what they had been raised to believe. Father Abram studied them briefly, then resumed walking and continued the speech that pained him to deliver, as he had so many times before.

"By law, only Armenians are allowed to enroll in Armenian schools. In the eyes of the Turkish government, one of the worst crimes possible is to convert non-Armenians to the Armenian ethnicity and religion. The consequences for those who dare to do so are serious."

Both the school and the patriarchate had to conform to stringent and oppressive laws targeting minorities, Father Abram explained. The Interior and Education Ministries in the Turkish capital, Ankara, rigorously enforced these regulations by imposing severe penalties on those who flouted them. These included confiscation of property and imprisonment of transgressors, among others. Every Armenian school was assigned a government-appointed Turkish vice principal to ensure compliance with the laws and instill fear in the patriarchate, the school administration, and the student body. The instructors taught *everything* in Turkish, with particular emphasis on Turkish history. Only three hours a week were devoted to the Armenian language.

"The government absolutely forbids the teaching of Armenian history," Father Abram said in a grave voice.

Once they had arrived at the school, the priest entrusted the children to the care of the principal, who directed them to take their places with the other students, already lined up and grouped according to their grades, for the morning ceremonies. Hanna stood with his other classmates and sang the Turkish national anthem as the Turkish flag was raised. Then starting with the youngest students, they filed inside to go to their respective classrooms.

In the hallways and classrooms loomed the same austere portrait of Ataturk, the founder of the fatherland.

"This…this man has our blood on his hands!" Hanna recalled Musa Tchengo's rage when he had brought home a picture of the "Father of Turkey" from the village school. Musa had used his teeth and only hand to shred the picture of Ataturk to pieces.

Several hours later, as the Turkish flag was being lowered and that day's school session brought to an end, Hanna thought once again of his great-uncle. He missed him terribly, as he did his grandmother, his friends, his neighbors, and the village, the only home he'd ever known. Most of all, he missed his mother.

Two weeks in the church basement turned into six months. Haiko, it turned out, was not adept in the ways of the city and was still struggling to find a job. One evening, however, he returned in a celebratory mood with chocolates for the children, as he had back in their village following his long absences.

"It's a construction job with a Japanese company that pays good salaries," he announced. "I will be part of a team assigned to build the bridge across the Bosphorus. I will quickly save enough money for us to move to Almanya." Proud, cheerful, and playful, he was going to make history by joining Europe to Asia.

Two weeks later, after Haiko had settled into his job with the Japanese company, he moved the family from the church basement to an apartment in the city's Kumkapi District. Hanna, like his siblings, had never seen anything like it before. It had more rooms than he thought possible.

Ever since Seta's death, Haiko's muse had been mute. But encouraged by the promise of better times with his employment and a fine new apartment, he found his spirits lifting and resumed his storytelling. The tales enchanted Hanna and the others, transporting them back to their safe and cozy home in the village.

But their happiness was short-lived. A courier arrived one evening at their apartment door with news of Muksi Sarah's sudden and unexpected passing, and just like that, the newfound charm of city living turned to ashes. Grandma Sarah had, according to the message from Hanna's aunt, "died of a broken heart" which had "ached for Seta's children."

Haiko left for the village in order to attend the forty-day requiem Mass. When he returned, he brought Ani with him. Levon, now just a year old, was left in the village to be shuttled from one aunt or uncle to the next.

For Hanna and the children, Grandmother Sarah's death was a cruel reminder that the village and the fragile associations that still bound them to their mother would soon be a thing of the past. And the past, like one of Haiko's tales, grew murkier by the day.

CHAPTER 8

The family had hardly recovered from the tragic loss of Muksi Sarah when Haiko came home from work one evening, looking pale. Hanna thought he appeared on the verge of tears.

"We need to save more money," his father announced. He drew in a deep breath and then managed a smile that had nothing cheerful or spontaneous about it. "We must move again. But the new apartment will not cost as much."

Asto stormed out of the room and even Hanna, now six years old, sensed that something was missing in his father's justification for this detour on the road to Germany.

In fact, although a good worker on the job site, Haiko had failed to show up for work once too often. His excursions to the coffeehouses had taken their toll on his reputation as a sincere and dependable employee. His supervisor, not nearly as lenient or forgiving as his brothers had been in the blacksmith shop back at the village, had cut him loose. Without a source of income, the family could no longer afford the rent.

They packed their meager belongings, climbed into a waiting Volkswagen van, and drove through one Istanbul district after another on their way to their new home in Tarlabashi. This was Hanna's first glimpse of Istanbul beyond Kumkapi and he sat spellbound, as they drove down the wide boulevards of Aksaray, past the ruins of Byzantine walls and forts, and over the Galata Bridge with its breathtaking views of Hagia Sophia. He was amazed at the sheer number of people, from hagglers at Galatasary's bazaars to the throngs overcrowding the plush shopping districts and squares of Taksim.

There was little trace of Istanbul's beauty and prosperity, however, as they reached Tarlabashi, its entrance marked by unpaved roads and dilapidated homes. The signs of deprivation and deterioration grew more pronounced as they moved deeper into the district, which was notorious for its ghettos that overflowed with Anatolian peasants and threatened to overrun Istanbul.

Grimy, barely clad children played in the streets under the hot July sun. Elderly matrons sat on the stoops of their ramshackle homes and hollered to their neighbors across the street, their shrill voices shattering the calm. Women everywhere staggered under the weight of large buckets of water, trays stacked with food, or baskets piled high with fruit, somehow managing to balance their burdens either on their shoulders or on their heads that were covered with colorful shawls. The women also wore thick wool stockings, mere flashes of which were visible under long, wide skirts that swept the ground.

The men, meanwhile, stood alone or gathered in small groups, some squatting, others standing, all of them smoking pensively as they twirled their amber *tesbiehs*, worry beads threaded into a ring. The more energetic among them engaged in card games or backgammon, excitedly calling out in Kurdish the numbers of the dice thrown, and the chips could be heard up and down the street as they banged against the boards inlaid with mother of pearl.

Hanna stared, wide-eyed, as they passed a voluptuous woman flaunting her curves to a group of men sitting on someone's front stoop. She stopped to linger in front of them, her hands on her hips, turning just in time to lock eyes briefly with Hanna as the Ibelin family drove by. The boy had never seen anything like her and he stared in wonder at her bleached blond curls, her skin-tight miniskirt, and her ridiculously high heels. But soon, they passed others who, like her, wore heavy makeup and low-necked blouses as they sauntered up and down the streets.

Finally, the Volkswagen van came to a stop in front of a building. Hanna noticed that it had neither an entrance door nor all the front steps leading to it. Only a couple of the windows had panes and shutters. The rest were either broken or boarded up. The driver killed the engine and the children sat in stunned silence, contemplating their new home with a growing sense of unease.

"Welcome," a stooped old man said as they piled out of the van. "This way. Watch your step."

He led them through a filthy hallway that reeked of urine and down a dim stairway to their new home: a dark, dank basement apartment with dirt floors. Unequipped with either kitchen or bathroom, the one-room apartment overlooked a small backyard that was littered with trash thrown from the upper floors of the building.

A rat scurried past and Hanna felt hot tears streaming down his cheeks. "No!" he cried. "Not this! Not here! I want to go back!"

Nazeli, now fourteen and the closest thing he had to a mother, took him in her arms and rocked him back and forth, gently stroking his hair and face to pacify him. Her soothing caresses momentarily transported Hanna to another world, long lost and threatening to fade from memory, where he had once felt so safely rooted. Gradually, his sobs subsided into sniffles and then into a restless doze in Nazeli's comforting embrace. Hanna was only dimly aware of his surroundings as his sister lay him down on a makeshift mattress, supported his head on a bag, and covered him with a blanket.

The rats swarmed all around him. They stared at him with squinting, frightening eyes. Wicked eyes. He tried desperately to shoo them away.

Where is my mother? Why is she letting this happen?

The rodents metamorphosed into wolves and the vicious gray monsters bore down on him. He tried to run, to escape, but his legs betrayed him. He tried to scream for help, but his voice was gone. He was paralyzed. He felt sharp fangs rake across his chest, legs, and arms. The warm saliva drooling from the beasts' jaws oozed down his cheeks.

The fitful struggle finally snapped him awake when he jerked his arm. He managed a muffled cry. Nazeli arrived shortly at his side.

"Where were you?" he asked, stifling another round of tears.

"In the backyard, cleaning," she said sweetly. "You've been asleep since yesterday."

Due to the distance and lack of money to buy bus tickets, the boys started to skip school most days. The truancy alerted Father Abram to their dire circumstances. He began visiting Haiko and his family frequently, bringing along parcels of food. Unexpected attention came from another caller as well. Samir, a seventeen-year-old Assyrian who hailed originally from a village near Palu, would often stop by when Haiko wasn't around and visit Nazeli. She seemed to enjoy having him around, especially when he took Hanna and Ani out for ice cream or pastries.

For Haiko, Samir's visits only spelled trouble. "You can't come here anymore!" he warned the boy one day, when he came home unexpectedly and found him alone with Nazeli.

Having dismissed an embarrassed Samir, Haiko angrily chided Nazeli. "I absolutely forbid you to see him!" he warned her.

But Samir was not easily deterred, as Haiko would later discover.

Revered, and by now regarded as the family guardian, Father Abram came calling one day in August with a determined look on his face.

"I have a proposal for you," he said to Haiko, taking him gently by the elbow and escorting him out to the backyard.

They spoke quietly for a long while and although Hanna couldn't hear a word of their conversation, he noticed his father wiping tears from his eyes.

When the mysterious talk was over, Father Abram wrapped his arms around Haiko in a comforting hug and then put his hand on the other man's head in a gesture of blessing.

"Father Abram actually imagines his blessings will keep our father from gambling," Asto said with a sneer.

"Father Abram won't stop visiting us," Hanna said anxiously, "will he?"

Nobody answered, but the prospect of the priest never coming again was unsettling.

That night, Haiko feigned cheerfulness, but the story he had spontaneously begun to relate rang hollow, and after struggling with it for a few minutes, he fell silent, leaving it unfinished. Hanna wondered if another detour was imminent on their journey to Almanya, although he did not think it was possible to move to a place worse than the one they already lived in.

The next day, Haiko sauntered off to a coffeehouse and the children fell into their usual routines, with Hanna intent on roaming the streets.

Ani, now four years old, followed her older brother everywhere. Hanna, though, was in no mood to entertain his little sister.

"Go away!" he barked.

Ani ignored the order, but dropped a few paces behind.

When a bus pulled up to the curb, Hanna hopped on, sneaking in through the rear entrance to avoid paying the fare. Ani climbed on as well and sat a few seats back.

After a few stops, Hanna jumped off the bus. Ani wasn't quick enough to anticipate her brother's move and the bus took off, with her standing by the door, her eyes wide with fear. Hanna stuck his tongue out at her and watched triumphantly as the bus lumbered away. He then strolled aimlessly for a few blocks, his hands in his pockets and his head held high, feeling smug. He even whistled at the scantily clad women as he had seen other young boys do.

But eventually, he grew bored and his mind turned to thoughts about his younger sister's safety. Suddenly, he didn't feel so complacent anymore. He remembered a little girl drowning in the village lake and the helpless shrieks of the mother. He shrugged off the memory and tried hard to put it behind him, but his feelings of guilt over leaving Ani to fend for herself only grew.

When he could stand it no more, he rushed back to the bus stop, then raced along to the next bus stop and the next, but to no avail. Ani was nowhere to be found.

He ran home and announced in a shaky voice, "Ani is lost."

"What? Where?" stammered Nazeli.

She immediately dispatched Chelo to locate their father. "Search every *kahve* until you find him," she ordered, knowing a coffeehouse was the most likely place to locate Haiko.

She seized Hanna by the hand and dashed outside, running here and there to see if Ani would reappear. But it was a futile quest. The siblings returned to the apartment, exhausted and in tears.

An hour later, Haiko came running home with Chelo. He was visibly distraught. "Where is Ani?" he demanded.

Hanna was silent.

Haiko slapped him across the face. The blow stung, but less from the physical pain it had inflicted.

"Let's go!" his father commanded harshly. He grabbed Hanna's hand and dragged him along to the nearest police station. "Sit here!" he ordered angrily as he went inside with an officer.

In the waiting room, which was directly across from the room where his father was speaking with the officer, Hanna studied a portrait of Ataturk on the wall. The Father of Turkey stared back at him disapprovingly. Hanna was terrified, but refused to blink or drop his gaze, lest the implied surrender leave him vulnerable to the power of the dark eyes boring into him.

Fifteen minutes later, the officer and Haiko emerged, all smiles. Hanna followed them to a police cruiser and they drove to another police station where they found Ani sitting on an officer's desk eating chocolate. She ran to her brother and gave him a big hug.

Realizing how perilously close he had come to losing his little sister, Hanna felt a sudden spasm of remorse in his stomach. He knew he didn't have the strength to bear another loss.

Later that evening, Haiko gathered the family around him.

"Istanbul is a dangerous place," he began.

Hanna noticed all eyes turn in his direction, but it became clear soon enough that his father had no intention of further reprimanding him.

"Do you recall Muksi Sarah's story about her pilgrimage? Her visit to Jerusalem?" Haiko asked.

Exhausted by the day's events, the children simply nodded.

"Muksi Sarah and her mother left a pot of gold there; a gift to the Armenian Monastery in Jerusalem. It was for the orphans and young children that attend the seminary there." He turned to his three boys, hoping, perhaps, to inspire them, but his voice lacked both enthusiasm and conviction. "Our family practically owns that seminary."

He paused expectantly, but the children said nothing.

For his part, Hanna was too tired to care about the faraway and unfamiliar place, even though it had been dear to Muksi Sarah.

"On Father Abram's advice, I am sending you to the seminary," his father announced.

"You are sending us away?" Asto asked in disbelief.

"Father Abram says it is a nice place. A great place for boys."

"Bull!" spat Asto angrily.

"Watch your language!" Haiko snapped. "I said it will be good for you."

"You mean good for *you!*"

"Enough! It will be safe. You'll receive food, clothes, and a good education."

"This is my fault," cried Hanna, tears beginning to stream down his face. "My fault, again! I am sorry I asked Mother to pick the wildflowers from that bush. I am sorry I lost Ani. Please don't send us away. I don't want to leave my sisters!"

"Shush! This is only a temporary arrangement," his father said in a reassuring voice. "I will work hard, save money, and relocate to Almanya. And then I will take you there."

"You'll never go to Almanya," Asto said with a scowl.

"I will. *We* will. Trust me. It will happen soon. Every day, I hear of more and more people making their way to Germany. Even some bungling fools—"

"You will never—"

"I will!" Haiko shouted, striking his rebellious son on the cheek with the back of his hand in one swift motion.

Asto didn't flinch, but his face reddened instantaneously.

Haiko too flushed with embarrassment. He opened his mouth to speak, but unable to muster an apology, simply skulked away, leaving the children alone in the apartment.

Hanna turned to his siblings, tears of guilt still glinting in his eyes. As they huddled together and cried, he wondered how much more he could take before the wolves devoured the last of him.

CHAPTER 9

It seemed as if all of Tarlabashi had queued up outside the municipal building and its jam-packed waiting room. The Anatolians—Kurds, Assyrians, Yezidis, Laz people, Turkmens, tribespeople, and mountain Turks—were there to apply for passports and exit visas.

"Are they all going to Germany?" Hanna asked.

Asto smirked.

Despite the surging crowd, it was eerily quiet. Fear of the officials, fear of rebuff, fear of being unable to afford the unavoidable baksheesh necessary to grease the palms of the officials made the atmosphere oppressive.

After a long wait, Father Abram and the three boys were finally ushered into an office. Ataturk's ubiquitous portrait hung on the far wall. Dressed in a Western suit, the leader still stared sternly at Hanna.

The public servant sitting behind the desk, apparently busy with the papers submitted by the previous applicant, did not look up. "What are you here for?" he growled.

"I am here to obtain passports for these three brothers." Father Abram handed the official the boys' identity cards. A fifty-lira note stuck out of each booklet.

The official leafed through them. "*Ermeni?*" He raised an eyebrow, then nodded his head slightly. "It is not often that I see Armenian applicants." He looked at the pictures, studied Hanna and his brothers, and then reexamined the pages that branded their ethnicity, religion, and birthplace. He was clearly intrigued. "Armenians from the Mardin District?" His tone was one of astonishment mixed with a healthy dose of contempt. "I thought we had solved the Armenian Question and no *gavours* were left in Anatolia."

Hanna didn't quite grasp the underlying menace of the official's remark, but his pointed use of the slur "infidel" had been impossible to miss.

An awkward silence followed.

"Why do you need passports?" the official finally asked, nonchalantly pocketing the fifty-lira bills.

"These boys have lost their mother and their father is poor and unemployed. He is unable to care for them and has decided to send them abroad to an orphanage."

"Where is this orphanage?"

"In Jerusalem."

"Jerusalem? If they are *pezeveng yahudi*, why are they identified as Armenian on their identity cards?" snarled the official, confident in his assumption that they were "Jewish bastards" trying to conceal their origins.

"They are not Jewish," Father Abram replied firmly, his chubby cheeks turning red with indignation. "They are Armenian."

"Why would an Armenian go to Jerusalem? They must be Jewish!" The official pointed at Hanna. "This one—he doesn't look like an *Ermeni gavour*. None of the three do, in fact. They all look Jewish. Are you taking them to a kibbutz?"

Father Abram stood there, flabbergasted.

For the Turkish official, the absence of a response from the priest was clear confirmation of his suspicion, and he appeared to be savoring the successful exposure of a fraud.

"There must be a riddle in this one: how much does a stingy Jew pay an avaricious Armenian priest to do his dirty work for him?" He waggled his eyebrows repeatedly as he unfurled a sly smirk.

"*Effendi*," Father Abram now replied with a heroic effort at composure, "these boys are *Armenian*. The Jews have nothing to do with this. I am not getting paid for it. It is charity work."

"Lies! All clerics are liars." The official grinned malevolently, rose from his chair, and leaned down to take a better look at Hanna.

Hanna felt his underwear grow damp and tried hard not to burst into tears.

"He is not Armenian. And I'll prove it." The official opened Hanna's identity card and drew a line through the word "*Ermeni.*"

"*Effendi*," Father Abram protested, "but——"

"Shut up! Do you think you're dealing with an idiot? Jews have all the money and Armenians are the merchants. You're probably getting one thousand liras for every person you send to the kibbutz. And you have the audacity to give me only *fifty!*" He waved the documents in Father Abram's face to drive home the point.

"It's not——"

"What do I care if the Jewish bastards go to Jerusalem or not? As far as I'm concerned, it would be so much the better for Turkey if they did. We need to get rid of all of you! Jew, Armenian, Greek, Assyrian, Kurd—all the same despicable vermin! Now go away, think about this, and come back tomorrow. If you have a more *reasonable* approach, then we can talk." He took a deep breath, put the identity cards in the drawer, and then spat, "*Siktir!* Get lost!"

Once outside, Father Abram reassured the boys that they were not going to jail. "By tomorrow, I will have the situation resolved."

He bought them *lokum*, a Turkish pastry, and sent them home in a taxi, with word to Haiko to remain unruffled.

They returned the next day to see the passport officer and this time, Father Abram handed him a thick envelope.

The official counted out the baksheesh of three hundred liras and looked pleased. After retrieving the identity cards from his desk drawer, he started leafing through them again. He turned to Hanna and asked in a buoyant voice, "Hanna Ibelin, are you Armenian?"

Hanna nodded fearfully.

"Say something in Armenian as proof of your religion."

Hanna was stricken with anxiety. One year at an Armenian school and he was unable to utter a single word to prove his ethnicity.

Father Abram nudged Hanna. "Come on, my boy. Don't be afraid. Speak up."

"*Aboush!*" Hanna blurted out, reciting the only Armenian word he could recall at that moment. The word, which the boys at school often used to taunt Hanna with, meant "stupid."

The expression of shock that appeared on Father Abram's face did not last long enough to alert the official who smiled broadly, apparently satisfied with the boy's response. He took out his pen and wrote "*Ermeni*" in Hanna's identity card, right under the same word that he had struck out the day before.

"Come back in two weeks and the passports will be ready," he said pleasantly and this time, he dignified Father Abram's presence with a reverential Ottoman bow.

"*Effendi*, thank you," the priest said in parting.

The official rubbed his palms together and winked at Father Abram. "Kindly pay the cashier the processing fee on your way out. *Insh-Allah*, they will be happy in the Bible Orphanage."

Two weeks later, Father Abram arrived with a driver to transport the boys to the port. Hanna felt numb in Nazeli's disconsolate arms, her fierce embrace squeezing the breath out of him.

Moments later, the cab was maneuvering around the Tarlabashi potholes and the children at play. As he stared out the back window, Hanna's gaze was trained on the receding silhouettes of the two fragile figures standing motionless in the middle of the street. Ani clung to Nazeli's dress, not grasping the implication of this separation. As the cab turned the corner, Hanna caught one last glimpse of the anguished Nazeli. *Mother,* he thought.

Street vendors hustled their wares at the crowded port and the families and friends of passengers argued with shipmates to board the ship so they could say their farewells. Mostly joyous, some in tears, the passengers climbed the ramp while porters shoved aside anybody who came in their way as they rushed to load and restock the huge, ten-deck-high ship.

Father Abram had arranged for stewards from the ship to assist him in boarding the ten young boys he was accompanying. All ten novices, including the three Ibelin brothers, were new recruits to the Armenian Seminary in the Holy City. The stewards showed them to their cabins, three to four boys per cabin.

After Father Abram had settled the future seminarians, he called the three Ibelin brothers aside and led them to a quiet corner of the deck. "In Istanbul, we are forced to conceal our Armenian identity," he told the boys.

"In the village too," Hanna volunteered.

The priest smiled at the eager boy. "No more. You are leaving Turkey and you can leave your fears behind too. You're going to Jerusalem for a new life. There, you can be proud of who you are."

"Is all of Jerusalem Armenian?" Hanna asked.

"No, my son. There is an enclave within the Old City of Jerusalem that is completely Armenian. That's where you are going. You'll be happy, safe, and *free*." He paused to see if the boys had understood him. "You must leave your fears, along with your past, behind you. And that includes your names."

"Our names?" Asto asked, curious.

"From now on, you can—and *should*—use your Armenian names. Asto, your name is Azad; Chelo, yours is Kalousd; and Hanna, yours is Jonah."

Until this moment, Hanna had never understood why some of his relatives in the village had occasionally referred to each other by names other than their given ones. Father Abram's pronunciation of these "new" names sounded similar to the ones he'd heard back at the village.

"I'm simply converting your names to their Armenian equivalents," the priest continued. "Your family name is Ibelinian and not Ibelin."

Hanna searched his brothers' eyes for affirmation. Asto's expression was one of indignation. He was too proud to betray his relations, discard the family name, and assume a new one. But the brothers trusted and loved this priest and were resigned to accept a rechristening.

"It is very important that you use no other names but these. Starting now."

Jonah Ibelinian. My new name is Jonah Ibelinian. I am Jonah Ibelinian, the young boy kept repeating to himself as he scanned the port.

Why didn't Father say good-bye? He doesn't even know my name now. Am I still the son of Haiko Ibelin?

From the deck, Jonah searched the crowd below, hoping his father would emerge from the multitudes cheering and waving to their loved ones. But Haiko had disappeared two days before their departure.

When the horn of the cruise liner blasted the air at a volume that was deafening, Jonah felt a sudden emptiness pervade him. He was alone and for that, he felt angry with his father. He left the crowded deck, went back to the cabin, and collapsed, face-down on the bed, his tears soaking the pillow.

"Hanna," someone called in a faint voice.

Jonah looked up to see Haiko standing at the cabin door, his eyes brimming with tears. The boy leapt up from the bed and ran into his father's open arms.

Haiko hugged Jonah tightly and kissed the boy several times on the head. Only the ship's final whistle could force them to break the embrace.

CHAPTER 10

Jerusalem, August 1968

Jonah lifted a hand to shield his eyes from the searing glare of the Mediterranean sun as the group descended the gangplank at Haifa to join the sweltering masses.

"Blessed are the feet that walk on the land of Canaan!" an outlandish figure greeted the passengers in a booming voice. Bundled in layers of tattered clothing and a black woolen robe, he stood atop a crate in the middle of the wharf, leaning on a long wooden cane as though it were a bishop's staff. His matted gray beard hung down to his chest and his long, scraggly hair extended to his lower back. "Blessed are those that enter the land of Abraham, Isaac, and Jacob."

When the hermit spotted Father Abram and the group of novices, he bolted from his perch and bounded in their direction, the cane held high in his right arm. The crowd parted to make way for him, with several people wrinkling their noses as he passed. He crossed the square in a flash and stretched both arms wide, blocking Father Abram's way. He then peered intently at the priest and asked him a question in a language Jonah did not understand.

"They're orphans," Father Abram answered quickly. "Novices for a seminary."

"Save thy people, O Lord, and bless thine inheritance."

The strange man paced in front of the children and examined all ten of them intently, stopping in front of Jonah and

Karnig. The oldest among the children, Karnig had been assigned to look after the youngest, Jonah. The man closed his eyes, lifted his face and arms skyward, and declared, "Not shepherds, but errant sheep and sacrificial lambs they will become."

Father Abram appeared unnerved by the pronouncement. "Let's go!" he commanded and struggled to push through the crowd, shepherding the children as he did.

"Do you bring the children to the promised land? Do you believe they will inherit the earth? Do you think these are the chosen few?" The strange man's voice reverberated behind them.

It disturbed Jonah that the hermit had upset his beloved priest. *Somebody should tell the lousy nat off.*

"What language was that man speaking?" Jonah asked Karnig.

"Greek, I think," Karnig answered.

Jonah pried his hand loose from Karnig's grasp, as if to get around the crowd, and brushed by the hermit. "You stink!" Jonah hissed at the man in Assyrian.

The man stiffened and bristled at the remark, but his expression quickly eased into a smile. "So did Job," he retorted cheerfully in Aramaic, a language that Jonah recognized as the ancient Assyrian dialect used in the Assyrian church in his village. "I see you speak the language of the Lord," said the man more tenderly. "But why the fear and the caution?"

The reply and comment startled Jonah. He rushed to rejoin his group and clasped Karnig's extended hand to avert a scene.

"Remember, nothing remains hidden," the man blasted after Jonah. "All secrets shall be shouted from the rooftops!"

As they boarded the minibus, Jonah breathed a huge sigh of relief. Soon the vehicle cleared the city and headed for Jerusalem. Jonah stared out the window at the barren landscape as it went by in a blur. The dry, rocky countryside reminded him a little of the land around Palu, but his thoughts lingered only briefly on his home and his family. He was more concerned about what was to come: Jerusalem, his new home, the future... Everything was unknown.

As they approached the Old City of Jerusalem, Jonah could see a mighty wall rising around it. *If Palu had had such a wall,* he thought, *we would have been safe from the Turks and the Kurds.*

They entered the Old City through Jaffa Gate, one of the seven gates piercing the high, stony walls. The Golden Gate, Jonah would subsequently learn, had been permanently sealed shut. According to Jewish tradition, the Messiah would use the Golden Gate to enter Jerusalem victoriously. The Christian faith, meanwhile, upheld the legend that Jesus had used the gate for his final entry into the Holy City, while the Muslims viewed it as the gate through which the just would pass on Judgment Day.

Once inside the Old City, Jonah stared in disbelief at a world that looked as if it had not changed in centuries. The bus carrying him and the other nine novices veered right, away from the bazaar on Via Doloroso, and entered an alley just wide enough to accommodate it. The alley ran like an asphalt canyon between towering walls, with those on the right side shielding a notorious police station and those on the left enclosing the Armenian patriarchate. At the end of the deep chasm lay the entrance to their destination, nestled within the Old City of Jerusalem and safely insulated from the rest of the city and the world: the *Vank*, the monastery.

"You can live there as Armenians without fear," Father Abram had promised.

Our new home, Jonah thought.

CHAPTER 11

Elijah, His Eminence, the patriarch and head of the Vank, embraced Father Abram, welcoming the group warmly with a hearty laugh. "Sit, sit," he invited with a smile, indicating the large, ornate chairs and sofas in the room that served as his office.

The ten children, with Jonah bringing up the rear, waited in line to kiss the patriarch's right hand and his beautiful amethyst ring before taking their seats.

Said to be in his late sixties, the patriarch was a handsome, imposing man, whose silver hair, goatee, and large black eyes were complemented by a warm, deep voice. His silk pastoral robe, with a collar snug around the neck and a single button to the left of it, was patriarchal white and flowed freely down to his white slippers.

As soon as the patriarch was seated, he reached for an over-size cigar that rested on a crystal ashtray, placed it between his lips, and lit it with a long matchstick, taking several quick puffs. Then, with the pungent smoke from the cigar billowing grace-fully toward the ceiling, he tossed the match, still lit, into the ashtray on his desk, its flame flickering briefly before going out.

The patriarch did not smoke the cigar, however. Instead, he let it perch stiffly between his clenched teeth for a while and then set it in the ashtray, where it slowly went out. He then proceeded to repeat his actions, striking another matchstick to reignite the cigar, before casting the still-burning matchstick into the ashtray.

Jonah watched with fascination as the patriarch repeated this ritual numerous times. Then he glanced around the room and noticed several ashtrays, each harboring a half-finished cigar and several burned matchsticks. He also noticed the elongated match-boxes on every available piece of furniture.

After enduring ten minutes of conversation in Armenian that he couldn't understand a word of, Jonah was surprised when the patriarch cheerfully beckoned to him, saying something once again that the boy couldn't decipher.

"He says you remind him of a time long ago, when he had just arrived at the Vank," a beaming Father Abram translated.

Jonah smiled back at the patriarch, whose obvious affection for him needed no translation.

"I was born in Van and became an orphan during the deportation marches," the patriarch said in Turkish.

"My great-uncle talked about the marches," Jonah offered, glad he could put some of his learning to use. "Did you pass by Mount Ararat too? Uncle Musa was a fighter then."

The patriarch gently pinched the boy's cheek. "You know a lot, don't you? Your great-uncle must have taught you many things."

Jonah smiled and looked at his brothers for affirmation. None came. Instead, he saw that Azad and Kalousd were blushing in embarrassment.

"You are going to be the patriarch's son. You will be my little boy, my son!"

The patriarch's affection transported Jonah back to the warmth of his home in the village, and he remembered sitting around the hearth with his family and listening to his father's stories.

"Now go see your school," the patriarch urged, "and tell everyone you are my son."

As they left the patriarch's office and descended the stairs, Jonah glanced into the long, elegant reception hall to the left.

Plush sofas and armchairs upholstered in deep reds and purples lined both sides of the room, while paintings of saints and scenes from the Holy Scripture hung on the walls. At the far end sat a lone, high-back black and gold armchair unlike any of the others. Behind it was a painting of Christ, larger than life and standing tall, one arm outstretched. Jonah stared at the open hand and beckoning fingers, but then a painting on another wall caught his eye. It showed a mountain—the same one featured in the picture hanging on Uncle Musa's wall.

His great-uncle's words, "Never forget Ararat!" rang in his ears and he wondered how Uncle Musa's painting had come to be here. It was exactly the same, with the same twin-peaked, snow-capped mountain where Noah's Ark had landed.

"Ararat is ours," his great-uncle's voice echoed in his mind.

The Vank, the Armenian Quarter of the Old City, was an enclosed sanctuary. Within the confines of this ancient bastion stood a labyrinth of narrow, blind passageways, cloistered archways, steep stairwells, and rugged cobblestone courtyards. Diminutive, squat doors opened into hidden, cavernous residences. Hallowed cathedrals, monastic living quarters, and libraries housing valuable illuminated manuscripts and antiquities intermingled with the austere apartments of the lay population. Traversing through this web, Jonah envisioned the locations described in his father's fairy tales. They felt familiar. Like their village home. Jonah felt safe.

In one of the alleyways, they passed a small shop frequented by pilgrims eager to pay for the tattoo of a cross. Jonah thought of his grandmother. *Is this where she got the mark of a* muksi*? Did she and her mother know their gift of gold to the seminary would help us?*

Father Abram left for Istanbul after a two-week stay, having been assured that the young seminarians he had escorted to Jerusalem were beginning to put down roots in their new environment.

The three brothers were careful to use only their new names and nobody seemed the wiser. Being unfamiliar with the Armenian language posed a problem for only a short while, but during that period, Jonah realized that it was safer for him and his siblings to converse in Turkish than in Assyrian. At first, this seemed odd to him, given the deep fear and mistrust with which the Armenians viewed the Turks. In Jerusalem, however, as Jonah was beginning to discover, the Armenians' bitter rivalry with the Assyrian patriarchate was centuries old. The young boy's instincts told him, moreover, that his roots in an Assyrian village were something he must hide as carefully as he had concealed his Armenian identity back in Turkey.

In any case, it wasn't long before he and his brothers had become fluent in Armenian and the fear that someone might discover their Assyrian associations evaporated. As for the Assyrian language, it would take the boys considerably longer to forget it, despite the abrupt disuse into which it had fallen owing to their forced renunciation of it.

Even with these nagging concerns occupying his mind, Jonah adjusted quickly to his new surroundings. He felt connected to the Vank through his grandmother, whose gift to the monastery he assumed gave him special rights to this sanctuary. Moreover, his "adoption" by the patriarch gave him a sense of security that had eluded him since his mother's death. The feeling of comfort and acceptance he enjoyed within this Armenian part of Jerusalem and the secure walls that enclosed it seemed capable of protecting him in the future from all possible dangers.

CHAPTER 12

Mornings began abruptly at the seminary, with the club-wielding deacon delivering a blow to the sheet of tin at the foot of each bed as he strode down the long corridors where the students slept. Jonah, who slept in one of two stark dormitories, each lined with a double row of beds, twenty cots to a row, had learned to anticipate the rude awakening and would be standing by his bed by the time the deacon approached. It was a jarring way to start each day, especially at five thirty in the morning, but leaping out of bed while the deacon was still noisily making his way through the adjacent dorm spared his bed the dreaded whack and his nerves the early morning assault.

Just as he did every morning, the deacon shooed the seminarians out into the chilly open-air corridor for five minutes of exercise drills, followed by ten minutes of washroom and dressing time, during which Jonah and the other students hastily changed into black woolen hand-me-down uniforms to go to church. Each jacket, reminiscent of Chinese Communist Party attire, buttoned up to the neck. A special cap, made from the same material as the jackets, completed the standardized uniform.

By a quarter of six, everybody was in the courtyard, lined up in pairs according to height. Jonah led the march to the cathedral for morning services starting fifteen minutes later.

Housing the relics of countless luminaries of Christendom, the Cathedral of St. James was a great source of pride at the Vank. Built at a time the Armenian colony in Jerusalem was just being set up, the church had somehow escaped the encroaching influence of modernity and retained much of its medieval charm. Three wide, heavy wood and iron doors opened into a soaring nave that lacked benches, but offered plenty of plush carpeting for the pious to kneel upon in prayer. A small chapel by the left entrance that served as the sanctuary was also the burial site of the younger apostle James's head. The grand main altar, festooned with glittering gold and silver candleholders, flower vases, Bibles, and chalices, rose majestically above the burial sites of the elder St. James and some of the more notable patriarchs of the Brotherhood of St. James.

Decorative ceramic tiles, the work of the renowned Balian family artisans who had made a gift of them to the church, adorned the interior walls. As Musa Tchengo had pointed out to Jonah on more than one occasion, his family shared its lineage with the celebrated architects that dated back to the early 1600s. The striking, richly colored tiles would be a constant reminder to the young boy of his ancestry.

Murals, frescoes, and oil paintings of religious scenes covered the walls above the tiles. The cathedral was dark and particularly so in the early morning. Beams of sunlight poured in through the few windows set high in the dome, but most of the illumination came from hand-held candles and oil lamps hanging from hooks in the ceiling or on the walls, transforming the cathedral into a mystical and inviting place of worship.

The acolytes formed a semicircle around a lectern during part of the daily service to read or sing from hymnals. As the youngest seminarian, Jonah sat under the lectern, hidden from the congregation's view. Cradled amidst the chanting members of the group, lulled by the soothing hymns, and caressed by the warm, scented air, he dozed off from time to time.

Six years old—a good four years younger than the next-youngest seminarian—Jonah presented a challenge to the institution. The seminary was forced to grapple with the issue of caring for the boy and educating him. Was it appropriate, given his tender age, to subject the young boy to the strict regimen of the seminary? The headmaster's solution was to enroll "the patriarch's son" in the School of St. Tarkmantchatz, the local elementary and secondary school for Armenians in Jerusalem that practically abutted the walls encircling the seminary.

The first-grade class consisted of twenty students. The teacher, Mrs. Maritsa, a short, heavyset, and cranky elderly woman, had a low tolerance for misbehavior. On his first day of class, Jonah sat watching in amazement as the stern teacher pulled out a small round snuffbox, which had been tucked somewhere inside her bulging clothing, and opened it ceremoniously. Taking a pinch of snuff from it, she packed it well by tapping it a few times against the lid. Then, holding the reddish orange powder between her discolored fingertips, she brought it to one of her wide nostrils and sniffed vigorously. Jonah's eyes continued to widen as she repeated the ritual for the other nostril, for he had never witnessed such a thing and couldn't imagine why it pleased her. The sniffing triggered two monstrous sneezes and, not bothering to cover her nose or mouth with her hand, Mrs. Maritsa sprayed snuff and spit everywhere. The children in the front row, clearly familiar with the routine, ducked to make sure they were not in her line of fire. Jonah could barely contain his giggles.

Despite Mrs. Maritsa's strict rules, Jonah didn't feel obligated to fall in line. After all, he wasn't just some local student but a guest, the pet of the seminary headmaster, and the patriarch's son. He ignored assignments, became disruptive, and a constant nuisance to the teacher schooled in Dickensian methodologies.

To his surprise and unlike the headmaster, she disciplined him, but to no avail. Her idea of punishment involved making him stand against the wall for the duration of a session or write a particular word on the blackboard a hundred times. Sometimes, she took it a little further by rapping him on the knuckles or palms with a ruler. Jonah took it all with great aplomb, often mocking the teacher while her back was turned to him, all the while enjoying the mischievous laughter his antics elicited from the other children.

He walked into class one morning, confident and ready for a fight.

"Who did not finish his homework?" the teacher asked tersely.

Jonah eagerly raised his hand.

"Jonah," Mrs. Maritsa said in a reproving tone, "come up to my desk."

He hurried to the front of the classroom, all smiles, and extended his hands, expecting the ruler to descend smartly on both palms.

"Turn around and face the class," the teacher commanded him.

Puzzled, Jonah did as he was told.

Mrs. Maritsa then calmly addressed the class. "Everybody repeat after me: *Amot kezi dzuyl deghah!*" It was the Armenian equivalent of "Shame on you, lazy boy!"

The whole class repeated gleefully and in unison, "*Amot kezi dzuyl deghah!*" Shrill laughter and giggles followed.

Jonah felt his face burn with humiliation. Despite his best efforts to contain them, tears flowed from his eyes, embarrassing him further. He ran to his desk, sobbing, and hid his face in shame. The disgrace would transform him.

CHAPTER 13

As Neshan began his story, uttering each word with dramatic effect, he pounded on the stone for maximum theatrical impact with his long, rectangular club, which had a metal handle and a metal point at its tapered base.

Jonah sat with the others in the courtyard and listened to the old man spinning yet another story about the traditions of the Vank. Neshan's tales always glorified the Vank, its guardians and, most of all, its patron saint. Nobody doubted their veracity.

The children lovingly referred to Neshan as the "town crier." He had earned the title for his dedicated commitment to the perpetuation of one of the most beautiful traditions in the Vank. On especially auspicious days or those marked by certain religious rituals, he traveled all morning from courtyard to courtyard, from one rooftop to another, to sing proclamations. His charming, melodic voice would wake everyone before sunrise on those particular mornings. Jonah would hear him in the seminary courtyard, singing the Armenian verse from the major hymn of the day. Upon finishing the song, Neshan would bang the tip of his heavy wooden stick on the stones and exclaim, "*Ov Paree Kristonya, artentsek yev. . .donetsek.*" It meant: "O good Christians, rise to celebrate. . ."

That particular day's story was related to the lore of the younger apostle James interred in the Cathedral of St. James. According to legend, the younger James had been beheaded on the Mediterranean coast near Haifa and his body washed away to the shores of Spain. Meanwhile, a faithful follower had brought the head to Jerusalem. In the early years of Christianity, a prominent Armenian monk and preacher had brought the head to its current resting place, a side chapel within the Cathedral of St. James.

Neshan brought his stick down with a thud and paused deliberately before continuing. "In this land, there are constant skirmishes and occasional wars to acquire and retain rights and privileges to the holy sites. During one unforgettable incident, we almost lost one of our prized possessions to the scheming Assyrians."

The children gasped. Jonah, whose spine was already tingling with suspense, felt a twinge of self-consciousness.

"Through the centuries, the Assyrians had secured privileges to perform services in our cathedral," Neshan stated in a more subdued voice. "Following a celebration, they claimed they had not been given enough time to collect their vestments, staffs, banners, and other religious possessions and requested permission to return the next day to do the needful. To ensure the safety of their valuables, the Assyrians also requested that two of their priests stay behind and sleep in the cathedral."

Neshan paused to take a deep, dramatic breath. Then he smiled, raising his eyebrows to give his audience a suggestion of a hint as to what was in store. "Do you realize what this meant?" he inquired. "In this city, once you grant a privilege, it acquires the permanence of tradition and becomes an irrevocable right. Nonetheless, we consented to this peculiar request."

Jonah squirmed impatiently on the cobblestones. Did Neshan's raised eyebrows mean that the Armenians had figured out ahead of time what the Assyrians were planning to do?

Finally Neshan continued. "In the dead of night, the Assyrian priests prepared to carry out their monstrous deed. They removed axes from their treasure chests and attempted to break the marble under which the head of the younger St. James now lies. They wanted to dig out the relic and hide it among their belongings for removal the next day!" Neshan tapped the metal end of the club against the stone three times very deliberately. "The noise of the ax cracking open the marble roused the patriarch from deep slumber and he opened his eyes to see an apparition standing at his bedside." Neshan deepened his voice to mimic the ghost's.

"'*The Assyrians are stealing the head of St. James! Rise and defend the holy relic!*' declared the phantom." Neshan's voice shook with anger as he spoke. "The apparition, the patron saint of the Vank, St. James the Elder himself, had woken the patriarch to reveal the plot. The patriarch, in turn, rallied others to subdue the Assyrians." Neshan beamed confidently. "The beating they received was very satisfying too," he said with a chuckle. "That was the end of them! All their rights to the cathedral were repealed!"

Jonah had come to the realization that in the Holy City, right was might. The more rights—to property, access, entitlements, and representation, among other things—a community had in relation to the holy sites, the more power it wielded. The number of churches it owned, the number of chapels or domains it was responsible for, and the number and types of ceremonies it held in different locations indicated the extent of a faction's power. A community's privileges may well have been acquired centuries or even millennia earlier by its forbears. In Jerusalem's world of entrenched traditions, it was imperative to adhere to the customs and rules established many hundreds of years ago, including those dictated by imperial proclamations. Those emperors and their empires were long gone, but the dictates were still enforced meticulously. Any deviation from the norm led to interdenominational strife and jeopardized perpetuation of the faction's rights. Any lapse, such as nonperformance of a service or failure to observe its rituals at the agreed-upon time and place, could well lead to the surrender of that privilege.

These traditions and rituals did not just pertain to property ownership within a specified area. The right to be the first to carry out a procession or determine the number and size of the candlesticks to be placed in a certain location during feasts were issues of major import. The number of chairs to be placed in a particular location and the right to sit there at a certain hour of the day became key points of contention. The absurdity of these privileges even descended to levels that were mundane and frivolous in the extreme. The right to clean bird droppings in a belfry, for instance, could lead to a Byzantine quagmire of discord between fractious denominations that often festered for generations. While most outsiders had difficulty comprehending the preoccupation with such trivial matters, to the defenders of the holy sites, it was a matter of upholding the faith and protecting their heritage as well as their pride.

As a round of applause from the children marked the end of Neshan's story, Jonah felt more determined than ever to defend the Vank and its relics, and avenge injustices done to the Armenian nation. While he experienced a surge of pride, he couldn't suppress a twinge of ambivalence either; he was overcome by remorse, anxiety, and a diminution of self as he thought of his village and his Assyrian links.

The Armenians and the Greeks were equal partners in the ownership and custodianship of the principal sites of Christian worship in the Holy Land. The most notable among them included the cathedrals of the Holy Sepulcher in the Old City, the Church of the Nativity in Bethlehem, the Chapel of the Ascension atop the Mount of Olives, and the tomb of the Virgin Mary by the Garden of Gethsemane. The uneasy truce between the two patriarchates often degenerated into open hostility.

During certain periods in history, the Vank had seen its number of monks dwindle along with its financial wherewithal to sustain its holdings. Subsequently, the Greek community and the strength of the Greek Patriarchate in Jerusalem had outmaneuvered their Armenian counterpart. Thus, over the centuries, the Armenians had lent usage rights to the Assyrians, a similar Eastern Orthodox denomination, to avoid erosion of influence and loss of custodianship of domains at the holy sites.

As with the Greeks, the Armenian communities outside Jerusalem had established close ties with the Assyrians who were the Biblical neighbors of Armenia, the descendants of Babylon, and inhabitants of Mesopotamia or modern-day Iraq. The three shared several millennia of history and now, a common enemy: the Turks. Even as the genocide of the Armenians was at its height during the First World War, the Turks did not spare either the Pontic Greeks or the Assyrians of Anatolia. In Jerusalem, however, centuries-old intercommunal rivalry was tied to the ascendancy or decline of a community's standing within the hallowed grounds and cathedrals.

The feuds and bitter disputes were as old as the edifices themselves and no amount of shared suffering and martyrdom could eclipse the religious and national zealotry each group manifested. Neshan's stories only highlighted the obvious to Jonah: the expulsion Neshan had referred to had dealt a severe blow to the Assyrians.

CHAPTER 14

New York, 1969

"Thanks to your support," said an ebullient Archbishop Sevantz Aminian, "the Vank is thriving. The number of seminarians has gone up. There are plenty of priests now to tend to the needs of the Vank and defend our rights in the holy places. We are also making better use of our real-estate holdings to generate more income."

His audience occupied ten chairs in a well-lit Manhattan office. Like their host, Mr. Haitourian, they were wealthy Armenian businesspeople who had, through sheer determination and effort, risen from their humble position as mere survivors and refugees from a distant land to become illustrious individuals in their adopted country.

"To further strengthen the Armenian presence in the Holy Land, we need your continued support...in new ways."

"We've already donated large sums to the Vank," Mr. Haitourian interjected. "Still, my friends and compatriots here are more than willing to underwrite worthwhile projects. Do you have anything specific in mind?"

Highly respected by his guests, Mr. Haitourian could speak without fear of being contradicted. Nobody argued with him or turned down his suggestions.

"The seminary used to be filled with novices from Syria, Iraq, and Lebanon," Sevantz answered, without directly addressing the question. "Following the 1967 Arab-Israeli war, that source dried up. The post-war approach is to recruit from Turkey."

The Turkish connection, in fact, suited the purpose of the school's potential sponsors better. The diaspora Armenians, particularly those in the U.S. community, still carried the deep scars of the genocide and recalled with nostalgia their towns and homes that had either been razed or appropriated and resettled by Turks. They knew that Armenians living in Anatolia, the interior of Turkey, would not survive the Turkification and Islamization of their communities.

"Who are these students?" Mr. Haitourian inquired.

"Mostly orphans," Sevantz answered. "In fact, the seminary operated as an orphanage following the genocide. Why, our current patriarch himself was a child refugee who had been given shelter by the Vank."

The archbishop calmly looked around at the benevolent faces staring up at him. Things were proceeding better than expected.

"I have been rescuing these children from certain Turkification. Without your support, we can't feed, house, or educate these boys. As you know, there is a great need in the Vank."

"My father sends his apologies for not attending this gathering," said the only woman present. "He is on a business trip, and I am here to represent him. He is specifically interested in *direct* assistance to the students."

"Ms. Paravonian," Sevantz said, addressing the blond American, "that is exactly why I'm here. I'm soliciting sponsorships for the students. Every benefactor will be responsible for a designated student. The sponsorship should cover the entire period, starting from entry into the seminary and ending with the ward's ordination into the priesthood."

"My father went through the list of students and selected three boys with the Ibelinian surname. Are they brothers?"

"Yes, they are."

"My father will sponsor all three."

"Why specifically them?"

"My father said it was their family name that caught his attention."

"Thank you for your kindness. I'm more than happy to offer you their pictures and I'll send annual updates on the progress they make." Sevantz handed the picture of the youngest boy to Ms. Paravonian. "His name is Jonah. Here are his brothers," he added, passing her two more photos.

"He's beautiful. They all are," Ms. Paravonian gushed, examining the photos intently. "My children would love to have more brothers."

In Chicago, Sevantz redoubled his efforts. The response was the same with each group he met.

"He's adorable!"

"His name is Jonah," Sevantz said to a prospective sponsor. "He has curly blond hair and blue eyes."

CHAPTER 15

San Francisco, one week later

Archbishop Aminian heaved a long sigh as he exited the elevator. Exhausted and still suffering from jet lag, he stepped outside into a brisk wind and hailed the first cab he saw.

"Where to?" a grizzled cabbie asked him as soon as he'd plunked himself down in the backseat.

Too drained to waste another breath, Sevantz handed the cab driver the card to his hotel, and then leaned back in his seat. Selling the Vank's preservation to wealthy Americans was tiring but relatively easy work, and as he closed his eyes for a quick cat-nap, the archbishop recalled more perilous times...

Beirut, 1967

"Lord God of hosts and Creator of all things," Sevantz sang from the altar, "Who hast brought all things into visible existence out of nothing; Who also in Thy love of man hast ordained us to be ministers of a mystery so awful and ineffable..."

Somewhere along the line, what had begun as a calling had degenerated into a mechanical routine. He remembered his early years as an acolyte in a Beirut seminary, when he had actually felt secure and cocooned in the small, snug altar, despite the soaring cathedral ceiling above him. As someone who had embraced the elaborate rituals of the seminary and felt comforted by the warmth of the ornate garments of the church fathers, he had never tired of inhaling the fragrant aroma of the incense or watching the smoke rise through the shafts of sunlight that penetrated the long, narrow windows of the expansive dome. Compared to his life in the ghastly refugee camp, his years in the seminary had felt like a divinely inspired fairy tale.

"By the grace and loving kindness…"

Like heat rising in the distance, colors danced across curtains, marble pedestals, and tiled walls. Oil lamps of all sizes, shapes, and colors glowed from their perches on the walls and ceiling, while the faithful clutched their flickering candles. As the light shifted, the faces of saints appeared in paintings and then disappeared, as if ethereal beings from beyond had come forth and vanished again. The chanting of the ancient hymns provided him the comfort and security he had missed in his own home.

"Peace unto all." He turned halfway and made the sign of the cross, gesturing toward the congregation with broad, benevolent strokes of his right arm.

Then the deacon spoke, chanting, "Christ, the spotless Lamb of God, is offered in sacrifice."

Sevantz Aminian thought of the opportunity that had presented itself. He felt it could only have been by God's will. *I deserve it. Should I deprive myself further in His service?* He was quick to see the gift that God had bestowed upon him. *The Palestinian had to sell his property and the Israeli had the money.* He had simply mediated—*facilitated*—a preordained, unavoidable transaction.

"With fear and with faith," chanted the deacon, "draw near and communicate in holiness."

Holding the chalice, Sevantz dipped tiny pieces of the host in the wine before offering them to the waiting mouths of the week's penitents. One by one, they knelt in front of him and prayed for forgiveness and absolution.

"Say, 'I have sinned against God,'" the deacon muttered each time Sevantz dispensed the host.

An attractive young woman approached the altar. As she leaned forward to accept the communion, Sevantz couldn't help but stare at her exposed cleavage. His fingers lingered in her mouth and then gently brushed her tongue as he withdrew. She opened her eyes and blushed under his roguish gaze. Her mouth went dry—he could see it in the way her lips quivered, in the look of arousal that animated her face—and she swallowed the host with a gulp before retreating in an uncertain flurry of steps.

When the long line of communicants had come to an end, Sevantz hoisted the chalice as high as he could reach. "Save Thy people, O Lord, and bless Thine inheritance..." He stopped when he caught sight of a tall, dark, bearded man in the front pew staring at him intently.

The deacon standing next to Sevantz whispered the next verse, assuming, perhaps, that Sevantz needed a reminder.

Haltingly, Sevantz continued with the entreaty. *Who is he? Why is he here?*

He searched the congregation quickly and what he saw made his legs tremble. Two other dark, bearded men stood in the vestibule with legs spread and hands clasped in front. Each had the same hard look on his face. *These aren't parishioners. They don't look Armenian.*

The pleasurable excitement he had felt in his loins only a few moments earlier had disappeared, replaced by painful contractions in his abdomen. In his haste to turn away from the strangers' unsettling scrutiny, Sevantz tripped on the surplice draped over his shoulders and almost dropped the chalice.

Once the altar curtain had been drawn, the unnerved Sevantz unceremoniously poured the contents of the Lord's vessel into his mouth.

The deacon, meanwhile, was clearly perplexed by the bishop's utter disregard for the most sacred moment of the Mass. An officiant first prayed for the purification of thoughts, body, and soul, and then demonstrated meekness by bowing and touching his forehead to the base of the chalice three times. Only then could the imperfect, adulterated human vessel be offered to the Lord.

Too preoccupied with his predicament, Sevantz ignored the deacon's disapproving glare. Today, his heart did not rejoice as the fermented, muddy red sap of the grapes coated his parched throat. While gripping the chalice with his right hand, he squeezed his prominent Adam's apple with his left hand to finally swallow the flesh and blood of Christ. The usually sweet and appealing rivulet tasted bitter and did not douse the fire in his throat.

The rest of the Mass was anything but exaltation in the glory of the Lord. Sevantz tripped over his vestments, his fingers were clumsy as he leafed through the pages of the Bible, and his voice cracked as he read the day's verses. He tried desperately to mask his tension, but his right hand lacked grace whenever he turned to bless the congregation.

The back door of the church opened and a man wearing the black robe and steeple-like hood of an Armenian priest stepped outside. It was a cold, rainy day in Beirut and the small courtyard's overhanging vines blocked out the little available light. As the man reached the rectory, a blow struck him between the shoulder blades and he went down with a thud.

Two men began to kick him. One of the assailants swore in Arabic as he delivered another kick.

"Ungrateful swine!" the other snarled. "We Arabs saved your father and mother from the Turks and you betray our cause!"

After another vicious blow, the priest's hood came loose.

"It's not him!"

"The pig deceived us!"

The men looked at one another and then bolted toward the front of the church.

Having stepped out of his liturgical garb and dressed in lay clothes, including a wide-brimmed hat, Sevantz held an umbrella as he waited for the two men to descend on the parish priest. He then stepped outside and turned in the opposite direction, blending in with parishioners and passersby. His head bowed, he managed to pass acquaintances without them recognizing him.

Then he spotted trouble. Just ahead was the third man, the one he had first seen in the church. He was scrutinizing the face of every passerby.

Sevantz unfurled his umbrella and held it low. Then at a pace that was brisk, but not hurried enough to arouse suspicion, he crossed to the other side, turned the corner and ran to the next block, where a taxi was waiting for its next fare.

Without wasting a moment, he dropped the still-open umbrella onto the curb, jumped into the car, and slammed the door shut. "Drive!" he ordered, slumping sideways on the rear seat.

The driver grumbled to himself, anxious, no doubt, to avoid becoming entangled in a never-ending feud, of which Beirut had witnessed too many. He stomped on the gas pedal, and aggressively navigated his way through the maze of people and traffic.

Sevantz remembered his father's paranoid adage, always uttered in a hallucinatory haze: "When you least expect it, *they* will dig your ditch."

The Lord giveth, but before the Lord taketh away, I must leave Beirut. It's time to take up Elijah's offer and go to Jerusalem.

CHAPTER 16

Jerusalem, January 1970

Archbishop Aminian's visit to America set the stage for the opening of an annex to the seminary, which, in the absence of an official name, quickly became known as the Haitourian School. The "school" functioned largely as a dorm, and provided room and board for the younger boys who were housed on the first floor of a building across from the seminary compound adjoining the St. Tarkmantchatz School. The second floor of the building housed the priests, members of the St. James Brotherhood. For their actual schooling, the Haitourian boys attended the St. Tarkmantchatz School with local Armenian students, but only up to the sixth grade, after which they transferred to the seminary.

Kalousd and Jonah made the Haitourian School their new home, while Azad decided he was too mature to join them and stayed behind in the seminary. Jonah was still the youngest of their class of recruits, but with the arrival of more children, rescued by Father Abram from Anatolia, he could no longer claim such a distinction in the school at large.

Run independently of the seminary, the Haitourian School had lay guardians and a secular approach. The headmasters were Mr. and Mrs. Shakarian, a refined and well-educated couple who were good friends of the patriarch and respected community leaders. Their son Raffi was Jonah's classmate and soon became his best friend. He had a sister named Shahnour. Mrs. Arousiag

Shakarian, a charming and attractive woman, impressed Jonah
and the others with her attentive and caring demeanor. While she
took care of the Haitourian boys as though they were her own,
she couldn't help betraying her obvious preference for Jonah and
offered him opportunities not available to the rest of the students. Raffi also interceded on Jonah's behalf so the latter could
join him on trips and excursions and even visits to movie theatres.

The Haitourian School was the newest inner layer of a tranquil Armenian presence atop Mount Zion, and, as such, brought
more children to the Armenian Quarter. Thomas and Enoch
were in one of the groups that Father Abram had brought to
the seminary. After he put them both in Jonah's class, the three
boys quickly became friends. They did everything together, from
homework to exchanging stamp collections, breaking school
regulations, and disobeying the institution's rules that forbade
them from trespassing in areas clearly beyond its boundaries by
exploring the environs outside the Vank. The trio often huddled
in a corner, with Jonah and Thomas listening intently as Enoch
spun his imaginary tales about three Texan cowboys and their
heroic deeds. The stories always ended the same way, with the
cowboys saving the maidens in distress. While Enoch's storytelling had neither Haiko's flair for narration nor Neshan's depth, he
nevertheless managed to keep Jonah and Thomas hooked.

The boys often regretted living in a building where the priests
occupied the second floor. The students preferred not to be under
the constant scrutiny of their elders. Although, the older priests
occasionally complained about the noise the children made, most
of the younger ones cared for the students and, along with men-
toring them during their study sessions, often interacted with
them during their leisure activities.

There was one priest, however, who had earned the students' antipathy. Jonah and several others had been milling around the Vank's Calouste Gulbenkian Library one day, when this priest approached them.

"Wasting time again?" he had remarked in his typically condescending manner. He seemed to take a distinct pleasure in patronizing the boys.

"We're discussing this English book." Jonah had held up an anthology of short stories entitled *The Gift*.

The first story in the book was O. Henry's "The Gift of the Magi," a tale about an impoverished young couple's deep love for each other. Both husband and wife had, without informing the other, individually sold a possession each cherished in order to buy the other a gift for Christmas. Ironically, the husband had sold his precious watch, an heirloom, to buy his wife a hair clip, while she had cut off and sold a portion of her long, beautiful hair to be able to afford a gold chain for the very watch her husband had sold off.

"Ah, let me see." The priest had taken the book, looked at its cover, flipped the pages, and returned it. "English used to be one of my strongest subjects while I was in school," he boasted casually.

Jonah saw the opportunity to bring the self-important priest down a peg or two. "We can't agree on the pronunciation of the title. Can you help us?"

The priest took the book back and studied the cover briefly. "The Djift—yes, yes, I am certain it's pronounced *The Djift*."

Barely able to hold back their snickers, the students exchanged sly glances, even as they feigned admiration for the depths of knowledge the priest proudly claimed credit for.

"What does that mean?" Jonah persisted with a straight face, his eyes apparently earnest with keen interest.

"It means ghosts," the priest answered pompously.

"Ghosts!" Jonah repeated. "Now I get it. It must be about the ghosts of Christmas! Oh, thank you so much," he said with an exaggerated show of gratitude, bowing repeatedly. "I was having trouble understanding it. Now it will be so much easier to understand the book."

The priest left with a dismissive smirk on his face, apparently satisfied that he had educated a few ignorant students.

As soon as his back was turned, however, the students ran into the library and, no longer able to contain themselves, burst out laughing and chanting, "Djift, ghost, djift, ghost, djift, ghost!"

The librarian rushed out of his office and drove them out, but the nickname stuck. The priest whose arrogance had become legendary would be known from then on as Father Djift or "the Djift," for short, and years later, alumni of the Haitourian School and the seminary would be hard-pressed to remember his actual name.

Although the Djift considered himself aristocracy, his family hailed from the same province to which Jonah and the families of many other students belonged. But while the priest's arrogance was annoying, it was not as dangerous as his other shortcomings. He frequently stopped by Mrs. Shakarian's office to curry favor or to flirt with young female visiting teachers. But mostly, his visits were motivated by his urge to intervene in disciplinary matters, always to the students' detriment. To their dismay and resentment, he behaved as though it were his prerogative to take matters into his own hands and punish them. In a loud voice, he would lecture hapless students for a few minutes, and then, for good measure, slap them around.

Everyone preferred the discipline meted out by Mrs. Shakarian which, at the very most, amounted to an expression of mild reproach, followed by the effort to soften the impact of her words by stroking the guilty student's face as she murmured in a beseeching voice, "Please, my boy, don't do that again." Although the offender promised not to repeat the misdemeanor, he often did so deliberately just to elicit the kind caresses and smiles she was so generous with. The strategy backfired, of course, when Father Djift intervened to spare Mrs. Shakarian the responsibility of enforcing discipline and the heartache she associated with it.

CHAPTER 17

Istanbul, February 1970

Bright-eyed and radiant with smiles, Jonah, Kalousd, and Azad peered from the black-and-white photograph which had been taken a month earlier in Jerusalem. Dressed in formal attire, they were lined up in order of height—and age—in front of a Christmas tree.

Haiko tried to force a smile as he gazed at the picture pinned to the living-room wall. The passage of time had not dulled the pain of separation, least of all for his two girls. Ani, the usually bubbly, happy little girl, was obviously lonely, despite Nazeli's doting presence and constant care. Both had become quiet and withdrawn, except when Samir visited to provide them with some diversion and accompany them on walks outdoors.

Haiko frowned upon the boy's visits. He had scolded Nazeli on numerous occasions, making it more than clear that he disapproved. But after each argument he had with her on the subject, Samir would briefly disappear, only to return, more persistent than ever.

Eager to marry off his fifteen-year-old daughter in keeping with established tradition and thereby avoid a scandal, Haiko began entertaining offers for her hand from matchmakers and acquaintances negotiating on behalf of the families of prospective bridegrooms. But Nazeli turned away each suitor, pronouncing them too young, uneducated, or ugly. She even refused one on the pretext that he wasn't Armenian.

"She is making fools of us!" a frustrated matchmaker muttered to Haiko one day, before leaving in a huff.

That same day at a nearby coffeehouse, Haiko's card partner said nonchalantly, "Today's youth show no respect for our customs and traditions. My neighbor thinks your daughter will eventually elope with someone."

Haiko came home, incensed, and he had hardly shut the door before he began hollering at his daughter. "How dare you dishonor me and the whole family!"

"Father?" Nazeli looked at him, bewildered.

"You had better ditch all your plans," Haiko warned. "You will not marry Samir!"

"But I have no such plans!" Nazeli cried.

Her tearful denials did nothing to quell her father's rage. "I'll deal with him!" he threatened, wagging his finger menacingly at her.

Haiko rushed from the house, determined to find Samir. But after twenty minutes of fruitlessly stomping down one street and up another, oblivious to the stares of passersby, he angrily took up his position a block away from the boy's apartment and waited for him to appear.

He didn't have to wait long. A few minutes later, Samir came strolling around the corner in a carefree manner, whistling a love song.

Haiko accosted the unsuspecting youth, shoving a fist in his face. "You are ruining my family!" he growled. "You are ruining our name and honor! How dare you!"

"*Amdja* Haiko, I-I'm not sure I understand," Samir stammered. Addressing the other man as "Uncle" was an obvious attempt to placate him.

"I heard of your abduction scheme!" Haiko thundered.

"But I…I have no such—"

"Don't *ever* come to our house again! In fact, don't you even dare set foot in our neighborhood!" Haiko drove the point home by repeatedly jabbing Samir in the chest with his finger.

"But my uncle is your neighbor," Samir protested feebly. "I visit him."

"I don't care if your *mother* is my neighbor! If I ever see you around our house, if I even *hear* you have visited my daughter, I will break both your legs! Do I make myself clear to you?"

Samir started to walk away, but stopped short and turned back abruptly. "You can't scare *me!*" he said, glaring at Haiko defiantly. "I think what I'll do is rent an apartment across the street from yours!"

Haiko hadn't anticipated the boy's rebellious response and took out his frustrations on Nazeli as soon as he returned home, slapping her and warning her, once and for all, to stay away from Samir.

A few days later, a determined Samir visited his uncle and sent word to Nazeli to come and see him there. When she turned up, he proposed to her in front of his aunt and uncle. "Let's run off and get married," he suggested.

"Do you think you're still in some backward village?" Nazeli protested. "We're too young and I don't really know you. Besides, you'll be enlisting in the military soon." Her father had frightened her and she no longer had the courage to consider her own happiness. "And I really don't want to get married," she concluded.

"Your father *will* marry you off soon," Samir persisted, "and to a *complete stranger!* Is that what you want? Don't you think you would be better off with me?"

"If I do as you suggest, my father will kill me," Nazeli said nervously, "and you as well!"

"Your father won't find us," Samir retorted in a flippant tone. "Let's pledge ourselves to each other *right now, right here.*"

Samir's uncle and aunt nodded in approval.

In her heart, Nazeli knew Samir was right. It was better to get married to him than to meet a stranger at the altar. They shook hands to seal their decision, with Samir's uncle and aunt serving as their witnesses.

When Haiko learned of his daughter's engagement later that night, he exploded in anger. In a fit of rage, he kicked over a chair in the living room, before venting his frustrations on the nearest wall.

"How dare you! How dare you!" He paced back and forth. "Your word and promise mean nothing! It is the man of the house who makes such agreements!"

Nazeli and Ani crouched against the far wall, holding on to each other fearfully.

Then their father suddenly stopped pacing. "Tomorrow, you are both going back to the village." He was relieved at having come up with a solution. "Ani, you can rejoin Levon and live with your uncles and aunts like you used to," he said in a tone that was more contemplative than angry. Then he told Nazeli in a calm voice, "I will send word to your aunt to get you a passport from the regional office. She will have to make sure they record your age as eighteen. You are going to Germany."

It was as simple as that. In that one moment, an epiphany had come to him: this was the perfect opportunity to get the entire family to Germany. It wasn't the way he had envisioned it, but perhaps his long-held dream would materialize after all.

Turkish citizens were immigrating to Germany in droves. The *Gastarbeiter*, guest workers, typically established a foothold in that country as family units, but occasionally, they did so individually, one member at a time. Young men and, very occasionally, women paved the way for the promise of a better future for entire families.

Germany, for its part, was still accepting *Gastarbeiter*, especially from Turkey, its former World War I ally and tacit ally of the Nazis during World War II. Their special relationship had endured and continued to be more firmly entrenched over the years.

Haiko was envious of the many families from his province who had successfully migrated to Germany. They were mere *peasants* and had not even *heard* of Europe when he first aspired to go there; yet they had succeeded, while he still languished in Istanbul.

He put Ani and Nazeli on the first available bus to Diyarbekir and, within three weeks of their arrival at the village, the aunt had secured a passport for Nazeli.

While she was packing to return to Istanbul, from where she would make her way to Germany, Nazeli heard a knock at her aunt's door. It was Samir and his parents. The visitors persuaded the aunt to give Nazeli's hand in marriage to their son to prevent Haiko from sending the young girl to a far and foreign land all by herself. Samir's family then rushed Nazeli to their own village, where a quick matrimonial ceremony, officiated over by the local Assyrian priest, took place.

The news spread quickly, reaching Tarlabashi in no time and Haiko at his favorite coffeehouse. He couldn't have imagined a worse insult to his honor. He rushed to the village, where he embroiled himself in a bitter fight with the aunt whom he accused of trampling upon family traditions and humiliating him by giving Nazeli away without even seeking his consent. Haiko and his brothers then formed a posse and marched on Samir's village to salvage the family honor in a reenactment of the Biblical story of Dinah. Fortunately, Haiko didn't resort to the same tactics as Dinah's brothers, who had summarily slaughtered an entire village of men to avenge the honor of their sister for her rape by the "most honorable" young man from the neighboring family.

Instead, Haiko and his squad shouted insults in front of Samir's family home, hurled curses at them, threw stones over the wall, and eventually broke down the front door. After intervening to prevent bloodshed, neighbors and other villagers summoned the village *Mukhtar* and the priest to mediate a settlement. In a symbolic admission of guilt that was simultaneously intended to restore Haiko's pride and assuage his hurt feelings, Samir's father agreed to a dowry of one rifle and an undisclosed amount of money. The sum was not significant, but Haiko saved face by proclaiming, before he left the village, that he had been vindicated and suitably compensated.

Later that night, to his great discomfiture, well-wishers streamed through Haiko's house back in Palu. As if to make a mockery of the grave insult he had suffered, some even brought wedding presents. Haiko put on a brave face, bragging about the dowry. Finally, when the last of the visitors had departed, he went to the stove and wearily threw more wood on the fire. He lit another cigarette and sat cross-legged on the divan.

Musa Tchengo sat across from him, twirling the worry beads around his fingers. "I am leaving the village as well," he finally mumbled, breaking the silence.

"Why?" Haiko asked. "Where would you go?"

"To Beirut."

"Beirut?"

"I left a good friend behind. He saved my life."

"But that was over forty years ago. How will you find him? You don't know if he is still in Beirut or even alive."

"I will search for him."

"But why? Here, you have a home—"

"No!" Musa shot back, his voice cracking. "You don't understand." He wiped his eyes. "I lost my home fifty years ago and now I have lost my family."

"I did what I thought was best for my children," Haiko said softly.

A long pause followed and as the burning wood crackled and hissed, he recalled the old days, before Seta's death, when everybody had sat around the hearth, absorbed in the fantasy world he created.

Haiko did not return to Istanbul. Nor did he remain in Palu. Instead, he traveled to Midyat, the largest town in the Mardin region, after entrusting Ani, now six, and Levon, four, to his relatives.

Separated from their siblings and their father, Levon and Ani clung to the only possessions each of them owned: a small blanket and a few items of clothing. Every few days, when something happened that Ani found disagreeable, she would wrap their belongings in the blankets, throw them over her shoulder, seize her brother's hand, and stomp out. Another relative's house was only a stone's throw away. The nomadic child-mother often returned to the aunt or uncle's house she had so unceremoniously left only a day before.

Haiko drifted as well. He went from home to home in Midyat, staying with acquaintances and distant relatives. His hosts were obliged to entertain the many visitors from surrounding villages that came to lose themselves in the beguiling tales of the famed storyteller.

"*Chiroke, Chirvanoke, Khajkhajoke*," was how the sage of Mardin began each story.

While the guests sipped frothy coffee, smoked cigarettes, and twirled their worry beads, Haiko predicted their fortunes by reading the markings left by the dregs in their demitasse cups, often subjecting unsuspecting visitors to good-natured tricks with his sharp tongue and wordplay.

His friends pressured Haiko at every opportunity. "You are young," they would tell him. "You can't mourn forever. You have two young children that need a mother's care."

Haiko laughed off their entreaties. But his attitude changed one day, after a visitor, belittled and offended by one of his ploys, challenged Haiko, bringing up the subject of what he referred to as the storyteller's hypocrisy.

"Given your own success," the visitor said caustically, "of course it's easy to bestow on your audience such nuggets of lofty wisdom while denigrating the rest of us. I wonder what prevents you from acquiring a wife. Is it your exaggerated sense of self-esteem that comes in the way or your intolerable arrogance?"

Haiko ended the session abruptly and left the house.

For the following seven months, he went from home to home and village to village, accompanied by matchmakers and friends, determined to end his widower status. But there was no perfect match. He found fault with every woman shown to him.

"I give up," one exasperated matchmaker finally said. "I never met your deceased wife, but it's obvious no one will ever be able to match up to her."

After the woman left him standing alone in the street, he left the village on foot, head hung low, crying softly to himself.

He walked aimlessly through the evening and night. At dawn, he was shocked to find himself in Shushe's village. He headed to his estranged sister's house, where he was welcomed warmly.

"She is tall and ravishingly beautiful," promised a gypsy in a distant village.

Shushe and her Kurdish husband accompanied Haiko and served as his guarantors and interlocutors.

Haiko glimpsed the young woman from a distance, through a doorway. Wearing a long robe, the bridal candidate stood a head taller than the other women gathered around her and appeared young and attractive.

Haiko did not take long to make up his mind.

The girl's parents generously offered to forego the dowry in deference to Haiko's reputation, as well as to show their kindly feelings for his two youngest children.

The date of the wedding came around quickly, and Haiko arrived for the church ceremony without ever having spoken a word to his future mate. He was shocked to discover a *very* different woman waiting for him at the altar.

CHAPTER 18

Jerusalem, summer 1970

One Friday afternoon, as Jonah and the other children were lining up to go to church, a deacon arrived at the Haitourian School, accompanied by a man who clearly appeared out of place. Azad trailed behind reluctantly.

"A visitor from Istanbul for Jonah and Kalousd," the deacon announced.

Visitors and emissaries to the seminary were scarce. News from families came through the mail or via Father Abram, when he arrived with new students.

It had been two years since Jonah's arrival in Jerusalem and he hardly thought of his family back in Istanbul, much less at his village, now only a distant memory. His father had, so far, sent only one letter addressed to his sons: a poorly written litany of identical questions for each one that had begun and ended with the same prayer and good wishes.

"Can you point them out to me?" the man requested in heavily accented Turkish.

"Step out of the line," the deacon gestured to Jonah and Kalousd.

The man, whose attire and accent identified him as belonging to the Mardin and Diyarbekir region, turned to the brothers and, to Jonah's horror, started speaking in Assyrian.

Barely able to conceal his panic, Jonah shrugged his shoulders and pretended not to understand a word of what the man was saying. He didn't welcome a visitor, especially one who would draw attention to his old association with Assyrians in an environment where this particular ethnic group was reviled.

"How quickly they forget their mother tongue!" the man mused in broken Turkish.

"We do speak our *Armenian* mother tongue *very* fluently!" Azad quipped sharply.

The man seemed to understand and did not press the matter.

Perhaps sensing the awkwardness, Mrs. Shakarian ordered the students to start marching to church, a decision for which Jonah felt grateful. She then escorted the three brothers and their visitor to her office. Speaking in broken Turkish, which, to Jonah's ears, sounded European and refined compared to the visitor's uncouth accent, she welcomed the man and left them alone.

"I have come to Jerusalem for a pilgrimage—and to become a *muksi*," the man explained to the boys. "I'm a guest at the Assyrian monastery and have taken the afternoon off to come and visit you. I am a compatriot and a friend of your father's."

Eyeing the stranger with suspicion, Jonah remembered the Turkish official back in Istanbul who had threatened to reveal his "true ethnicity." Without being able to settle on a specific reason for his animosity, he already found himself disliking the visitor.

The man handed a letter to Azad, who proceeded to unfold it and read it aloud, tentatively at first, but soon with great speed and impatience. Even from a few feet away, Jonah recognized his father's poor handwriting. As for the contents of the letter, they were identical to that of the last one he had sent: short on news and long on good wishes.

"Now, let me tell you what is *not* in the letter," announced the man in a troubled voice. Ignoring the surly looks directed at him by Jonah and his brothers, he went on to describe their sister's hasty marriage and the subsequent plight of their father and their two youngest siblings.

Jonah avoided looking at their unwelcome visitor, his father's emissary, but he listened attentively to every word he uttered. The man seemed under an obligation to convey every detail he knew and Jonah was shocked to hear what had happened to his family. More concerned about his own predicament, however, the young boy tried hard not to acknowledge this man or his message. *How am I going to explain this to my friends?* he thought.

A few students teased Jonah about the strange visitor and his "mother tongue" comment, but relief came soon with the arrival of an amazing distraction.

Jonah was playing with his friends in the courtyard when he suddenly became aware of an extraordinary woman surveying them. He was the first one to notice her, but was soon joined by the others, as they all stopped their game and gawked at her. Youthful, attractive, and perhaps in her late thirties, the woman had short blond hair and a round, pretty face that exuded confidence. Dressed in white bell-bottoms and a colorful blouse, she scanned the students with a gentle, engaging smile. Jonah thought she was looking at him more intently, almost as if she recognized him.

"Where is Mrs. Shakarian's office?" she asked no one in particular. Her Armenian was good, but she had an accent that was clearly American.

Everyone volunteered to walk her there, but Jonah was hesitant. He sensed or, at the very least, *wished* she had come for him.

After slinging her handbag over her shoulder, she took a boy by the hand and motioned to Jonah to take her other hand. The whole group then walked down to Mrs. Shakarian's office and, after letting the American enter alone, hovered just outside.

The office door closed and everyone started speculating about the visitor's identity and the purpose of her visit.

"A passing tourist," offered one student confidently.

"English teacher?"

"Do you think she has come to take a student with her to America?"

That prospect excited everybody the most and Jonah found himself hoping that Dickens's stories about orphans and destitute children being adopted by wealthy, charitable people were not all fantasy, but held a grain of truth.

When the office door opened again, Mrs. Shakarian's face wore a broad smile. To Jonah's surprise, she asked him to follow her inside. The other boys pushed an astonished Jonah forward.

The mysterious lady was sitting on the sofa and looked at him with a gentle smile as he entered.

Standing behind him, with her hands on his shoulders, Mrs. Shakarian said, "Ms. Paravonian, this is Jonah."

"I recognized him from the pictures when I saw him outside. He is so handsome and I love his blue eyes." She addressed Jonah directly. "Please call me Nora."

Jonah suppressed a nearly irresistible urge to squeal with delight. "Hello, M-Ms. Nora," he stammered.

The American stifled a laugh and offered an affectionate smile instead.

"Jonah, my son, Nora is your benefactor's daughter," Mrs. Shakarian said in a reassuring voice. "In fact, her father sponsors your two older brothers as well. She has come all the way from America to meet you."

Jonah sensed the significance of this introduction and suspected that this woman could somehow determine his future. "I would like to fetch my brothers!" he said excitedly.

The ladies hesitated, but before they could say a word, Jonah was out the door and on his way to search for Kalousd and Azad. After negotiating his way through the gathering crowd of curious students, he found his siblings and was back in five minutes, dragging a reluctant older brother and a shy middle one.

"This is Azad and this is Kalousd," Mrs. Shakarian said, introducing the boys to the visitor.

"They look so much alike!" Nora marveled, still smiling.

Jonah relaxed, feeling pleased with himself.

"Why don't you recite a poem for Ms. Nora?" Mrs. Shakarian suggested.

Jonah quickly assumed his favorite posture, his right leg in front, his right arm resting on his hip, and recited with great flair a poem he had memorized recently for class. When he had finished, both Mrs. Shakarian and Nora applauded enthusiastically. He grinned proudly.

"Mrs. Shakarian tells me you want to become a doctor," Nora observed.

Jonah nodded.

"You have to be very smart to become a doctor, you know," Nora said.

"I am the smartest in my class," Jonah said with poise, before turning to his two brothers for confirmation.

Azad gave him a reproving look, while a blushing Kalousd smiled shyly.

Nora laughed approvingly. She got up and kissed Jonah on both cheeks and then turned to Mrs. Shakarian and said, "I like his confidence. I'm *sure* my two children will like him as well."

Mrs. Shakarian offered an uneasy smile. "Ms. Nora tells me that an Ibelinian saved her father's life—during the genocide. He has felt eternally grateful to that family ever since. Because of your name, they want to help all three of you."

"Thank you, Ms. Nora," Azad offered in a tone that conveyed gratitude, but was tinged with defiance.

"We will do more than just help," Nora said with unmistakable certitude in her voice.

"It is complex and will take time to resolve," Mrs. Shakarian replied quickly. Then she ushered the boys out, explaining, "I have some things I need to discuss with Ms. Nora."

The boys joined their envious friends outside, as the office door closed behind them.

His mind racing, Jonah ignored the questions his excited friends were asking him. He was unsure as to what Mrs. Shakarian had meant by "It is complex," but soon his thoughts were elsewhere. An Ibelinian had helped Ms. Nora's father during the genocide, and Jonah's imagination wandered to the village and Musa Tchengo. He fancied that his legendary great-uncle was the hero who had saved the life of his benefactor and immediately regretted not offering that explanation to Ms. Nora. Then again, he hadn't been afforded the opportunity, considering Mrs. Shakarian's uncharacteristically hurried dismissal of the boys.

Nora Paravonian left Mrs. Shakarian's office favorably impressed by the woman, but with her enthusiasm somewhat dampened. She was a determined woman, however, and wouldn't give up on her plan, despite the warnings from the principal. She could and would overcome the obstacles in her way and knew exactly who the real opposition would be. Quite taken by the children, she also felt inspired to do this for her father who, after all these years, deserved the peace of mind that could come only from accomplishing something grand.

Her father, Arkan, was a kind and gentle man, soft-spoken, generous, and stable as a rock. While he was clearly proud of all that he had accomplished, he had scant respect for fanfare and pomposity. He spoke with great humility whenever he recounted the story of his arrival at Ellis Island with nothing but the shirt on his back and a twenty-dollar bill in his pocket. When asked about his life before New York, however, his mood would turn somber and he would lapse into a grim silence.

What Nora knew of her father's past came from her mother. An engineering graduate from Roberts College, a school in Istanbul affiliated with Columbia University, he had been drafted into the Turkish army at the beginning of 1915 and assigned to a German unit in Anatolia. He had served as an engineer and interpreter for the Berlin-to-Baghdad railway project. Over the years, his wife had pieced things together by listening to his friends' stories, absorbing whatever she could in those brief moments when he let his guard down, and being there for him during his nightmares and panic attacks. One episode, in particular, had always stood out.

New York, November 1938

After handing their tickets to the young boy dressed in a smart red uniform with matching cap, Delilah and Arkan Paravonian took their seats in the middle of the movie theater just as the lights were being dimmed.

Charlie Chaplin appeared on the screen, moments later, wearing a bowler hat, his signature baggy pants, and a mustache no longer than the breadth of his nose. The whirling cane aggravated his clumsy gait instead of helping him to improve it, and the audience cheered and applauded as he bumbled onscreen. As though afflicted with a strange tic, the "dictator" saluted ceaselessly with an outstretched arm, all the while goose-stepping and mouthing an inaudible, yet apparently eloquent speech. The more outrageous Chaplin's antics became, the more clamorous the crowd grew.

Arkan's spirits were high. No wonder *The Great Dictator* had been touted as *the* film to watch. But as he sat next to his wife, his mind began to wander. Soon his thoughts had turned to his Jewish business partner and the news from Europe. Arkan's mood and vision suddenly darkened. The scene in front of him turned blurry and the bowler hat morphed into a turban, then a Turkish fez, the whirling cane into a slashing scimitar and the dictator into Talaat Pasha, the prime minister of Turkey and leader of the Young Turks.

Arkan shut his eyes and shook his head to ward off the specter, but a torrent of images from his past, more vivid than the film itself, flooded his memory. The silhouettes of a dozen naked girls circled the towering flames of a bonfire, craven gendarmes prodding the petrified girls until they danced. Emaciated mannequins they were, with the outlines of their bones clearly visible under their taut, almost translucent skin. They were young, some prepubescent, and their breasts were mere buds—when present at all or not sunken into the chest from near starvation. Each had a long mane of hair. Curiously enough, some appeared as white as his grandmother's hair. They were bereft of family, orphaned by untold massacres, piteous survivors of deportations. Sobbing in quiet shame, they gyrated awkwardly, while the lecherous soldiers poked and prodded them with tongues, fingers, penises, and bayonets.

For God's sake, they are only—

He was unable to finish the thought. Without warning, one forlorn soul broke rank and simply walked into the flames. The halo from her burning hair illuminated her trance-like gaze.

Arkan shrieked and discharged his rifle, and the salvo that followed from every direction pounded in his ear.

Brandished Turkish scimitars imitated the ceaseless salutes and the whirling cane. Pledges to the Almighty to butcher the *gavour*, the infidel, and battle cries of *"Allah-ou-akbar"* became one with the image of Chaplin silently bellowing.

If it hadn't been for Petros and Movses...

Arkan shifted in his chair as his forehead broke out in a sweat. He loosened his collar to relieve the invisible grip around his neck.

I need air. I have to get out of here.

He tugged at Delilah's arm.

"What? What's wrong? Why are we leaving?" Delilah looked around to see if somebody had bothered her husband.

Arkan pulled her up harshly and she recoiled in surprise.

They helped me escape. Did they survive?

They were outside now and he didn't even notice the frigid air—or the fact that he had left his coat in the theater.

CHAPTER 19

Sinai Peninsula, July 1970

The driver revved the engine as he made yet another attempt to free himself and his passengers, but it was futile. The blue Mercury sedan's front tires remained stuck in the sand.

The situation looked hopeless from the back seat, where Nora Paravonian sat. She watched as the driver stepped out with the archbishop to examine the problem more closely. They tried to rock the car out of the pothole, but it wouldn't budge. Exhausted and frustrated, they sat down on the sand and leaned against the car.

When the temperature in the car's interior had climbed above one hundred degrees, Nora joined the men outside for some much-needed air. She was ill prepared for the desert, where the sun smoldered relentlessly in the cloudless sky. She had needed time with the archbishop to ensure the success of her plan. And when he promised that he could personally show her some of the most ancient monasteries in the Holy Land, she had been convinced the trip would be worth it. But for some unexplained reason, he had been edgy the entire time.

"Where are we?" she asked.

He waved off the question, a gesture which only succeeded in infuriating her.

"Why did you invite me here in the first place?" the American demanded. "We're stranded, aren't we?"

"Yes, but someone will come by soon." He removed his black robe and unbuttoned his collar. He was sweating profusely.

"This place is in the middle of nowhere," Nora said anxiously. "I didn't notice any other cars the last half hour we were driving. Should we walk?"

"We can't leave the car."

"Why not? It's stuck. Let's walk."

"I said somebody will come soon," the archbishop replied brusquely.

"And how can you be sure of that?"

"I have...uh...*packages* in the trunk. The intended recipient will send someone after us."

"How would they know we're stuck?"

"I had an appointment," he replied absentmindedly.

"The sightseeing was a ruse, wasn't it?" When he didn't reply, she knew she had been duped. "What's in the packages and who are you meeting?"

Ignoring her, he got up, walked around the car, and stared out at the horizon, shielding his eyes from the sun with his hand.

Nora hurled a few sarcastic remarks in his direction, the outcome of her feelings of frustration, but upon receiving no response, fell silent. She stared into the distance, following the direction of the archbishop's gaze. Nothing moved.

After they had been quietly baking under the sun for an hour, the driver stirred. He stood up suddenly, his expression nervous, his posture tense with anticipation. "There!" he yelled in Arabic, pointing toward a mountain.

The archbishop sprang to his feet, straining to spot whatever the driver had pointed out. "Get up," he said hurriedly to Nora. "Look your best. I need to impress them."

"I don't care who you're impressing," Nora retorted. "I came to see the boys my father is sponsoring. Why did you have to drag me into this mess?"

"If I am not mistaken, you had an agenda yourself."

"Not a selfish one."

"Selfishness motivates everything we do."

"For some, it seems it is the only motivation."

He let out a laugh that sounded anything but genuine, and then turned to look at the approaching party.

A camel rider appeared, towing three other camels with him. They exchanged the customary salutations, bows, and gestures.

"Ms. Paravonian, I hope you don't mind riding a camel," Archbishop Aminian said with a snicker.

"I've been around the world several times," she retorted indignantly. "I've ridden camels, elephants, and horses. Don't worry about me. For you, they should have brought an ass."

The camel rider helped Nora onto one of the camels, while the clergyman and the driver unloaded the trunk. They placed several packages of different sizes and shapes on the other camel's back and tied them down securely.

After an hour's ride, they reached an area dotted with a few palm trees and a well. There were several tents nearby. They were quickly ushered into the largest tent, which was cool inside and dimly lit.

Once Nora's eyes had adjusted to the gloom, she noticed an elderly Bedouin sitting cross-legged on a plush rug.

"*Salaam-u-alaikum,*" the archbishop said and bowed.

"*Alaikum-us-salaam,*" the Bedouin replied with a nod, and then motioned for them to sit. "*Itfaddal,*" he said and offered a smoke from his water pipe, the *nargileh.*

The archbishop took a drag and passed it to Nora, who declined. The archbishop appeared perturbed by her refusal, but covered for her by making a charming comment to the Bedouin as he passed the pipe back.

"Who is he?" she asked.

"A friend." The archbishop smiled. "It is very important that we not offend the host. Follow my lead and simply do as I do."

Three Arab servants entered the tent with decorative pitchers of water, washbasins, and towels for the host and his guests. After everyone had washed, the servants spread a white cloth on the rug. Two other servants appeared, carrying a large tray with a huge mound of steaming rice and chunks of roasted lamb. They placed the tray on the cloth in the middle of the seated party.

Nora was aghast when the Bedouin and the archbishop reached for the rice and meat with their bare hands. However, she was simply too hungry to allow her squeamishness to get the better of her. Frowning with distaste, she scooped up a handful and popped it into her mouth. She was surprised to find it tasted as good as her mother's delicious Armenian rice pilaf.

When they left three hours later, a jeep was waiting for them. Nora watched suspiciously as the packages were loaded into the trunk of a car.

Jerusalem, the next day

A trio of black limousines drove up and parked in front of a shop built into the outside wall of the seminary, opposite the Zion Gate. With its windows boarded up, the shop appeared to have gone out of business and wore a deserted look.

A group of well-dressed men jumped out from the first car and the third, and took up positions next to the vehicle in the middle. One of the doors to that car opened and a stout, bald man stepped out and hurriedly strode into the store through a metal door that magically opened for him from inside. A half hour later, he was back in his car. The trunks of the other two cars were then loaded with the packages the archbishop had collected from the Bedouin.

Paris, the next day

Several time zones away and just a block from Sotheby's Auction House, a young man stood inside a public phone booth and dabbed nervously at his perspiring forehead. "Mr. Haitourian," he said in a frantic voice, "you must bid on these. You must!"

"Andrew," said the voice on the other end of the line, "how do you know these are Armenian? They could be Byzantine bibles or even Ethiopian. The Ethiopians and the Byzantines were sufficiently inspired by some of the Armenian styles to copy them. And I'm sure you're aware of the strong similarities between the Ethiopian and Armenian alphabets."

"In the auctioneer's list, they are identified as 'manuscripts from the Byzantine era', but Mr. Haitourian, you have to believe me, these are Armenian illuminated manuscripts!"

"Who is the seller?" the wealthy New Yorker asked skeptically.

"He isn't identified. If you don't buy them, they'll probably be snatched up by some European collector. They'll be lost to us forever."

CHAPTER 20

Jerusalem, summer 1971

Father Abram brought new recruits to Jerusalem in September; Levon, Jonah's youngest brother, among them. He was not quite six years old, younger than Jonah had been at the time of his entry into the seminary.

As the newcomers entered the Haitourian School compound, the entire student body examined them, their curiosity piqued. Levon's expression was quizzical as he looked straight at Jonah. There was no mistaking the family resemblance. Jonah said nothing. He felt embarrassed and nervous around the unfamiliar younger brother he had last seen as an infant. Jonah had one particular memory of his little brother that made him shudder. He recalled their mother, along with other women, doing their laundry by the shore of the lake. They had scrubbed and scrubbed the clothes before pounding them against the rocks while the younger children played around them. Jonah was supposed to mind his younger sister, Ani, and the newborn. He had just learned about Moses at church and thought of sharing his information with his sister.

"They put Moses in a basket, just like the one Levon is sleeping in, and sent him down the river. Just like so," Jonah had said, giving the basket a gentle push.

"Look, Mama, look! Levon can swim like Moses," Ani had squealed excitedly.

Seta had let out a frightened scream and jumped into the water, fully clothed, to retrieve the basket.

Jonah brushed aside the memory, while Father Abram carried out the formal introductions. The brothers warily eyed each other. Jonah wanted to hug Levon, but felt unsure about the response he would elicit from the boy who now looked quite different from the little brother he had known.

Energetic and free-spirited, Levon was smartly dressed and looked healthy and happy. Father Abram explained to the boy's three older brothers how he had taken Levon into his house upon his wife's urging, soon after Haiko's relocation to Istanbul.

Azad, Kalousd, and Jonah were pleased that Levon had finally found the loving and secure environment he had lacked since birth. It was quite apparent that the boy loved Father Abram, who cared just as deeply for him.

The boys learned that after the birth of their first half brother, Haiko had moved the remaining members of his first family, along with his growing second one, from Midyat to Istanbul. This time, he had left no one behind. He had placed Ani in a boarding school run by Austrian nuns.

Father Abram gave the boys Ani's address, and soon they began corresponding with her. Jonah enjoyed receiving her letters, especially when she sent pictures. In return, he mailed her the few he had.

Soon after Levon's arrival, Kalousd joined Azad at the seminary, while the two younger siblings remained Haitourian boys, attending the St. Tarkmantchatz School. Azad assumed his role as the family patriarch and protector, while Jonah was entrusted with the responsibility of watching over their youngest brother. Content that his whole family had finally settled down, Jonah immersed himself even further in the nurturing surroundings of the Vank.

Jerusalem, spring 1972

Swimming in the briny waters of the Dead Sea and floating on its surface held its own peculiar pleasure, but Jonah was now keen to explore the dolomite cliffs above its brownish salt-laden shores. Before he could do so, however, he heard Bishop Cyril, the principal of St. Tarkmantchatz School and the children's escort during this school outing, call out to the students. "Everybody gather up your belongings! It's time to climb to Masada."

With the sun blazing above them, they began the steep ascent toward the fortress ruins at the top.

Bishop Cyril was *the* authority on the Vank's rights and privileges at the holy sites. His encyclopedic knowledge and love of the region had led to his being appointed the grand sacristan of the Armenian sections. As such, he ensured that traditions, practices, prestige, privilege, and the structures themselves were preserved. Moreover, he constantly sought new approaches to improve the Vank's standing and expand its rights.

Midway up the hill, the bishop stopped to catch his breath. "Let's rest a moment," he suggested between gasps for air. "Who has read Franz Werfel's novel, *The Forty Days of Musa Dagh?*"

A few hands went up, Jonah's among them.

"The saga of Masada is very similar to the heroic fight of the Armenians of Musa Dagh," the bishop said, still panting from the heat and the steep climb. "The Israelites lasted a long time, but eventually, the absence of water and food, on top of the continuous Roman assaults, broke the resistance. The rebels chose death and suicide over captivity. The Armenians of Musa Dagh fared better. A French navy ship rescued them from certain martyrdom at the hands of the Turkish army."

He pointed to the gaping holes in the barren mountains. "The hills you see house the Qumran caves, where the Dead Sea Scrolls were discovered. In 1947, a young Bedouin shepherd chased one of his goats into a cave and discovered the scrolls and fragments of the Bible's Aramaic text."

"He's an encyclopedia!" Thomas whispered in Jonah's ear.

After they had reached the summit, a handful of the boys crawled in and out of the small openings in the citadel's ruins. Jonah, in particular, seemed to be able to fit into just about any crack.

"I have a job for you when we get back," the bishop said to him with a broad smile.

A week after the outing, the bishop summoned the boy to his office. Jonah was surprised to find the usually pensive and somber man in an ebullient mood.

"Helena, the mother of Emperor Constantine the Great, discovered the cross in a dump not far from Golgotha," the bishop said guardedly.

Jonah was well versed in the centuries-old legend and was at a loss as to why Bishop Cyril had summoned him simply to repeat the story.

"Helena sponsored the construction of the Holy Sepulcher Church," the bishop continued, "to encompass the sites of crucifixion, the burial grotto, and the site where the cross was discovered."

It was obvious to Jonah that preserving the Vank's history and tradition and ensuring the passage of its legacy to future generations mattered more than anything else to the bishop. His mission in life, it seemed, was to uncover actual evidence in support of the prevailing theory on the unearthing of the cross of crucifixion. He had spent years in research and pursuit of the actual location. Invariably, this passion had earned him the labels of "obsessed" and "eccentric" from some.

The bishop fell silent as he studied Jonah. "Can you keep a secret?"

The boy flinched, unsure as to how he should respond. *I have harbored secrets all my life. My family survives on secrecy.*

"At Masada, I noticed you had no difficulty fitting into tight spaces."

Jonah grew more puzzled. "Your Grace, I don't understand—"

"You must have noticed that despite the completion of the Holy Sepulcher Church renovations, the scaffolding behind the altar of the St. Gregory Chapel remains in place."

"Yes, Your Grace, I have."

The unfinished work, as far as Jonah could tell, perplexed the whole community. Although the altar appeared fully renovated, Bishop Cyril insisted that more work was needed in the space behind it. But no one ever saw any workers at the site. To many, this seemed to confirm the bishop's mental instability.

"Well, can you keep a secret?"

Jonah became curious. *What might it be?* "Yes, of course. Why do you ask?"

"I'm in the midst of a highly sensitive operation. If it becomes public knowledge, the Vank stands to lose a significant advantage. The other denominations, particularly the Assyrians and the Greeks, must not get even an inkling of it. Absolutely no one should know about it. I need to warn you that it's a dangerous mission. It must be carried out at night, when nobody is around."

Intrigued, Jonah thought of his great-uncle, who had most likely engaged in such operations. Now it was his turn. His heart beat faster.

"Are you afraid?"

Jonah noticed the bishop's facial muscles tightening and his lower jaw moving ever so slightly; the old man had a habit of parting his lips and grinding his teeth.

"Afraid?" the boy replied. "No."

"Remember, this must be kept a secret," the bishop stressed. Then he reached out with both hands and grasped Jonah tightly by the shoulders, peering into the young boy's eyes and hissing through his grinding teeth, "I will crucify you if you utter a single word about this—to anyone!"

Jonah knew the threat was not a hollow one. "I swear on the cross," he said firmly. Then he crossed himself to prove to the half-skeptical bishop that he was firm in his commitment.

Bishop Cyril stared Jonah down for a few more seconds and then released his grip on the boy. "Behind the altar, I have unearthed a tunnel," he confided. "It's too narrow for an adult to pass through. I don't know where it leads. Before we expend an enormous amount of energy digging, you could save us some time by crawling through."

"What am I looking for?"

"You will know when you find it."

A week later, Bishop Cyril summoned Jonah to the Holy Sepulcher Church one evening.

"What for?" asked a curious headmaster.

"He will serve at the altar for the usual midnight services."

When Jonah arrived at the church, the anxious bishop directed him to the sleeping quarters. "Go take a nap. You will need all your energy. I will wake you when it's time."

A little past midnight, the bishop and Jonah quietly slipped away. The only audible sounds came from the church services of several denominations, the droning murmurs echoing softly from every corner.

"It's eerie," Jonah remarked.

They passed Golgotha, unnoticed by the Greek priests that staffed the actual site of crucifixion at all times, and then descended the steep steps leading to the cathedral's ancient bowels. St. Gregory the Illuminator, one of the Armenian chapels, was at the bottom of these steps. Beyond it, another set of steep steps led to the cave where, according to legend, the cross had been discovered. This site lay hidden beneath the pavement and bazaars, under several subterranean layers of history, meters and meters of dirt, and the ruins of other historical structures.

Two Arab construction workers, dressed as Armenian deacons, waited for them behind the altar. They removed a few stones to reveal a gaping hole in the wall.

The tension of anticipation was palpable.

"We went as far as we could," the bishop explained. "We removed dirt and fortified the walls and ceilings of the passageway. But it narrows abruptly."

The bishop gave Jonah a flashlight and sent him into the tunnel with a small hand pick and a bag to collect the dirt.

Jonah quickly entered through the opening and soon, the bishop's whispered warnings to be careful were hardly audible. The tunnel turned a few times before Jonah hit a dirt wall, which he carefully excavated. Then he worked his way backward and returned with his bag full of dirt and his lungs choked with dust. He handed the bag to the Arabs and coughing to clear his lungs, took an empty one back into the tunnel. After his fourth trip, the bishop helped him to his feet and offered him cool water to drink.

"Well?" the bishop asked eagerly.

"Sorry. There's only dirt. Are you sure the cross is in there?"

"This may take a while," the bishop said and nodded for him to go back into the tunnel. "Don't lose hope."

On his hands and knees, sometimes prostrate, Jonah dug deeper into the tunnel, but to no avail. Thick dust covered his clothes and sweat turned the dirt clinging to his body into mud. Exhausted from lifting the pick and filling the bag, Jonah began to regret his eagerness to participate in the bishop's mad obsession.

Then fear crept through his body. *What if the ceiling collapses on me? Am I going to be buried alive?*

"Your Grace, there is nothing in there."

"Don't give up, my son. Just a little while more. Then you can rest."

Six feet later, the pick went through the dirt and hit the ground with a clunk. The noise startled Jonah. He reflexively raised both arms to protect his face, bracing himself for the worst. For the next sixty seconds, he remained motionless, aware of only his rapid heartbeat. Once certain the ceiling hadn't collapsed, he cleared the rest of the dirt and shone the light into a chamber that had been entombed for many, many centuries.

With the help of a few trustworthy people who worked through the nights to gradually remove the soil and debris and fortify the site, Bishop Cyril continued his clandestine and dangerous excavation. If any of the other denominations were to find out about it prematurely, they would surely prevent the bishop from proceeding further, until they had negotiated their rights to the new site. The negotiations would, in all likelihood, last generations and lead to further acrimony, recrimination, and fighting—all in the name of religious rights.

Seven months later, on a cold November day, the scaffolding and wall coverings came down during High Mass to the surprise of the congregation and the dismay of rival denominations. Bishop Cyril led a jubilant procession through a gaping void in the wall behind the altar and into a large, excavated chamber.

The bishop rewarded Jonah by asking him to lead the pageantry. "My son, hold the chalice high," he directed him. "It is *your* chalice! You will be the first to receive communion and drink the blood of our Lord from it."

Jonah, with both hands clasping the chalice—the very treasure he himself had unearthed from the cavernous bowels of history—raised it as high as he could reach. *His* exquisite prize, intricately carved and studded with rubies and emeralds, would soon host the Lord and signify not only purity and penance for sins committed, but also victory over rivals.

For the community and the bishop, it was, indeed, a proud day. While Bishop Cyril hadn't discovered the Holy Grail, he had stumbled upon an ancient Roman antechamber. One of the stones inside the chamber displayed a carving of a vessel with a Latin inscription underneath it that read: *Thank you, Lord, for our safe arrival at the port.*

CHAPTER 21

Jerusalem, spring 1973

"Rejoice, O Jerusalem, and adorn thy bridal chamber, O Zion, for behold thy king: Christ, seated on the new colt, who showeth meekness and cometh to enter into thy chamber."

As the seminarians chanted, the choirmaster slashed his baton through the air with vigor and flourish.

Easter marked a beautiful time of year in Jerusalem, and this year's celebrations, close on the heels of the excavation of the chamber and the chalice, had begun with much promise. Filled to capacity with students, the seminary and the Haitourian School were thriving, while the St. Tarkmantchatz School had a large contingent of young men and women who planned to pursue higher education.

The holiday season had begun in earnest fifty days earlier with the onset of Lent. It had stepped into high gear on Palm Sunday. Holy Week had been grueling. The seminarians had spent practically every waking moment, as well as several nights, in church.

Throughout the period, the Vank flaunted during elaborate rituals its treasure trove of precious jewel-laden vestments, crosses, banners, staffs, Bibles, and ancient Armenian illuminated manuscripts. Unchanged for more than a millennium, the services were marked by soulful supplications, lilting hymns, and voices rising to a crescendo as they recited psalms that lifted the seminarians' spirits and alleviated any semblance of exhaustion.

"And we cry aloud: Hosanna, blessed is He that cometh in the name of the Lord, Who hath great mercy."

The grand processions of Palm Sunday and now, Easter Eve, had brought out every single member of the Armenian community and attracted Armenian tourists and pilgrims. The pomp and pageantry began at the Vank and accompanied the processions through the alleys and bazaars and finally, the Via Dolorosa, right up to the Holy Sepulcher Church. The congregation formed a massive column led by the Boy Scouts, marching bands of local Armenian clubs, and the uniformed students of Tarkmantchatz School. Following them were the *kavazes*, the patriarchal escorts, dressed in full Ottoman regalia reminiscent of a Sultan's carriage guard: colorful knitted shirts and vests and Ottoman-style baggy pants; red Turkish fezes, the unmistakable Ottoman headgear, provided the finishing touch. Magnificent swords with intricate carvings hung at their sides. A vestige of Ottoman rule, the *kavazes* served as the patriarch's private guard and official escort and marked time by vigorously pounding the pavement with the metal ends of their ceremonial scepters.

After the *kavazes* came the ranks of the clergy in a double-line formation that, pressed to the edges, left the middle empty. The Haitourian boys and seminarians led the way, followed by the deacons and the priests. As the ranks reached the bishops, the lines gradually converged toward the middle, meeting at the point where the patriarch stood flanked by two priests holding the trail of his magnificent red robe with gold embroidery. The pontiff held a large ornate cross in his right hand and the bishop's staff in his left; a bejeweled miter rested on his imperial head. The community followed.

Saturday, Easter Eve, marked the culmination of the week-long celebrations. On that auspicious afternoon, the procession moved off after the incense had been blessed and the Lord's Prayer sung. The students chanted as they slowly and deliberately advanced to the Holy Sepulcher Church. Other denominations were doing the same and converging on the same destination. The closer they got to the site of worship, the thicker the crowds grew. All jockeyed for position, and although the specified rights granted to each group determined at what precise hour and location they could stand or wait and in what order they could enter the church, the pushing and shoving by rival camps did not abate. With several fights breaking out in years past, Israeli police had begun guarding the area surrounding the labyrinthine structure that housed Christendom's holiest shrine. The police, though, were not allowed inside the venerable cathedral.

At the appointed time, a cacophony of church bells pealed from many different locations and towers, and the Muslim family that had been entrusted with the keys to the church since the thirteenth century unlocked the door to let in the crushing waves of the devout. The various communities quickly claimed their designated territories and defied rival denominations either in defense of their domain or while attempting to encroach on another's. The most coveted spot was around the grotto, a circular, domed crypt set in the middle of the cathedral's large and soaring rotunda. Throngs of pilgrims and clergy encircled this holiest of holy temples in excited anticipation of the divine light of resurrection. While the police kept order outside, inside the church, rights, rituals, traditions, and brute force separated the different denominations and the clergy from the faithful.

"Boys, don't leave gaps in the line for dimwits to break through!" Father Djift hollered repeatedly over the drumbeat as he marched up and down the column formation, acting more like a drill sergeant than a priest.

The clergy and the seminarians defended their ground against the swelling crowd, which was pushing against the barricades as pilgrims sought to get closer to the holy site. Owing, perhaps, to their unfamiliarity with the rules governing the celebrations or their incomprehension of the zealous devotion to religion or rights, tourists added to the fray by elbowing neighbors aside and moving around as they sought the best vantage point for their cameras.

Gradually, however, the chaos gave way to a semblance of order and with two hours to go, everyone had secured a position from which to watch the anticipated miracle: a flash of fire from Christ's grave, the actual site of interment inside the grotto.

This brief respite, though, was not marked by prayers or peaceful reflection on the emergence of the Holy Light of Resurrection. As in previous years, the lull merely provided an opportunity for more swagger and bluster and jockeying for position. Ringleaders rekindled ancient feuds, and groups of young men—Armenian, Assyrian, and Greek—tried to provoke each other into an altercation. It was all part of tradition. The youths sang nationalistic songs, carried members of their respective groups high on their shoulders, and jostled with their rivals in an effort to goad them into a fight. The clerics, meanwhile, were galvanized into action. There was pushing and shoving among them, but this was customary as well.

By now a veteran observer of these proceedings, Jonah was astonished, nevertheless, by the nonreligious fervor the occasion generated.

"Hold your positions!" Father Djift barked. "Do not be intimidated by the sons of bitches!"

"What an agent provocateur the fellow is!" Jonah heard a civilian remark from behind the barricades.

Following the practice of many centuries and in a reenactment of the vision that had appeared and the miracle that had occurred two millennia earlier, Bishop Cyril entered the grotto, accompanied by his Greek counterpart, a bishop of equal rank. The grotto was then promptly sealed shut. The two clerics remained inside to witness and capture the spark of God Reincarnate and deliver it to the multitudes present.

The faithful waiting anxiously for the moment of rapture clutched their unlit candles and murmured prayers. As the moment approached, an eerie silence permeated the rotunda and those present were gripped by feelings of anticipation and apprehension. Then suddenly, two small oval portholes on opposite sides of the grotto were flung open. From the darkness, thick bundles fastened with colorful ribbons and holding thirty-three flaming candles each came into full view. A thunderous roar of exaltation acknowledged the proclamation of Christ's resurrection.

As always, the Greek and Armenian communities had chosen their strongest and swiftest young men to participate in the spectacle that followed. As the two bishops thrust the bundles of smoldering and dripping candles into eagerly outstretched hands, the young men snatched the radiant flares and with lead and backup support, dashed through their territories to reach their respective patriarchs enthroned high in the rotunda dome above the Grotto. It was the race to win the right to be the first to worship.

The excitement, the commotion, the collision of bodies, the screaming, the cheering, the cursing, the cocktail of different languages and dialects, the muffled entreaties to the Virgin Mary—all reached fever pitch. The men sprinted through the delirious crowd, up staircases, and over hurdles, trampling pilgrims and unsuspecting tourists who had unwisely crossed the barricades. Then a triumphant roar greeted the outstretched arm of the Armenian patriarch as he offered the light to the masses below.

Jonah happily howled cheers of victory. As in all the years he could remember, this year too, the Armenians had won the privilege of leading the Easter procession around the grotto.

The faithful clambered to reach the source light and within minutes, thousands of flickering flames lit up the rotunda like a bonfire.

"Christ is risen from the dead! He trampled down death by death and by His resurrection, He granted life unto us." The Armenian hymn reverberated in the rotunda, mingling with the murmurs of prayers and the clamor of the crowd.

A half dozen Armenian youths fetched their exuberant bishop, the prince of lights, and hoisted him high on their shoulder for a victory lap around the grotto—to a chorus of cheers, jeers, and howls. Swept up by the surging crowd and the festive atmosphere, the seminarians abandoned the hymn and joined the boisterous celebration.

"Glory unto Him for all ages," the choirmaster chanted, his solitary voice nearly drowned out by the din. "Amen."

The Greek clergy and pilgrims—the losing side—pushed and shoved their way through the crowd to make a quick exit, their shoulders slumped in resignation and resentment writ large on their faces. Bedlam ensued, and it was just the beginning.

The Armenians still had to contend with the phalanx: the Assyrian and Coptic contingents. Relegated to the fringes of history—and the holy sites—these two Eastern Orthodox denominations had submitted to Armenian patronage in order to retain a semblance of a presence and to survive the political and historical injustices heaped upon the weak. Hence, they also constituted the winning side and worshipped simultaneously with the

Armenians. The three denominations rounded the rotunda at a snail's pace as they chanted in three different languages, the members of each group straining their vocal chords to overpower their rivals' prayers in order to ensure that their own reached God's ears. Jonah was certain that a similar pandemonium had prevailed in the Tower of Babel.

Resentful of their status, the descendants of ancient Egypt and biblical Mesopotamia had leveraged the Greeks. The Armenians, of course, considered this reliance on the Greeks, particularly on the part of the Assyrians, as nothing short of treachery. After all, they used Armenian chapels and performed services based on the rights ceded to them by the Armenian patriarchate.

The scuffles preceding the run of the lights were a mere warm-up. And this Easter, following the covert, yet undeniably spectacular discovery of a chapel and a chalice by the Armenians, there were scores to settle. The bitterness of the Assyrian side did not dissipate once the procession started.

"Gavour! Gavour! Gavour!" a group of unruly Assyrian youths howled, rhythmically pumping their fists or fingers in the direction of the Armenians.

The term "infidel" used so freely by the Turks did not distinguish Armenians from Assyrians or Greeks, but in this combustible setting, the meaning was irrelevant and the emotions it incited were everything.

"Shut up, you scum!" Father Djift shouted at them in a voice dripping with disdain.

"Your mother is a Turkish whore!" one of the Assyrians shot back, following up his words with an obscene gesture.

Reacting with surprising speed, Dijft shoved aside the few people separating him from the impertinent fellow, grasped the

Assyrian's shirt with his left hand, and unceremoniously punched him on the nose with a powerful right fist.

The young man collapsed backward into the arms of his comrades.

Stupefied, the crowd in the immediate vicinity fell silent, but only for a split second. An instant later, the grotto shook with the sounds of crashing bodies and cracking bones. Arms flailed, fists sought targets, and blood splattered on people and stained the floor.

"God arose and all His enemies scattered!" the choirmaster called out in a booming voice as he tried to control the acolytes. "They who hated Him fled from the sight of His face!"

Despite his efforts to steer clear of the bloody tussle, Jonah was shoved around and roughed up quite a bit. He felt worse for the elderly pilgrims that were trampled underfoot and fell headlong in front of the Grotto.

The Israeli police rushed in to restore order, and when the melee ended, it was evident that the Armenians had overwhelmed the Assyrians and Father Djift had emerged unscathed. Others did not fare as well.

"The holiest of all places," a dejected Mr. Isaac, the choirmaster, concluded as they left the sanctuary, "defiled by the spiritually depraved."

Jonah couldn't agree more. After reveling in the week's glorious adorations, its sacred and mystical melodies, and the profound spiritual transformation it had wrought in everyone, Jonah wondered why it had had to end on such a profane note. The inner conflict and confusion welled up within him once again. *Neshan would most certainly, in a future tale, convey today's exploits to generations of seminarians. Am I the victor or the vanquished? Should I take pride in the thrashing we Armenians delivered to the enemy and celebrate, or should I empathize with the Assyrians, the underdog, which I am in some measure?*

The desecration, unfortunately, did not end there.

In the dead of night on Easter Sunday, a distant, rhythmic chant seeped into Jonah's consciousness, disturbing his dreams.

"*Ov joghovurt artentsek. Asorineroun kunetsek!*" It meant: "Rise up, O people. Damn the Assyrians!"

He sensed the Turkish gendarmes closing in as his mother struggled to break free of the thorny bush. Moments later, he was sitting up groggily in the family courtyard, awakened by gunshots in the distance. Haiko, father and defender of home and family, snatched up his rifle and left for the village outskirts to hold off the intruders.

"*Ov joghovurt artentsek. Asorineroun kunetsek!*"

The chanting grew louder. Closer. Had the bandits already scaled the court-yard wall?

"*Hye joghovurt artentsek. Asorineroun kunetsek!*" Rise up, Armenian people. Damn the Assyrians!

Jonah shook himself awake and the illusion vanished. But the chant was as real as it was unsettling.

"*Hye joghovurt artentsek. Asorineroun kunetsek!*"

It was a call to battle.

"What is it?" asked a tentative Thomas, whose bed was next to Jonah's.

"I don't know."

Jonah, Thomas, and Enoch quickly dressed and left the dormitory. Moments later, they spotted a large group of men entering the Haitourian courtyard on their way to fetch Father Djift, their hero. The noisy mob pounded the concrete with their wooden sticks and clanged them against the metal railings as they climbed the stairs.

"Hye joghovurt artentsek. Asorineroun kunetsek!"

The ominous undertone of the refrain grew louder as the rabble congregated in front of Father Djift's door. Most chanted in unison, but a cacophony of other epithets from certain individuals drunk on something more intoxicating than the fervor of the looming conflict competed with the chorus.

Father Djift answered the door moments later and soon, the men were on their way down the stairs, carrying their champion on their shoulders.

"Hye joghovurt artentsek. Asorineroun kunetsek!"

The three young boys followed at a safe distance.

Jonah was distraught. "They're ruining Neshan's beautiful tradition," he said angrily. "Why are they doing this?"

Thomas responded with a question of his own. "What's going to happen?" he whispered.

"Another fight with the Assyrians," Enoch stated, a note of amazement in his voice.

"This is crazy!" Jonah declared, suddenly feeling alarmed.

One of my grandmothers is Assyrian, my family lived in an Assyrian village, and most of my extended family is well on its way to assimilating with the Assyrians. Even my first language was Assyrian. He thought for a moment. *Nazeli eloped with an Assyrian. And father's second wife is Assyrian!*

Jonah shuddered as he recalled the visit of the Assyrian man who had come to the school to deliver his father's letter. "Your Assyrian mother tongue," he had said. The words, which rankled even more now, still rang in his ears. *It was a simple letter. Why hadn't Father mailed it? There was no reason for him to send it with a courier, was there?* Jonah cursed the Assyrian pilgrim *and* his father. *It was only a darn letter!*

"Hye joghovurt artentsek. Asorineroun kunetsek." The profane words faded in the distance as the mob carried Father Djift away.

The brawl inside the church was a mere prelude to several days of tense and, at times, bloody skirmishes. One seminarian ended up in the hospital with a broken nose and a gash on his scalp. But sleepless nights, injuries, and the presence of an increased number of policemen in the vicinity had a sobering effect: the explosive tension subsided, only to give way to an uneasy truce, with things returning more or less to normal. The sporadic violence gave way to the same undercurrents of animosity that had simmered between the two communities throughout history.

Two weeks later, still riding high on the greatest accomplishment of his life, Father Djift instigated another confrontation. This time, the loathed opponents were his former admirers. With Djift accompanying the patriarch and a small entourage of bishops and priests to one of the local Armenian clubs for a special community event, Jonah and another seminarian were entrusted with the duty of lifting the patriarch's robe from either side. For Jonah, it was yet another opportunity to be close to his beloved patriarch.

The clerical party arrived earlier than planned and witnessed a young couple dancing an arabesque. Despite the demands of protocol, the music continued playing; the dancing did not come to a halt either.

Infuriated at the insult, an indignant Father Djift decided once again to dispense justice. He approached the dancers, pushed the woman aside, sending her hurtling to the floor, and then turned around and slapped the befuddled young man across the face. Blood spurted from the man's nose.

The musicians, who had been drinking, charged at Djift, forcing his fellow priests to come to his aid. Chairs flew and tables were upturned in the chaos that followed, with drinks spilling onto the already messy dance floor. Some fell on the slippery surface and the patriarch himself wound up prostrate, with a mortified Father Djift landing right on top of him.

Jonah marveled afterward that despite the intensity of the scuffle, there were no serious injuries, barring hurt pride and strained relations between the community and the clergy. The lasting effect, however, was more serious: the local population shunned the seminarians and the Haitourian boys, marking the beginning of an internecine dispute that would last much longer than the immediate hostilities with the Assyrians.

"We, especially, should watch our step," Azad advised his three younger brothers a few days later. "This is an unholy place."

It was beginning to dawn on Jonah that in these ancient surroundings and institutions, apparently insignificant differences between groups widened hairline fissures into dangerous chasms.

CHAPTER 22

Jerusalem, late April 1973

As Jonah approached the end of the sixth grade, he realized how much his preoccupations had changed since the beginning of the school year. Just months earlier, he had hardly noticed members of the opposite sex. Now he watched with envy as Enoch and other classmates met secretly with their sweethearts in a peaceful park nearby that hid a damp, quiet cave believed to house King David's tomb.

David, history's most celebrated personality to have beaten the odds, had used a slingshot and his own ingenuity to vanquish the colossal Goliath. His triumph had propelled him to his anointment as the second king of Israel. According to legend, James the apostle, the bedrock of the Vank, had been a descendant of King David. The park's proximity to the Vank made this location ideal for the recreational activities of its children. Sometimes, Enoch would ask Jonah and Thomas to accompany him, although Jonah was never sure whether they had been invited along to play with him or to act as lookouts.

During one of these excursions, Thomas and Jonah stumbled upon each other in the cave after a short chase and decided to stay there awhile and observe the Israelis light their candles and murmur their prayers. They sat silently for a long time, watching the shadows of the visitors and the dancing flames of their candles.

"My birth certificate says my name is Heidar," Thomas finally whispered, shattering the silence. "It's a Turkish name. A *Muslim* name."

Jonah was surprised at the announcement and focused on his friend's words.

"Nobody knows," Thomas continued, raising his eyebrows and looking askance at Jonah. "I thought you might want to know."

Jonah *did* want to know, but tried not to appear too inquisitive. He felt a certain vindication in discovering that he and his siblings were not the only ones in the Vank with dual names—one assumed, the other a secret withheld from those around them.

"Did Father Abram ask you to change your name to its Armenian equivalent?" he asked, without divulging his own secret.

"No, Thomas was the name I had been given. So I'm using it now."

"What did your parents call you in the village?"

"Heidar, my Turkish name. They were forced to."

"What do you mean?"

"Our village is very remote and isolated. It was the only one around the mountains of Sassoun that survived the genocide. After the Turkish government emptied the surrounding villages of their Armenian inhabitants and drove them into the desert of Der Zor, the government gave the homes, fields, and all other Armenian properties to Muslims, Turks, and Kurds. They even resettled Muslims from the Balkans into what had originally been Armenian villages." Thomas took a deep breath and went on. "Our village had an Armenian church and an old priest." He paused, longer this time, before finally continuing in a hushed voice. "But things changed a few years ago."

Jonah knew a bit about the Sassoun region, which was legendary among Armenians and known as the land of the Armenian

Titans. The Armenian equivalent of *The Iliad*'s Achilles and the *Niebelungenlied*'s Siegfried was David. In the epic *Sassountsi Tavit*, David of Sassoun was the famed slayer of dragons, beasts, and dictators alike and the defender of the nation from conquering hordes and barbarians. True to the myths, the men of Sassoun had, over the centuries, made the best Armenian soldiers and fighters.

With his Sassoun lineage, Thomas enjoyed much respect from Jonah and his classmates. Short, muscular, and strong, he boasted a dark complexion, a big, flat nose, and an excellent knowledge of the Kurdish language, by virtue of which he had earned the nickname "Kurdo"—the Kurd. Jonah knew that Thomas preferred to be called "Sassountsi Thomas" (Thomas of Sassoun), but since his friend loved teasing others and playing pranks on them, Thomas had good-naturedly tolerated the slightly derogatory nickname he had been given. In fact, he frequently introduced himself as Kurdo.

Thomas continued in a grave tone. "Overnight, our village was Armenian no more. It became Turkish. The pictures of the saints were ripped from the church walls, the cross was replaced by a crescent, and the steeple was torn down. In its place, a minaret was erected."

"And the priest gave up his robes and dressed like a mullah," Jonah added in jest.

"Correct."

Jonah sat in stunned silence, unsure as to whether this was another of Thomas's attempts to pull his leg.

"After being trained to do it, the old priest started calling the faithful to prayer five times a day, like a *muezzin*, from the top of the minaret." Thomas put his right hand behind his right ear and started imitating a mullah on a minaret. "*Allah-ou-Akbar, Allah-ou—*"

"Shh!" Jonah reached out quickly and clasped his hand over Thomas's mouth. He then looked around furtively to see if there were any Israelis present who might have overheard the Muslim call to prayer. There were none. "What utter nonsense!" he exclaimed, still wondering if this were some kind of a joke.

"I'm serious. The whole village converted! My *whole family*! I still have a sister and her family back there, going to the mosque every Friday!"

"How is that possible? And why on earth would they do that?" Jonah was still skeptical. *Is he teasing me? Is he fishing for information, hoping, maybe, that I've been through the same experience?*

Thomas's eyes narrowed. "The Turkish army came and the commander gave the villagers three days to decide," he said, his voice trembling with suppressed anger. "The order was: convert, get circumcised, and become Turkish Muslims—or else."

"Or else what?"

"Or else they would destroy the village. The commander also hinted that if things came to such a pass, he wouldn't be able to guarantee the people's safety."

"Just like that?" Jonah snapped his fingers.

"No, not *that* simple," Thomas answered, mocking his friend by snapping his fingers too. "Several young men disappeared, even before the three days were up."

"My God. But why?"

"It was a *warning*. The commander would not be crossed. They didn't even try to carry out the executions of the young men in secrecy; the commander just accused them of joining the Kurdish guerillas. He said everybody in the village would pay for what they'd done. He called it 'treason.' The Turkish troops took the village elders in for 'questioning' and roughed them up pretty bad."

A long silence followed.

"But isn't that what they did during the genocide?" Jonah asked. "We obeyed them like sheep. Nobody fought back. Well, almost nobody. I know Sassoun put up a great resistance in 1915 and my great-uncle fought back. Why aren't you fighting back now? I thought Sassountsis fought to the bitter end—to the last man?"

"This is a continuation of the 1915 struggle for survival."

"No, it's not. You *surrendered*. You betrayed your nation *and* your religion!"

"Don't be so self-righteous," Thomas snapped. "We *are* fighting back. We are gradually leaving the village. Once in Istanbul and beyond, we are rediscovering our nationality and religion."

Jonah immediately regretted his hurtful comment. Back in his village, his own family had assimilated without the duress of an inquisition. He suddenly had more respect for Sassoun and his friend.

The sound of a girl's voice dispelled the somber mood. "Hey, what are you two doing in there?"

Two of the girls had discovered them.

Jonah suggested walking out of the cave arm in arm with the girls to make their sweethearts jealous. It worked and the girls were happy.

At the end of the school year, Thomas, Enoch, and the other sixth graders transferred to the seminary. For reasons unknown to Jonah, he gained a reprieve and was allowed the option of continuing at the Haitourian School. The unexpected opportunity fostered in him the hope that he could continue indefinitely as a Haitourian student and finish his schooling at St. Tarkmantchatz. He had other reasons for wanting to stay, not the least of which was Shahnour Shakarian, the principal's daughter.

Jonah, now eleven, had fallen deeply in love with the pretty, smart, and quite popular eleven-year-old Shahnour. Every girl wanted to be like her and every boy was infatuated with her. Shahnour, though, was unaware of Jonah's interest in her. In the Vank, open relationships between boys and girls were discouraged until the students were old enough to marry. Formal pre-engagement discussions between parents preceded public courting. Nevertheless, relatively innocent clandestine contacts were common—and the reason for much embarrassment when they were discovered.

Jonah's staunchest ally and accomplice in his pursuit of Shahnour and her affection was his dear friend and Shahnour's brother Raffi. Raffi became Jonah's emissary in this mission. In the privacy of their home, he informed his sister that Jonah was desperately in love with her and needed his feelings reciprocated if he were to live at all. Jonah could not contain his excitement when Shahnour sent word that she harbored feelings of deep affection for him as well.

The year went by in a blissful, dreamlike blur, as Jonah and Shahnour secretly took their relationship further. They were more cautious than most other couples, given the Shakarians' status in the community and the fact that they were Jonah's principals. Jonah had a hunch that Mrs. Shakarian knew and did not disapprove, since she often sent him on errands to their house. Shahnour would be waiting to receive the packages or messages and Jonah would arrive feeling shy and overly nervous. They were both delirious with excitement, though their secret rendezvous never amounted to more than a fleeting touch or an affectionate glance as the package changed hands. When her fingers lightly brushed against Jonah's hand, his whole body would thrill to her gentle caress and as they parted, he felt her loving gaze on the back of his neck. She waited longingly by the window, pretending to stroke her Persian cat as she watched him stride away. He knew as much, because at every opportunity, he looked back to steal another glance at her.

The same club where Djift had instigated a brawl held an annual dance party. On Raffi's insistence, the Shakarians took Jonah along. While the band played popular Armenian songs, Jonah sat with his hosts late into the evening, fidgeting nervously as he eyed the beautiful girl across the table. Shahnour kept moving her body and shaking her hair to the music, trying desperately to send him signals without being too obvious, but he was unable to summon up the courage to invite her for a dance. Finally, growing impatient, she got up and walked over to him. Jonah sprang to his feet a little too eagerly and then, not wanting to be disrespectful, looked at Mrs. Shakarian for approval. She gave him an encouraging nod and a smile.

Although they were the same age, Shahnour was taller than Jonah by several inches. Their first dance was to a disco tune, but soon, they were moving to a tango. Jonah kept his distance, not wanting to seem too forward, especially in front of Shahnour's parents, but gradually, she breached the space he had maintained and started holding him closer and tighter. Occasionally, her leg rubbed against his inner thighs, heightening the intensity of his first encounter with passion. Soon, he was oblivious to his surroundings, no longer cognizant of how many songs had played or how long they had been dancing. When it was all over, his head was on her shoulder and her cheek was resting against his hair.

Jonah continued to feel her body in his arms for several days after the dance, the weight of her head lingering on his. He hoped the sensation would never end. But to his dismay, the pressure points eventually eased to nothingness, leaving him only his memories to cling to. Thus he lived for the moments when he would catch a glimpse of her, at school or in church, certain that this carefree, blithe state would last forever.

The fairy tale ended unexpectedly one day, when Jonah's oldest brother took his three siblings aside to share with them a decision he had made.

"I'm leaving," a determined Azad announced. "I'm getting the hell out of here."

"But…but…why?" Jonah stammered in disbelief.

"It's time we spread out to different countries and prepare for other eventualities." Azad, now seventeen, seemed to know more than he wanted to disclose to his brothers. "In any case, the priesthood isn't for me."

"I'm happy here!" Jonah protested. Why would anybody leave *this* and return to the Tarlabashi lifestyle, he wondered.

Azad simply shook his head. "There is no future for us in this place. I wish I could take you all with me."

"You'll be drafted," Jonah warned, trying to dissuade his brother. "You must have heard of the horrific treatment meted out to recruits in the Turkish army, especially if they are Armenians and other Christians."

According to the date of birth in his passport—falsified to make him several years older than he actually was—Azad was of age for the military draft. But this was not enough to deter him from returning to Turkey.

"I will get away before they nab me. Maybe our father was right: Germany is the answer."

As the news of his decision spread, Archbishop Aminian seemed pleased, while many others, including the Shakarians and the patriarch himself, intervened and asked him to reconsider, but to no avail.

Jonah feared the separation would be a difficult one. Azad was his idol, protector, and friend.

On his last day in Jerusalem, Azad pulled his brothers aside. "Be careful. This place may not be the haven it seems." Then he turned to Kalousd. "You're the oldest now. I leave them under your protection. I hope you use your fists, when needed."

Soft-spoken, kind, and gentle, Kalousd avoided fights and the kind of trouble Azad and Jonah frequently embroiled themselves in. He uncomfortably shifted his weight from one leg to the other and averted his eyes, refusing to meet Azad's stern gaze.

"At the very least, don't lose that canary of yours," added Azad with a smile.

Jonah laughed as he recalled the story Haiko had often related about Kalousd's gift of speech. Kalousd had made it to the age of six without uttering a word. Fearing he might be mute, Haiko had taken him first to a village healer, and then to a doctor in Kamishli. Neither had offered any remedies for the apparently voiceless boy.

Determined to do something for Kalousd, Grandmother Sarah took him to the gypsies camped near the village cemetery. She had returned from her visit in a state of great excitement and immediately dispatched Haiko to Syria to look for a *Hazaryan bulbul*, an Arabian canary that could sing a thousand songs.

After a two-week search deep inside Syria, Haiko returned with a canary that supposedly sang endlessly. The bird was taken to the gypsies, who mixed their potions while reciting ceremonial incantations, slaughtered the chirping creature, and, after boiling it, fed it to Kalousd. The boy uttered his first words soon after.

Jonah's love for Shahnour tempered his despondency over Azad's departure. Kalousd did his best to protect them, which was not a difficult task, at least during those years. Levon and Jonah were both popular and assertive among their peers. For his part, Jonah also had plenty of protectors in high places, not to mention lofty expectations for the future—a future that seemed all the more promising when the blond American returned.

Jonah was playing in the courtyard when Ms. Nora appeared. Although he recognized her immediately, he was briefly transported to the family courtyard back in the village—a place he scarcely thought of anymore—where his mother had often watched him play. He quickly dismissed the flashback and concentrated on the visitor who hadn't reappeared at the seminary since her first visit three years earlier.

He greeted her and she hugged him warmly. She had not changed.

"You remembered me! It is good to see you, *again*," he said in English, emphasizing his disenchantment with her prolonged absence, then continued in Armenian, "I hope you are doing well."

She seemed pleased to see him looking so well. As they walked to Mrs. Shakarian's office, she asked about his school and his brothers.

After a short exchange of the usual niceties with Mrs. Shakarian, Ms. Nora stated abruptly, "I am very disappointed at the way things have progressed."

Her blunt comment was followed by a moment of uneasy silence. Jonah was not sure what the criticism had been leveled at, but he knew Mrs. Shakarian would not intentionally harm anybody, least of all, him. He wanted to defend her, but kept quiet.

"You know I would do everything I could to help," Mrs. Shakarian replied, blushing in embarrassment. "These are complicated matters. It is not really in my hands."

"I had even agreed to take all *three* brothers, but I hear Azad has left and gone back to Turkey." The American was clearly perplexed.

"We tried to stop him. Be assured that these boys are like our own. We would hate to lose any of them."

"My father will be absolutely *devastated* to hear that a young boy under his sponsorship—entrusted to your care—has gone back to Turkey."

"We tried everything, Ms. Nora. We do our best to house them, feed them, educate them, and keep them here. However, some simply want to return and we can't keep them here against their will."

"Yet we could have prevented this loss. Why can't I take the boys with me? When I come to see them, I'm told, yes, it will happen—soon. But after I leave, nothing happens."

Jonah felt his heart beat faster. *Could it be? Am I going to the United States?*

"Jonah," Mrs. Shakarian said sweetly, "I'm going to have to ask you to step out of the office. I need a moment alone with Ms. Paravonian."

He left reluctantly. And soon afterward, Ms. Nora did the same—without saying good-bye. Jonah was disappointed, but the visit gave him hope that she would come back for him. He prayed it would be soon.

CHAPTER 23

Tel Aviv, summer 1974

Rising from the barrels of his pistols, serpentine swirls of smoke slowly drifted upward before dissipating beneath the glaring sun. Three vile leaders of the Young Turks party suitably dealt with. Satisfied, Jonah dropped the pair of six-guns back into their holsters, securely attached on either hip. He tipped the wide-brimmed hat on his head slightly to one side, settled himself in the saddle, and dug his spurs into his horse's flanks. The beautiful white stallion reared up before galloping off in a cloud of dust.

Jonah and his faithful steed glided over desolate landscapes and quickly reached the green hills of his ranch where herds of cattle roamed and grazed freely. And just as he had imagined it, there on the porch of a dark log cabin stood his sweetheart, waiting. Her long black curls rested on her shoulders, stirring when a gentle breeze lifted them.

He reined in his horse and leapt off the saddle.

Shahnour smiled. . .

A sudden, paralyzing blast ripped Jonah from his fantasy, followed immediately by a disorienting silence. But the lull lasted hardly a second before the terminal at Tel Aviv Airport erupted in shrieks of panic far louder than the explosion. A command issued in Hebrew for everyone to lie down on the floor didn't penetrate Jonah's temporary state of confusion and he remained rooted to the spot. But he went down quickly when a heavyset policeman caught hold of him with his big, strong hands and pulled him to the floor.

Once again, an eerie quiet descended on the crowd, with everyone facedown, hugging the floor. Finally, the bawl of an infant shattered the silence. Those around Jonah lifted their heads and a few murmured softly. When the possibility of another explosion seemed remote, Jonah followed the lead of the others in the crowd and stood up, dusting off his clothes and glancing about him.

The culprit was discovered seconds later: a balloon had popped nearby. Nobody laughed. Such was the atmosphere that summer in Tel Aviv, thanks to a series of hijackings of El Al planes, along with several acts of terrorism around the globe that had heightened people's fears and sensitized security forces to lurking dangers.

A reluctant Jonah was en route to Istanbul after a six-year absence. Mrs. Shakarian had insisted he visit his father.

Jonah had resisted. "My father hasn't sent a ticket for me to visit him," he protested.

"Unlike the other parents, your father doesn't have the means to do so," Mrs. Shakarian had replied.

"More reason for me not to visit."

"I am buying your ticket," Mrs. Shakarian said firmly, adding in a more casual tone, "besides, it would serve as a much-needed break before your next phase in life. Look at it as an opportunity that might not come your way again."

Jonah remained unconvinced. His love for Shahnour was blossoming, and he was resentful of any intrusion in their court-ship. At the end, it was Shahnour who convinced Jonah to take up the offer. On one of his errands to the Shakarian house, he was surprised when Shahnour invited him in. No one else seemed to be at home. Dizzy with excitement at being alone, they were, nonetheless, a little nervous about the unsupervised encounter.

"Your mother is insisting I visit Istanbul," Jonah finally told Shahnour.

"I know. Don't you miss your father?"

"I don't even know him."

"This is your chance to reconnect with him," she said. "You may not get this opportunity again."

Jonah was surprised by the comment that appeared to be an eerie echo of what her mother had said earlier. "I would miss you if I went," he persisted.

"I would miss you too," she responded. "But we will be spending part of the summer in Istanbul as well. We could see each other there, couldn't we?"

Later, Mrs. Shakarian had explained that her family would be enjoying a three-week vacation in Istanbul and that Jonah was welcome to join them on their excursions. That had been enough to sway the boy, although he had, despite the added incentive, only grudgingly agreed to the trip.

Father Abram met Jonah at Istanbul's Yesilkoy Airport.

"Are you a little nervous about meeting your father?" the priest asked, hugging the young boy. "Six years is a long time."

They got into a hired car and rode mostly in silence. As Jonah absorbed the sights through the window, he tried to recall the Istanbul he had once known. But he realized his only memories of the city centered on the patriarchate school, apart from the Kumkapi and Tarlabashi apartments.

Father Abram lived in a lovely apartment in Bakirkoy, a middle-class neighborhood.

"What a handsome boy he has grown into!" the priest's wife observed cheerfully as he led Jonah inside.

Father Abram's mother-in-law, endearingly called Yaya or grandmother, patted Jonah's cheeks, enveloped him repeatedly in affectionate hugs, and smothered him with kisses.

The priest and his wife had no children of their own and referred to Jonah's brother Levon as their son. The boy, who had arrived two weeks earlier, was not home.

"Your brother is visiting your father," Father Abram explained. "You can stay with us this week while he is away."

The week passed quickly. On the day Levon was due back, Father Abram took Jonah to work with him for the exchange, which would take place at the church office.

An extremely nervous Jonah had seen nothing of his father in six years. Not even a picture. *Do photographs of him exist? My mother vanished without a trace. Not a single picture. Not a single memento.*

During the ride to the church, he tried to recall what his father looked like.

Will I recognize him?

Will he recognize me?

Then memories of his mother overwhelmed his senses: her fragrance, her touch, the lilt in her voice, the sight of her standing in the dark on the rooftop, waiting for Haiko to come home.

Jonah fidgeted as he sat in the hall outside Father Abram's office, waiting for his father's arrival. Every time a man walked in, he would half rise to his feet—he did not want Haiko or Levon to think that he could not recognize his own father—but when he didn't see Levon alongside the stranger, he sat back down.

When the two finally appeared hand in hand, however, Jonah could only stare at them, transfixed. He forgot about rising to his feet to greet them. He simply sat there and stared. If Levon had not arrived with his father, would he, Jonah, have recognized him at all? Had the past six years aged him so? Jonah could not recall the face well enough to decide if it had, indeed, changed. His father's deep wrinkles and sunburned face offered a stark contrast to Jonah's pale, freckled twelve-year-old countenance. People often said Jonah bore a striking resemblance to his father, but he himself could not see it. Perhaps he had. At some point in his life.

Levon pointed Jonah out to Haiko, but he need not have. It was obvious that his father knew him from the moment he had set eyes on him. He walked straight up to Jonah and pulled him into his arms.

Jonah put his trembling arms around his father for a brief moment, and then let go. He felt limp.

Haiko said a few things in Assyrian that Jonah did not understand, but the boy recognized "Hanno," the endearing name his father had called him in the village. With that word uttered, the years melted away Jonah was five years old again and listening to his father's engrossing stories.

They sat in Father Abram's office and drank tea. The priest had a pleasant chat with Haiko, while Levon filled Jonah in on news about Ani and her school. Jonah stole frequent glances at his father.

"Jonah can stay with Levon in our home for another week," Father Abram suggested. "The Shakarians are arriving soon and they want to take him to Bursa with them."

Haiko never thought to disagree with Father Abram. They all respected and loved the priest, the family's chosen patriarch.

The Sheraton Hotel in Istanbul's plush Taksim district overlooked the magnificent Dolmabahce Saray, an Ottoman palace and a most remarkable edifice that had been built by Garabed of the distinguished Balian family.

Father Abram accompanied Jonah to the Shakarians' suite, where they found the reception room full of visitors, including Father Djift and his inseparable friend, another priest from Jerusalem.

Jonah's presence clearly irked the two priests. The feeling was mutual.

Raffi smiled upon seeing his friend and offered Jonah a seat between him and Shahnour. Jonah craved Shahnour's attention, but with several conversations going on simultaneously, the girl he loved so dearly had her head turned away from him and was busy listening to the dreaded Djift.

Djift, meanwhile, was busy thanking Mrs. Shakarian for her invitation to join the family on its vacation. "Oh, sure. Thank you. Of course we'll join you in Bursa."

Unable to hide his disappointment over this new development, Jonah became sullen and withdrawn.

During a break in the conversation, Shahnour rose and went over to her mother to whisper something in her ear.

A few minutes later, Mrs. Shakarian pulled Jonah aside and asked, "My son, when did you last bathe?"

Jonah blushed and whispered, "Not since the week before I left Jerusalem. Father Abram goes to the *hamam* to bathe every two weeks. He will take me next time."

"Let's go into Raffi's room so you can take a nice bath," she suggested, walking him over to an adjoining room, where she handed him a towel and clean underwear and a shirt from Raffi's dresser. Mrs. Shakarian managed all of this discreetly, but Jonah was embarrassed nonetheless.

As soon as she had left, he paused a moment to take in the bathroom, the likes of which he had never seen before. *So big! So many faucets, handles, and dials!*

He could neither figure out how to use the shower nor how to set the proper temperature. So he filled up the tub and sat in the lukewarm water for a long time. Using the scented soap in the tray, he washed his hair and body in the tub water and then let it drain, leaving an ugly ring. He tried desperately to scrub it off, but it just wouldn't budge. He lingered for some time in the bathroom, hoping that the stain would miraculously disappear by itself and not cause him further embarrassment. But nothing of the sort happened. Eventually, he shrugged his shoulders and joined the rest in the reception room.

"Should we leave?" Father Abram seemed to have had his fill of the chatter.

"I'm ready," Jonah replied eagerly.

"I'll bring Jonah back to the hotel tomorrow morning," Father Abram promised as he said good-bye to the Shakarians.

Over the years, Bursa had served as the vacation spot for the region's most powerful individuals, from the sultans to Ataturk and the Turkish elite. Now it was a resort that attracted tourists to its natural beauty, especially its hot springs. Mrs. Shakarian's back and joints bothered her, she explained to Jonah, and she hoped the hot springs would do her good.

Jonah found the water too hot, especially under the blistering summer sun. Despite his love of water and swimming, he could not tolerate the steaming pools. Instead, he preferred the walks and hikes with Raffi. To his chagrin, Shahnour did not join them. At twelve, the precocious girl was drawn to the semi-flirtatious, adult conversations of the twenty-five-year-old Djift.

One evening, Jonah found himself lounging on the hotel's balcony with Raffi, Shahnour, Djift, and the other priest. Despite the warm evening breeze, the occasional rustling of the leaves, and a beautiful white summer moon, he felt tense. The self-important Djift was, as expected, monopolizing the conversation and, to Jonah's dismay, sharing amusing anecdotes about the Haitourian boys that expressed his utter contempt for them.

"Did you hear about Nazar?" he asked with a chortle.

"Tell me, tell me!" a giddy Shahnour pleaded, flapping her arms at her sides in excitement.

Djift chuckled. "You know Nazar."

"The short, stubby fellow?"

"Yes, that's him. He is not the brightest of boys." He laughed again, looked at Jonah askance, and continued, "but then again, which one of them is?"

"You should know. You are one of *them*."

Jonah's caustic rejoinder stiffened Djift's spine. "Don't get huffy. I am discussing Nazar, not you," snapped Djift quite high-handedly.

An angry Jonah tried to appear nonchalant. "Nazar isn't here to defend himself. In any case, he is a real gentle soul. He's very strong and plays marbles like no other person. What's more, he's generous; he makes it a point to distribute his winnings after the games end."

"That doesn't make him smart, does it?"

"Oh, do tell me the story!" Shahnour interjected.

"As you know, these boys are either from destitute peasant families or orphans. Or…," Djift, relishing Shahnour's interest in his stories, throws a perversely amused glance at Jonah before delivering the punch line, "or, half orphans but with fathers gone astray." Djift clears his throat then continues. "A wily emissary of the Jehovah's Witness sect converts Nazar's father. For a few pennies the poor ignorant soul is born again."

"How much?"

"Certainly not enough to get me interested in proselytizing for this cult." A boorish laugh follows. "They promise more if Nazar drops out, leaves the seminary, and returns to Istanbul."

"Really?"

"Nazar's illiterate father has sent a letter to the boy. You won't believe what it says."

"What? What?"

"In the letter, he writes in Turkish, '*Oghlum, okudughun yeter, diplomani al gel.* My son, you have studied enough. Ask for your diploma and come back home.'" The priest snorted with laughter. "A diploma for his genius boy!"

After each such anecdote, Djift would wink at Shahnour or squeeze her arm. She would giggle back, which perturbed Jonah more. Even if he had had any stories to match the priest's, the boy had little confidence that Shahnour would find them half as interesting.

"I'm going to bed," Raffi said curtly, visibly annoyed by the way Djift was flirting with his young sister.

With his friend's abrupt departure, Jonah felt completely out of place. "Good night," he muttered and followed Raffi.

A peeved Jonah stretched out on his cot and mumbled a curse.

"I agree," Raffi said. "But I think she is doing it on purpose."

"What do you mean?"

"You will know when it's time."

"I don't get it."

But Raffi wouldn't say anything else, except "Good night."

That night, no matter how hard he tried, Jonah could not sleep. All he could hear was Djift and Shahnour laughing.

Is she losing interest in me?

"I've promised your father to drop you off at his house," Father Abram informed Jonah the day before the Shakarians' planned departure from Istanbul.

"We'll all drive you there," Mr. Shakarian insisted. "We'll see more of the city."

The traumatic memories of the squalid Tarlabashi house still haunted Jonah. "Why ruin your last day in Istanbul on an unnecessary trip?" he said, doing his best not to sound desperate. "Father Abram can take me."

They would have none of it. That very afternoon, everybody piled into three separate taxis and headed to Haiko Ibelin's residence. Father Abram, Raffi, Levon, and Jonah sat in the lead car.

"Where does he live?" Jonah asked Levon nervously.

"In the Yenikapi District."

It was a different neighborhood from the old one. What if it was just as sordid? Or—worse—sleazier? *How embarrassing if he still...* Jonah shook his head glumly. *Why can't he be like the Shakarians?*

They passed through neighborhoods with tree-lined streets, wide boulevards, and upscale businesses.

Jonah became more cheerful. "Levon, are we almost there?"

"Baba, don't you think we have another twenty minutes or so to go yet?"

The priest nodded in response to Levon's question.

Soon, the townscape began to change. Dramatically. The roads grew narrower and the neighborhoods less attractive. The trees had disappeared. Elegant boutiques gave way to rows of tenements. Secondhand clothing stores sat alongside shops with pots, pans, and all sorts of tin containers hanging from their doors. Flea-infested butcher stands, with stray cats and dogs lurking by, added to the noxious smells. Street vendors frequently blocked the roadway, with some of them pushing carts laden with old household items, while others sold different colored drinks from elaborate dispensers strapped to their backs. The noise level increased, potholes became the norm, and barefoot kids in grimy clothes played in the streets. There was filth everywhere.

It still was not Tarlabashi; no women of disrepute walked the streets. But Jonah's hopes began to wane. It was clear that his prayer for a miracle—to see his father living in an apartment similar to Father Abram's or the Shakarians'—would go unanswered. What mattered most at the moment, however, had little to do with concern for his father; he was determined to prevent the Shakarians, especially Raffi and Shahnour, from being eyewitnesses to his family's abject living conditions.

Jonah worriedly rubbed his clammy palms together. He could feel his heart pounding, but could everyone else hear it too?

Please stop this caravan! Even if I have to walk the rest of the way! Ten, twenty miles—it doesn't matter!

Relief came unexpectedly.

"I'm sorry, sir," the driver said to Father Abram in an apologetic tone, "but I cannot drive any further. I'm afraid that if I continue to drive on these roads, I'll end up landing the car in a ditch."

"It's OK," Levon said cheerily. "We can walk from here. The house is only two blocks away."

Jonah said a hurried good-bye and jumped out of the car, dragging his brother out with him.

Raffi made to get out as well. "Wait for me!"

"No!" Jonah said sharply. Instinctively, he had thrust his arm out to stop his friend and inadvertently pushed him right back into the car. "Stay where you are! Levon can take me."

"And who will accompany Levon back?" asked Raffi, clearly irked by Jonah's unexpected rudeness.

"My father!" Jonah was adamant.

"What if he's not there?" Raffi seemed oblivious to Jonah's predicament. Was it mere obstinacy on his part or unhealthy curiosity?

"He *is* there!"

"Let's go," Levon said. He pulled on Raffi's arm to lead the way.

Convinced that his eight-year-old brother was deriving pleasure from seeing him squirm, Jonah hurried after the two boys, glancing anxiously around him as he walked. Young children were playing in the street and using a rod with a "U" at its end to roll along a large, rusty iron ring. *Tarlabashi!* It was exactly how he had spent his time in the streets of Tarlabashi. Jonah could hardly breathe.

Levon stopped at the steps leading to the entrance of an apartment building that looked slightly less dilapidated than the Tarlabashi tenement. Two young boys, Jonah's half-brothers, were sitting on the steps, playing. They would toss a small stone into the air, swiftly gather up the few remaining ones on the ground, and then reach out to catch the airborne one. As soon as they spotted Levon, they abandoned their game and ran to him. They looked at Raffi and Jonah curiously.

Jonah did not acknowledge them.

"Here we are!" Levon said.

Why is he sounding so smug? Jonah had the sudden urge to slap his younger brother. "Thank you," he said tersely. "Now you two should go back."

"Oh no," Levon countered. "I want to go inside. Maybe Ani is here. I'd like to see her."

"Please, go now!" Jonah pleaded.

Levon ignored him and led the way inside.

Their home was a street-level apartment with two rooms and a small kitchen. Jonah did not see a bathroom. The second room was being sublet to a young man from the village, Levon explained, while their father and his new family lived in the larger room. The room had one large window overlooking the street. A pair of sofas faced each other in the foreground, while pushed against the far wall were a table and a couple of chairs.

Jonah heaved a sigh of something close to relief. Not the Kumkapi apartment, certainly, but it was not the Tarlabashi basement either.

Raffi, who had led a sheltered and comfortable life in relative luxury, looked confused. "Is this it?"

Jonah felt his eyes sting with tears. This was a nightmare, but all too real. "No! No, this is just—"

"When I visit, I sleep against the wall on the mattress with the boys!" Levon exclaimed jubilantly.

Was he really this stupid, Jonah wondered, or was he deliberately making the situation worse?

"Will you shut—"

As Raffi watched slack-jawed, a short, heavyset woman with a dark complexion and dark, coarse hair came forward and smothered Jonah in her arms. For Jonah, there was nowhere to hide.

"Hanna, *Oghlim, hoshgeldin. Nasilsin?* Hanna, my son, welcome. How are you?" Several gold teeth flashed as she spoke in a dialect with a heavy Turkish accent, both typical of the Kurdish and Assyrian regions in the interiors of Turkey.

"This is our mother." Levon introduced the woman with a naughty snigger.

"Please," Jonah begged in a shaky voice, trying hard to hold back the tears, "go!"

Raffi put his arm around Jonah's shoulder and said in a consoling tone, "See you soon—back in Jerusalem."

He and Levon left Jonah standing in the middle of the room, with two curious little boys, an excited stepmother, and a swaddled baby in the corner screaming for attention. Haiko, Jonah's stepmother explained, had gone to buy meat for the special occasion.

Jonah retreated to a corner, sat down, pulled his legs up close against his chest, and rested his forehead on his knees. He did not budge or talk, despite his stepmother's incessant pleading.

The minute his father walked through the door, Jonah's tears burst forth in a flood.

"What is it, my son?" Haiko kneeled next to him to hug and kiss him.

"How can you ever get to Almanya, if in six years, you couldn't get back to the Kumkapi apartment?" Jonah pushed his father away and continued sobbing.

"*Oghlim*, can I give you something to eat?" his stepmother asked.

"Woman, shush!" Haiko said sternly. "Leave my son alone."

He sat next to Jonah and gazed blankly at the ceiling for a while before removing the strings of amber worry beads from his pocket. Then he twisted and flipped them forcefully around his index and middle fingers.

Finally, he addressed his son again, speaking softly. "Hanno, do you want to go outside and play with the ring? Just the way you used to in Tarlabashi?"

Jonah sobbed more violently than ever.

"Can I tell you a story?"

The boy was too devastated to respond.

Haiko rose from the floor and paced the length of the room a few times. Then he stopped in front of Jonah and patted the boy's curls. "I will go fetch your sister," he said and left in a hurry.

Jonah cried disconsolately for another hour before the sobs gradually subsided into whimpers and eventually settled into silence. He lifted his head, rested it against the wall, and stared ahead sullenly, still in a near catatonic state.

Several hours later, Haiko returned with Ani.

The sight of his sister broke the spell. Jonah ran to her and the two embraced, gently rocking each other from side to side as they cried softly. They clung to each other for several minutes until the six years of pent-up longing gradually eased off into a feeling of lightness, followed by curiosity. Oblivious to the commotion around them, they sat under the window and talked quietly.

Jonah had been forced to bid Ani farewell when she was only four, but the separation, a whole lifetime in terms of their tender years, had not managed to loosen their strong bond. Away for half his young life, Jonah was now estranged from his father, but not from his sister.

When it was time for Haiko to take Ani back to the Island of Burgaz, her summer school, Jonah stood up as well and said defiantly, "I am going too."

"You can't stay there," his father said gently. "It is for girls only."

"Take me to Father Abram's house, then," Jonah insisted. "I'm not staying here!"

They dropped Ani off at the ferry, and Jonah and his father took the bus to the Bakirkoy District where Father Abram resided.

"What are you...?" Father Abram's wife could not hide the shock on her face as she answered the doorbell.

Yaya, her mother, seemed to grasp the situation, however. "Come. Come," she said, pulling Jonah inside. "You and Levon should spend the summer together."

CHAPTER 24

War broke out that summer. Turkey invaded the small island of Cyprus and the drumbeat of propaganda reverberated everywhere. The war was being waged to avenge the persecution of the Turks in Cyprus, quash the loathsome Greeks, and punish the infidels—all in the name of justice, of course. With help from the media, generals and politicians fanned the flames of nationalism. Slogans invoking the glory of the fatherland and Ataturk's courage in Gallipoli were ubiquitous. When the war was in full cry, the same chorus sang the heroic deeds of the Turkish GI Joe, endearingly called *Mehmetcik*, little Mehmet.

The tug of Turkish nationalism, which extolled the virtues of the fatherland and its heroes, while portraying the enemy as the evil incarnate, had a direct impact on the Armenian community. Turkish military men descended upon Armenian church halls and community centers to praise the heroic deeds of the *"Ermeni Mehmetciks,"* brave Armenian soldiers. In turn, Armenian businesses, churches, and community leaders held fund-raisers for the war effort, with the propaganda machine questioning the community's loyalty and patriotism if the contributions were not generous enough. All the while, European journalists and eyewitnesses reported atrocities perpetrated by the Turkish military against the Armenian and Greek populations of Cyprus. Northern Cyprus was ethnically cleansed—"Cyprus for Turks only," went the battle cry—and Armenian and Greek monuments, schools, cemeteries, and churches were razed by Turkish troops.

The war coincided with Azad's first anniversary in the army. At first, he had written diligently to Father Abram, but after a few months, the letters dried up.

"Is he safe?" the priest's wife asked worriedly one day. "Have they sent him to Cyprus? Why doesn't he write?"

Azad never wrote to his father. Thus the barrage of "good news" about Mehmetcik coming from the Cyprus front did nothing to alleviate Haiko's anxieties.

Though concerned about his older brother, Jonah was deeply preoccupied with the temporary joys of youth. Over the summer, he had befriended Arto, a relative of Father Abram's who was Jonah's age and of a similar bent of mind. They often went to the slums of Bakirkoy to rent mopeds, which they rode at full throttle, like two daredevils, through the dangerous maze of alleys teeming with cars, carts, children, and stray animals. There were no traffic lights. The unpaved roads, replete with ditches and potholes, added to the thrill. Their youthful delusions of invincibility somehow protected them from serious harm.

During one of these reckless excursions, they saw Levon running down the street after them.

"That's strange," Jonah remarked to Arto. "Father Abram's wife *never* lets Levon roam the streets by himself."

Still a hundred yards away, Levon yelled in Armenian, "Azad is here!" He waved to them to return home.

Arto and Jonah angrily signaled to the boy to shut up. But he continued to speak Armenian in his high-pitched voice. "He is here!" he yelled.

"Idiot!" Jonah muttered through clenched teeth. "Stop yelling and speak in Turkish!"

But Levon was too far away to hear his brother.

The xenophobia and racism espoused by the Turks and their government were far from understated, with official banners and graffiti, splashed all over the city, issuing the same commandment—"*Vatandash Turkche konush!*"—exhorting compatriots to speak Turkish. Fervently nationalistic for the most part in times of peace, the Turks became even more strident when war broke out. With the political climate so hostile, the last thing Jonah and Arto wanted to do in the crowded streets of Bakirkoy was to attract undue attention to their Armenian ethnicity.

They rushed back to Father Abram's home and found Azad sipping tea at the kitchen table. Jonah hugged his brother hard. Azad was smiling and looked well.

"The first three months were rough," he explained cheerfully.

"What was it like?" Jonah asked.

"Yes, tell us," Father Abram chimed in.

"Our drill sergeant pushed us beyond our limits—and beat anyone who couldn't keep up," Azad said. "When we weren't drilling in the snow, we were peeling potatoes, clearing roads, or gathering firewood." He turned to Father Abram's wife. "I wore the wool hat, gloves, and socks you sent me, keeping them hidden under my uniform, but they weren't enough." He turned again to the others. "One night, when I was pulling guard duty in full sight of Mount Ararat in the distance, I got frostbite."

"Frostbite?" Jonah inquired.

"Another Armenian saved me. His mother, a devout Christian, had taken him as a young boy to Jerusalem where he became a Hadji. After he enlisted in the army, the Turkish sergeant ordered that his skin be flayed to remove the tattooed cross—an allegedly indiscreet display of an insignia that supposedly insulted the fatherland and Islam. As a result, he now had an ugly scar on his right forearm where his cross had once been. He advised me to keep my Armenian identity a secret and to ensure that no one came to know about my time in the seminary in Jerusalem. He was with me when I got frostbite and my legs became so numb I couldn't move. He ran to fetch help, while I lay hallucinating on the snow-covered roadside. I woke up in a hospital bed with bandaged feet. How they ached! The nurse who treated me gave me a shot of penicillin—right here!" He winked at Jonah and pointed to his backside.

"When she asked me how old I was, I told her I was twenty, but she said I didn't look old enough to enlist. She figured my father had falsified my age on my ID card—like all the other peasants back in the village do—so he could get me back home sooner to help till the land, harvest the crops, tend to the live-stock, and all that."

"Well?" Jonah asked.

"She was right. I *am* too young. That needle hurt!"

Everyone laughed.

Father Abram looked at Azad, curiosity lighting up his expression. "But things got better, no?"

Smiling broadly, Azad stood up and saluted crisply. "Sir, I am reporting for duty," he said in mock seriousness. "Today, we will do conversational English." He laughed heartily and sat back down. "I am the general's personal English tutor."

"You have benefited already from your education at the Jerusalem seminary!" Father Abram remarked with satisfaction.

"How are your feet now?" the priest's wife wanted to know.

"They're fine. They healed well."

"How about Cyprus, the war?" Jonah persisted.

"The general kept me out of it. I don't know what excuses he made. Thankfully, I'm not in Cyprus. I'm here on leave for a month." Azad chuckled. "The general wants to learn English badly, it seems."

"Doesn't he know that you're Armenian?"

"I'm certain he does," Azad replied seriously. "My guess is that he's helping me *because* I'm Armenian."

"What do you mean?"

"It turns out his mother is Armenian. I heard it from his daughter. By the way, she's *very* pretty; I think she's in love with me. The general's father was a Turkish military governor and plucked a pretty adolescent girl from one of the deportation caravans to keep as a domestic servant. Later, he decided to promote her to the harem and make her one of his wives."

During his month of leave, Azad stayed with a friend, a former classmate from the Jerusalem seminary. He explained to Jonah that he did not want to be a burden on Father Abram's family and refused to stay with his father with whom he was no longer on speaking terms.

Azad and Jonah visited Ani at her school as often as they could. On those occasions, they frequented the beach and swam in the calm Marmara Sea.

"Does this remind you of the village lake?" Azad joked as they lounged and sunned on the rocky beach that was strewn with pebbles.

"You mean our 'ocean'?" Jonah asked, then sat silently a moment. "Why don't you visit Father?"

"Oh, come on now!"

"Tell me. Why don't you visit Father?"

"Is that what matters now?" Azad looked away to watch a tanker with a Soviet flag passing in the distance. "There may be Armenian sailors on that Soviet ship. If Haiko Ibelin had planned on moving to Soviet Armenia instead of Germany, maybe the family would have remained intact. None of this would have happened—or would be on the verge of happening."

"What do you mean by that?"

"You're really naïve, aren't you? I have to go back to the army. You'll go back to Jerusalem. And poor Ani, she'll be left here, all by herself, at the mercy of an unsympathetic stepmother and of...of a backward—"

"Remember, you're his son."

"His stupid customs are passé."

"I don't understand a word of what you're saying."

"You will, soon enough." Azad picked up a fist-size rock and flung it into the sea. Clearly dissatisfied with the results, he shot to his feet, picked up as many rocks as he could manage with both hands, and hurled them into the sea with all his might.

"Bad throw," Jonah observed calmly.

"I know." Azad sat back down and hugged his knees. "We must find a way out for you."

"For *me*?"

"Jerusalem will come to an end. Probably a bitter end."

"You're talking nonsense!"

A long silence followed.

"Listen." Azad's eyes brightened. "If you ever need help, call the general. I know he will help."

Jonah was eager to put his dreadful summer vacation behind him, starting from his father's poverty-ridden apartment to Azad's alarming premonitions. He assumed the cold shoulder Shahnour had given him in Bursa was a temporary setback, and looked forward to returning to Jerusalem and resuming their courtship. He was also confident that his best friend Raffi would not tell others about the appalling condition of Haiko's apartment in Yenikapi.

But his hopes of picking up where he had left off were quickly dashed upon his return to the Vank.

"Jonah, my son," Mrs. Shakarian said tentatively, "it's time for your next phase of schooling." She seemed to be struggling to find the right words as she placed both her hands on his shoulders. "The plan is...the archbishop..." She frowned and looked away, near tears. "Things are complex and I have no control over them," she said and walked into her office.

Next phase of schooling? Jonah shook his head, puzzled.

The next day, the Haitourian boys lined up to start their march to church for evening vespers.

Instead of giving his usual orders to the boys to head to church, Mr. Shakarian spoke philosophically about growth and maturity. "I am privileged and honored to have nurtured seven more boys, now ready for their next phase of schooling."

Jonah cringed. *Next phase of schooling.*

"Seven of our boys," Mr. Shakarian droned on, "in fact, *sons,* since I feel so close to all of you, are ready. It is time to matriculate to the seminary."

Jonah was stunned. *How can they do this to me? I'm the patriarch's son!*

"...well equipped to tackle the rigors and challenges...the seven transferees..."

Jonah stopped listening. *Bastards.*

Shahnour was standing in the doorway of her mother's office. A distant eyewitness. A mere observer. Jonah turned his questioning gaze squarely on her. Their eyes met and locked. *To hell with discretion.*

"No! It's not what I want!" he shouted, surprising himself.

Mr. Shakarian was momentarily stunned into silence by the outburst.

"I won't transfer to that prison," glowered Jonah.

"Jonah, my son..."

"I'm the patriarch's son! I will speak to him myself."

"The archbishop has already obtained the patriarch's approval."

Jonah turned to Shahnour. There was pity in her eyes. He bowed his head in submission, as though in disgrace. Covering his eyes with his hands to hide the tears of humiliation, he headed for his room. *This,* he told himself as he stumbled through the hallways, *is Sevantz's doing.*

CHAPTER 25

Jerusalem, September 1974

Archbishop Sevantz Aminian had presence. At five feet ten inches, he was considered tall and imposing. He possessed a full head of jet-black hair, interspersed with streaks of gray. His handsome, aristocratic features acted as a magnet, drawing attention to his face, and his black eyes appeared to take in his surroundings at a glance and dominate them. Like the patriarch, he kept a well-trimmed goatee, although his own was more pronounced. His voice, while melodic and inviting, descended, sometimes, into a biting baritone. Always impeccably dressed, he usually wore white, purple, or black silk robes which were mostly new and always crisp and freshly laundered. A cross with a large medallion in the middle hung from his neck to denote his rank, while the large amethyst ring on his right ring finger was of the finest quality.

Highly educated, Sevantz was fluent in Armenian, Turkish, Arabic, English, and French and had a working knowledge of Hebrew. His expression exuded confidence and authority. He was the crown prince of the Vank, the unrivaled heir to the patriarchal throne.

Rumors abounded. Most pegged him as a consummate politician and shrewd businessman, but there were allegations of more sinister and nefarious conduct as well.

"He might as well be Cardinal Richelieu," Jonah had remarked more than once in conversations with friends.

Sevantz controlled the Vank in every respect. He, more than anybody else, held sway over the lives and futures of the young boys entrusted to his care. He was their puppet master.

Jonah found life in the seminary after his transfer restrictive, but his new regimented routine felt less stifling than the experience of being under the thumb of His Eminence, Archbishop Sevantz Aminian. To drown his anger and disappointment—and to better endure the drudgery of the seminary's daily routine— he spent his time reading and occasionally breaching, along with his friends Thomas and Enoch, the seminary's oppressive rules. Enoch still dared to scale the seminary walls to meet his sweetheart, with Jonah and Thomas serving as decoys and lookouts.

As they were returning from one of their excursions to King David's tomb, Thomas began teasing Enoch. "Did you kiss her?" he asked.

Enoch kicked Thomas in the rear and ran toward the Zion Gate, a massive tower in the Jerusalem Wall, just across the street from the western wall of the Vank and facing its side entrance. Thomas and Jonah chased after him, but did not get far. As they negotiated the turn, they came across a sight that stopped them cold.

Across the street on the Vank side, three long, black American-made cars were parked in front of a boarded-up store. A number of thuggish-looking young men in black suits stood beside the cars. Their stance suggested they were on full alert.

The three boys hid inside the tower.

"Who are they?" Jonah whispered worriedly. "What are they doing here?"

"That's strange!" Thomas observed. "That store is open."

Three others emerged from the store. The two flanking the man in the center looked like the agents outside, but the one in the middle appeared much older. Portly, completely bald, and sporting a short-sleeved khaki shirt, he walked briskly over to the car parked in the middle, that had a door open in readiness, and ducked inside. The rest of the men standing guard followed suit, jumping into the last of the three cars, and the motorcade sped off.

"Was that Moshe Dayan?" Jonah asked incredulously, referring to the legendary Israeli leader.

"The man didn't have an eye patch," Enoch quipped.

The three boys waited a few minutes in their hiding place before proceeding toward the Vank. They had just taken a few steps when they froze again; the door to the store had opened once more. Someone stepped out through it and began looking up and down the street.

In a panic, the boys ran back to their observation post. Jonah could feel his heart racing.

Thomas carefully peered around the wall. Then he snapped back, his face ashen. "Our English teacher!" he whispered.

"Nersotz Aghvesian?" Jonah was dumbfounded.

After looking around for a few minutes, Aghvesian seemed satisfied that the coast was clear and went back inside.

The boys waited and wondered. *What next?*

Aghvesian reemerged a moment later, this time, accompanied by Archbishop Aminian. The two of them locked the door of the store that had been opened after remaining mysteriously shut for so long. Then Aghvesian made a hasty entry into the Vank, while Sevantz headed straight toward the Zion Gate.

The boys scrambled up the steps of the fortress and hid behind an arch where they waited anxiously until the archbishop had disappeared.

"Let's follow him," Jonah suggested.

Sevantz headed in the direction of the Church of Pentecost, the site of the Last Supper, where a Bedouin was waiting for him. They walked into a side alley and the two engaged in a heated discussion. Soon, they appeared to come to an agreement. Sevantz reached inside his vestment, pulled out a package, and handed it to the Bedouin. The man, in turn, gave Sevantz a large, thick envelope. Sevantz stuffed the envelope inside his robe and turned around abruptly.

While Enoch and Thomas quickly slipped back into a crevice in the wall, Jonah, still absorbed by what he was witnessing, was late to react. Stunned to see the boy staring at him, the archbishop's face turned red with rage. After hesitating a moment, he walked briskly toward a terrified Jonah, who remained frozen in place. His eyes ablaze with fury, Sevantz walked past the boy without uttering a word.

Jonah felt obliged to justify his presence. "I was on my way to the chapel of the Last Supper," he yelled.

Sevantz was already ten paces past Jonah and continued his purposeful stride.

"I wasn't spying on your clandestine operations!"

Sevantz stopped in midstride, but after a moment's hesitation, thought the better of it and walked on.

Paris

The gavel came crashing down and with that, the session had come to an end. A fourteenth-century Bible, a magnificent illuminated manuscript from Cilician Armenia, had just been sold to No. 75 for $250,000. It had been the last item on the block.

Mr. Haitourian approached the purchaser-payments counter and turned in his paddle: number seventy-five. The ledger listed six items he had bid for. He made the payment and asked his young friend to join him for a cup of coffee.

Mr. Haitourian and Andrew went across the street from Sotheby's Galerie Charpentier in Paris to a small café, where they sat outside, gazing at the many elegant boutiques and lively pedestrians.

"It's a shame to see our national treasures being auctioned to the highest bidder," Mr. Haitourian said sadly. "There's so much history, pain, and suffering tied up in these artifacts. I cannot be everywhere to bid against anyone who tries to buy them."

"As you know, some experts think that these come from the treasury of the St. James Brotherhood in Jerusalem. Archbishop—"

"Sevantz? Just rumors."

"Perhaps," the young man said. "Nonetheless, they persist."

"Maybe propagated by rivals to the throne."

"Rivals or otherwise, there is enough fodder. It's clear that this cleric doesn't show much deference to his vow of abstinence." He stifled a laugh.

"Yes, yes, I know. Both Sevantz and the patriarch live rather extravagantly," countered Mr. Haitourian. "Perhaps they simply have a zest for life. When they travel, they stay at plush hotels and lavish expensive gifts on people. Elijah indulges in the best cigars and brandy. I have the same vice. That doesn't make one a thief or looter."

"Perhaps not, but something or someone pays for his life-style—and for the properties, homes, and hotels that Sevantz has acquired in France and Switzerland."

"Unsubstantiated conjectures. And I suppose these auctioned artifacts aren't sufficient."

"Agreed. I've heard stories that are even more worrying: that Armenian-owned lands and property in Jerusalem and on the West Bank are being sold off."

"That's a serious allegation."

"Well, the Vank used to be one of the largest landowners in the Holy Land and Archbishop Aminian acts as the sole proprietor."

"The sale of land in that viciously contested region would have serious political ramifications."

"The Israelis want to acquire more land to build *kibbutzim* and settlements in what they consider to be their ancestral homeland. The Arab nationalists, on the other hand, consider the sale of land to the Israelis high treason, punishable by death."

"Indeed. The Vank must be kept out of such a quandary."

"Exactly!" the young man exclaimed in an animated voice. "And our Archbishop Aminian sells Vank property to Israelis directly or acts as a middleman for Arabs who sell Palestinian land to the Israelis. The rumor is that the PLO has blacklisted Sevantz and he dare not visit any Arab country. I even heard that there was a bounty on his head!"

Mr. Haitourian shook his head in disbelief. "All these stories sound too farfetched to have a grain of truth in them. Elijah has always impressed me as someone deeply devoted to the Armenian cause. Not only would he not betray the Vank, he would certainly never tolerate behavior of this kind from anyone, not even Sevantz."

The young man thought the other naïve. "Sevantz is a rogue operator and doesn't seem to be answerable to anyone. He carries on with impunity." After some hesitation, he added, "Surely you've heard of his illegitimate son?"

"Hearsay."

"How about the current mistress?"

"A good deed misinterpreted," Mr. Haitourian shot back. "When a brother dies suddenly, what's one to do with the young family left behind?"

"One fine summer day, a strikingly beautiful young woman arrives in Jerusalem and takes up residence with Archbishop Aminian." The young man chuckled. "In his apartment, in the Vank. Out of the goodness of his heart, Sevantz moves his sister-in-law to Jerusalem, so that it is easier for him to care and provide for her and her children. Perhaps he is following the written word in the Bible: be the keeper of your dead brother's wife."

"You're angry about the auction."

"I'm angry about a lot of things."

CHAPTER 26

Jerusalem, October 1974

"To appease the patriarch or perhaps the Shakarians, Sevantz places me in the tenth grade," a sullen Jonah complained to Kalousd following his transition from the St. Tarkmantchatz School to the seminary. "A two-grade jump. But the course books, other than those involving religious studies, are equivalent to the seventh-grade level at St. Tarkmantchatz."

The tenth-grade class had nine students, of whom at least five felt themselves deserving and capable of more advanced studies. They met secretly one day, not long after Jonah's conversation with Kalousd, to debate their academic future.

Jonah, in typical fashion, was the first to speak up. "Even if we eventually join the priesthood," he said, "we should still acquire as much education and knowledge as we possibly can."

His statement was met by nods from the others.

"We should address our concerns to Archbishop Aminian," Jonah continued.

"Tsk, tsk, tsk." Houtah, a fellow student, shook his head skeptically. "I'm not so sure this is a good move."

"We're not causing trouble. Our request is not only the right thing for us, it is also for the betterment of the seminary—for the Vank. He'll support us."

"I'm afraid I see nothing but trouble ahead."

The five boys remained alert as they waited for one of the archbishop's occasional visits to the seminary. After several days, their patience paid off when they spotted Sevantz walking down to his office. Jonah and the others rushed to follow and a few moments later, stood breathlessly outside his office door.

After getting the nod from his accomplices, Jonah knocked tentatively.

"Come in," came a bad-tempered baritone voice from behind the closed door.

They entered with eyes downcast and, one by one, kissed the archbishop's amethyst ring before lining up in front of him.

"*Sirpazan*," Jonah greeted Sevantz, addressing him by his formal Armenian title of bishop. He paused awkwardly. He had practiced the opening, but was now at a loss for words.

"Speak up, boy."

Jonah was unsure as to whether Sevantz was annoyed or was actually encouraging him to speak up. "We are here..." He cleared his dry throat. "We would like our class to be split into two groups."

"That's interesting." Sevantz nodded attentively. "Why?"

"*Sirpazan*, we, the five of us..." Jonah motioned to the group. "We are unable to progress in our studies."

"Who is holding you back?"

"The rest of our classmates. They can't keep up."

"Splitting the class into two groups?"

"Yes, so we can advance in our studies."

"Hmm. You want to excel. Quite admirable! I'll speak to the headmaster and see what we can do."

The students left the office, some hopeful, others pessimistic.

After three weeks had gone by with no signs of feedback, Jonah approached the headmaster.

"The archbishop has not discussed this topic with me," was the curt reply.

"It's best we drop the issue," suggested Houtah, when Jonah reported back his conversation with the headmaster. The others agreed with Houtah.

Jonah wasn't willing to give up that easily. "Fine. You can stay out of it. I think Sevantz forgot to mention it to the headmaster. I will ask him next time I see him."

An eager Jonah approached Sevantz at the very next opportunity. "*Sirpazan*, have you considered our request? The headmaster—"

The archbishop whirled towards Jonah, eyes ablaze. Seizing Jonah by the nape of the neck, he pushed him into his office. "Listen, you punk!" he seethed, eyes narrowed, nostrils flaring.

Jonah wasn't perturbed at first by the vehement, if puzzling reaction. "*Sirpazan*, we were hoping we would be in a separate class by now."

The archbishop tightened his grip on him. "You better start behaving like my model students—or else!"

Jonah realized Sevantz was dead serious. He also knew exactly which students the man was referring to. "You mean the boys who are notorious for their submissive nature and lack of intelligence?" he shot back.

"You impertinent bastard! Students like you are a blot on the Vank!" The archbishop shook his finger in Jonah's face, nearly jabbing him in the nose.

Jonah felt his face turn pale, in stark contrast to Sevantz's, which was flushed with rage.

"This Vank has survived centuries of brutal history and flourished because of the dedication and unwavering, unquestioning loyalty of its residents. You...you arrogant and ungrateful bastard! What have *you* done for this Vank?" Sevantz's eyes were full of fury and his usually pleasant baritone voice had degenerated into a coarse growl. "Elijah's favoritism toward you doesn't go very far! The old man is cooped up in his office writing poetry. He's going senile. Your future is in *my* hands.

"Furthermore, if you are still harboring hopes that your American sponsor is coming to whisk you away, keep dreaming." He motioned to dismiss Jonah, but then stopped abruptly. "Don't be ungrateful for the food and shelter we give you, the clothing we put on your back, or the education you receive. Did you find any of this in *your* father's house?" He waved the boy off contemptuously, adding in vulgar Turkish, "*Siktir!*"

Jonah left the archbishop's office, disoriented and quivering all over with humiliation and anger. After running blindly outside, he sought shelter in the cemetery behind the seminary. There, hidden behind gravestones and trees, he threw himself, facedown, on a pile of freshly poured dirt and sobbed his heart out.

CHAPTER 27

Six long, lonely months had passed since Jonah's reassignment to the seminary. Any illusions he'd cherished about his future had long since faded away. His infatuation with Shahnour was the sole thread still connecting him to those hopeful days in the past when he had been a promising young Haitourian boy, and occasional sightings of her continued to nourish his heart.

He no longer minded the drudgery of church during holidays, for it meant that the student body from the St. Tarkmantchatz School attended. He would quickly locate Shahnour in the lineup of girls and then keep her in view throughout the service. Occasionally, their eyes met. While his gaze was sometimes pleading, it usually remained stern. Hers, on the other hand, was always playful. At times, she smiled without attempting to disguise it.

She likes me. Still.

While Enoch and Thomas remained Jonah's best friends, Korvat and Houtah gradually became his other two confidants. Jonah's romance with Shahnour seemed of great interest to his new friends and he spent long hours with his two classmates talking about her.

"She's just flirting," Houtah said in a dismissive tone when Jonah mentioned his eye contact with Shahnour.

"You're jealous."

"Unlike everybody else," Houtah said with a shrug, "I'm not interested in her."

"With your looks, it's good you realize there's no hope," Korvat quipped and gave Houtah a playful kick in the rear.

"Hey!" Houtah protested. "You should—"

Korvat covered Houtah's mouth with his hand to stop him from finishing his sentence. He then turned to Jonah. "Write her a letter. You'll find out how she feels."

A tall, handsome fellow, Korvat was the star of the school's soccer team and had many admirers among the Tarkmantchatz girls. He was a former Haitourian boy who, after leaving Jerusalem for good, had managed to return three years later.

Every student who had ever expressed a desire to leave the seminary had heard from his headmaster the same refrain: "Once you leave the Vank, you won't be readmitted." The policy was indeed rigidly enforced. Hence, Jonah, like the others, had been surprised when Archbishop Aminian had personally intervened and approved Korvat's return. The boy had then been enrolled in the tenth grade where the majority of the students were seventeen years old, like him. Thomas and Enoch, on the other hand, were fifteen, while Jonah was the youngest, at thirteen.

"Yes," Houtah said, chuckling as he goaded Jonah. "Yes, go ahead and write."

"I *will* write to her."

"Ooh! He's *so* daring. He's in love."

Jonah walked away, somewhat perturbed by the way his friends had teased him and made their lack of sympathy for his plight quite obvious. But he remained determined to get in touch with his love again and did so by using couriers. A Haitourian contact would pass each note addressed to Shahnour to a former Tarkmantchatz classmate of Jonah's for delivery to its intended recipient. After three successive letters—each distinguished from the one that had preceded it by a more acute note of desperation—he finally got a response. It was a disappointingly brief and impersonal note:

> *Thank you for the coded names in your notes. As you mention, they may fall into the wrong hands. The rendezvous you want is too risky. Please be careful.*

Jonah read and reread the note, bringing it to his nose and sniffing it, hoping to catch a whiff of Shahnour's fragrance. He then kissed it and hid it behind the wallpaper in the small built-in closet at the head of his bed. Every day thereafter, he would take it out whenever he was alone and read it all over again.

"Come on," Houtah said one day, "show it to us."

Jonah studied him and Korvat, who was standing nearby. "Why are you so eager to see it?"

"Maybe she hasn't sent it at all?"

Finally, Jonah gave in. Once in their hands, the note and the handwriting on it came under such serious scrutiny that it made him uneasy. They read it over and over again.

Jonah stirred and then woke up. The sound of Neshan pounding his stick on the courtyard stones outside was a welcome intrusion into his fitful sleep. He sat up in bed and waited for the soulful melody.

"*Ov paree kristonya, artentsek yev Diarintaratch donetsek!*" O good Christians, rise and celebrate the presentation of Baby Jesus.

The sound of Neshan's stick echoed again through the seminary.

The feast of *Diarintaratch*, Candlemas, the presentation of Baby Jesus to the old man Simeon at the temple, marked the beginning of Lent. In Armenian Jerusalem, the *Diarintaratch*

celebrations culminated in a bonfire, proving that the pagan worship of fire was still in practice 1,700 years after paganism had
been trounced as Armenia's state religion. In accordance with
pagan tradition, merriment and tolerance permeated the spirit of
the participants around the bonfire, making this the one holiday
in the year when the whole Vank community mingled freely, with
lay people joining the clergy, including the seminarians and the
Haitourian boys, in the revelry. There were no divisions.

O good Christian, rise and face your day of salvation, sang Neshan.

"Or damnation," Jonah mumbled to himself.

Perched on the roof of the very tall seminary building, Jonah
gazed at the horizon where streaky white clouds had begun to
absorb the glow of the rapidly setting sun. As the colors changed
and intermingled with each other, white gave way to pink, blue,
purple, emerald green, and finally, a fiery orange, like the sun
itself.

Jonah watched the sun dip toward the horizon and then
vanish. The luminous clouds continued to light the soccer field
below his dangling feet and he stared down at a pyramid of flam-
mable debris rising in the middle of the field. Broken furniture,
firewood, cardboard, and other trash had been hauled onto the
field and thrown on top of the already impressive mound. The
din from the growing crowd reached Jonah quite clearly; he could
feel the excitement and the celebratory mood. He searched for his
target and thought he caught a glimpse of her, but darkness was
descending fast.

Draped in a black robe and wearing his black pointed hood,
Sevantz approached the perimeter of the pyramid. In his left
hand, he held a tall, glistening staff with a two-headed snake
crowning it; in his right was a flaming torch. He stretched his

arms wide and raised the staff and torch as high as they would go. This was a signal for the crowd to fall silent, and gradually the noise subsided, followed by an eerie silence. Under a moonless sky, the only source of illumination was the torch Sevantz held.

"O Lord, let this light shine on the repentant souls gathered here. Let it cleanse them of their sins and guide them to salvation." Sevantz bent down and held the torch to the dry hay in front of him. "Burn and dissipate the evil and send it to its damnation many fathoms below Jerusalem."

The smoldering fire caught the gasoline encircling the mound and the pyramid burst into flames. Sevantz stepped back and cast the torch into the middle of the inferno. Soon, the flames had reached fifteen to twenty meters high and the blaze illuminated the faces of those encircling it, casting long shadows on the groups farther away.

It's time. Jonah swung his legs around and jumped off the parapet wall. After walking to the side of the building, he descended the long and narrow metal ladder.

On the field, at the periphery of the bonfire, some daring men were engaged in a friendly contest of jumping. The highest and longest leaps or the ones landing at the very edge of the flames elicited either cheers or gasps from the crowd of admiring girls. Nobody got seriously hurt, but loose shirts, hair, and eyelashes did get singed in the process.

Gillig, the Vank's notorious drunkard, let loose the vulgar words from a song about his imaginary lover. "*Yargule, yargule,*" he slurred, off-key. "*Balkoni partser e...*"

Two men restrained him as he attempted to jump right into the middle of the blaze.

Jonah moved swiftly to the periphery of the crowd and worked his way toward Shahnour. To his dismay, numerous admirers surrounded her. Her merry laughter was easily audible.

He lingered in her vicinity so she could not fail to notice him, waiting for a signal, perhaps a smile, inviting him into her circle. But then he locked eyes with Korvat, who stood close by her side and seemed to be getting the most attention. He winked at Jonah.

Scoundrel! Jonah strode toward Korvat.

Houtah materialized from the darkness and blocked Jonah's path. "Don't you dare!"

"What's it to you?"

"If you embarrass Korvat, he'll make you pay."

Jonah raised himself on his toes, brought his face as close to Houtah's as he could, and hissed, "Get out of my way!"

"Oooooooh, I am terrified." Houtah pretended to shake, but quickly and more sternly added, "Scoot!" and shoved Jonah back.

Jonah regained his balance and advanced on Houtah.

"What's going on there?" Korvat yelled in their direction.

"Hi, Jonah," Shahnour added as if she had just noticed him.

Feeling offended and betrayed, Jonah turned his back on them and stomped away.

After two weeks of indecision, during which Houtah continually goaded him to act, Jonah finally sent another note to Shahnour. While he ached for her reply, he tried to find solace in books—Enoch's romantic cowboy tales—and, most of all, in Neshan's anecdotes which provided Jonah with a much-needed respite from reality. But the seminary walls and Sevantz's ominous presence were perennial reminders of his confinement.

"She will write back." Jonah remained steadfast as Enoch and Thomas tried to get his mind off Shahnour. *But would she?*

Jonah clung to his hopes, until one day, he overheard a conversation between Korvat and Houtah.

"The meeting is set," Korvat said cockily.

"Where?"

"The park. King David's Tomb."

"Do you need me?"

"Of course. You're my best lookout."

"OK, OK." Houtah paused briefly and then laughed. "Maybe we should ask Jonah to be your lookout."

"Very funny."

"So you're telling me Shahnour didn't write that note to him."

"No. His friend did, to raise his spirits."

CHAPTER 28

Santa Barbara, California, March 1975

An impeccably dressed, silver-haired man walked into an exclusive restaurant and checked on his reservation.

"Sir, would you like to be seated?" the maître d' asked him. "Your guests have not arrived yet."

"Are you sure they haven't?"

"I am certain, sir."

"All right. I'll wait for them here."

"Would you like to order a drink while you wait?"

"No, thank you."

Nearly seventy, the man crossed the small foyer in a deliberate fashion, carefully patted his coat pocket to double-check the contents, and then turned to face the entrance.

Five minutes later, the door opened and two men entered. Their sharp American-made suits belied their position as diplomats, a breed that tended to favor European sartorial styles. When they saw the elderly gentleman, they waved and greeted him in Turkish with a broad smile.

He smiled back, removed a revolver from his pocket, steadied his aim, and fired repeatedly.

The two men slumped to the floor. Bright red blood seeped from beneath their lifeless, contorted bodies, forming a puddle near their erstwhile host's feet.

A moment of stunned silence followed the noise of gunfire. Then the restaurant patrons stumbled over each other to make a hasty exit, careful to avoid eye contact with the man standing erect and serene, still brandishing the handgun. Trapped behind the reception desk, the maître d' remained motionless.

Once the restaurant had fallen silent again, the assassin whispered, "That's to avenge the sixty members of my family your fathers slaughtered before my eyes." He calmly placed the revolver on the floor and turned to the maître d'. "Please call the police. Tell them I come in peace."

Jerusalem, April 24, 1975

Neshan, the town crier, entered the seminary courtyard as the sun was rising.

"*Hye Joghovurt artentsek, Medz Yegherni Hishetsek!* Armenian people, rise to commemorate the genocide!" For once, he neither sang nor chanted, but spoke clearly and somberly.

The glum message even had an impact on the deacon, who refrained from striking the students' beds, the way he was accustomed to doing with gusto each morning. Instead, he tugged at the boys' bedcovers or jiggled their feet, protruding from under the covers. Nobody complained that morning. Nor did anyone make excuses or feign illness to avoid church. All hurried to get ready and stand in line.

It was the sixtieth anniversary of the night of April 24, 1915, the bleakest date in Armenian history. That night, upon orders from Talaat Pasha, the interior minister of Turkey, and the ruling party of the "Young Turks," the Turkish gendarmes had arrested the Armenian community's cultural, religious, and political leaders, who were dragged from their beds and homes and thrown into prison. A few days later, they were driven in cattle cars to the interiors of the Empire and summarily executed. With that, the first salvo of a master plan for the mass annihilation of the Ottoman Empire's Armenian citizens—the Age of Genocide— began in earnest.

In years past, the Jerusalem patriarchate had conducted private church vigils at St. James Cathedral to commemorate the genocide, but this year, the patriarch had decided to show solidarity with the Armenian community worldwide and join in the more public commemoration activities. The Jerusalem patriarchate was ready to unshackle the yoke and shame of victimhood. It was time to celebrate *survival.*

"Let's learn from our Jewish brethren!" was the rallying cry. After all, the intent of the perpetrators in both holocausts had been to annihilate a whole race of unsuspecting, loyal subjects. "The Jews are no longer ashamed of their victimization," the Armenians reasoned.

With dozens of Israeli dignitaries, journalists, and foreign embassy staff in attendance at the commemoration, the patriarch officiated over the High Mass and gave a moving sermon, after which the community was brought to tears by the choir's poignant rendition of the requiem for the two million martyrs. The Mass was followed by a hushed procession from the Cathedral of St. James to the Armenian Cemetery, where fiery speeches were given and solemn prayers murmured at the foot of a memorial dedicated to the slaughtered victims.

The Turkish ambassador to Israel slammed the newspaper on Soluk Kurt's desk. "Colonel, have you read this?"

A clearly annoyed Colonel Kurt raised his eyes from his own reading and threw a cursory glance at the front page of the most widely circulated daily newspaper in Israel. "Armenian Genocide Commemoration," Kurt read with a sneer. "I have no time for distractions. I have more pressing business to attend to with the Mossad."

"But…but…these children are Turkish citizens!" the ambassador spluttered in indignation and bewilderment, pointing to the picture of the seminarians marching in the procession.

"You are the ambassador." The mockery in the colonel's voice was unmistakable. "They are your charges. Aren't they?"

"What is that supposed to—"

Kurt snatched up the paper, threw it against the wall, and shouted, "They are training terrorists like that madman in California! Right under your nose!"

The ambassador was not pleased at being rebuked so harshly, but Kurt was not one to be trifled with. He was a deputy director of the MIT, Turkey's National Intelligence Organization, and had the power to cut short the ambassador's career with one phone call to the Foreign Ministry in Ankara. The ambassador decided to use a more conciliatory tone with him. "The Interior and Foreign Ministries issue passports to these children and allow them to come to Jerusalem. What am I to do?"

"Do what an ambassador should be doing!"

"OK." The ambassador started to pace about the room. "I will personally visit this…this…this nest of terrorism. I will crush these Armenians!"

"Now I can see the Young Turk blood hasn't been completely drained from your veins."

The ambassador sent a curt note to the patriarch, demanding to be allowed to see for himself how the young and impressionable citizens of his nation were faring. In response, the seminary and Haitourian School were hurriedly spruced up and prepared in anticipation of the Turkish ambassador's visit.

Archbishop Aminian met the visiting dignitaries at the entrance to the Vank.

"The Turkish citizens in Israel are my liege!" declared the ambassador in a comment targeted more at the colonel than at their host, Archbishop Aminian.

"Dagh bashini duman almish, yuruyelim arkadashlar..." The seminarians, standing rigidly at attention for the ambassador as he entered their dining hall, sang the closest thing to the Turkish national anthem that would, at the same time, not violate Armenian sensibilities. "Smoke is rising from the mountaintop. Let's march on, comrades..."

Jonah remembered singing the song in Palu and hearing it echo across the surrounding fields and hills. He recalled the words of the Turkish history teacher in the village who had led the children on field trips to obliterate the last traces of Armenian and Assyrian monuments: "Turkey for Turks only!"

The visit began with a lunch in the dining room where the ambassador sat at the head of the table, next to Archbishop Aminian. On his right was the MIT colonel. The meal was as lavish as the Vank's kitchen could prepare.

The ambassador had a notebook in his hand and took copious notes, while the colonel coldly scrutinized the environs. As Jonah stole a hurried glance at the colonel, he felt a chill run through him. There was something familiar—and frightening—about him. The boy looked around the dining room and realization suddenly dawned: conspicuous by its absence was a picture of Ataturk. Paintings of Mount Ararat, religious figures, and Armenian heroes peppered the walls, but Ataturk was nowhere to be seen. The colonel's features didn't resemble the potentate's, but his general appearance and dour demeanor did, in what was an obvious attempt to emulate the look of the father of the Turkish Republic. Kurt wore a Western-style suit reminiscent of the one Ataturk had worn in the photographs Jonah had seen back in Turkey. And he had the same slick hair, combed back sharply. Most unsettling of all was his piercing glare.

After lunch, the archbishop offered to show the guests the library. He asked a few students, including Jonah, to join the entourage and serve as tour guides to the visiting dignitaries. While the archbishop and the librarian confidently pointed out the resources available to the students of Turkish nationality, the colonel focused on the books critical of Turkish rule and history. He picked up a couple of books that were prominently displayed and examined them.

"*Smyrna 1922: The Destruction of a City*," Kurt read aloud. "*The Forty Days of Musa Dagh*," he continued.

Jonah knew the books well. The first book, written by Marjorie Housepian Dobkin, was a chronicle of the destruction, pillaging, and burning of the city of Smyrna and the massacres of its Armenian and Greek populations by Ataturk's army. The second, authored by Franz Werfel, was the epic novel based on the heroic resistance of the seven Armenian villages of Musa Dagh against the Turkish deportation orders of 1915.

"Is this what you teach our citizens?" the colonel demanded, gesturing to the books in his hands.

"This is a libr—"

"Is it?"

"These are simply reference books. Historical—"

"History? Written by whom?"

"These are independently authored, scholarly—"

"It's anti-Turkish." The colonel threw in the stock party line, almost as if it were the mechanical response of a robot. Kurt reflected upon the wisdom of the decades-long Turkish policy of not only denying the genocide, but also avoiding all mention of Armenian presence in the former empire. Then his thoughts switched to the present, dwelling on the implications and consequences of exposing these children to the "reference books" he was contemplating. "I want to speak to some of these boys," he snapped. "Individually."

"Kurt *Effendi*, these are young boys—"

"That is obvious. More reason for me to question them— one by one."

Kurt used the librarian's office. The interviews were short, but the students leaving the office appeared shaken.

Karnig came out and it was Jonah's turn. As Karnig brushed against him, he whispered in a barely audible voice, "The bastard!"

Jonah recalled how Karnig had held his hand firmly while they were disembarking from the ship upon their arrival in the Holy Land. He longed for the same comforting reassurance now, but was embarrassed to reach out.

"What is your name?" Kurt asked Jonah, as soon as the interview had begun, already busy jotting down notes in his notebook.

"Jonah Ibel..." Jonah cleared his throat awkwardly.

"I didn't hear that!"

"Hanna Ibelin," Jonah said, correcting himself.

"Where are you from?"

"Mardin."

"Mardin? Are you Armenian?"

"Yes, sir."

"An Armenian from Mardin?" The colonel looked up from his notebook, leveling his knife-sharp stare at Jonah. "Highly unlikely."

Jonah averted his eyes and shut them tight, lest the Turk bore holes through his pupils.

"Are you sure you're not an Assyrian?"

"Yes, sir. No…I mean, I am not Assyrian." Jonah began to tremble.

"What do they call you here?"

"I don't understand."

"*Kopek!* Listen, dog! Don't play games with me! What did they change your name to?"

The boy swallowed hard. "Jonah Ibelinian," he muttered and tried to swallow again, but his mouth was too dry. He took a hurried breath, afraid he might stop breathing.

"Ibelinian?" He played with the word a moment. "Ibelinian. Ibelin. Where does the name come from?"

"My great-uncle says one of our ancestors was a French knight," Jonah replied meekly.

Kurt laughed heartily and drummed the desk with his palms. "How charming. The peasant, the peon is, in fact, nobility." He stopped laughing abruptly. "Why are you here?"

"To become a priest."

"Oh, yes. Just like the others. Why do you want to become a priest?"

"Why?" Jonah was stumped. He had never asked himself the question.

"Were you in the same group as the *kopek* that just left?" The man's eyes burrowed into Jonah.

"Yes."

The colonel scribbled a few more notes and then ordered Jonah out. "*Siktir, kopek oghlu kopek!*" he said, swearing in Turkish.

"What did he ask you?" Sevantz asked nervously.

"My name," Jonah answered. "Where I was from." He was angry with Sevantz for putting him in such a predicament.

"Did he ask you anything about me?"

Jonah looked up at Sevantz, incredulous.

"Answer my question," the archbishop demanded in a gruff voice.

"He wanted to know what you gave that Bedouin."

"What?"

"Why would he ask me anything about you?"

Sevantz's eyes widened. Then he turned away, apparently through with *his* interrogation.

To the Minister of Interior Affairs:

It may come as a surprise to you that many young Turkish citizens reside in the old section of the city of Jerusalem. A certain priest from Istanbul by the name of Abram Varujoghlu acts as their recruiter. This is a nest of sedition. Armenian history and the details of the Armenian genocide are taught here. Anti-Turkish books, pamphlets, and pictures are proudly displayed. I recommend action to put down, once and for all, this ongoing subversion against Turkey.

Sincerely,

Colonel Soluk Kurt

CHAPTER 29

The summer of 1975 began with the promise of a calm interlude, and by the end of June, almost the entire student body had gone home for the summer break. It included Kalousd and Levon who traveled to Istanbul to stay with Father Abram. Only seven students and a deacon remained at the seminary—a paltry number, Jonah thought, for attending to the compulsory tasks imposed by daily routine which was no less rigorous over the summer. When it came to the Vank's rights to the holy sites, vigilance remained a top priority, regardless of the number of people available at the seminary to maintain it.

Mid-August brought with it the feast of the Assumption of Mary, Mother of God. During this major holiday of the summer, the Armenian faithful would flock to the Cathedral of the Virgin Mary to celebrate the Assumption, thank the Lord and the Blessed Virgin for the abundant harvest, and share in the blessing and the consumption of freshly picked grapes. To the seminarians, the festivities meant more drudgery and sacrifice. For the two weeks leading up to the event, their already onerous schedule was crowded with more church services and liturgical events.

Following the daily early morning services at the Cathedral of St. James and a quick breakfast, the small band of seminarians trudged to the Church of the Holy Virgin. The thirty-minute march was a strenuous one and the boys, trapped in their black buttoned-up wool uniforms designed for winter, absorbed every blistering ray of the scorching summer sun.

"It's sweltering," Korvat, the most athletic among them, complained. It was his turn to carry the oversize Bible and he was now using it to fan himself.

"I'm drenched," Enoch added, not to be outdone.

"Damn these caps! Why do we have to wear them at all?"

They walked along the city walls, past the Western Wall on Temple Mount. The frustration mounted as the heat became more oppressive.

"This is like the fiery furnace of Shadrach, Meshach, and Abednego," Jonah mused.

The road skirted fortress walls on the left for part of the trip. As they passed the Golden Gate, sealed shut with bricks, Thomas added his own inputs to the conversation. "I think it would be easier for a camel to pass through the eye of a needle than for us to enter the kingdom of God—or through this gate to heaven."

Nobody had the energy to laugh at his feeble attempt at humor.

To the right of the steaming pavement was a deep ravine from which rose hills bare of vegetation. The surroundings were hallowed ground. Monuments and religious ruins were omnipresent—dotting the hillside, embedded in caves, and carved into the rocks.

The most notable mausoleum belonged to Judas Iscariot, the apostle who had been swayed by the devil—and money—to betray his Master. After witnessing the coronation of Christ with thorns, the traitor, wracked by guilt, had returned the reward of thirty silver coins to the high priest before attempting to hang himself. The rope had snapped, however, and he had plunged to the rocks below, the impact of his fall causing his blood and intestines to spill from his body and serve as fodder for wolves.

Past the accursed spot, at the foot of the Mount of Olives, an oasis of olive groves invited the weary into the Garden of Gethsemane, the site where Christ had wrestled with His fate just before His arrest. The Vank owned a significant portion of the coveted garden and a substantial portion of the Church of the Holy Virgin already visible through the twisted branches of trees.

"Kyrie Eleison," Korvat sang in a deep and reverent voice. "Lord, have mercy." He pointed the Bible in the direction of an Assyrian bishop and his entourage entering the church.

The students simply shrugged. In this church, as in others, many centuries ago, the Armenians had allocated to the Assyrians a chapel for worship. But the magnanimous act, instead of creating an atmosphere of cooperation and peace, had ended up fomenting friction instead.

Finally, the end of the initial leg of the first day of the tedious two-week-long trek was in sight. The church entrance, the shade, the water, and the rest were all a few steps away.

Just then, a large passenger van pulled up in front of the church and out hopped the deacon and the headmaster.

"I just can't believe this!" Korvat muttered with a scowl.

Jonah added, "This is unconscionable."

A two-hour-long Mass followed. After it was over, the deacon and the headmaster rushed to gather their robes and accessories. The van driver was waiting.

"How many people in the van?" Thomas asked.

The deacon frowned.

Jonah was blunter. "Can we ride back with you? Certainly there is plenty of space."

"Let's not break tradition," the deacon answered curtly.

The half-empty van sped off.

Like derelicts, the seven shuffled back, with the noon sun beating down on them.

Back at the Vank that evening, Korvat and Jonah were selected to be the spokesmen for the seven.

"We're humbly requesting a ride in the van," Jonah explained. "That's all."

"Is this a protest of some kind?" The headmaster shook his head, clearly annoyed at their impertinence. "This is unwise. Foolhardy." He shook his head again. "If you absolutely insist, I will ask the archbishop."

The reply descended from the archbishop's top-story residence. "No precedent will be set. They will walk." The deacon delivered the message blithely, adding with a chuckle, "Consider it a pilgrimage."

That evening, the seven decided to rebel.

The next morning, when the bell summoned the seminarians for the march to the Church of the Holy Virgin, instead of lining up, all seven changed out of their uniforms and dispersed.

The headmaster was stunned. "In the entire history of the Vank," he said, scolding the boys, "this seminary has never witnessed such insubordination."

An irate archbishop gave strict orders to withhold meals unless the mutinous seven returned to church. Accordingly, no lunch or dinner was served that day.

After morning services the following day at the Cathedral of St. James, all seven changed out of their uniforms once again and dispersed. Breakfast was not delivered. The gnawing pangs in their stomach did not diminish their resolve. They exhausted their candy, cookies, and bread, along with the rest of their reserves, while the Haitourian boys, sympathetic to the cause of their elder brethren, smuggled bread in to them.

Jonah read to keep his mind off food, losing himself in Victor Hugo's *Les Miserables*.

No lunch arrived.

"No church, no food," reiterated the headmaster.

At two o'clock that afternoon, relief came in the form of bread, biscuits, and jam, courtesy of a care package from Mrs. Shakarian. A stiff warning accompanied the delivery.

"Your behavior is appalling," she said in an admonishing tone. "If this continues, *someone* will pay dearly!"

The rebels ate, grateful to her.

On the third day of the standoff, Mrs. Shakarian summoned Korvat and Jonah to her office.

"The archbishop is furious and holds the two of you personally responsible for this situation," she said worriedly. "Please, please, for your own sakes, stop this childish game immediately! Don't let it ruin your future."

"But Mrs. Shakarian," protested Jonah, "we are just the spokesmen for the group."

Korvat nodded. "This was a group decision."

"The archbishop is convinced that you two are the leaders of the insurrection. He is considering some drastic measures to end it. And you will suffer the consequences."

Jonah and Korvat returned with the news. The seven held a summit and decided to remain steadfast in their mission.

That evening, Mrs. Shakarian sent more food. With their hunger temporarily appeased, the seven regained their confidence.

"We must remain resolute," Thomas said.

They paraded in front of the headmaster's office and chanted, "No van, no church."

On the fourth day, Korvat and Jonah found themselves once again in Mrs. Shakarian's office.

"I can do only so much for you," she said rather helplessly, appearing more anxious this time. "You do realize that this is an insult? A personal affront to the archbishop?"

"Why can't we go in the van?" Korvat asked.

"The archbishop has made his decision."

"So have we," Jonah retorted, his tone truculent.

"I would be less strident if I were you. I expect you to comply with his orders."

Jonah bit his lower lip. "We're not alone in this. It has to be a group decision." He took his role as emissary seriously. *They trust me to represent them.* "We can't desert our comrades."

"You foolish, foolish little boy!" Mrs. Shakarian sighed, throwing her arms up in frustration. "Integrity and loyalty are noble qualities, but your lives, your futures are at stake here. I will say it once again: you two are regarded as the ringleaders and will be held responsible for all the trouble caused by your group's dissent. You must think of self-preservation. You either obey the archbishop's wishes or you're out!"

"Out?" Korvat's knotted eyebrows and puzzled look conveyed alarm. "What's that supposed to mean?"

"Expelled!"

Korvat threw a perplexed glance at Jonah and then at Mrs. Shakarian. "He wouldn't dare!"

"Aren't we overconfident? If I were you, I wouldn't be quite so brash, you know."

"I can't go back to Turkey," Korvat said, suddenly sounding less defiant.

"I don't think either of you would want that." Looking more disappointed than angry, Mrs. Shakarian turned to Jonah. "You! You are throwing your future away. Your schooling, your education and...and...why not? I will say it: your chances of going to America that you're banking on!"

Jonah left with Korvat in a daze. *America*, he thought. *Why hasn't Ms. Nora come for me? Will she ever?*

The seven huddled in a classroom. "We made our point," Jonah began solemnly. "It has gotten out of hand. And Korvat and I face a terrible dilemma."

The two tried to sway the group to end the protest, but the others stood firm. "No van, no church."

Korvat, like Jonah, saw no other alternative. "We will have to break ranks," he announced grimly.

The next morning dawned radiant, with not a speck of cloud or even the slightest breeze. At 9:00 a.m. sharp, Jonah heard the clear, crisp echoes of the bell ringing in the courtyard to summon them to church. He reluctantly responded to the call, his head bowed, his steps heavy, to join Korvat in line.

The other five hissed and booed at their associates for having caved in to pressure.

"Get in line!" barked the headmaster, pointing at the five renegades.

"No van, no church!" yelled one, and they ran off to the cemetery in the back.

"The game is over!" the deacon declared. He and the headmaster trotted after them. "This is your last chance. You either come out or we'll drag you out."

"Thomas," the headmaster called out, "I see you crouching behind the gravestone. You better come out. You! Behind the tree. Enoch..."

The daily march took off again, although now, it resembled a funeral procession rather than the celebration of the resurrection and ascension of the Mother of God.

When they passed the Golden Gate, Jonah no longer believed it would open for him. *America, your doors are shut. I've lost all hope.* And as the group trudged by Judas's burial site, Jonah pondered the notion of repentance. *I don't even have thirty pieces of silver to throw back at the archbishop.*

In the deep caverns of the cathedral, on the granite plinth from where the Holy Mother of God had soared to the heavens, Archbishop Aminian officiated over a splendid, regal Mass. Then the archbishop, delighted with his victory over the rebels, led the flock to the Garden of Gethsemane, where he blessed a tray overflowing with harvested fruit.

Jonah thought the sanctified grapes contained an abundance of seeds; the fruit lacked the sheen and sweetness of previous years.

By the end of August, the vacationing seminarians were back in school. The newly returned Houtah seemed eager to deliver a message to Jonah. He did so one day, when he and Jonah were alone and waiting in line for their trip to the church.

"Your father *looks* Assyrian," Houtah muttered, after nervously clearing his throat.

Jonah's back stiffened and his cheeks flushed. He recalled the Easter mayhem around the Grotto and the pitched battles that had followed. "What do you mean?" he asked, his voice faltering. *When did Houtah meet my father? How is he going to use this against me? What's his motive?*

"Your father really does look Assyrian," Houtah explained nonchalantly. "He speaks Assyrian and travels in Assyrian circles."

"Well," Jonah stammered, as he searched for a suitable retort, "you are from Ourfa, not very far from Mardin. People from those regions are farmers and are under the sun constantly. They are sunburned and often have wrinkles." He knew he was merely waffling and his effort to explain his Assyrian associations was making little sense. "They don't know Armenian; they speak the local Kurdish and Assyrian dialects."

Houtah did not appear convinced. "Why are you going on the defensive? I just said he *looks* Assyrian." He ended the discussion by giving Jonah a sly wink.

Jonah felt cornered, but could not afford to betray his fear. He wanted to weep, but could not show any sign of weakness. He envisioned the unsheathed sword of Damocles hanging above his head.

CHAPTER 30

Four months passed without incident. During that time, the winter weather turned capricious. Balmy, sunny mornings alternated with gloomy, overcast afternoons. The nights were uncharacteristically frigid and the seminary's few heaters and thin blankets did little to provide sufficient warmth in the elongated, high-ceilinged dormitories. Frequent downpours drenched the seminarians' uniforms as they made their way to church every day. Even snow fell one morning.

Jonah's moods reflected the unpredictable swings in the weather. Confident and secure one moment, he struggled with paranoia the next, sensitive as he was to the growing chasm between him and Houtah. Avoiding each other's company, getting involved in testy exchanges and minor skirmishes, allowing tensions to escalate—these were all signs of the inevitable showdown that would take place between the two.

Then one dreary December afternoon, a thrilling announcement interrupted the solitude of the study period. "The American is here! The American is here!"

An elated Jonah sprinted to the gate. *I knew it! I knew she'd come back for me!*

Alas, it was not Ms. Nora.

A twenty-year-old American-born student had arrived at the seminary to study for the priesthood. The disappointment of not seeing his perceived savior refocused Jonah's thoughts of impending doom in Houtah's hands.

Houtah had increasingly disassociated himself from Jonah, while making a blatant show of warming toward Korvat. Houtah, Korvat, and the members of a newly budding gang began meeting each evening in a dilapidated and filthy unused outhouse in the back garden, where they prepared tea on a makeshift hot plate and gossiped late into the night. Jonah christened it "the Pigsty Camp" and the name stuck.

During this period, Thomas, Enoch, and Jonah strengthened the bonds of their friendship still further, concentrating on their studies and continuing to listen to Enoch's stories about the three cowboys in Texas. Jonah still dreamed of Ms. Nora and the life he would have some day in America.

Houtah, for his part, gradually managed to drive a wedge between the groups and two opposing camps emerged. Initially, the rift between Jonah's group and the Pigsty Camp appeared harmless, merely another expression of adolescent rivalry, but soon, the relationship between the two deteriorated alarmingly.

One day in church, as the scriptures were being read aloud, a stare, a smirk, and an expletive escalated into a nudge, a poke, and a sharp dig under the ribs. The confrontation ended with Houtah angrily throwing a liturgical book at Jonah and Jonah responding by throwing a whole stack of them back at Houtah, before the deacon boxed their ears and sent them to the headmaster for a dressing down. They both received several lashes on the palms from a thin reed and were ordered to stand on opposite sides of the door to his office, facing the wall, for the whole afternoon.

With that, the uneasy truce between the two groups degenerated into open hostility.

During a soccer game following the church incident, Houtah tackled Jonah while he wasn't handling the ball and pushed him to the ground.

Sprawled out on the muddy field, Jonah sized up his adversary and the rapidly growing number of Houtah's gang members arriving at the scene. *OK. Eat muck. No sense in starting—and losing—a fight against these wolves.* He rose slowly and walked away while dusting himself off.

"Coward!" Houtah raised his hand to slap Jonah.

Kalousd stepped in and pushed Houtah off balance. A tussle of pushing and shoving ensued.

Mercifully, the deacon refereeing the game stepped in and averted a brawl.

Houtah resorted to words to deliver the punch he had been denied. "*Assyrian* son of a bitch!" he hissed and then walked away with a smirk on his face.

The remark was clearly overheard by all present. The slur "Assyrian" remained suspended in midair.

In desperation, Jonah turned to the fellow closest to the scene of his humiliation. "What did he say?" he asked, choking on his own words.

"I...I...I didn't hear," came the response.

And just like that, within moments, a supposed friend of Jonah's had declared his allegiance by hurriedly trotting after Houtah.

The Pigsty Camp members had discovered their mission and Houtah spread the news, telling everyone who would listen, "His father looks Assyrian."

The Ibelinian brothers and Jonah, in particular, were marked as lowly Assyrians. Somebody had to bear the cross, the ineradicable smear left by centuries of simmering acrimony.

"Maybe they are moles, spying for the Assyrian patriarchate."

"Is it not enough that the Vank offers their faith sanctuary in the holy places? Do we now have to offer shelter to the bastards as well?"

Unsure as to why Houtah had launched this smear campaign against him, Jonah freely discussed with his brothers and friends the nature of the physical aggression his opponent directed at him. But he never mentioned the emotional torment and verbal assaults to which he was subjected nor the taboo word "Assyrian" that was flung at him. Neither did his camp.

Perhaps following the cue of others in the Vank's hierarchy, the headmaster turned a blind eye to the escalating animosity between the two sparring groups. The deacons, meanwhile, stayed out of the altercation. Kalousd, by now a deacon, remained above the fray, but was not spared the contempt shown to his sibling. Jonah knew Kalousd was concerned for him, but keen on keeping his brother out of the conflict, he stayed upbeat in his presence and pretended to exude complete confidence. Neither discussed the matter when they were together and behaved, instead, as if nothing was amiss.

Emboldened by the way the authorities feigned ignorance of their activities and let them continue unchecked, Houtah and Korvat started bullying others to join their group in order to isolate Jonah and his sympathizers. Most of the seminarians resisted them and tried to remain neutral, but the Pigsty Camp made it exceedingly difficult for them to do so.

One night, during a basketball game, Houtah instigated a quarrel with one of the boys who had not yet buckled under their pressure.

"We hear you're converting."

"What?"

"If you're not with us, you too must be an Assyrian."

The boy turned to walk away.

"Where are you going?" Korvat yelled. "We're not finished talking."

"I don't want to take part in this," replied the boy and continued to walk.

"I guess you need convincing." An offended Korvat grabbed him from behind and landed a punch between his shoulder blades. Before the boy could come up for air, other blows landed indiscriminately, with lefts and rights and occasional kicks raining down on the hapless fellow's head, chest, abdomen, and back. It was a demonstration of overwhelmingly superior power.

Jonah thought it imprudent to intervene, certain of his own inability to alter the vicious outcome. He also understood that a worse outcome awaited him in case he stepped in; yet he knew that he must. After all, he was the root cause of the brutal bashing.

Jonah tentatively approached Korvat, but his nemesis Houtah was waiting for him. Houtah raised his arms, pumped his fists, and started to hop back and forth like Muhammad Ali. "Come on, come on," he invited Jonah.

Jonah tried to evade Houtah to get to Korvat, but Houtah cut him off and swung. With one motion, Jonah ducked and lunged headfirst at Houtah's midsection. Houtah landed on the ground with Jonah right on top of him. Immediately, many hands descended on Jonah and pulled him off Houtah.

Meanwhile, the main combat remained completely one-sided as a mighty gladiator toyed with an abject foe who was no match for him at all.

The boy's blood-streaked face presented a frightening sight. Korvat's company held back the few other people who tried to intervene long enough for Korvat to land the decisive blow: a right uppercut to the chin that made the boy spin around completely. He fell flat on his face and remained motionless on the court.

Everyone thought it was over, but Korvat bent down, lifted the unconscious boy's head by the hair, and was about to deliver another blow when the headmaster finally arrived at the scene. Korvat's victim remained in the hospital for three days with a broken nose and three gaps where his front teeth had been.

Korvat's awe-inspiring manifestation of the rule of the fist forced everybody to make a choice. Despite the enormous risks involved, a handful of students surprised Jonah by refusing to align themselves with the Pigsty Camp. Jonah wasn't sure whether it was courage, integrity, or sheer insanity that drove them to his small, depleted camp.

Despite this encouraging show of solidarity, he began to feel increasingly lonely and his sleep was troubled as a result. The Pigsty Camp invaded his dreams, inciting stick-wielding mobs bent on his destruction. *"Hye joghovurt artentsek, Asorineroun kunetsek!"* they screamed, "Armenians, rise up and damn the Assyrians!" The nightmares jolted him awake and left him feeling bewildered and vulnerable. At just thirteen, Jonah was waging a battle for survival. His enemies were numerous, while his guardian angel was nowhere in sight.

Often, when Jonah passed one of the rival camp members, someone would mutter, "Assyrian," in a tone dripping with revulsion. He became the target of mockery, derogatory epithets, and veiled threats. Enoch, Thomas, and the others in Jonah's camp were, meanwhile, accused of being "Assyrian sympathizers." The unholy war of Easter had been rekindled; only now, Jonah was the focal point of his fellow Armenians' suspicion and anger. He felt trapped, but wisely ignored the insults, for it was safer to swallow his pride than provoke his detractors.

Finally, one evening in the dining hall, the invectives hurled against him were loud enough to generate responses up and down the table that undermined Jonah's reputation still further.

"Ignorant bullies," he muttered in spite of himself.

"Did I hear something?" Korvat asked with a chuckle, cupping his hands behind his ears.

"I think the Assyrian is challenging you." Houtah whooped and performed a drum roll on the table.

"An ass—Assyrian—is challenging *me*?"

"The filth of a pigpen is spouting from the mouths of some idiots." Even before it had left his lips, Jonah regretted the retort.

A sudden hush fell over the dining room as all eyes focused on Korvat.

Jonah was small, but agile. Four years his senior, Korvat was tall, strong, athletic—and merciless. Jonah could feel every muscle in his body tense. Only a table and a few feet separated him from the ruffian.

The screeching of a chair pushed back violently broke the silence and, wasting little time, Korvat leapt from his seat toward Jonah.

The younger boy jumped to his feet and backpedaled, keeping his eyes focused on Korvat's clenched fists. As the latter lunged at him, Jonah managed to duck just in time, with Korvat's elbow merely brushing a wisp of his hair. But Jonah's defensive maneuver landed him on his rear.

Korvat's momentum had, meanwhile, hurled him past Jonah and before he could recover, Enoch gave him a shove in the back that sent him flying to the floor.

In mere moments, the chaos of Easter Eve at the Holy Sepulcher Church was recreated. Several others rose and flung their chairs aside. Pigsty Camp supporters piled atop Enoch, with Thomas coming to his rescue. And Houtah flew at Jonah who braced himself for the worst.

Amazingly, no one was seriously hurt, thanks to the deacons who intervened just in time.

It's a miracle, Jonah thought, as order was restored. He turned to Enoch and whispered to his friend whose brave, speedy response had surely spared him severe injury, "Thank you."

Word of the brawl and the smoldering rancor between the two groups could no longer be ignored. Jonah and Kalousd were summoned to see the patriarch.

"I hear you're having difficulties," the patriarch said as he lit a cigar and sat next to Jonah on the sofa, the pungent odor of the smoke overwhelming his sweet-scented cologne. "I will tell them to stop." He smiled and then pinched Jonah's cheek. It was clear that he viewed the whole episode as nothing more serious than adolescent mischief and couldn't imagine the sense of isolation, rejection, and fear that overwhelmed the boy. This kindly, aging lion seemed convinced that his mild reprimand would put an end to "the difficulties," as he put it. Once he willed it, why would anybody fail to fall in line?

The two brothers thanked the patriarch, kissed his right hand, and left. They didn't get far before Nersotz Aghvesian, Jonah's English teacher, who was lurking in the foyer, accosted them and ordered them into Archbishop Aminian's office.

Into the wolves' den, Jonah lamented.

"You have to realize that the patriarch is not fully involved with these issues," the archbishop said in a friendly tone. "You need to be careful of what you tell him. I will have a chat with Korvat, Houtah, and the rest to put an end to this kind of behavior."

Jonah wasn't fooled. Despite the archbishop's pleasant demeanor, he still remembered the words Sevantz had used to dismiss him after he and his classmates had requested an advanced placement in their studies.

Mr. Aghvesian, meanwhile, lurked in the corner with a barely detectable smirk on his face.

Jonah felt a chill go down his spine. *If these are my protectors,* he thought, *I'm finished. Surely, it can't get any worse.*

With nowhere to turn, Jonah clung to the reprieve offered by books. The imaginary worlds they held within their pages were his only refuge, albeit an illusory one. He only regretted that he couldn't read twenty-four hours a day. He could then perhaps have escaped the insomnia, followed by the nightmares that plagued him when he went to bed

A few days later, while taking his class and struggling to explain the intricacies of Othello and Desdemona's complex relationship, Mr. Aghvesian's face suddenly lit up with a smile that was wider than usual. His eyes gleamed. "How should this class behave if, let's say, one of you belonged to a different race?" he asked, elaborating further with, "An inferior race? A race we despise?" He cocked his head and gave Jonah a sly glance.

The potentially explosive comment drew roars of approval from Korvat and Houtah who laughed heartily and beat their desks in excitement.

Jonah immediately identified with Othello's predicament and, in that moment, recognized the Iago of his life. With Mr. Aghvesian continuing to leer at him, he knew his protector, the patriarch, had failed in his attempt to rein in Jonah's enemies. Mr. Aghvesian had just given the Pigsty Camp *carte blanche* to unleash upon him whatever ugly forces they wished to.

A middle-aged bachelor who boasted on every occasion of his loyalty and devotion to the Vank, Mr. Aghvesian was tall and thin, wore round, black-rimmed eyeglasses, spoke with a lisp, and constantly used his tongue to retrieve the permanent drool that threatened to trickle down the left side of his chin. He was servile in the presence of his superiors, but strutted boldly in the classroom where he was merciless with his prey.

Aghvesian played no official role in the patriarchate, but in practice, he acted as Archbishop Aminian's personal secretary and liaison man with outside groups that needed historical or policy information on the Vank. Because of his solid grasp of the English language, he was often assigned the role of guide to visiting dignitaries. Despite his constant complaints of being overworked, he somehow made time to offer his services as a private tour guide to beautiful young Western women. During these personalized tours, he focused on the area surrounding the Vank and was frequently seen leading a woman to the top of the city walls where, at a certain point, he and his companion often disappeared from view. They typically emerged, ten to twenty minutes later, to continue the tour, although sometimes, the woman emerged *very* quickly, departing alone in a huff and leaving her "guide" behind.

In May 1976, the Vank celebrated the Feast of Ascension at the summit of the Mount of Olives. The location, overlooking the Old City of Jerusalem, was famous for two things: the structure that housed the Lord's Prayer in every written language that existed and the little domed chapel that stood on the hallowed ground where Christ had given His last sermon to the apostles before His ascension.

Liturgical services were held under tents in the circular walled-off area surrounding the domed chapel. As was the case with other holy sites, the Assyrians officiated over their Mass alongside the Armenians. The Armenian patriarchate owned a reception hall and an office at the entrance to the encircled holy site. While waiting for the services to start, the seminarians killed time by sitting on the steps of the reception area.

When the Assyrian patriarch and his entourage passed in front of them, protocol called for the seminarians to rise to their feet in deference to a church leader's presence.

"*Hye joghovurt ver getsek, Asorineroun kunetsek!*" Houtah hissed, throwing a fiendish look at Jonah. It was the old insult: "Armenians, stand up and damn the Assyrians!"

Several students turned toward Jonah with scornful smiles.

Hoping to reverse the course of recent events, Jonah remained firmly seated in place as the Assyrian clergy passed.

"Uh-oh," Houtah said with a chuckle, his tone revealing his utter disdain for his prey. "If he doesn't stand up and respect his own ilk, why should we?"

Jonah had the urge to punch Houtah as hard as Korvat would have, if he had wanted to make an example of him. *Damn you! I should have had the courage to stand and show proper respect*, he thought.

It was too late to undo the shameful act.

A few weeks later, the patriarch called Kalousd and Jonah to his office once again. This time, Houtah and Korvat were also present.

The patriarch paced back and forth, clearly annoyed at the situation he had to deal with. He did not light his cigar. "You will stop this nonsense immediately!" he ordered, addressing the two thugs.

Jonah wondered how the patriarch had finally found out about his plight and his brother's. The most likely source was Mrs. Shakarian. A few days earlier, she had invited Jonah to their house for his first visit since his transfer to the seminary. Jonah hoped to gain a glimpse of Shahnour, but she wasn't present.

Raffi was there to show solidarity with his old friend. She had wanted to know how he was holding up and had asked about his relationship with Sevantz. It had been clear from the nature of her queries that she was aware of the tension and wanted to help.

The patriarch wagged his finger at the boys as he continued to pace. "Whether these brothers are Assyrian or not is irrelevant."

Jonah cringed. *What's he doing? He knows I'm not Assyrian! Why doesn't he just tell them the truth?*

"You are not here to bully others," the patriarch continued. "Concentrate on your studies, serve the Vank, and do God's work!" He stopped pacing, turned angrily to Houtah and slapped him across the face. "I want this vicious conflict to end now! And stop harassing my son!"

"They are Assyrian! It's confirmed."

The news spread and all doubts vanished. The Pigsty Camp felt vindicated. Moreover, it felt compelled to avenge the slap the patriarch had delivered to one of its members.

Barely a week later, Houtah found Jonah by himself and approached him tentatively. "You look just like the Assyrian priest we saw at the Mount of Olives," he said to him. "The blue eyes, the fair skin, the light hair…If you wore a beard like his, I would easily confuse the two of you."

"That's interesting," Jonah replied. "The Assyrians are a Middle Eastern, Semitic race. They have dark skin, black eyes, and black hair." He paused for effect. "Like you."

"Don't you dare insult me!"

"Just an observation."

"You know where you can shove that observation."

"Up yours."

"You will regret this!"

Jonah made an obscene gesture.

"You Assyrian bastard! I'm going to get you expelled!"

"With your moral standing?"

"Go to hell!" Houtah turned to walk away, but stopped. "Perhaps it's best you stay here and become a priest. The vow of celibacy would prevent you from marrying an Armenian and contaminating Armenian blood."

"What?" Jonah had faced such loathing before. He had seen it in the eyes of Turkish officials and heard it in the words they spouted every time he needed a document from them. "You hate me that much?" he now asked Houtah.

A month later, Jonah was called once again to the patriarch's office. Passing through the ornate reception area, the two gilded paintings, the majestic Mount Ararat and Christ pointing the way to salvation brought him little comfort as he saw Sevantz and Aghvesian already there.

The patriarch took no note of Jonah's entry. "Wasn't Ms. Nora supposed to take him to America?" he asked no one in particular. "She promised."

The archbishop remained quiet, but exchanged glances with Aghvesian, who was fidgeting uneasily.

"These Americans are so whimsical! They lack all sense of commitment. Sometimes I think it's truly a wonder their republic even lasted to see its bicentennial." The patriarch seemed beaten. He turned to Jonah. "She came twice and promised to adopt you. Where *is* she?"

Jonah, of course, was equally perplexed and had no answer.

"Listen, my boy, I have asked Sevantz to take you to Switzerland." The familiar cigar appeared, followed by the long matchstick, as the patriarch struggled to light it. "God knows

Sevantz has connections there," he scoffed, throwing a disdainful look at the archbishop. "He will make the arrangements over the summer and place you in a boarding school there. He will make sure you are well provided for. You can finish your education in Switzerland."

Sevantz shifted in his seat. "Switzerland has excellent boarding schools," he said with little conviction in his baritone voice. "We have a very rich Armenian there who'll be more than pleased to look after you. I'll get started on this right away."

"In the meantime, why don't you and Kalousd go to Istanbul for the summer?" the patriarch suggested, his tone suddenly buoyant. "Sevantz will arrange it so you go directly to Switzerland from Istanbul."

Jonah had serious misgivings about this idea, but did not dare voice them. Questioning his elders, especially church elders, particularly when they were planning such a brilliant future for him, was quite unthinkable.

He kissed the patriarch's right hand in gratitude and Archbishop Aminian's with revulsion. As he turned to leave, he caught a glimpse of Aghvesian. The wily, insufferable man stood aloof, his hands clasped in front, his shoulders hunched slightly. He locked eyes with Jonah briefly and then, after glancing away in an obvious display of aversion, flicked with his tongue at the drool that had collected in the left corner of his mouth and threatened to spill over.

Chapter 31

Jonah flew with Kalousd to Istanbul to stay at Father Abram's. There he waited anxiously for Archbishop Aminian to arrange for his future in Switzerland.

After settling in, Jonah decided to pay a visit to his father. Haiko, thanks to Father Abram's help, had landed a job as a sexton with the Armenian Church in a seaside parish, and lived on the premises. It was a beautiful church, with classic Armenian architecture. A wide boulevard named after U.S. President John Kennedy ran in front. On the other side of the road stretched the Sea of Marmara, vast and unending. Jonah recalled his childhood lake among the wheat fields, rocky hills, and barren and dusty deserts of his village, unable then to even imagine a broader expanse of water anywhere.

While waiting for his father to clean the vestibule, Jonah sat on the warm church steps and fixed his eyes past the sea. He wondered whether Switzerland or even America waited on the other side of the blue-green horizon.

That evening at the dinner table, his normally energetic and shrill stepmother was silent, hardly touching her food.

Jonah asked his father about Azad and Ani, both of whom had left Istanbul. But Haiko too seemed forlorn and was sparing with his answers.

"Azad has gone to London," he said with a wave of the hand.

"London? Why? What about Ani?"

"She is in Bavaria now."

"Almanya?" Jonah was struggling to keep up with all the developments that had taken place in his absence. "Why?"

"Her husband—Baruir—took her away."

"You mean you actually married her off?"

Haiko remained sullen. He looked twice his age—and utterly dejected.

"But she's only a baby!" Jonah protested.

Razeh's shoulders slumped and she began to cry inconsolably.

"What's wrong?" Jonah asked. "What did I say?"

"They stole my baby," she answered in a voice of doom. "They stole my baby!" She lifted her arms toward the ceiling, rocked sideways, and covered her forehead and eyes with her palms.

Jonah turned to his father. "I am sure she encouraged you to marry Ani off," he said accusingly, gesturing at his stepmother. "What's she crying about?"

Haiko shook his head glumly. "It's about your brother. I held the boy in my own arms."

"I don't understand!" Jonah said impatiently.

"I had a son. A year ago, Razeh bore me a son—a strong, healthy boy who took to his mother's breast right away. He looked much like you, Hanno. I held him in my arms a few hours after he was born. I then went to the coffeehouse and bought tea for everyone. When I returned…he was gone."

"When? How?" Jonah asked in disbelief.

"Liars!" Razeh said in a tired voice. Her anger made her voice rise a notch. "Baby snatchers! May the curse of God settle on their heads and on their families!"

Haiko gently placed a hand on his wife's balled-up fist. "Razeh fell asleep with the boy attached to her breast after a feeding. She was exhausted. When she woke up, the baby was gone."

"Gone?"

His father nodded. "They took him. When I came back to visit, the staff all trotted out the same lie—that Razeh had given birth to a stillborn. But I saw him with my own eyes. He was fine, I tell you! I said as much to the doctors and the administrators, but they insisted I was in shock."

"They told me I was feverish!" Razeh added angrily. "Hallucinating!"

"I accused them of stealing my son," Haiko continued, "and they called security. 'Who do you think the police will believe?' the administrator said. 'A Christian peasant, a *gavour* like you, or us, Turkish officials?' They threw me out—and sent Razeh home in a cab."

"Did you go to the police?" Jonah asked.

"Yes," Haiko said. "They threw me out too. I saw a lawyer and he told me I didn't stand a chance." He looked away stoically.

If God takes a child, that's fate, Jonah thought, *but to lose a son to child trafficking...* He felt helpless and had no words of consolation for his father or stepmother. *First Azul. Then Ani. Now the baby. Will my half brother grow up to become an Armenian-hating Turk?* The thought made him shudder.

"Father Djift is in Istanbul," Father Abram told Jonah a few weeks later. "Can you deliver these documents to him? He will be very relieved to see them."

Father Abram had secured with great difficulty and after paying a hefty bribe documents attesting to Djift's military service. With the help of one of his many contacts, he had also obtained exit visas for the man and his family.

Jonah welcomed the diversion from what was turning out to be a monotonous, depressing summer, but as he arrived at Djift's front door, he couldn't help resenting this particular errand, since it involved meeting with the Vank's most notorious troublemaker.

Djift opened the door and his expression immediately soured. "What are *you* doing here?"

"I..." Jonah peered inside. "What's going on?"

Father Djift moved to block the boy's view, but in vain, for several people carrying furniture outside to a van were trying to get by. Jonah's eyes opened wide in amazement. *I wish Shahnour could see this. Better yet, the Pigsty Camp!* Suddenly, he was delighted that Father Abram had chosen him as his emissary for this particular errand.

Father Djift's family did not look very different from Jonah's or from any other immigrant family from the interiors of Turkey. The men inside sat cross-legged or squatted as they chain-smoked and fingered the strands of their worry beads. The women, dressed in village garb that consisted of layers of blacks and purples, wore headscarves that covered their hair, foreheads, and chins. They spoke Assyrian and Kurdish—and Turkish—with the same heavy rural accent his stepmother used. In fact, the only person who spoke Armenian there was Father Djift.

"This is good news," Djift said, glancing hurriedly at the documents. Then he tried to shuffle Jonah back out the door.

The boy was reluctant to leave. "What news?" he persisted. Remembering how uncomfortable he had felt when Raffi had visited his father's apartment two summers earlier, he now relished watching Djift squirm. It had been a long time since he'd had the upper hand.

"Thank you!" Djift snapped rudely as he pushed Jonah out the door.

The boy smiled gleefully and bounded down the stairs.

A week after Jonah's visit to Djift's house, Father Abram came home, agitated. The boy overheard him whispering nervously to his wife.

Eventually, the priest sat down with Kalousd and Jonah. "Don't be alarmed," he said in a somewhat shaky voice, "but I was taken in for questioning today."

Jonah's mind went instantly to the fortified walls of the notorious Gedikpasha Prison, located only a stone's throw from Kapali Charshi, Istanbul's enclosed bazaar and a popular tourist destination. Atop the prison's steel gate and written ominously in Turkish was a simple warning: *Allah yok icherde*—there is no God inside. He shuddered at the thought of Father Abram ending up in a Turkish prison.

"The Turkish police seem to be focusing their investigation on the seminary in Jerusalem and the individuals who are in attendance there."

"Do you think this has anything to do with the Turkish ambassador's visit to the seminary?" Jonah asked.

"Well, they are confiscating the passport of any former seminary student who attempts to renew it." Father Abram's voice rose in alarm. "I need to see the expiry dates of your passports!"

"April 1977," Kalousd read aloud, glancing at the stamped date on his passport. He took Jonah's and examined it. "It's the same for both passports."

Father Abram made the sign of the cross and sighed in relief, but beads of sweat were visible on the kind man's forehead. "You must immediately return to Jerusalem." He seemed more concerned about the boys than himself.

Jonah had concluded, weeks earlier, that he wasn't going to Switzerland. Sevantz, in fact, had never contacted him about this matter. While it was possible that the patriarch had been sincere in his intentions when he suggested the transfer, Jonah assumed Sevantz and Aghvesian had found a way to thwart any constructive plans made for him. He had been considering staying in Istanbul and seeking employment in the jewelry section of the Kapali Charshi, where many young boys his age found work. The worried look on Father Abram's face convinced him that it was no longer a viable option. While his life in the seminary in Jerusalem had brought him to the edge of the precipice, Turkey was the abyss. In order to survive, he had no choice but to return to Jerusalem, the lesser of the two evils.

Within days of Father Abram's interrogation by the police, the priest purchased return tickets for Jonah and Kalousd. His parting words at Istanbul's Yesilkoy Airport left no room for misinterpretation.

"You are not to come back to Turkey," he said in a grave voice. "Neither one of you. *Ever.*"

CHAPTER 32

Jerusalem, August 1976

"Maybe they forgot," Kalousd said in an uncertain voice, "or got the day wrong."

Jonah and his brother had arrived at the Ben Gurion Airport in Tel Aviv, only to find no driver waiting for them. The seminary always sent a driver to pick up new arrivals.

"Maybe," Jonah murmured. He had a sinking feeling, but said nothing to his brother.

After phoning the headmaster's office in vain—and waiting two long hours at the airport—the two brothers took a taxi to Jerusalem. It was past midnight when they finally arrived at the seminary.

The doors were locked and when they knocked, no one responded. They waited ten minutes in the dark.

"Help me get to that ledge," Kalousd commanded him.

Jonah helped his brother scale the wall and enter the building through a window.

Five minutes later, the door opened and a man stepped out, holding a flashlight. Kalousd was right behind him.

"I'm so sorry!" the man said apologetically.

Jonah recognized the voice of his mathematics teacher, a layman from Bethlehem. "The headmaster is away. I was asked to officiate in his place. Several of the boys had warned me that some people were arriving to cause trouble." He shook his head in dismay. "Let me help you with your bags."

Other than Levon, no one welcomed Jonah back.

"Things have deteriorated," explained Enoch, the only other person to even acknowledge his presence.

Jonah listened dejectedly to the update. "I had hoped—"

"You are suffering from delusions. Even Thomas has switched sides."

Jonah couldn't hide his disappointment

"You can't blame him," Enoch said. "They threatened to break both his arms. At least they leave your little brother alone. I guess they think he is still too young to be of any consequence."

"What about you?"

"I am with no one and against everyone," Enoch answered with a shrug. He shoved his hands into his pockets and left.

I just want to belong, Jonah thought. Left alone, he sat in the classroom to read a book to get his mind off his plight. He'd only been reading a few minutes when out of the corner of his eye, he noticed Thomas pacing outside in the hallway.

His former friend glanced nervously in both directions before stepping inside the classroom briefly. "I'm very sorry," he mumbled and then left without waiting for a reply.

Shunned by everyone, Jonah passed his time in solitude, a despondent fourteen-year-old. The lonely days bled into dreaded nights, and he supplemented the group prayers preceding bedtime with his own supplications, pulling the blanket over his head before he went to sleep, as if hiding from the world. But no prayer could shelter him from the demons that invaded his dreams.

While all was quiet and the others slept peacefully, Jonah tossed and turned. Each moment stretched into an eternity of misery as he conjured up images of multiheaded wolves and monsters, engaged in self-pity, or imagined wild, calamitous scenarios. At the moment when his body and mind seemed ready to collapse into darkness from sheer exhaustion, his senses came violently alive, as if every nerve ending in his body were attached to a sizzling hot electrode. The painful sensation began at the apex of his skull and discharged itself in spurts that caused his brain to pulsate. From there, the prickly shockwaves engulfed the rest of his body in a massive convulsion that brought with it quivering flashes of color and debilitating panic as powerful as anything he'd ever experienced. Then, as suddenly as it had manifested itself, the pain vanished.

With each passing day, the tormenting trance at the moment of transition from consciousness to darkness—that agonizing moment when he was frozen by fear and unable to move or make a sound—only increased in frequency. Alone, one day, Jonah searched the space beneath his bed to allay his suspicion that somebody was electrocuting him. He found nothing. *Are these seizures?* he wondered. *Am I losing my mind?*

Before graduation from high school and in preparation for a more committed form of service to church, God, and nation, Jonah and his classmates were elevated that October to the rank of deacon, with Archbishop Aminian performing the ordination ceremony.

Jonah served at the altar as a deacon for the first time, the following Sunday.

"Peace be with you," the priest said, blessing the congregation of a hundred or so faithful with broad strokes that described the sign of the cross.

Timing the ritual with precision, Jonah artfully swung the censer in perfect, pendular movements. He spread the fragrant smoke in peace and harmony. Years of observing the rites had imprinted the details of the ceremonies in his subconscious. He felt proud of himself, despite all that had transpired. *I wish Muksi Sarah could see me. Would she have been proud?* How he wished his mother were there as well to share the gratifying moment!

The tension at the seminary appeared to be waning. Would the ostracism end soon, he dared to wonder. Would Houtah retract his lies? Who knew—perhaps the priesthood would be his calling, after all.

Toward the end of October, Jonah sat in class one Monday and listened to his history teacher review the Crusades and their impact on Armenia.

"Many of the leaders of the Crusader movement, along with their followers, settled in Armenia after surrendering Jerusalem to the Muslims," the teacher said. "The Lusinian kings of Cilician Armenia were descendants of Guy de Lusignan, the French prince."

"My great-uncle says our family bears the name of one of these knights," Jonah offered with newfound confidence.

"Balian de Ibelin?" the teacher asked. "He was the French knight that led the final defense of Jerusalem and negotiated the terms of surrender."

"It's only family lore."

Houtah startled Jonah and the rest of the class by bringing his fist down on his desk. "Damn!" he yelled and feigned a look of exaggerated surprise. "All this time, we thought he was a lowly Assyrian peasant. He's a prince! A French prince!"

The room erupted in shrill laughter. Had the insult been aimed solely at him, Jonah would have brushed it aside, but he deemed this a slur on the reputation of his legendary great-uncle.

He rose from his desk with clenched fists, but a raspy knock on the door put a quick end to Houtah's antics and Jonah's intent.

Already tense, Jonah stiffened even more when he saw Nersotz Aghvesian wedge his pointed, balding head through the slightly opened door. The man nodded to Jonah and beckoned him to step out and follow him.

Jonah considered for a moment whether he should ignore the command and continue his advance on Houtah or even deliver the punch to Aghvesian. Eventually, he unclenched his fists and submitted. He stepped out and followed Aghvesian morosely, keeping a few paces behind the man as he led him toward the patriarchate. They went up the stairs and entered the antechamber where Aghvesian indicated that Jonah should sit in the middle of the room, exposed and vulnerable. There were several people in the office, but most of the discussion was taking place between the patriarch and Archbishop Aminian.

"They offered me the catholicosate, head of the global church," the patriarch said with a chuckle. His hearty laughter rang through the office. "Move to Soviet Armenia? Why would I leave this throne and put myself under the thumb of the communists?"

Those present feigned equally exuberant laughter. They had heard this story many times.

The lighthearted conversation and the laughter should have set Jonah at ease, but Aghvesian, a cold, cunning grin replacing his usual smirk, looked ready to pounce.

"Sevantz, what do you think?" the patriarch asked.

"I'm glad you chose *this*. I enjoy serving as the grand vizier of this throne."

"With the games you play, you are most like the head of the eunuchs guarding the harem of the Sultan."

Laughter followed the jibe. Aghvesian seemed to enjoy the last comment as well. His shoulders lifted, his head withdrew deeply enough into his collar for his neck to disappear entirely and his upper body shook with a quiet chuckle. He was drooling, as usual.

"*You!*" came a booming voice.

Jonah was startled to see the patriarch standing in the doorway of his office, several steps above, pointing down at him ominously. "Why are you here?"

Shocked by the suddenness and vehemence with which the question had been directed at him, the boy was unable to utter a word in reply.

"Why did you come back? I told you to go to Switzerland! Why did you come back? *Why?*"

Framed by the doorway, his eminence the patriarch, Jonah's bulwark and surrogate father in Jerusalem, continued to peer down fiercely and bore his pointed finger at the boy.

Jonah could only tremble in response, which merely seemed to fuel the patriarch's anger.

"Sevantz arranged *everything* for you!" he said, shaking his finger at Jonah. "How many more opportunities can I offer, only for you to squander them recklessly?"

What arrangements? What opportunities? Jonah was astounded.

"Go!" the patriarch exclaimed, making no effort to hide his disgust. "I don't want to see you anymore!" He waved the boy off and turned away.

Still dazed by this outburst, Jonah blindly followed Aghvesian back to the classroom and sat down again in his place. As he replayed the scene of what had just transpired over and over in his mind, he became aware of probing glances from his classmates. He wanted to run outside, to seek some space so he could think things through.

Thirty minutes later, there was another knock on the classroom door and for once, Jonah was actually relieved to see Aghvesian's sly grin, as he motioned for him to step outside once again. Anything was preferable to the inquisitive gaze of his classmates.

Aghvesian was drooling excessively, which meant, Jonah assumed, that he was anxious about something.

"I need your passport," the man stuttered.

Jonah eyed him suspiciously.

"You forgot to turn it in upon your return from your summer vacation," Aghvesian insisted.

They went to the dormitory and fetched Jonah's passport and Aghvesian snatched the document from the boy's hand.

"Thank you," he said abruptly and scurried away.

"Do you still have your passport?" Jonah asked Kalousd during lunch.

"Yes. Why?"

"Aghvesian just collected mine."

"Hmm."

As the afternoon progressed, Jonah's angst subsided. *Could he have taken my passport to obtain a Swiss visa? The patriarch was certainly infuriated enough. Will they send me to Switzerland right away?*

The religion teacher, meanwhile, was droning on and on from the *Book of Daniel*:

"Daniel was preferred above the presidents and princes because an excellent spirit was in him. . .then the presidents and princes sought to find occasion against Daniel. . ."

For the third time that day, a knock on the classroom door jolted most of the students out of their stupor. Aghvesian cautiously poked his snout inside and peered at Jonah. He did not have to gesture to him. The boy rose indifferently and walked out.

Without uttering a word, Aghvesian turned hurriedly and began walking in the direction of the dormitory.

"Where are we going?" Jonah demanded to know.

"You'd better pack your bags quickly," Aghvesian snapped without slowing his pace. "The flight leaves in three hours and the drive to the airport alone may take two hours."

Jonah froze. *Have they arranged for my schooling in Switzerland that quickly? I would need a visa for Switzerland. This trip can't be to Switzerland.*

"Quick, boy! As I said, there is not enough time!"

Never before had Jonah seen Aghvesian so peremptory, so commanding. The devious, cowardly fox had suddenly become a wolf, and his demeanor shook Jonah out of his listlessness. Father Abram's parting words rang in his ears: *"You are not to come back to Turkey. None of you! Ever!"* Rage replaced Jonah's bewilderment.

Aghvesian took two cautious steps back when he saw the fire in the boy's eyes. "Don't be un-un-ungrateful," he stammered. "Ar-Ar-Archbishop Aminian will take care of you."

Ungrateful? The archbishop is taking care of me all right! There are no doubts about it at all.

Jonah turned around and started heading in the opposite direction. He went straight to his brother's classroom, with Aghvesian scampering after him. When Jonah stopped and looked at the man threateningly, Aghvesian stopped short to keep a safe distance between them.

Kalousd came out in a hurry.

"It's decided!" Aghvesian sputtered. "It's the patriarch's order."

Kalousd's eyes widened, but he appeared too shocked to speak.

"He is going!" Aghvesian told Kalousd. "If I were you, I would not make a big deal out of it. If you do, you will put your own future at risk."

Without saying a word, Kalousd turned around and started walking, almost running, in the direction of the patriarchate. Jonah hurried after him. He had never seen his brother so determined and angry.

Sensing trouble, Aghvesian scurried ahead. He was not the athletic type, and his large feet slid awkwardly on the pavement as he ran.

When they got to the patriarchate, Archbishop Aminian and Aghvesian were waiting in front of the antechamber.

"If I were you, I would go no farther." Sevantz, the consummate politician, feigned a note of concern in his voice.

"Do you realize where you're sending me?" screamed Jonah.

"Keep your voice down!" ordered Sevantz emphatically in his scratchy baritone.

"Do you know what Father Abram told us when we left Istanbul?" Jonah's tone was more pleading than combative this time.

Sevantz nodded in understanding and exaggerated compassion, but turned to Kalousd. "The patriarch is in quite a temper and is likely to make another rash decision and dismiss you as well." He paused to let his words sink in. "I will intercede after he is calmer and will bring Jonah back in no time."

"Just like you were going to take me to Switzerland?"

Sevantz reached out to pat him on the cheek, but Jonah recoiled in revulsion.

Jonah tugged Kalousd's arm. "Let's go." He didn't want to put his brother's future at risk as well.

A sense of helplessness descended on Jonah as he and his brother quietly walked away.

"I will call for the driver," Aghvesian said, trailing them now. They ignored him.

Levon looked perplexed when Jonah stopped by to say good-bye. He simply stared at his older brother in bewilderment, saying nothing.

When Jonah went to pack, Korvat was in bed, ill with the flu. Without hesitation, Jonah went over to him, shook his hand, and said good-bye.

Korvat was uncharacteristically quiet. Jonah thought he saw regret in his eyes.

"Maybe someday..." Korvat left the sentence unfinished.

During the ride to Ben Gurion Airport, Kalousd murmured encouraging words to his younger brother, but Jonah could neither hear nor feel nor even think. Nor could he cry.

CHAPTER 33

Istanbul, fall 1976

A vivid blue sky, the color of his mother's eyes. Not a cloud. A sea of incendiary gold shimmered all around him. He ran, arms spread, like a partridge in flight, stroking the wheat stalks and the velvety wisps of hair surrounding the kernels. Threads of silk ready for weaving into a prayer rug, a golden sash, a flowing robe. He remembered the location of the nest.

The sky changed with every approaching step, suddenly filling with angry gray clouds. The wheat bowed and then broke under the swirling wind, losing its luster, and the stalks turned into spikes and the leaves into sharp blades that slashed at his face and bare arms.

He tripped and tumbled into a ditch in front of a cave which was dark, but for specks of glitter. Two at first, then four, then six. Round, glistening whiteness. Empty holes of reflecting light within the blackness of the cave. A snarl. Then a snout appeared, the glinting eyes turning an angry black. Tense paws. Stiff, pointed ears. Fangs bared, sharp and long. Dripping tongue...

Jonah shook himself awake and sat upright on Father Abram's sofa, exhausted. He desperately needed sleep—deep, restful sleep—but dreaded the disorienting transition and the surreal nightmares that awaited him on the other side. So he fought to stay awake.

It wasn't fear. It wasn't the bleak road ahead. It wasn't the danger bearing down on him. It was the expulsion. Not the expulsion from the seminary, but the expulsion from belonging. He simply wasn't.

His world had been reduced to Father Abram's living-room sofa. There he brooded, day and night, letting his mind slowly sink into despair.

"I have a job for you," Father Abram said with a hopeful smile one morning, after rousing the boy. "In fact, you have a choice. You can work either for an electrician or for a jeweler in Kapali Charshi. They are both friends of the family and will take good care of you."

"Kapali Charshi," Jonah repeated listlessly.

Istanbul's enclosed bazaar, a notorious tourist trap, was infamous as well for its entrapment of children. It was the vocational university of the *gochmen*, immigrant and internally displaced children, as young as eight years old, who were employed for token pay. Recently, it had become the refuge of most of the Armenian boys returning from Jerusalem. Most worked for some jeweler or the other, polishing or repairing. The luckier ones were hired to design and mold, but the most fortunate worked the sales counters. Those who professed to know English were posted to hawk the wares to tourists.

"We need to find the least conspicuous environment for you," Father Abram said, a few days later.

The least conspicuous! The words hit Jonah like a hammer. In Jerusalem, despite all his efforts to blend into the student body, he had remained a striking blemish. Now in Istanbul, it was the same. He was an obvious alien, an outsider, and would have to resort to the tactics he had loathed in Jerusalem: ceding ground and identity. *How to become invisible?*

Attending a school would lead to immediate discovery. The Turkish officials at any Armenian school would alert the authorities the moment he enrolled. In the seminary and now in Turkey, Jonah was deemed different and thus, somehow, a threat. Like the Pigsty Camp members and their sponsors, the Turkish authorities in Istanbul were hunting down "dangerous and subversive" individuals who didn't belong.

Jonah wondered how anyone could live, much less carve out a future, while in self-imposed exile. It seemed an impossible goal, yet precisely the sort of challenge he'd needed to clear his mind. He began thinking about his studies in Jerusalem, the boarding school in Switzerland, Ms. Nora and America, and even tentatively contemplated a job in Istanbul. He dreamed of becoming a priest, a lawyer, a doctor—even a master architect like his Balian ancestors.

He was given a few more days to languish on the sofa before his guardian prodded him gently.

"Too many Jerusalem boys are in Kapali Charshi and some have already had their passports confiscated by the Turkish authorities," Father Abram said one day, resuming their discussion. "They are monitoring your schoolmates and grounding them to prevent them from leaving the country."

Jonah decided on the electrician's job.

"He's too small," the electrician said. "He looks too weak. I can't use him."

Father Abram gave the man a warm smile and placed his hand on his shoulder. "Give the boy a chance. He is one of *my* boys."

The electrician relented. Father Abram had touched the lives of many. He was everybody's *Baba*—father.

Jonah tried to be a good apprentice, but was a hindrance to the master electrician. He lacked the strength and endurance to walk the steep streets of the seven hills of Istanbul or climb stairs while carrying heavy electrical wires and tools. He was also uninterested in his work. The job lasted a week.

The man took Jonah back to Father Abram on Friday. "Maybe you can place him in a library," he suggested.

For the next two weeks, Jonah's emotional state hovered between desperation and dejection. Although he resisted, at first, he was ultimately relieved when Father Abram dragged him along to the office each morning. Jonah simply sat in the office most days, but he occasionally sought some diversion by going to the movies, although afterward, he usually couldn't recall anything he had seen.

One day, while Jonah was engrossed in his own thoughts and staring at the wall in Father Abram's office, a parish council member walked in and asked the boy to follow him.

"We need help. It's the funeral of a community leader and we expect a very large turnout. The person who takes the donations in lieu of flowers is sick."

"But—"

"It's simple. They give you the money and you record it on a receipt. Give them a copy of the receipt and keep the original with the donation."

Jonah opened his mouth again to protest, but the parishioner waved him off.

"Be sure you clearly record the source and also the designated recipient. Here's the attaché case for the money and receipts."

Jonah's new career skyrocketed as he went from church to church, as well as to the occasional cemetery, and staked out a position at the entrance to collect money. His only real concern was walking the streets of Istanbul with an attaché case full of liras as he delivered the donations to the nearest Armenian church. At the end of each week, he was paid for his time.

He was busy collecting donations at Father Abram's church on a bright, sunny November afternoon, when he heard a familiar voice.

"Jonah? What a surprise to find you here! How are you?"

The pen fell from Jonah's fingers. He instinctively slipped his arms under the table to hide his trembling hands. There, standing directly in front of him, were Korvat and Houtah.

"Jonah, it's us!" Houtah said, giving him a jab in the shoulder. "Have you forgotten us already?"

Forget them? How could he? Jonah stared incredulously at his former tormentors.

"We can form an alumni club in Istanbul with the other Jerusalem boys," Houtah suggested with a smile that looked strained.

The Pigsty Camp? Am I a member now?

"Jonah, the past is history," Korvat said quietly. He sounded sincere.

"Sure," Jonah mumbled, still dazed by their sudden appearance. *There are still camps,* he thought. *But here, it's the Turks hunting the boys of St. James.*

"Is Father Abram inside?" Korvat asked.

Jonah pointed numbly in the direction of the office and watched as the two boys disappeared inside. He then turned to face the line of donors forming in front of him, distractedly writing each donor a receipt before stuffing the cash into the case without counting it.

Korvat and Houtah emerged from Father Abram's office a half hour later.

"It's very unfortunate what happened at the Vank," a clearly embarrassed Korvat said. "We *will* meet again."

"Yes, let's stay in touch," Houtah said with a nervous chuckle. Korvat waved good-bye before they disappeared.

As soon as Jonah had finished with his duties, he hurriedly closed the briefcase and bounded into Father Abram's office.

"Those who live by the sword die by the sword." Father Abram was melancholic. "Sevantz phoned this morning. He requested me to help Korvat."

"What happened? Why are they here?"

"Apparently, this was a payback of sorts. The patriarch was very upset with your expulsion. During one of Archbishop Aminian's absences from the Vank, the patriarch decided to exact his revenge."

"The patriarch was upset with *my* expulsion?" Jonah asked bitterly. "*He* was the one who told me to get lost. He was the one to throw me out!"

"The patriarch dismissed you from his office, not from Jerusalem. Sevantz took liberties with his intent."

Comforted by the patriarch's remorse, Jonah recalled the story from the *Book of Daniel.* Would God deliver him from the lions? "Sevantz deliberately disregarded the patriarch's wishes to send me to Switzerland," he said slowly. "I became a liability."

"Yes."

"What did they want?"

"Help to get them out of this country."

"Are you going to help?"

"I will do what I can."

"But—"

"How can I not? They are mere boys. They are *my* boys. I am the shepherd who must not leave any sheep untended." Father Abram paused a moment and then added quietly, "You must forgive them. They knew not what they were doing."

Jonah doubted whether he could.

He ran into Korvat and Houtah the next day by the bus stop near the church.

"I need some money for the bus," Houtah said awkwardly, "and I'm too embarrassed to ask Father Abram again."

Jonah searched his pocket and fished out a five-lira note.

After Houtah had boarded the bus, Korvat stayed behind with Jonah. The two stood and chatted for several minutes, oblivious to the steady stream of people getting into and out of each subsequent bus. The once confident and proud Korvat, the gladiator of the Vank, was now a frightened adolescent. Jonah could see as much in his eyes, which were full of fear and reminded him of his own shortly after his return to Istanbul. They talked casually about some of the people from the seminary and their friends in Kapali Charshi.

Jonah met Korvat again a few days later. At the other boy's insistence, they went to meet his mother who worked in the Sheraton Hotel as a waitress. She was a beautiful woman who had never married. Korvat was evasive about his father's identity and Jonah decided it was best to leave the subject alone. He too had many family secrets that were best kept private.

"We must leave this country without delay," Korvat said quietly, sipping the tea his mother had brought them.

"I know. Father Abram tells me the same thing on a daily basis."

"I'm truly sorry for the way I treated you in Jerusalem."

Jonah didn't reply. *Why the sudden change?*

"Sevantz is self-serving. You were a threat. He wouldn't hesitate doing anything to neutralize you."

"That's clear. He fed me to the wolves."

"I hate—"

Having just finished serving the adjacent table, Korvat's mother had arrived in time to cut him off. "Hey, hey. Show respect. After all, he is—"

"He doesn't deserve it!" Korvat snapped.

A long, uncomfortable silence followed.

Finally Korvat continued. "Sevantz and Aghvesian won't let up until you're silenced." He reflected for a moment. "But that's only a small part of the problem. The Turks won't relent until we're all gone."

"Silenced? Gone?"

"Here in Istanbul, it's all too clear who the enemy is."

Hoping to find out if there was cause for Korvat's misgivings, Jonah decided to join him for a visit to some of the former Jerusalem students now working in Kapali Charshi.

The visit only heightened the boys' caution. Most of his former schoolmates preferred not to talk about Jerusalem or of any of the difficulties they were facing with the authorities. The few who did, spoke in worried whispers.

"They confiscate our passports."

"They prevent us from leaving the country."

"We former students of the seminary are being targeted."

"Did you hear what happened to Kichikirik?"

"My classmate in the Haitourian School?" Jonah asked. Kichikirik had always struck him as defiant back in Jerusalem, where he had bowed before none, be it classmate, principal, or priest. "What happened?"

"He dared to question the denial of his request for an exit visa. He was detained for two days. They flogged the soles of his feet and for several days after his release, he could barely walk.

He had a broken nose, a fractured collarbone, and a few missing teeth. Two weeks after his release from detention, he vanished."

"Yes. Some think he was nabbed by the MIT and imprisoned."

"Others say he has gone to eastern Turkey to join the PKK."

"The PKK?"

"The Kurdish insurgents. Sixty years ago, the Kurds became the tools of the Young Turks to annihilate us; now Kichikirik joins them to fight the Turks for an independent Kurdistan on our ancestral lands."

"Vanished?" Jonah asked, still struggling to come to terms with the news of Kichikirik's disappearance.

"No one's seen him since."

As they left the bazaar, Korvat gave Jonah another worried look. "I'm working on a plan to escape. You shouldn't wait too long. If you ever need help, come and stay with my mother."

"I really do appreciate your wanting to help."

"We're all in danger. *Trust me.*"

Colonel Soluk Kurt sat at his massive wooden desk, its glossy surface reflecting the afternoon sun that beat against the windows. Behind him was the ever-present portrait of his idol, Mustafa Kemal Ataturk. That Kurt emulated the appearance of the potentate was no mere accident. His father had served directly under Ataturk. In an attempt to perpetuate the illusion of direct lineage, Kurt dressed like the father of the Turkish Republic.

After reading the latest documents from the MIT and Foreign Ministry files, he picked up a folder sitting on the corner of his desk and decided to leaf through it once more. He had read the highly confidential contents so many times, he knew them by heart. His agents had discovered nascent Armenian terrorist cells in Beirut, and his contacts with Mossad and the CIA had corroborated the results of his investigations. The CIA and Mossad, however, disagreed with his assertion that the Armenian Seminary in Jerusalem was a fertile ground for recruitment, an initiation camp for these cells. *The Jews don't want a scandal involving Israel, and the Americans are protecting a Christian enclave in Jerusalem.* He knew better. *I witnessed it with my own eyes. With the returnees, the vermin is spreading in my country now. I will eradicate these enemies of the state. I will chop them off as I would a gangrenous arm.*

The hatred he felt—now an intrinsic part of his personality—had been bred into him as a young boy by his father, then a military commander in the Turkish army. Kurt had sat quietly in the living room with his brothers, hanging on to his father's every word, as he told them stories about the treacherous Armenians.

"The Armenian infidels controlled our commerce and our professions. They enjoyed the magnanimity of the Sultan. But they were not satisfied. They built alliances with the West to pressure us for political equality and freedoms similar to that of the Turkish subjects."

At this point, his father would hesitate for a moment. "These were the first steps toward seeking independence from the empire. We did what we had to do to keep the fatherland intact and for Turks only."

Kurt had timidly tried to explain to his father that there was an Armenian boy in his class who seemed no different than the others. The riposte was sharp and unequivocal.

Dogs! That's all they are! When the dogs attack their master, they are shot. It should be the same with these...these...infidels.

His father's words continued to ring in his ears.

"You are always in the service of the great leader. Even Hitler admired the Young Turks and Ataturk. Yes, Hitler had respect for the way we dealt with the Armenian Question. Hitler studied our methods and then perfected them."

Kurt's chest swelled with pride. Here, at the MIT, he could implement the wishes of Turkey's great leaders. He could carry out arrests, interrogations, torture, and even executions. He could crush people, bury evidence, rewrite history—or unleash, fabricate, create. *The priest and his boys must be crushed!*

Despite the warning from Korvat, Jonah was not only growing accustomed to his new life, but almost becoming comfortable with it. The daily trips to the different churches and cemeteries to collect donations were not burdensome. He was enjoying his work and he could feel the turmoil inside him abating. Jerusalem, Switzerland, and America were less on his mind than ever. He couldn't help thinking that perhaps things were finally working out.

One morning, when Jonah was turning the corner to enter the church with Father Abram, somebody reached out for the priest's arm and pulled him back, stopping the boy in the process.

It was the driver Father Abram often hired. "There is a secret service agent in your office!" he whispered.

The priest nodded calmly in Jonah's direction. "Take him home," he ordered the man.

"What about my work?" Jonah protested.

"There is no time to lose. Take him—*now!*"

The anxious driver seized the boy by the arm and swiftly led him toward his car, forcing Jonah to run, lest he be dragged along the pavement.

Father Abram waited on the corner until Jonah and the driver had ducked into the automobile and sped away. Then he went into his office.

"I am Colonel Soluk Kurt." The colonel was sitting in Father Abram's chair behind the desk. It was apparent he had been going through his files.

"Good morning, *Effendi*. How may I help you?"

"Funerals, baptisms, church services, visiting the sick—you're a busy priest, aren't you? How do you make time to recruit—or is it conscription?"

"*Effendi*, I don't understand—"

Kurt raised his hand to silence Father Abram's protestations. "Spare me. How do you want this to proceed? We can have a frank discourse or the usual drivel."

"In my profession," said Father Abram, "we uphold the virtues of truth, honesty, and openness."

Kurt smiled with one lip upturned, making him look even more sinister. "Excellent. I can't say my profession upholds the same virtues, but I, for one, prefer the blunt instruments. OK. Why do you ship our young citizens to that Bible orphanage? Are you aware that they teach them to become agents of subversion against the fatherland?"

"Everything I've done—and to my knowledge, this goes for the teachings of the school in Jerusalem—has been for the betterment of Turkish citizens and in the *service* of Turkey. We take orphans and poor children from the slums of Turkish cities and provide food, shelter, and an education for them."

"Education?" Kurt snapped. "You mean brainwashing. *Incitement.* They are taught subjects we forbid in this country. They march against their fatherland! They commemorate a so-called Armenian genocide."

Father Abram began to sweat. "They're taught history—"

"Teaching *Turkish* history means conforming to *our* standards."

"But it's not Turkish history they're teaching."

"Of course it is! Any mention of Turkey, Turkish leaders, or Turkish lands is part of Turkish history. Mentioning a genocide slanders Turkey, its history, and its leaders. Don't you think that's Turkish history?" Kurt pounded his fist on the desk and rose from his chair, training his steely eyed gaze on Father Abram. "What is being drilled into their young minds? They are indoctrinating these children and raising them to *despise* the fatherland."

Father Abram tried desperately to retain his composure. "That's not possible. These students come back to Turkey and serve in the military. They are loyal citizens."

"Loyal? Joining the PKK is loyalty? Do you call marching in the streets of Jerusalem with banners comparing the Young Turks to Hitler loyalty?"

Father Abram could think of nothing to say in the face of such fury.

Kurt sat back down. As he spoke, a smirk appeared on his lips. "I'll make sure they don't harm the fatherland."

Jonah sensed the anxiety in the whispers coming from behind the closed door.

Following a lengthy discussion with his wife, Father Abram emerged from his bedroom and telephoned Karnig. "Please come over right away. I will send my driver to fetch you."

Karnig, Jonah's fellow matriculant to the Vank and now an ordained priest, was in Istanbul to accompany three new recruits to the seminary.

At the dinner table, the talk was casual at first.

"Do you recall our voyage to Jerusalem?" Father Karnig asked Jonah. "The ship?"

"Very clearly. I still remember that mystic."

"You mean that ghastly recluse," corrected Father Abram. "All ten of you were so young."

The table fell silent, save for the scraping of knives and forks against plates. Father Abram was clearly troubled. The sight of him glumly pushing his food around his plate set Jonah on edge. He imagined the wolves from his nightmares closing in on him. They were hiding behind the couch, the chair, in the closet, waiting to strike.

After dinner, they retired to the living room.

"The colonel from the intelligence agency questioned me about the seminary," Father Abram said bluntly. "He questioned our loyalty to Turkey."

Father Karnig released a deep sigh. "I served in the Turkish military."

"Karnig, I'm not sure when they will take action. You should return to Jerusalem. Very soon." Father Abram turned to Jonah and continued in a deliberate tone. "We can't keep you here, my son. Not in our home and *definitely* not in this country."

"Is my presence putting you at risk?" Jonah asked.

"No, quite the contrary. I am concerned that as they investigate me, they will stumble upon *you*. Confiscating your passport or not renewing it will be the *least* of our problems." He was clearly more worried about Jonah than himself. "The Turks are determined to stop the flow of students to the seminary and send a message to the world that they are dealing with the terrorism issue. They are searching for a scapegoat. They are intent on making an example out of somebody. *Anybody!*"

A long silence followed.

"I wonder who the victim will be," Father Abram sighed. "God have mercy on that poor soul."

God doesn't exist inside a Turkish prison, Jonah thought, remembering the inscription on the front gate at the Gedikpasha Prison.

"We have to find a way to get you out of this country," Father Abram said. "As soon as we can!"

Jonah and Korvat met briefly at the church office the next day.

"I heard you had a close call," Korvat said.

"Father Abram says I should get out of the country as soon as possible."

"He's absolutely right. You should. In fact, that's why I stopped by. I'm leaving for Paris tomorrow. You should do the same."

Jonah didn't respond.

"You can't stay here," Korvat said. "It's far too dangerous."

"How will you manage in Paris?"

"It's taken care of."

"How did you get your visa?"

Korvat looked away. "It was arranged."

Silence followed.

Then Korvat met Jonah's gaze. "You must get out of here. Join me in Paris."

"How will *I* manage in Paris? I have no place to go. No money."

"You just get there and I'll take care of the rest."

"Who's taking care of you?"

"It's arranged. I must go now. Good-bye, my friend. And please, be careful."

With that, Korvat gave him an awkward embrace and left.

CHAPTER 34

At Istanbul's Yesilkoy Airport, Jonah hugged Father Karnig. "Wish you a safe journey."

"I wish I could take you with me."

"Perhaps this way is best."

"Be on your guard."

"Make sure the boys don't babble at passport control," Father Abram cautioned.

Jonah and Father Abram took their leave, lingering a moment to watch Father Karnig and the three new recruits get in line at the security checkpoint.

"Let's go," Father Abram said, when all seemed to be going smoothly.

They returned to the busy airport's passenger-loading zone where the driver had slipped a ten-lira note to a guard, so he could wait by the curbside.

As Jonah and Father Abram hopped into the car, a black sedan with government plates pulled in behind them. A well-dressed man with slicked-back jet-black hair jumped out of the car and raced into the terminal, tailed by two other similarly dressed men.

Jonah pointed to the entrance and frowned. "That man..."

"Who?" Father Abram asked, turning to look in the direction in which the boy was pointing.

"He looked familiar."

"We must leave."

"Stop him!" Colonel Kurt yelled, flashing his secret-service badge as he ran through the security checkpoint.

Police and undercover agents seemed to come out of the walls to converge on the young priest.

Father Karnig and the three terrified boys raised their hands in the air in an attitude of surrender. In a flash, they had been knocked to the floor. The priest went down hard and two agents, their knees crushing his spine, forcibly wrenched his hands behind him and fixed them there with handcuffs.

Jonah arrived early the next morning at Father Abram's office, but the priest was not there to give the boy the day's assignments. Jonah glanced at the morning paper lying open on Father Abram's desk and what he saw on the front page struck terror into his heart.

"Armenian priest arrested for subversive activities," read the headline. Karnig, "the traitor cleric," was pictured being led away in shackles.

Jonah did not bother reading further. He started for the door and ran into Father Abram.

"You better make yourself scarce," the priest said. "Forget work."

"Should I go into hiding?"

"I don't know yet. Go to your father's house and wait for a call from me. Don't come here again."

"What about Karnig?"

"I'll get him a lawyer. There is not much I can do. In fact, the less I am involved, the better for him."

There truly was little the priest could do, but just the same, he had always been there for his boys, and seeing him for the first time like this—powerless and harried—brought a lump to Jonah's throat.

Disillusionment, though, wasn't the primary emotion nagging at him; he had become inured to it. Fear, debilitating and total in its scope, threatened to freeze him in place, to catch him before the authorities could. He concentrated simply on keeping himself on the move. He hurried back to Father Abram's apartment to pack his belongings.

"I'm his lawyer. By law, you must let me see my client."

The guard ignored him.

"You cannot detain the priest without any charges."

"Hey," the irritated guard fired back. "My job is to guard." He ripped the documents from the attorney's hand. "Let me see," he said, throwing a cursory glance at the papers. "It will be some time before you can see the pig."

"But—"

"Come back next week."

"I must—"

"That wasn't a suggestion."

The lawyer left, unsurprised by the reception he had received. He had expected as much, in fact. Nonetheless, he'd felt compelled to try. *They will work him over first.* Despite protests from Amnesty International, human rights lawyers, and antitorture groups from around the world, Turkish prisons continued to use torture as a routine tool of interrogation. The prison at Gedikpasha had honed its craft of "extracting confessions" with terrible efficiency. No one ever came out—if they came out at all—unchanged. The person who had gone in was virtually unrecognizable, physically and mentally, when he emerged. *And if Karnig survives the interrogations, his mind and internal organs will forever bear the wounds.* Forever, with such injuries, would not be for long.

When out in public—in the streets, on trains—Jonah hung his head, averting his face, hoping to remain invisible. Whenever he saw police officers, he turned around or veered off into a side street. When conductors in trains came around to collect tickets, he got off before they could reach him. And when he left a station, he sought exits that circumvented turnstiles and Turkish officials. He ran from moving shadows, slunk against walls, and hid in alleyways. He avoided speaking Turkish in public or any other language, for that matter, which might attract attention to his Armenian accent. *I am a fugitive,* he conceded.

The night terrors Jonah had suffered from in the seminary and following his expulsion tormented him now with greater intensity, Talaat Pasha and other perpetrators of the Armenian genocide slithering their way from the recesses of history into his subconscious. Often, one of his torturers would assume the face of Ataturk, Sevantz, or Kurt. Each time, he would wake up bathed in sweat and weighed down by a sense of impending doom.

The arrest made the front page of every major Turkish newspaper and stayed there for several days. Most headlines incorporated the reviled term "traitor," but one made an even bolder statement: "Nest of Armenian terrorism uncovered at Jerusalem school." The chilling headlines and stories alleged that the St. James Brotherhood and Father Karnig had committed a series of unspeakably vile acts against Ataturk and the state of Turkey. The articles spoke of subversive books, falsification of Turkish history, demonstrations against Turkey, and virulent Armenian nationalism. In short, the seminary was a training ground for terrorism against Turkey, the fatherland.

Two weeks after the arrest, Jonah arrived early at Father Abram's office to discuss their next move. While waiting for the priest, he picked up a copy of the morning's newspaper sitting on the desk. As he read of Father Karnig's purported confessions, he began to shake violently, unable to stop his teeth from chattering.

The priest in question first went to Jerusalem with nine other young boys. Among this group were three brothers who bore the name Ibelin. These brothers were Assyrian, but were converted to the Armenian religion and raised to be terrorists and enemies of the state of Turkey.

The paper dropped from his hands. Jonah quickly grasped the edge of the desk to keep from fainting, the room suddenly swirling around him. As he reached for the paper, he vomited the contents of his stomach onto the floor.

Weak-kneed, he crumpled into the chair. *Three brothers... Ibelin...terrorists and enemies of the state of Turkey...*

He had heard of the methods of torture resorted to. Beatings with metal knuckles and rods. Thick, rigid canes on the back and thin, pliable rods on the soles of the feet. Paddles and blunt instruments for the head and abdomen. Hanging upside down. Stretching. Electrical shock. Waterboarding. Bludgeoning, flogging, whipping. Exposure. Isolation. Pit bulls. Starvation. Mental torture. Rape.

Jonah heaved once again and the force of it propelled him to the floor, where he remained prostrate, his face in the newspaper and his own vomit until he could regain enough strength to gather himself and clean up the mess.

That night, as he slept in his father's home, the persecutors visited Jonah to subject him to especially harsh and protracted methods of torture. He woke up gasping for air.

The lawyer returned to the prison with Father Abram. Despite the warden's initial show of arrogance, he let them in, although they were not allowed into Father Karnig's cell. Instead, he was brought to them in the reception area.

Father Abram was aghast. Karnig looked gaunt, weak, and listless, his eyes downcast and his face wearing a blank expression. The exposed areas of his skin showed large gashes and bruises, while his hands and feet were chained and locked with heavy brackets. He shuffled in, dragging the chains, barely able to walk.

The guards prodded him with their rifles and forced him into a metal chair behind an old, rickety wood table across from the two visitors.

"We have petitioned the Turkish courts for your release," the lawyer said.

Both guards snickered.

Father Abram whispered a prayer. *Only three weeks in prison and already, he looks decades older.*

"We will have you out of here just as fast as we can," the lawyer continued. "They cannot keep you. It is against the law. There is outrage throughout the Western world. Everyone is behind you."

Father Karnig shook his head slightly. Had he smiled? Was that a ray of hope? His lips quivered slightly.

Father Abram leaned over and whispered to him, "Speak, my son."

A tear streamed down his face and disappeared in the gash that had been chiseled into his cheek with an instrument of torture.

Father Abram wiped his own eyes and whispered again, hoping to comfort him, "Karnig, we know you didn't turn anybody in."

The statement seemed to bring the young man alive. He lifted his head and spoke in a hushed, conspiratorial tone. "There was nothing to confess nor anybody to betray. They had already concocted an elaborate plan. As you had warned, they're looking for scapegoats." He stopped to catch his breath. "Get out of this country—as soon as you can. They want you. They want Jonah."

Father Abram shuddered as he recalled Kurt's visit to his office. "It will be over soon," he said. "God is with you."

"I am not expecting God's help. There is no God in here."

In mid-December, the dragnet tightened. Two detectives came to see Jonah's father.

"You are Haiko Ibelin?"

"Yes?"

"Let's go. The colonel wants to see you."

The detectives dragged Haiko into a waiting car and drove him to the MIT offices.

"Where is your son?" demanded Colonel Kurt as soon as Haiko was seated.

"Which son?"

"You peasant scum! Don't you play games with me! Where is Hanna?"

"He left..." Haiko searched for the word. "Almanya. He went to Almanya."

"Almanya? Why?"

"To work."

Kurt was skeptical. He could beat it out of Haiko, but after the international uproar over that scum priest's arrest, things had to be done painstakingly, surreptitiously. It was only a boy he was looking for. He would get him sooner or later.

He aimed his next questions at Haiko. Was he really Armenian? Who had persuaded him to send his children to Jerusalem? What were they teaching in Jerusalem? Did his children express anti-Turkish sentiments? Did they ever mention terrorism or terrorist groups? Was he expecting his children to return and serve in the army? Had he been paid off?

After listening to a string of unsatisfying answers, Kurt dismissed Haiko. "I'll get your *kopek-oghlu-kopek* son!" he said, referring to Jonah as a son of a bitch.

When the boy came home that evening, his father was frantic.

"Son, you have to leave! They will come back. You must leave the country as soon as you can!" Trembling, he hugged Jonah hard.

The boy hurried to Korvat's house, arriving without warning, his small suitcase in hand.

Korvat's mother welcomed him warmly. "You can stay as long as you need to, but my advice to you is to leave this country immediately. Go join my son in Paris."

"How?"

"Find a way. Ask Father Abram. You must not wait. They will find you."

Time was running out. His passport would expire in April, barely four months from now, and a valid passport with at least three months to go was needed in order to obtain a visitor or student visa from any country—if, that is, he could get out at all.

Jonah went back to talk it over with Father Abram.

"Maybe I *should* try Paris. Korvat was able to get a visa and has invited me to stay with him."

"Paris? Hmm."

There was nothing reassuring in Father Abram's reaction. The shepherd himself was lost. How could he protect this endangered sheep of his?

"OK," the priest finally said. "Let me see what I can do. For this, I will need to call the general that helped Azad."

Jonah let his shoulders slump. Was that the best he could do?

Despite pressure from the West, the Turkish prosecutor and judge delayed the public hearing to allow sufficient time for the visible signs of torture inflicted on Father Karnig to heal. Irate that his tactics were coming under scrutiny, Colonel Kurt was now more resolute than ever about carrying on with his mission.

When eventually filed, the charges covered the full spectrum of allegations, ranging from the very serious (terrorism and treason) to the merely illegal (naming a dog Ataturk) to the absurd (insulting the very notion of Turkishness by taking part in a demonstration that commemorated the so-called Armenian genocide).

"No due process," Karnig's lawyer protested. "No merit."

But so much anger and furor had been generated against this "ungrateful, insolent, and treasonous" son of Turkey that no reasonable defense stood a chance. Kurt, the government ministries, the prosecutor, and the judge had decided that Turkish pride and honor needed to be salvaged at all costs. Father Karnig, the perfect scapegoat, would suffer the consequences.

"Slander," the defense argued. "All lies. Baseless charges."

"Did he or did he not march on April 24, 1975?" bellowed the prosecutor.

After a three-day farce of a trial, the verdict was pronounced: guilty. Still young and with his whole future ahead of him, Father Karnig was given a life sentence, with no possibility of parole.

CHAPTER 35

"I greatly appreciate your help in this, General. Without it, I fear this boy would be lost."

"His brother served me well. And I hope these small measures on my part will constitute the first steps of redress on behalf of my country for the injustices it has meted out to your people."

"Thank you," Father Abram said earnestly, clasping the general's hand to express his gratitude. "And I understand this activity exposes us all to grave danger, but none more so than you and your family."

"True," the general agreed solemnly. "If the authorities ever got wind of my involvement, they would hang not only me, but my entire family in the middle of the town square."

"What is your plan to get the boy out of the country?"

"I will take care of his exit from the airport. But he needs a visa for his destination."

"He wishes to go to Paris."

"I can get him a German visa."

"Even better. His sister lives there."

"I will get in touch with my contact in the embassy. Make sure he's the only person you deal with. I don't have to remind you to exercise the utmost caution. Make sure the boy is aware of this too. I hope he is as astute and courageous as his brother."

The German Embassy official stared at the passport for what felt to Jonah like an eternity. He seemed edgy. Uncomfortable. He looked up at the boy briefly, only to return his gaze to the passport.

Finally, he turned to Father Abram and addressed him. "The picture in the passport is of a very young child. I need a second form of ID."

Jonah felt crushed. *Are all government officials the same?* "I have only the passport," the boy mumbled. "The gen—"

"Listen!" the official snapped. "This is already an irregular case involving extraordinary circumstances."

"I understand," Father Abram interjected quickly. "And we appreciate the help. We'll get you another document." The priest put his hand on Jonah's shoulder. "Let's go. We'll find a way."

As they turned and left the embassy, Jonah felt doomed. "I'm not going to get out of here, am I? I will meet Father Karnig's fate."

"We are not defeated yet. He said you just need another form of ID. It is an obstacle. It is a mountain, to be sure, but you need to have faith."

Damn it! A second document that will verify my identity? Jonah knew that a birth certificate was out of the question. None existed. Back home in the village, babies were delivered in stables and without documentation to record the event. Under normal circumstances and through the transforming power of a baksheesh a birth certificate could be magically procured. Under the current circumstances, however, they could not afford to either imperil any of Father Abram's usual contacts or unwittingly reveal Jonah's whereabouts to the MIT.

"I will go to the village," Haiko offered, when he heard of his son's dilemma. "A hefty bribe should be enough to produce a birth certificate."

Father Abram shook his head vigorously. "Too risky. Besides, the successful outcome of your efforts is anything but assured, however tempting the bribe may be."

They worked out an alternative plan to obtain a baptismal certificate.

Jonah took a bus to the patriarchate offices in Kumkapi where he found young children playing in the courtyard. The scene reminded him of the six months his family had spent in the building's basement as new migrants to Istanbul.

Once inside the documentation office, he found the desk of the old, hunched Armenian who maintained the archives; it was located next to the Turkish official's desk, an arrangement that ensured the patriarchate abided by Turkish laws. Nothing was documented and no certificates were issued without the scrutiny and approval of the Turkish official. Consequently, information about actual events disappeared from the records and history was rewritten from a perspective that glorified Turkey. People, incidents, and places were lost in time at the discretion of the appointed official, while obstacles to the issuance of certificates remained so insurmountable that few were ever released.

"Good morning, *Effendi*," Jonah said softly to the Armenian archivist, hoping the Turkish official would not overhear him.

"What can I do for you, young man?" The reply from the old man was kind, but loud enough for the Turkish official to hear without straining his ears. It was clear he thought it wiser to conduct his business out in the open.

"Please, *Effendi*, I need my baptismal certificate to be reissued," Jonah said, still speaking softly and attempting, this time, to conceal his accent.

"Where is the original?" the old man asked.

"I lost it."

"If you give me another form of documentation to support it, I can go search the archives and locate the retained duplicate copy."

"I'm sorry, but I've misplaced *all* my documents," Jonah said without hesitation and according to plan. "I need a duplicate of my baptismal certificate so that I can start the entire process of having my other documents reissued as well."

"Why don't you obtain a birth certificate instead?" the Turkish official asked, jumping into the conversation. He did not seem pleased with Jonah's request.

The first thing that struck the boy was not the Turkish official's overbearing attitude, but the portrait of Ataturk above him. The threatening stare held disapproval and with his probing eyes, the official looked just as ominous. Jonah recalled his visit to the passport office eight years earlier and was, once again, overcome with fear and confusion. The plan was unraveling already.

"I said, you should get a *birth certificate* instead!" the Turk repeated gruffly after getting no response from Jonah.

"That would be very difficult." The moment the words left his lips, the boy realized his mistake. "Um...I am sorry. I meant to say, '*Effendi*.'" It was useless to hide either his fear or his accent at this point.

The Turk arched his left eyebrow. "It seems to me it would be easier than getting a baptismal certificate. And it's more official."

"I can go and look for a copy," the archivist offered in a conciliatory tone.

But before he could leave his desk, the Turkish official stopped him. "*No!*" he barked. "Let me hear *why* it is harder to get the preferred document."

"*Effendi*," Jonah began, pausing to grope for an answer, "for that I would have to travel to Mardin. I don't have anybody back in the village to stay with."

The official shrugged his shoulders, unconvinced by his argument.

Jonah considered his options. Instinct told him that dashing out before being discovered would be the most sensible one, except that he would probably run straight into the hands of the MIT colonel. He thought of another approach. "I would need documents to travel to Mardin. Those areas are dangerous. The Kurdish terrorists are killing travelers and our soldiers."

The hazards on the road to Mardin were well known. The twenty million Kurds in Turkey were agitating for equal rights and with the encouragement and support of Kurdish tribes in Syria, Iran, and Iraq, the fledgling resistance movement was gaining momentum in the contested regions of Diyarbekir and Mardin.

The Turkish official's features hardened. "We will quash them," he snarled. "We will wipe them out." The frown on his face disappeared, replaced by a smirk. "We have done it before," he said in an amused tone. "We know how to do it. And you know how we did it. Right?"

As the Turk, seeing himself in the role of conqueror, reveled in the past in the presence of the vanquished, his stance visibly softened.

The archivist seized the moment and rose without hesitation to his feet—too quickly, in fact, for his advanced years and frail build—and gently asked Jonah to follow him. All the while, he kept his gaze averted from the Turkish official, knowing full well that if he were to ask the man for his opinion, he might still deny him permission to look up the boy's baptismal certificate.

"What is the year of your birth?" the old man asked Jonah as he made his way to a back office, his voice loud enough, once again, for the Turk to overhear.

Jonah gave him the answer.

"Write out your name," the old man requested, once they had reached the back office.

Jonah wrote "Hanna Ibelin" on the piece of paper he had been offered.

Taking the slip from him, the archivist began noisily rummaging through cabinets and drawers.

Jonah started sweating again. *There's no way he'll find any documentation here. I was baptized in the Assyrian church in the village!*

"It must be in the other room," the old man said hurriedly after fumbling through a few cabinets. "Follow me."

Jonah cautiously followed him into a room located farther away and when they were out of sight, he whispered, "You won't be able—"

"Shh!" the archivist said and cupped his hand over the boy's mouth.

He went to a typewriter, inserted a form, and started typing. In one minute flat, he was done. He signed the document, marked it with the patriarchate seal, and folded it. Then he placed it in an envelope, sealed it, and handed it to Jonah.

"I found it!" he said, loud enough to be overheard by the Turkish official. "Don't lose it again."

Jonah could not resist the urge to bend down and kiss the old man's hand.

The archivist gently pushed him away and the boy hurried out without looking at the Turkish official.

Kurt nabbed Houtah as he attempted to board a bus. "Come with me!" the colonel demanded.

Everyone on board looked the other way.

The colonel dragged Houtah into a dark and narrow alley littered with garbage. The foul odor of excrement hung in the air.

"Where are your friends?"

"I…I…"

Kurt slapped the boy hard across the face with the back of his hand before grabbing him by the throat. "Answer my question!"

The colonel was tall and muscular, and his tight grip had his prey struggling for air. Houtah nodded and blinked to indicate submission.

"Where is Hanna Ibelin?" Kurt loosened his hold enough for the boy to answer, but not enough for him to breathe comfortably.

"Please don't hurt me!" Houtah started to sob.

"Shut up! Where is he?"

"Jonah Ibelinian?" Houtah asked, choking as he spoke.

"Tell me before I lose patience! *Where is he?*"

Houtah knew he had no choice. Besides, why should he risk *his* life for an Assyrian? "I heard he's staying at a friend's house."

The grip tightened.

"He's staying with Korvat's mother," Houtah answered, coughing. "I don't have the address."

"Get lost! Remember, I'll be watching you!"

Korvat's mother unbolted the door and opened it only partially, but Colonel Kurt threw his weight against it and knocked her to the floor.

"Where are your son and his friend?" He scowled down at her and then, without waiting for a response, brought his foot down hard between her breasts.

"Get your foot off me!" she demanded, struggling to remove the heavy boot from her chest.

"Whores should have better manners when addressing a gentleman caller!"

"If you're a pimp," she spat, "you have come to the wrong place!"

"Really? Do you think we don't know about you and your oh-so-holy lover? Where are the boys?"

"They're gone."

"I've heard that story before. I didn't believe it then and I don't believe it now."

"It's true. They *have* left."

"OK, *where* did they go?" The colonel began to unbuckle his belt.

She was already frightened, but felt that Jonah was probably at the airport by now. "They took a train to Germany," she said, praying he would believe her.

Kurt studied her carefully, clearly unconvinced. "His father said the same thing, but later, I heard he was with you. Now tell me! Where are they?" He twisted his boot deeper into her chest.

"They went to Germany!" she gasped between coughs, as soon as he had relieved the pressure. "I am confirming what his father reported to you already."

"If you're not telling the truth, I'll be back."

He slammed the door and raced to his car, its tires squealing as he sped away.

On a sunny morning in early January, in front of his father's residence, Jonah paced nervously in the cool air as he waited for Father Abram and the transport to arrive. Since the priest was not scheduled to turn up for another thirty minutes and the traffic on the boulevard named after the assassinated American president was light, Jonah decided to cross the street and take a short walk along the shore. He found the six foot rocky incline from the street level to the water littered with fish washed ashore, dead seagulls, and refuse. He spotted the decomposing carcasses of a cat and a dog wedged between the rocks below.

A little distance away, he climbed on a formation of rocks to a vantage point high above the grime at his feet and gazed far away. The taste of the saltwater in the breeze, the rhythmic lapping of the tranquil waves, and the expansive sea soothed him greatly, and, for a few fleeting moments Jonah felt free of the tight lair of the gray wolves. He wished and hoped that fulfillment of distant promises and dormant dreams lay just beyond the horizon.

After fifteen peaceful minutes on his perch, he headed back. Across from the pick-up location, Jonah paused to look up and down the boulevard before crossing. The road was empty to his left. On the right, he saw a tractor trailer approaching in the distance. He started to cross the road at a leisurely pace before realization dawned that he had misjudged both the distance and the speed of the truck. He quickened his pace and soon found himself dashing madly across the pavement. The truck was only twenty feet away when Jonah finally cleared the highway. As he stepped up onto the walkway, he heard the truck screech to a stop about fifty yards from him. The driver came around the cab and ran straight at Jonah. Was he worried he'd nicked him? The boy felt guilty and thought it best to acknowledge his blunder.

"I'm truly sorry—"

"*Pezeveng herif!*" the truck driver hollered at Jonah, referring to him as a bastard. "Are you trying to kill yourself?"

"I'm sorry. I didn't realize—"

"*Pezeveng herif!*" the driver screamed again, still charging at the boy. "Are you trying to put my neck in the noose?"

He unleashed a withering right hook and Jonah, unprepared for the savagery of the attack, just managed to block it. Then came the left, which Jonah barely blocked with his right arm. But he miscalculated the space between them and the man's forehead landed squarely on the bridge of his nose with a thud.

Before Jonah realized what had happened, the driver turned around and darted away, still cursing.

There was no pain at first, but his upper lip felt warm and wet. He ran inside to wash the blood off and then applied pressure on his nose to stop the bleeding. It wasn't long before he felt the stinging and throbbing pain.

By the time Father Abram had arrived, Jonah's nose had stopped bleeding, but the throbbing had grown worse.

"What happened to your nose?" the kind priest asked.

"Just a parting gift from Turkey," Jonah said without elaborating further.

The priest was far too apprehensive to worry about Jonah's nose. "When we get to the airport," Father Abram said nervously, "please do exactly as I instruct. We have no room for error."

They checked his luggage in at the Lufthansa counter, but to Jonah's surprise, the priest did not take him to the security and passport-control location. Instead, he led him briskly to the end of the terminal where a police officer and a military official were waiting for him.

Father Abram spoke briefly to the military man, after which they exchanged a firm handshake.

Then the priest turned to Jonah and whispered in Armenian, "This man is the general that helped Azad. He's putting his career and perhaps his life on the line for you. Follow him blindly and don't ask any questions. He will lead you to the boarding gate. Once there, do not leave the airline gate area! Make sure you board without attracting attention." He hugged Jonah tightly.

This seemed to be the signal for Father Abram's accomplice. The general, accompanied by the police officer, started walking through the corridor at a rather rapid clip.

Father Abram gestured to Jonah to follow them.

The young boy did not need any convincing. He hurried after the general and did not look back.

Chapter 36

Bavaria, May 1977

They walked on in silence, with Jonah pushing his niece along in a stroller. Ani's daughter, a toddler, squealed in excitement each time they passed a cow grazing by the road. Jonah thought of the village where he had grown up and shook his head in wonderment. This one, in the heart of Germany's Bavaria, couldn't have been more different. Charming brick and stucco homes with lush, overwintering gardens lined the village's paved thoroughfare, interspersed here and there with picturesque little farms, complete with green grass, bales of hay, and wooden water troughs. Plump Bavarian cows with swollen udders lazed beneath the unusually mild spring sun, the bells hanging from their necks ringing in a carefree chorus at the foot of the Alps. The cows were bigger and healthier than the ones back home. The grass was so plentiful, it was like a carpet underfoot and could be lain upon contentedly, with no shepherds standing nearby, watching, guarding.

Jonah remembered the lean cows of his now faraway village. The Mardin animals had always been in a hurry to get somewhere to forage for the scant food available. As a child of five, he had led the only cow his father owned through the dirt streets to join the herd waiting at the edge of the village. From there, cowherds had led the village cows to distant mountains and pastures, where they remained for weeks at a stretch, protected from wolves, other predators, and the most dangerous hunters of them all: gun-toting brigands.

Jonah shuddered as he recalled a childhood scene. One of the village cows had fallen into a deep, wide-mouthed, overflowing watering station. About a dozen men had desperately tried to pull her free by coaxing the exhausted, panicky animal to bite the ropes and branches thrown to her. Nobody had dared jump in to help rescue the frenetic animal. He could still hear its pitiful bellowing as it drowned.

"Aren't they pretty?" Ani stroked her daughter's cheeks fondly.

The baby squealed again and flailed her arms and legs in delight.

"We're an awfully long way from home," Jonah observed.

"Home?" Ani repeated in an amused tone.

"Are you happy here?"

His younger sister smiled as she gazed down at her daughter, but did not answer.

Still in a state of confusion after his escape from Istanbul, Jonah had been staying with his sister and her in-laws since his arrival in Germany. He had told Ani about Archbishop Aminian and his other detractors at the Vank, but had refrained from mentioning the torment of ostracism he had been subjected to there. He had also told her about Father Karnig's imprisonment and the fear and despair that now gripped Armenians in Istanbul. But he was still waiting to hear the story of how she had found her way to this green paradise.

"Tell me how you got here," Jonah said, gesturing at the surrounding countryside. He gave his sister a smile that had little humor in it. "And how you ended up living under the thumb of that tyrant mother-in-law of yours, Mrs. Yazik." He knew a bit about Ani's story, but only the version his father had told him.

"I don't know where to start."

"Start at the beginning."

"OK." She paused thoughtfully. "I was happy in school, but people started talking, claiming I was too old to be still there. They called me 'Papa's little professor' and said it would be scandalous if I didn't marry soon. So Papa pulled me out of school and I was left to fend off Razeh all day."

Jonah grimaced. "She is difficult to take," he said of their stepmother.

"She would watch me constantly and criticize everything I did. Papa would always take my side when we argued, but as soon as he'd left the house, she'd try to find ways to settle the score. I missed school and Burgaz so much! It had been so peaceful there on the island, and the nuns from Austria who ran the school had been so good to me.

"Things got better when Azad came home from the army, but he didn't stay long. He was angry at Papa who kept trying to matchmake on his behalf and send him to Germany with some peasant family's daughter. They argued terribly when Azad told him of his plans to leave for England. Papa declared there was nothing in London but hippies, but Azad was defiant and left anyway. Their last words were bitter."

Jonah let his sister take his place behind the stroller. He was still getting used to the idea of Ani as a mother and at times like this, with her humming softly to herself as she pushed her baby daughter along, she still seemed like his kid sister. But she'd clearly done a lot of growing up in the last few years, even if she still was, like him, hardly a teenager.

"Did Father try to play matchmaker with you too?"

Ani laughed sadly. "That's why I'm here. The family that wanted to marry their daughter off to Azad set their sights on me for their son."

"You?"

"Yes, that was two years ago and I was only twelve at the time. Papa set a ridiculous price for the dowry, assuming they would never agree to it. But they did. I felt like cattle." She slowed her pace long enough to stare at a Holstein a few feet away, just on the other side of a split-rail fence. "And so I married Baruir Yazik."

Jonah's eyes widened. "You mean the same peasant family that wanted to marry their daughter to Azad ended up marrying their son to you?" He frowned bitterly. "Imagine Azad having to tolerate Mrs. Yazik!"

"He wouldn't ever!" Ani said wearily. "Baruir and I were married in an Assyrian church in Istanbul. I cried through the whole ceremony, and even during the reception afterward. But it got worse. The minute I stepped into my mother-in-law's realm, I realized how good things had been with Razeh. Yes, she was a nag, but at least I had Papa to defend me then. Now..." She stared down the road numbly. "Mrs. Yazik dominates everything and everybody. From the moment we left the church after our wedding, she has run our lives. She tells us how to live, what to eat, when to sleep..." She blushed. "Even when to consummate our marriage."

"No!"

"We have no privacy," Ani said, nodding glumly. "Coming to Germany was her plan. We were to join Baruir's sister here, start working, and then send for the rest of the family. The Yaziks bribed officials to have my date of birth falsified on my passport so that I could be taken as a sixteen-year-old. They also lied about Baruir's age and claimed he was nineteen. When we got to Frankfurt, I was so nervous, I forgot every bit of German the nuns had taught me back in school. I tried to explain to the official questioning us that we'd just been married and were on our honeymoon, but no one believed me. They thought we were child laborers. They put us on a plane and sent us straight back to Istanbul.

"Mrs. Yazik, though, was determined. We tried again three weeks later. This time, they tried to make me look older. They made me wear rouge and black eyeliner and big hoop earrings and they put my hair up in a bun. I even had to wear a cheap imitation fur shawl around my shoulders. I looked like a fool—and a Tarlabashi whore. The man behind the counter at the airport in Frankfurt took one look at me and burst out laughing. Then it was the same thing all over again, with the same people interrogating us and then putting us on the first plane back.

"Finally, we took a bus to the Balkans and Austria and tried to enter Germany by that route. But the officials at the border reacted in the same manner and assumed I was a child laborer. So we went to Switzerland to visit Nazeli and Samir."

"Nazeli!" Jonah said excitedly. It had been ages since he'd seen his older sister. Then his expression grew somber as he thought about his fragmented family.

"From Switzerland, we tried again," Ani went on. "We were questioned again at the Swiss-German border. But Nazeli and Samir had proper Swiss documents and were able to convince the border guards that we were all traveling to Germany as tourists. A week after our arrival, Baruir and I applied for asylum. And now...here we are."

Jonah gave his sister a wry smile. "Papa's dream is coming true after all, at least for one of his children."

"*Haraam olsun.* May you choke on that cursed morsel!" the elderly woman reprimanded her young grandchild in a loud, cracked voice.

"Tell him, *Oma*," an older boy said, goading his grandmother.

"You, shut up! Don't give me that '*Oma*' rubbish. One year in Germany and I'm not a *Nene* anymore?"

Ani's in-laws, indeed, the entire Yazik family—parents, children, daughters, sons-in-law, and grandchildren—lived together in a three-bedroom apartment. Ani's living quarters, which she shared with Baruir and the baby, were a closet that barely accommodated their small single bed and the baby's crib. And they were the fortunate ones.

As the guest of honor, Jonah slept in the living room, thus displacing a sub-family of five who were forced to move into the kitchen.

"This is such a stifling environment!" he complained one day to his sister.

He did not feel he had outstayed his welcome. Nor had he become weighed down by guilt for dislodging the know-it-all father of the sub-family. He simply could not tolerate any longer the iron-fisted rule of Mrs. Yazik, who controlled the household and the lives of its members. Not only did she collect the wages of those among them who were employed and assign tasks and chores to those staying home, she even dictated the terms of the relationship her children shared with their spouses. She was feared by everyone, particularly Baruir who, much to Jonah's consternation, believed in absolute obedience and unquestioning loyalty to his mother.

Ani and Jonah escaped the chaos of the house by going for long walks in the countryside that offered them some respite from the perennial clamor and clutter. For Jonah, these walks were a diversion from the terrible memories of his recent past, which still haunted him in his sleep. He also enjoyed the chance of becoming reacquainted with his sister.

"You can't continue living like this," he said during one of their excursions. "You must get out of that house."

"We can't," Ani said glumly. "Baruir is devoted to his mother and has promised to always take care of her."

"The way she lords over everybody," Jonah said bitterly, "she hardly needs looking after." He needed a better approach to persuade his sister to confront her husband and her much-feared mother-in-law. "Do you want to raise your child in this apartment?"

"We have no money to go out and set up on our own."

"If Baruir stopped handing over his salary to his mother, you'd be able to afford a place."

Ani remained silent.

"Use me as the pretext," he persisted. "Say you need your own apartment so I can stay with you. I am sure they don't want me around anyway. I can sense they see me as a troublemaker."

"I agree," she said playfully. "They do think you're one. Aren't you?"

Jonah laughed. "I can't help it!"

Ani giggled and reached up and mussed his hair. "Actually, they want you to stay."

"Why? To make sure you stay in that house?"

"Oh, no! The possibility of us moving out does not even cross their minds." Ani smiled coyly. "They think you would make a good match for their younger daughter."

Jonah stopped in his tracks and stared at her in disbelief.

She nodded to dispel any doubts he might have.

"You should tell them not to get their hopes up," he said harshly. "They should have learned their lesson from Azad. Marry this young? No way!" He quickened his pace. "In any case, I plan to marry an *Armenian* girl, not an *Assyrian!*"

Ani reddened and turned her face away.

Jonah immediately regretted his words. "I'm sorry," he said sheepishly. But it was too late to take back the condescending comment.

"I know," she said sadly. "I know what you mean."

They walked on in silence, with Jonah pushing the stroller now.

"Will you stay?" Ani asked, gazing into the distance, her voice just shy of a whisper. She was clearly missing her family.

"I don't know. *Can* I stay?"

"I will make sure we leave her house, set up on our own. And then, of course, you can stay with us."

"I didn't mean that. Can I stay in this country?"

"Oh, sure. The German government is very hospitable. They allow everybody to stay."

I need to stay, he thought. *I can't go back to Turkey.*

Ani seemed to sense Jonah's apprehensions. "Once somebody manages to enter this country, he stays. Nobody is turned away."

"I don't think it's that simple. Things have changed. The German economy has slowed down. This country is suffering from a high rate of unemployment and doesn't need more *Gastarbeiters.* There's a backlash against foreigners. The skinheads are becoming restless."

"We're Christian; they will keep us. They are already overwhelmed by Muslim Turks in this country."

"Don't be so sure. The actions themselves may be justified in the name of God, but politics always trumps religion."

"I don't agree. We faced no problems when we asked for refugee status. They welcomed us. I believe it was because we were Christians claiming persecution by the Turks."

"I don't think religion had *anything* to do with it. Two years ago, the Germans were still in need of laborers. They welcomed Turks and Kurds just as readily."

Ani shrugged off her brother's cynicism. "We'll move out of her house, get an apartment, and then we'll go and apply for refugee status for you."

Despite his sister's confidence, Jonah resisted for several weeks the temptation of declaring his intentions to the immigration service. He was distrustful of all officials and wary of the consequences of coming out in the open. Would he be extradited? Fear of such a possibility consumed him.

Ani did not relent. "I'm optimistic," she continued to proclaim, day after day.

Finally, Jonah acquiesced. *Do I have an alternative?*

June 1977

The blond, blue-eyed German immigration official leafing through Jonah's passport was as tall as he was forbidding. Finally, he looked up from his inspection. "How did you manage to get a tourist visa?"

"He wanted to be with family," Ani answered in a confident tone.

"Let him speak for himself," the German said curtly. "Clearly, tourism wasn't your goal. You were not eligible for a tourist visa. Did you bribe somebody for the visa?"

"No."

"Why did you come to Germany?"

"I am here to seek asylum."

"Why didn't you inform the German Embassy officials in Istanbul of your intentions?"

"Istanbul?" Jonah shifted in his chair. A sharp pain shot through his temples.

"Yes, Istanbul," the official said and pressed the point home. "Why didn't you ask for asylum when you had the opportunity of doing so?"

"I couldn't," Jonah said hesitantly. Then he added hurriedly, "I couldn't wait indefinitely in Istanbul for a decision on the matter of asylum."

A long pause followed. The man leafed through Jonah's passport again. Then he got up and disappeared into the back office.

Jonah felt his face turn pale. *Is there a list back there? Has Colonel Kurt passed on my name to Interpol? Do they have me listed as a terrorist?* He briefly considered making a run for it, but had no control over his legs. He remained anchored to his chair but instinctively cast a paranoid look around the room in case the menacing photograph of Ataturk materialized through the walls.

Ten long minutes later, the official returned with a grave look on his face. "I'm sorry, but we can't treat your case as an appeal for asylum."

"But...I am an Armenian from Turkey. We are a persecuted—"

"Your sister claimed she was an *Assyrian*."

"My *husband* is Assyrian," Ani explained with tears in her eyes. "That was the reason we applied for asylum under that ethnicity. I, on the other hand, am Armenian, as my brother states."

"It's irrelevant. For us, you are a *Turk*. You were born in Turkey."

"I am Armenian and a Christian. Armenians were subjected to geno—"

"You were born in *Turkey*. You hold a *Turkish* passport. You are a *Turkish* citizen. *You are a Turk*."

Recalling the image of Father Karnig behind prison bars and fearing the same fate, Jonah struggled not to show his despair. *I must avoid deportation to Turkey.* "I am *not* a Turk," he said in protest. "Please, I can't go back..."

The official raised his hand to silence Jonah. "You had every opportunity to declare your status in Istanbul. You sought and were given a tourist visa. Hence, we have to assume you are not persecuted. We cannot consider you a refugee."

He rummaged through a drawer in his desk and pulled out a stamp. He then opened the inkpad and rested the stamp on it, pausing long enough to allow Jonah and Ani one more chance to plead his case.

Fully recognizing the finality of the official's decision, Jonah remained silent. He would debase himself no further.

"Do we have any other options?" an openly tearful Ani asked meekly. "Perhaps a *Gastarbeiter* visa?"

"Not in Germany," the official stated firmly. "There is no justification for him to stay in this country. Your petition is rejected. Asylum status denied. You must leave Germany within thirty days."

He pressed the stamp hard onto the inkpad, opened a page in Jonah's passport, and brought the stamp down with a thud. Satisfying himself that the mark was indelible, he removed the stamp and wrote "*Ausreisepflicht*" below the stamped area.

Expelled.

CHAPTER 37

Beirut, one week later

Civil war ravaged the Mediterranean port city of Beirut, its buildings reduced to skeletons of their former selves, its streets lost under the rubble.

Sipping coffee with Petros Aminian at a beachside tavern, Musa Tchengo pointed to a jeep nearby that was charred black and still smoldering from the latest shelling. "The neighbors are angry again," he quipped.

A mortar exploded a block away, but neither man flinched.

"So they take each other's land," Petros remarked calmly as a Katyusha rocket blasted overhead and landed several hundred yards north on the beach. "In God's name, of course."

"Of course. And to claim title to their land, each side waves a copy of the deed: the Koran, the Old Testament, or the New Testament."

"The holy books all say the same thing: it's God's property; we're just tenants."

Musa smiled weakly. "But most of us will be homeless if this keeps up."

"Perhaps that's God's will."

Five years earlier, Musa Tchengo had arrived in Beirut searching for his comrade in arms. After a long and difficult search, he had found Petros in the city's Armenian ghetto, locating him in a half-ruined hostelry. The joy of discovery had been short-lived.

In April 1975, a senseless spark of hatred had ignited Lebanon's ferocious civil war, with the conflict dividing local warlords, militias, ethnic groups, and religious sects. The Phalange Party and other competing camps of Maronite Christians in Beirut and Mount Lebanon, the Druze in the south, the Shiites and the Hezbollah Party in the slums of Beirut and in the rural areas, the Palestinians in their refugee camps, and the Sunnis all battled over an imaginary green line. The Israelis and the Syrians assisted their respective pawns overtly, while the CIA and the KGB did their bit covertly. The proxies were difficult to tag because of the region's ever-shifting alliances; the bitter enemy of a certain week became a close ally in the next.

Lebanon's sizeable and heavily armed Armenian community had declared neutrality, but there was no escaping the surrounding chaos. The warring factions pressured, demanded, and sometimes cudgeled the Armenians into abandoning their neutrality. The Maronite Christians, in particular, wanted the Armenians to show solidarity with the Lebanese Christians. But the Armenians remained steadfast.

An early casualty of the war was the influential Armenian political circle, which left a power vacuum in its wake. Individuals of dubious origin with ominous missions sprang up to fill the void, and the nascent splinter groups, armed with Western-style populism, vied for the support of Musa and Petros whom they championed to their followers.

"Freedom fighters, *fedayees,* from the most heinous period of our history will inspire us."

"Torchbearers of the *fedayee* legacy."

The two former *fedayees* encouraged each other.

"We can motivate the youth to serve and protect the community," Petros had told Musa one day.

The two men were paraded from one meeting to another, and the reactionary forces emerging around them urged them to make speeches and sing nationalistic and revolutionary songs about the heroes and martyrs of 1915.

At first, Musa and his friend had assumed they were providing a valuable service to the community. "We must be ready. At any moment, the rage of one Lebanese faction or another may be directed against the Armenians."

But the duo slowly began to realize that these blocs had not been formed to restore the Armenians to political power in Lebanon.

"Their ultimate goal is to establish a guerilla movement targeting Turkish interests," Musa Tchengo said one day in disbelief.

"We should try to influence the misguided."

Thus, they had decided to remain engaged.

A pair of Israeli F-4s swooshed overhead in the bright spring sky, the roar of their jet engines trailing them by a full minute as they circumscribed a steep arc over the calm sea.

"More bloodshed," Musa observed.

"It'll just make things worse."

"How long do you think Lebanon will remain a hostage to this violence?"

"It should conform to the Middle East cycle."

"Never-ending, then?"

"Like our struggle for justice and recognition."

Petros took a sip from the thick coffee and sighed. "Defending our lands and people was a lost cause then, and it will be a losing battle for the guerillas today."

"We're caught up in a movement we'll regret," Musa Tchengo said quietly.

"Heroes, *fedayees*, legends," Petros observed with derision. "We're just a tool to facilitate recruitment."

"I never thought these hotheads would exploit us and the memory of the *fedayee* so blatantly." Musa Tchengo, like Petros, was convinced they were ensnared in a clandestine operation. Neither man was comfortable with the gratuitous attention showered on them or with the radical fervor generated.

"You're being kind," Petros countered. "They're opportunists wearing the cloak of nationalism."

Musa drained the last of his coffee. "They're puppets."

"Yes. The KGB and the CIA are funding and training the rival Armenian groups."

"And we're pawns," Musa concluded.

The thunderous engines of the returning F-4s, now bearing less weight, seemed to split the sky open.

Petros glanced askance at the smoldering city. "So are the Lebanese."

Musa nodded and watched as his old friend waged another internal war. On the outside, Petros maintained a calm façade. But on the inside, he fought a never-ending war with the past...

Beirut, November 13, 1938

A fog rolled in from the Mediterranean and descended on the twisting blind alleys of the refugee camp. Standing on the threshold of his shambling house, Petros Aminian watched the mist swallow the ramshackle dwellings. *The past is a fleeting fog,* he reminded himself.

He expanded his chest and widened his nostrils, taking a deep, restorative breath. Then, after straightening the collar of his coat to cover his neck and ears, he put his hands in his pockets and tentatively stepped into the fog.

It was too early to stake out a spot in the queue of southeast Beirut's day laborers. Petros headed for the café instead.

He had hardly sat down beneath a green awning with tattered edges when the proprietor placed his tea and the daily newspaper on the table.

"Why so early today?"

Lost in thought, Petros heard nothing. *I must forget.*

He settled under the dingy canopy and reached for the glass teacup with both hands. The warmth in his palms was soothing. As he took a sip, he absentmindedly scanned the front page of the paper. In the bottom left corner, a photo of a formerly posh storefront, now smashed, caught his attention. *Jewish homes, stores smashed in Berlin*, read the caption.

He put the teacup down hard, spilling some of the contents. After straightening the paper, he read beneath the dateline the foreboding headline: *Nazis arrest Jewish leaders.* Beads of sweat formed on his forehead. His hands shook. With each new line, his heart pounded faster.

The present is the past, he suddenly realized. He would never be able to forget the brutal past: the arrests and executions of the Armenian intelligentsia and elite, the confiscation of property, the conscription and then elimination of able-bodied men, the death marches, the mass slaughters, the eviscerated corpses, the rapes, the orphaned children, and the vultures feasting on the mounds of the dead and unburied. History, including that which had yet to be recorded, would never let him forget.

He dropped the newspaper, lifted his gaze, and glanced nervously around him. But as he stared at the other customers, all preoccupied with their morning routines, he was unable to focus on anything. Nor could he decipher the words escaping from their mouths. He rose to his feet warily and left for home.

It took him only a few minutes to reach his house. He lingered a moment on the front stoop to ensure no one had followed him. He looked up and down the dirt alleyway before pushing his tin door open. Once inside the small, cramped house, he was seized by panic. He pulled down the sheet curtain separating the children's sleeping corner from the one he shared with his wife, trampled over it, and vigorously shook the two little boys from deep slumber.

"Up, up! Climb out!"

His wife rolled over and reached for her husband's coat. "Petros?"

"Damn it! Why is nobody keeping watch?"

He grabbed hold of both of his children, Sevantz and Benjamin, and dragged them off the bed. Sevantz, the younger boy, fell to the ground.

"Petros!" pleaded his wife.

"We must climb out of the ditch. Now!"

"Petros! Please, it's finished!"

"Yes. Yes, the *digging* is finished. Now they will rain dirt on us."

"Petros! Petros! You survived! We're safe now."

"Shh. We must run."

"There are no more ditches. There are no Turkish soldiers or gendarmes to bury us alive in the ditches."

"Turks? Soldiers? Where? You see them coming?" Petros spun around to face the onslaught.

Sevantz was getting up off the floor when his father's flailing arm caught him across the face, sending him tumbling back to the floor.

"Stop! Please, Baba, stop!"

His son's cries shook him out of his frenzied determination and Petros felt his face fall. *They don't understand. The past is never the past.*

He hunched over, dropping his limp arms to his sides, and plunked his numb body down on the bed. *New ditches are being dug. New graves for the living dead.*

Before long, he had slipped into a fitful sleep, transported in his subconscious to the haunting recesses of 1915, replete with the recurring traumatic scenes that fed his nightmares and that he so desperately wanted to erase from his memory.

They were fleeing from that horrific scene of the bonfire of the maidens. He and young Movses tried to dodge bullets and outrun the Turkish gendarmes. However, the boy's injury slowed them down. Movses's shattered bone rendered his left arm useless from the elbow down. It had been several days since he had sustained the bullet wound and in that time, his skin and exposed flesh had gradually turned a putrid greenish black and begun to ooze puss.

It has to be done. Petros pinned Movses down and sat on the boy's left shoulder and chest, straddling his limp arm.

The young boy wanted to be brave, to keep their hideout hidden from the soldiers. Would he give them away? He dug his teeth into his lower lip and cupped his mouth with his right hand to muffle the screams to come, praying he would pass out before he could feel any pain.

Petros applied the tourniquet and then, using the outside curvature of the dagger, began the gruesome operation, slicing through skin, flesh, veins, and arteries. Finally, he hit bone.

The young boy thrashed his legs and kicked his heels against the rocks to dull the pain.

With each arterial pulse, blood spurted from the incision and drenched Petros's hands, arms, clothes, and even his face. The smell of blood mingled with the odor of raw flesh, the festering wound making his stomach turn. He quickened the pace of his sawing. But there was too much blood loss and the soldiers were coming for them.

The arm has to come off! Petros pressed harder.

The boy couldn't control himself anymore and started to howl.

"*Shh!*" Petros stuffed a bloody handkerchief into the boy's mouth.

When he looked down, he noticed the edge of the dagger lodged midway through the bone. *Press harder. Saw faster.*

Finally, the bone snapped clean with a sharp crack.

Petros stopped to catch his breath. Then, with a surgeon's diligence, he finished cutting through the remainder of fleshy muscle and skin fascia. When the separation was complete, he lifted the bloody appendage like a trophy over his head. Blood ran down his arm and splattered his shoulders, but he felt only elation.

Petros let out a triumphant cheer that jerked him awake from his nightmare. He sat upright, soaked in sweat, and completely disoriented.

CHAPTER 38

Bavaria, late June 1977

The town green swarmed with colorfully outfitted young-sters, troupes of dancers in ethnic garb, a few town officials and German residents, and what felt to Jonah like the town's entire immigrant population. Greeks, Italians, Yugoslavs, Kurds, Turks, Assyrians, Pakistanis, and one lone African, among others, were setting up tents and tables on the periphery to display their national wares, while a German brass band provided background music in anticipation of the official opening of the international festival. The mayor was slated to arrive shortly, accompanied by a traditional oompah band in lederhosen and dirndls.

Ani, Baruir, and Jonah stood by the Assyrian tent, trying to plan the next move Jonah should make. He himself remained silent, overwhelmed by his seemingly inescapable destiny in the hands of a Turkish warden. His thirty days were nearly up, after which he would be forced to leave Germany. *I'm finished.*

If Jonah was despondent, Baruir appeared upbeat. "I agree with Azad," he said in an animated voice. "I can drive him to West Berlin today."

Azad had called just days after the German immigration official had denied Jonah asylum status, and had suggested that Ani and Baruir escort his younger brother to West Berlin, where he could live under the official radar with a cousin for as long as needed. For his part, Azad no longer lived in London. After two years there, he had visited a friend in Sweden, quickly fallen in love with the country, and decided to stay on.

Ani shook her head worriedly. "We should call him again. This is a big risk."

"Azad is impetuous," Jonah said, "but he's right in this situation. One thing is certain: if I remain here, I'll be extradited. The police won't be able to find me in West Berlin. I can blend in with the other foreigners and the thousands of illegal aliens."

"How do we manage the border crossings?" an anxious Ani asked.

"As long as the East Germans don't suspect espionage, they wave every West German car through," Baruir said. "We've made this trip many times and never had an issue so far."

West Berlin

As Baruir had predicted, the trip to West Berlin was uneventful. Ani and her husband took their leave and there, in front of his cousin's home, next to the curb, Jonah stood for several seconds to wave good-bye to his sister and brother-in-law.

Finally, after their car had disappeared from view, Jonah turned to Abi, his older cousin, without uttering a word.

Sensing, no doubt, the fear and confusion engulfing Jonah, Abi gave him a big bear hug and gently led him inside. "Just as I took care of you in the village a dozen years ago," he said cheerily, "I will take care of you now."

Jonah had not seen his cousin since leaving the village, where he had called him *abi*, older brother, a nickname that had stuck. Indeed, he had been a big brother to all of the Ibelinian boys.

Abi had received a technical education in Kamishli before moving to West Berlin in 1971, where he had studied further and become a mechanic. Now married and the father of two, he worked as an expert mechanic and taught at a technical school.

Jonah spent the next two weeks with Abi, visiting relatives and family friends all over West Berlin. By the end of their long tour, Jonah couldn't help marveling at how many of his compatriots had ended up in the German city. His father, despite being the first person in the Mardin region to dream about Almanya, remained in Istanbul, while the whole village seemed to have relocated to Germany.

During these leisurely calls, Jonah sat quietly absorbed in his own thoughts, while the men chatted, twirled *tesbiehs*, and smoked unfiltered cigarettes. Elderly matriarchs sat with the men, rarely participating in the discussions, while the young women stayed in the kitchen and served thick, frothy coffee in small demitasse cups or tea in curved glass cups.

"Smile!" Abi finally said one day. "Stop worrying. I'll find a way to keep you in Berlin and you can stay with us."

When a family friend offered to take Jonah along to his summer school class, Abi excitedly slapped his cousin on the back. "I'll keep you here on a student visa!" he declared.

The next day, Abi went to the *gymnasium*, the local high school, and obtained the necessary papers to apply for a student visa. He filled them out the same night and hand-delivered them the next day to the immigration office.

"It will take a month," he said upon his return. It was obvious he could barely contain his excitement. "Don't worry about being sent back to Turkey anymore. You will be safe here."

But Jonah wasn't so sure. *Once they process it, they'll uncover the Ausreisepflicht order.* His nightmares continued unabated.

Jonah had been in West Berlin for two weeks when Azad arrived by train with his Swedish girlfriend Anika and a plan.

"I will not allow it!" Abi said crossly after listening to Azad sketch out his idea. "You were brash in the village and you have not changed at all!"

Azad remained resolute. Sweden was the answer for Jonah.

"It puts both of you in jeopardy." A calm and composed fellow by nature, Abi started to pace restlessly. "It's too risky," he said in an agitated voice. "You will get caught. It is a sure way of being immediately deported to Turkey."

"It's our only option," Azad replied firmly.

"He can wait until we hear from the immigration office on his student visa."

"He'll get turned down," Azad countered.

"We can apply for asylum."

"The rejection of that petition is already on record," Jonah said bluntly.

"It will be safer for him to stay on illegally here in Germany, than to get involved in your mad and dangerous scheme." Abi sat down in frustration. It was obvious Azad was not going to budge. "Your plan will not work."

"It's a solid plan. Anika will be the decoy."

"It is insane. Your passport says you're twenty-five. He couldn't pass for sixteen. It's a dead giveaway!"

"My picture in the passport was taken when I was ten and we look so alike, we can pass for twins."

Desperate now, Abi turned to Jonah. "Are you going along with this madness?"

The boy nodded silently.

They waited two weeks—for Jonah, two agonizingly slow weeks—to put the plan into operation. To kill time, they toured the city's parks and visited friends and relatives, with Azad repeatedly trying to sell his plan to Anika. Jonah did not understand Swedish, but he could tell from Anika's reaction that she was a reluctant collaborator. Her protests were met with calm, but persistent reassurances.

Outwardly, Jonah remained apathetic, but inside, he felt torn between optimism and deep despair. Azad's plan was, if nothing else, an adventure—one that would either lead to freedom or, quite possibly, imprisonment. It was the latter scenario that haunted Jonah who, in his darkest moments, saw Colonel Kurt everywhere he looked: in a peaceful park, in a crowded street, behind the cages at the Berlin Zoo...It was in those moments that capture and incarceration seemed imminent.

But when his future looked its bleakest, Jonah closed his eyes and imagined himself back home in the village, clawing his way to the rooftop to find his mother. The sight of her—still and straight and slender, but steady, draped in a flowing white robe, her long golden locks shimmering beneath the moonlit sky and her blue eyes showing nothing but resolve—sustained him.

A few days before their departure, the dialogue between Azad and Anika changed tone and tenor and Jonah's older brother stopped trying to persuade his girlfriend and started sketching out his plan instead. For Azad, it was clearly a mission, a thrill. Anika, though, seemed to see it more as a looming catastrophe.

CHAPTER 39

Jonah had let his already long hair grow since Azad's arrival, and when the time finally came to execute his older brother's plan, he had begun to look a bit like a hippie. Azad said this new look would help him to pass himself off as a young vagrant gallivanting around with his older Scandinavian girlfriend. Anika, after much pressure, had achieved a similarly disheveled look, although she looked more refined than Jonah, whose already bushy curls were an unruly mess.

Meanwhile, when they reached the train station, an anxious Abi made one more attempt to dissuade Azad and Jonah from going ahead. "Are you sure about this?" he asked anxiously.

Azad's dismissive glance and Jonah's blank stare sealed the debate.

"God help us all," Abi muttered, crossing himself. He handed Jonah the ticket and the passport. "The ticket is to Malmo. You two have your own cabin. Don't leave it. Speak to no one. I mean *no one!* If conductors come by, keep your mouth shut. If immigration officers come by, keep your mouth shut. If they ask you questions, pretend you don't understand. Let the girl answer all questions. It doesn't matter what language they speak; you keep quiet." Abi crossed himself once more and whispered, "I hope your mother is watching over you."

"You'd better mail my passport back," Azad interjected, shaking his finger good-naturedly at Jonah in an apparent attempt to defuse the tension. "And don't have any designs on my girlfriend. Any funny business on your part and I'll send the Turkish police after you." He chuckled. "You're a blacklisted terrorist, remember?"

No one else laughed.

Azad reviewed the instructions in Swedish with Anika one last time, and after they had all exchanged hugs, the two "vagabonds" boarded the train.

As soon as Jonah and Anika had found their cabin, the train pulled away and gradually picked up speed. The two looked out their window and waved to Azad and Abi until they were out of sight.

Without the two of them to give him courage, Jonah shuddered. Alone in a speeding train that was taking him on a journey that would determine his fate, he felt utterly powerless.

As the train roared along at full speed, Jonah sat across from Anika and silently gazed through the window, absorbed in his own turbulent thoughts. Anika did the same. They didn't have much to talk about anyway, Jonah thought, and would hardly have been able to converse, even if they had tried. English was their common language, but Anika's grasp of the language was poor and Jonah's wasn't much better.

Before long, the train slowed down and came to a standstill. From the signs and banners outside their window, it was clear they had arrived at the border checkpoint for East Germany. Nervous tension settled upon the entire train, with even the noisy teenagers from the cabin next door falling silent. The East German officials not only instilled fear in their own citizens, they intimidated even the bold youth from the West.

"*Pasaport!*" The order shot through the passenger-car corridor after a long, uneasy wait. It was followed by the echo of footsteps as the border guard marched from cabin to cabin, demanding passports.

Jonah flinched moments later, when the door to their cabin flew open.

The uniformed guard stretched his arm in their direction and snapped open his hand. "*Pasaport!*" he barked, a disapproving frown on his face.

They quickly handed over their tickets and passports. Jonah felt his stomach lurch when the officer opened his passport and inspected the photograph, his eyes darting from the photo to the boy and back.

During an uncomfortable pause, he studied Jonah's face even more intently before abruptly shutting the passport.

Then, as quickly as he'd come, he left with their passports and stopped at the next cabin. "*Pasaport!*"

That wasn't so bad, Jonah thought. The guard was collecting everybody's passports. Routine procedure, to get them stamped, most likely.

Twenty minutes of eerie silence followed before the same menacing footsteps were heard again. The guard was making his way back down the car, opening and closing each cabin door to return the passports.

When the guard passed their cabin without opening the door, Anika threw Jonah a worried look. It was not an oversight and the guard was not shunning them. He was sending a clear signal.

Jonah felt a searing pain in his stomach, but did his best to keep his fear to himself.

The East German border guard continued on down the car, opening and closing doors. Then there was silence.

After ten long minutes, Jonah heard the guard approaching in his heavy boots. A few seconds later, the door flew open again.

The officer filled the doorway, legs spread, hands clasped behind his back, the rim of his cap pulled down to his eyebrows. After staring them down for a good minute, he tossed Anika's Swedish passport onto her lap. He then opened Azad's Turkish passport containing a Swedish residency permit stamp and alternately studied the photograph and the young boy.

"You!" he said gruffly and pointed at Jonah. "What is your name?"

His brusque manner sent shivers down the boy's spine.

"Answer my question!"

Jonah shook his head and motioned with his hands to indicate he did not understand German. The boy had, in fact, become proficient in the language since his arrival in the country.

The guard turned to Anika and demanded a reply from her.

"*Deutsch nichts. Kein Deutsch.* German no." Then she continued to blabber timidly in Swedish. Jonah did not detect his name or his brother's in her nervous chatter.

"*Name? Name?*" the guard barked. It was clear he didn't appreciate a response in a foreign language. He shifted his attention back to Jonah who shrugged his shoulders helplessly.

"Ibelin?" asked the guard, pointing to the picture in the passport.

Jonah nodded sheepishly and pointed to the passport and then to himself.

The guard stepped into the cabin for a closer look at Jonah, while still holding the passport open at the page where Azad's photograph was affixed. "How old are you?" he asked in German. At another shrug from Jonah, he demanded, "Pull your hair back!"

Jonah feigned an even more puzzled look, but his fear was real.

The exasperated guard proceeded to remove his own cap bearing the proletariat epaulets, put both his palms on his forehead, and pushed his hair back to demonstrate. Then he motioned to Jonah to do the same.

The boy maintained his mystified expression.

The official gestured again.

This time, it was a clear order, and Jonah thought it best not to act too dim-witted. He gathered up his locks and pushed them back to expose his face and forehead.

The East German studied him intently and then returned his gaze to the picture on the passport. After glancing from one to the other a few more times, he indicated to Jonah that he had seen enough.

Jonah dropped his hands.

"How old are you?" the guard demanded.

When the boy didn't answer, the irritated guard turned to Anika and asked her for her companion's age.

She lifted her palms to indicate she did not understand.

The border guard aimed his contempt once again at Jonah. "Do you think we're idiots?" He smoothed his cropped hair and carefully replaced and adjusted his cap. "This is not you," he said with a sneer. "I don't believe you're over fifteen." Without waiting for a response, he turned on his heel and strutted off without returning Jonah's papers.

Arrest and extradition. Jonah fought off dizziness as a parade of frightening images raced through his mind: the gate at the Gedikpasha Prison in Istanbul, with its sign that read: *There is no God inside*; the tortured and emaciated face of Father Karnig, his schoolmate and friend, now locked away for life; and his own hands in handcuffs, as he was being manhandled by Colonel Kurt.

Jonah wasn't sure how long they had waited, but soon, the scowling East German was filling the doorway to the cabin once again. He was muttering to himself and shaking his head in dismay.

"*Scheisse! Idiot!* The stupid captain doesn't want to jeopardize his next promotion." He shook his head in disgust. "*Scheisse!* He says it will be a headache and embroil us in a scandal." He turned to Anika and asked in a more subdued tone, "Is he your friend?"

She shrugged her shoulders in confusion.

The exasperated border guard looked ready to give up, when a twinkle appeared in his eye. He brought his index fingers together, rubbed them, and then with a naughty smile pointed at the youngsters.

Anika smiled and repeated the gesture.

"The idiot may be right," he huffed. "It is not our problem. Let Sweden deal with these dregs." He tossed Jonah's passport at him and lumbered down the car.

When the train finally began to move again, Anika ran to the bathroom. Jonah wasn't sure whether it was to relieve her bladder or her bowels, but she looked awfully pale when she returned. He looked out the window and pretended to be unperturbed, but he could feel his whole body trembling and sweat pouring from his armpits.

Soon, the rhythmic motion of the train clattering along the rails had rocked him to a restless sleep and he was suddenly transported to his childhood, where he found himself sitting next to his sister in the family's wooden tub. His mother hummed a song while she gently and lovingly rubbed them down with her soft hands. Then, to the children's delight and surprise, she undressed and climbed into the warm water, singing all the while.

"Will you pour the water over my head?" she asked Jonah.

He was happy to do so, stroking her smooth white skin as the water ran off her shoulders. Then he ran his hands through her long, blond hair, parting the silky strands as she laughed playfully.

She seemed quite happy at that moment. So was he.

"Hey! Hey!" Anika poked Jonah nervously. "Up! Wake up!"

The train had stopped on the West German side, but no border guards had come through for passport checks.

After a ten-minute stop and complete silence, the train started moving again, and Jonah and Anika breathed a huge sigh of relief. As the train started heading north toward the German-Danish border, drawing closer to their destination, Jonah whispered the Lord's Prayer over and over. Soon, he had lost track of the litany, the lines, the beginning and the ending, and the prayer shrank to an appeal: "Deliver us from evil and Thy will be done." Then, with a degree of misgiving, he reduced it further to a single refrain: "Deliver us from evil."

At the Danish border, a female officer came around to check their documents. The cabins were anything but quiet, especially the neighboring one.

The young men next door, who must have seen Azad's Turkish passport in the officer's hands, called out, "*Schau mal!* Look."

"Turks leaving Germany?"

"Good riddance."

"*Ein Gastarbeiter*, a guest worker for Denmark!"

The German youths laughed lustily.

"*Wunderbar!* You take them in. God knows we have enough."

The Danish officer clearly had no difficulty understanding them and joined in the laughter. She then returned Jonah's passport and Anika's, without commenting on them. The train lurched forward, the sound of its metal wheels screeching against the tracks effectively drowning out the slurs from next door.

Chapter 40

Husqvarna, Sweden, 1978

Olof Palme's voice echoed over the loudspeakers as the candidate for prime minister addressed a full house at Husqvarna Stadium, a medium-sized arena.

"We must not jeopardize this blessed country," he said from the podium. "Its riches, entitlements, enviable living standards…"

The crowd roared and chanted, "Olof! Olof! Olof!"

"And…" He paused for effect. "And we must stand for social justice. Stand for the underdeveloped countries, the poor and the hungry everywhere, the underprivileged, the downtrodden, the persecuted…"

"He's my idol!" Azad yelled to Jonah in between the loud cheers.

"Is he good for the country?" Jonah shouted back.

"Palme is good for the world. If there's one world leader who will recognize the Armenian genocide, it will be *him*." Azad pointed in the direction of the stage and looked at Jonah intently. "He will remain true to his principles. He will not buckle under the pressure of business interests and political expediency."

Jonah was skeptical. "When the time comes, realpolitik will override ideology and morality. It always does."

"Not with Olof Palme!"

Azad was the only Armenian in Husqvarna, but there were many Assyrian immigrants from the Mardin District and even a few families from the village. They had welcomed him into their community and recruited him for the Assyrian soccer team. By the time Jonah arrived, his eldest brother had become fluent again in the boys' childhood language and was deemed a respected member of the Assyrian club. His teammates referred to him as "the Armenian mole," but they were clearly fond of him.

Azad rented a sparsely furnished studio apartment overlooking a park near the center of town. The lone form of decoration on the walls was a painting of Mount Ararat that whisked Jonah back in time whenever he stood before it. He missed his great-uncle dearly.

Azad spent most of his evenings at the home of Anika's parents. They lived in an old Scandinavian farmhouse surrounded by woods and sheep farms, hardly a twenty-minute drive from the city. Jonah usually declined the invitations to join them and sought solitude, instead, at his brother's apartment, silently staring at the ceiling or looking past the images dancing on the television screen. The nightmares had begun to recede and sleep, something he had dreaded before, no longer frightened him.

Azad's fun on the soccer field came to an abrupt end one day when he tore the cartilage in his right knee joint and was forced to undergo an operation.

A few days later, the team's captain approached Jonah and asked him to consider leaving the sidelines and join them. "We need a player," he said, "and we've seen how well you handle the ball."

The boy was hesitant, but his brother immediately warmed to the idea.

"You can replace me," Azad chimed in. "Under my name."

"What if I get injured?" Jonah recalled the deliberate tackles in Jerusalem.

"Won't happen. In any case, you have assumed my identity to tide you over."

"Come on," the captain begged. "We need you."

Jonah became the striker and soon, the team's highest scorer. Playing the game he loved steadily tore him away from his self-imposed seclusion, and he soon found freedom in the bonds of friendship established on the soccer field. After the games, he joined his teammates at the Assyrian club, where they played cards and discussed the four-millennia-old histories of Babylon and Armenia. Their conversations carried on late into the evening and left no stone unturned: the shattered alliances and the wars waged; the common tragedy of genocide suffered at the hands of the Turks; the loss of statehood, land, and homes; dispersion to the four corners of the world; and the cultural and religious ties that still bound the two ancient nations together.

In this country, in this club, on this team, and for the first time in Jonah's life, diversity wasn't an impediment. He didn't have to lead a cloistered existence. He felt safe, as long as he used Azad's name and documents. But his fear of the Turks never left him.

Sweden endured one long winter, interrupted only briefly by its short-lived seasonal changes. The temperament of its people seemed to follow the weather. When temperatures were at their highest or dipped to freezing point, there was a perceptible equanimity to the country and its people, who were serene and aloof when sober, and changeable when inebriated.

As had been the case in Germany, foreigners, even the light-skinned and fair-haired, were clearly distinguishable from the

Swedes. But unlike in Germany, xenophobia never surfaced. As a result, Jonah was able to enjoy freedom and peace for the first time. Yet his illegal status in Sweden served as a constant reminder that his newfound happiness was superficial and temporary. There was no extricating himself from the past—or from Colonel Kurt's grip.

Jonah's cousin Jasmine lived four hours away from Husqvarna and was eager to help. "Come to Sodertalje," she said one day over the phone, insisting they visit her. She wouldn't share her plans with him, but requested that Shabo, a close family friend, accompany them.

Although Jonah was skeptical of whatever it was she had in mind, he agreed to visit her, deciding to take advantage of this opportunity to get to know his cousin better.

"This should be fun," Azad said knowingly. He kept Jonah in suspense by not disclosing what the "fun" might entail.

Jasmine, meanwhile, was excited to see them. "There is no time to waste. I suggest we call on them today."

She insisted Jonah dress up nicely, which piqued his curiosity, and off they went to visit "friends."

With Jasmine providing the directions, they traveled to the home of a hospitable family and there they enjoyed a sumptuous meal.

Jonah, however, couldn't help noticing how he was being treated: like the guest of honor. What was going on? What was behind the secret winks and wide grins coming from Azad?

The women of the house were constantly in and out of the kitchen, insisting on serving bigger helpings, while the father of the family engaged Azad and Shabo in lengthy discussions and debates in Assyrian.

Jonah understood much of the discussion, but was too uncomfortable to participate. During the meal, he noticed a young girl, perhaps fifteen or so, giving him coy looks. She was quite attractive, with pretty brown eyes and an engaging smile, and he couldn't help being flattered by the attention.

After the meal, family and guests retired to the living room where rugs depicting the Last Supper and other religious motifs hung on the walls. Jonah found a seat next to Azad on a sofa. A distinct hush settled over the gathering when the young girl arrived to serve coffee. She offered Jonah a cup, glancing flirtatiously at him once again.

He raised his hand in a gesture to indicate he did not want it, but a frown of disapproval from the father and a nudge from Azad told Jonah that refusing the coffee would offend the host as well as the server.

"Thank you," he said reluctantly, accepting the cup. He wasn't used to the thick, sweet Middle Eastern coffee and sipped it cautiously.

The girl retreated to the kitchen, leaving her father and the guests to contemplate the frothy brew. For a while, only the sounds of slurping and the chink of china, as coffee cups were set down on saucers, could be heard.

Finally, Shabo ceremoniously cleared his throat and said deferentially, "Uncle, I mean this with the utmost respect, but I couldn't help but notice your beautiful and graceful daughter."

Jonah winced and turned to give his cousin a quizzical glance.

But Jasmine, staring down at the coffee cup in her hands and gently swirling its contents around, appeared quite oblivious to the conversation.

"She's the apple of my eye," her father said proudly. "She's very good in school and very helpful at home. She cooks, cleans, and helps her mother."

"My cousin Hanna is an educated man," Shabo said. "He knows English, German, Armenian, Turkish, Arabic, and Hebrew and has already learned Swedish. And although it may not be apparent, he knows Assyrian as well."

Jonah's hands began to shake, causing his cup and saucer to clatter. Shabo glared at him disapprovingly.

Jonah finally put the demitasse cup down. When he looked up, he caught a big grin on Jasmine's face. He turned helplessly to Azad, who was obviously just as amused by the proceedings.

"What are his plans for the future?" the father asked.

"He may continue with his education and become a doctor or start a business with his brother." Shabo paused and then added gravely, "At the moment, he is mulling over the merits of starting a family."

Jonah felt sweat beginning to creep down from his left armpit. His face flushed and his lungs struggled to expand against his constricted rib cage.

"Is he mature enough for marriage?" probed the father.

"Uncle, my cousin is a well-traveled and learned man. He has seen many countries, lived on his own from an early age, and read extensively. He has matured and will value the girl he marries."

"How can I help you?" the father asked, apparently satisfied with all he had heard.

Jonah wanted desperately to bolt from the room. Only his desire to keep from being further embarrassed kept him glued to his seat.

"We thought your daughter, the young lady who served the coffee, would make a very good match for my cousin. We wanted to ask for her hand in marriage, with your blessings."

A silence followed.

The father pondered the proposal as he twirled the worry beads around his fingers. He folded his right leg under his left on the sofa and then stroked his chin pensively. "Your proposal is attractive. But I don't know this young man. I'd like to see him a few more times and also have a chat with my daughter and wife before I give you my word."

The visit lasted another ten minutes, but the conversation was now desultory and subdued.

"What an arrogant SOB!" Shabo seethed, grinding out the words through his teeth. "A complete disaster!"

"I don't agree," Jasmine interjected. "It was a very good first impression."

"Yes. Yes. We should visit again tomorrow," Azad added playfully. "We should give the family a chance to get to know Jonah better."

Jonah wasn't sure what had humiliated him more: the whole incident or the fact that the girl's father had not consented to the proposal there and then.

"We're going back home. *Now!*" he snapped.

Azad had always aspired to be a businessman. With Jonah's encouragement, he borrowed money from Anika's parents and the two brothers purchased a grocery store and converted it into a Mediterranean-style delicatessen. Jonah minded the cash register and the books, while Azad did the purchasing. Not surprisingly, a steady stream of Middle Eastern and East European customers frequented the store. And after a while, even the Swedes began stopping by to try the exotic spices and delicacies. The business thrived.

"Ibelin?"

Jonah was busy arranging the wares on a shelf and didn't immediately respond to the question.

"Ibelin?"

The boy turned around and saw two policemen by the counter. He dropped the container of feta cheese he was holding. It landed on his foot, bounced off it and fell to the floor. But Jonah hardly noticed the stinging pain in his foot; he was too busy gulping air.

"We didn't mean to startle you," one of the officers said. "Is your name Ibelin?"

The policemen's youthful faces looked distressed, rather than stern.

"He isn't...ahem." Jonah swallowed hard. "Yes, how can I help you?"

"Do you know this man?" the other officer asked, unfolding a picture. It was a photograph of a friend from the Assyrian club. Jonah nodded.

"Do you know his girlfriend?"

He nodded.

"She is dead."

"What?"

"She was killed."

"*Javla*. What the devil! Are you...? A murder in Sweden? Not possible!"

"Shocking, isn't it?"

"Not him!"

"He's not a suspect. Why don't you come to the police station tomorrow morning at nine? Perhaps you can shed some light on our investigation."

When Azad came home that evening, he found Jonah sitting in the dark. His packed bag was by the door.

"I need your passport. I'm taking the night train to Paris. Korvat has promised to take care of me."

"Stop your nonsense! They'll arrest the murderer."
"By the time they do, I'll be discovered."

The earth shook as the wolves pounded the dirt behind him, gaining steadily. The little boy ran as fast as his feet would carry him, but still the beasts gained ground. They multiplied and some grew several heads. Then their faces metamorphosed and Jonah saw Colonel Kurt bearing down on him, followed by Ataturk and Talaat Pasha.

The angel of Haiko's tale did not descend from the heavens to vanquish them.

CHAPTER 41

Lebanon, July 1978

Vrej, the newly promoted commander of a clandestine group, the Armenian Liberation Army, drove the two aging *fedayees* to a suburb of Beirut. It wasn't long before they arrived at a walled-off compound in a wooded area, a mile off the main road. At the end of a dirt path, two machine-gun-toting sentries wearing hooded masks appeared from behind the bushes and motioned for the automobile to stop. Recognizing the driver, the guards waved them through after an exchange of passwords.

Vrej drove into a courtyard complex of three buildings and pointed at the one on the left. "This one is our training facility."

Musa and Petros followed him through a tiny side door into the building in the middle, a small warehouse sparsely filled with all manner of weaponry and equipment organized in separate piles, including rocket-propelled grenades, machine guns, hand grenades, pistols, ammunition, camouflage fatigues, and helmets.

These people are serious, Musa thought. *Dead serious.* "If only we'd had these back then," he mused aloud.

Petros chuckled. "Can you imagine what we could have accomplished?"

"Certainly many more of us would have survived."

"Yes. I often think about our comrades who never made it."

"Do you suppose Arkan ever made it? I mean, to America?"

"We'll never know."

"Gentlemen," Vrej interrupted, "this is the seat of the new *fedayee* movement. This is the ALA—the Armenian Liberation Army."

"Where do you get the funds to acquire all these?" Musa asked.

Vrej ignored the question. "We're well trained and well armed. We keep the Armenians of Beirut safe, but more importantly, we have plans beyond Beirut."

"Oh, yes. Seek revenge by assassinating unsuspecting Turkish diplomats."

"Aren't you flattering? The silver-haired fedayee in Santa Barbara is certainly an inspiration. However, we consider that amateurish. That's a headline for one day on the newswires. We plan to aim for much more spectacular targets, more dramatic impact. Noteworthy coverage for a month!"

"It won't bring our martyrs back."

"It is retribution, all the same."

"To what end?"

"The aim is to elevate the genocide to the forum of international discourse."

"I'm afraid it may be to our detriment."

"We disagree. Our actions will stoke the dormant volcano and set a cascade of events in motion that will lead to the recognition and acknowledgment of irrefutable historical facts and pave the way for eventual reparation."

Yes, thought Musa, *this is a very determined group of people.* He shook his head and wondered if they really could accomplish the impossible.

"Let's go to *your* office," Vrej said and led Musa and Petros to a room furnished with two desks.

Musa was the last to enter and paused to take in the Spartan room.

Vrej pointed to a large map of historic Armenia hanging from one wall. "It used to be a sprawling country—from the Caspian to the Black Sea and all the way to the Mediterranean. That's what the ALA will recreate!"

"We all dream that one day, our tiny landlocked country will once again spread its wings from sea to sea," Musa said.

"It's time we acted on that dream." Vrej pounded his fist on the desk closest to him. "The ALA will. As one of its soldiers, I will."

The three stood silently for a moment and studied the map.

Then Vrej looked at his watch. "Duty calls. I must leave now. I have an important mission to organize."

"And just what *is* this mission?" Musa asked.

"I'm not at liberty to discuss it. Make yourselves comfortable here. One of our commanders will brief you on some of our accomplishments and give you an idea of the kind of operations we're planning for the future." He shook hands with them on his way out. "Musa, I think you will be particularly pleased with my new mission!" He winked and was gone.

Jonah entered Korvat's Paris apartment, dropped his luggage on the plush carpet, and stared in amazement at his new surroundings. Large paintings with ornately carved frames hung from the walls and antique furniture, the likes of which could be found only in museums and palaces, decorated the space.

"My mom said you left Istanbul just in time," Korvat said. "Someone must have tipped off the authorities."

Jonah didn't hear him. He was still in awe. "Who owns this place?"

"My father," Korvat replied hurriedly, before changing the subject. "Since they arrested an Azeri illegal alien in connection with that girl's murder, your brother will keep hounding you to return to Sweden."

"If your father is this rich, why did you ever come to Jerusalem?"

Korvat sighed resignedly. "It's complicated."

"I'm sorry. I didn't mean to pry. I'm very grateful to you *and* your father."

"You? Grateful to my father?" Korvat laughed. "If you only knew…"

A long silence followed.

Jonah was confused. It was clear there was much about Korvat he didn't know. But like him, the former bully from the Pigsty Camp seemed preoccupied.

"Listen," Korvat said, "I have joined a secret organization, an offshoot of a well-known Armenian party."

"You love anything that verges on the subversive."

Korvat didn't seem perturbed by the jab. "I've joined a cause," he said passionately, "not some underworld gang. They're entrusting me with a mission. Will you join?"

Jonah sat down in an antique chair, both intrigued and perplexed. The whole situation—the apartment, Korvat's mysterious father, and this clandestine group—had him off balance.

"Jonah," Korvat said, his voice trembling with excitement, "the heroes of our books, songs, and dreams…the *fedayees* are back."

After a weeklong, often heated debate, Jonah felt himself being swayed by his friend's patriotic arguments. One evening, they hailed a taxi to keep a carefully arranged rendezvous, with Korvat giving the address of their destination to the driver.

Twenty minutes later, they got out in front of the New Beirut Restaurant, which stood in a dingy alley in one of those Paris slums teeming with immigrants from Morocco, Algeria and, most recently, Lebanon.

Korvat approached a man standing at the door and whispered something to him. The man showed them inside and pointed to a table where a young man in his late twenties sat, heartily eating a bowl of lentil soup. Korvat motioned to Jonah to follow him and they approached the table.

As soon as he spotted them, the man invited them to join him at his table. They did so, taking seats across from him.

"Hello. My name is Vrej," he said, extending his hand to Jonah. "Hanna? Hanna Ibelin?"

The reference unsettled Jonah. He shot a quick glance at Korvat, who seemed just as surprised as he was.

The man pressed further. "Hanna Ibelin. Your father is Haiko Ibelin. You have family all over the place, it seems. How were you ever admitted to an Armenian seminary? You were expelled because of your Assyrian lineage. You—"

"Hey," Jonah said cautiously, "I don't know who you are. I thought—"

"No, you don't know who I am. But I know who *you* are." Vrej looked at Korvat in disgust. "Is this the best you can do? We have no need for turncoats."

Korvat, who was sitting across from Vrej with a blank look on his face, didn't quite seem to know what to do.

Jonah did. "This is an insult!" he said angrily. "I don't know where you got your information from. I assure you—"

"Answer my question!"

"I don't remember you asking one."

"Are you an Assyrian?"

"No!"

"Your sisters married Assyrians, did they not?"

"As you said, my sisters are married to Assyrians. That doesn't make them or me Assyrian, does it?"

"Your father married an Assyrian as well."

"I didn't come here to defend my nationality," Jonah shot back.

"Our only goal is to defend our nationality!"

"Then why are you questioning mine?"

"Your origins are murky. I want to be sure your commitment is not."

"I am very proud of my—"

"You are desperate. You were written about in the Turkish papers as a terrorist and the MIT is on your heels. You will do anything to get away."

"I'm not desperate. I came to join a cause. To help my people."

"Prove it!"

"You seem to have made up your mind already."

"Then it's true. You *are* Assyrian!"

"No! I am Armenian and a staunch nationalist." Jonah rose from his chair threateningly.

Vrej was noncommittal. "The burden of proof is on your shoulders."

"I don't have to prove anything to anyone!" Jonah shouted.

Vrej remained unmoved.

"It's you who need me." Jonah's tone was less aggressive this time.

"Maybe you didn't hear me earlier," Vrej replied calmly. "Let me repeat myself: I have no use for turncoats of questionable origin."

Jonah grasped the edge of the table, unsure as to whether the maneuver was to prevent himself from lunging at the fellow or to brace himself against a fall. His knees felt weak and his hands trembled.

"Korvat made an error of judgment," Vrej said. "He tried to pass you off as an Armenian. The Turkish newspapers clearly identified you as Assyrian."

Jonah glared at Vrej, his temper rising by the minute. His impulse was to run out of the restaurant, but something the man had said kept him rooted in place. *He knows the MIT are after me.*

"Are you also the son of an Assyrian mother?"

The comment stung and Jonah fought with everything he had to keep from swinging at the man.

"What?" Vrej said, goading him.

"I...I..." Jonah stuttered. "This is unbelievable." He fought to regain his composure, ignoring the tremors in his hands and the beads of sweat dripping from his armpits. "My family has been fighting the Turks and running from their terror for one hundred years. I come from a long line of great Armenians."

Vrej shrugged his shoulders.

"My great-uncle fought with the *fedayees*," Jonah declared, pounding his fist on the table.

"To claim a noble heritage isn't the same as earning it or demonstrating that one is worthy of that legacy," Vrej said in a grave voice. "We are engaged in a struggle for justice. Why would you join our cause?"

"My mother was killed by the Turks—*in front of my eyes!*"

The comment silenced Vrej and left Korvat wide-eyed with incredulity.

"I have more to avenge than any of you!" Jonah said after a long silence.

Vrej rose slowly from his seat and put his hand on the boy's shoulder. "I'm truly sorry," he said softly. "We'll help you exact your revenge."

Korvat breathed a sigh of relief.

"I will persuade the leadership to bring you into the fold," Vrej said, suddenly looking and sounding tired. Perhaps he hadn't enjoyed the inquisition either. "You'll make a good *fedayee*, just like your great-uncle. I will be proud to have you as a partner in our planned mission."

Jonah stared at Vrej intently. He didn't know what he was signing up for, but felt ready for whatever awaited him.

CHAPTER 42

The suburbs of Paris, August 8, 1978

Jonah gazed out of the small Fiat's passenger window, watching the landscape fly by in a blur. Fluffy white clouds on the horizon appeared to chase after them. Could they keep up? It was a question Jonah would answer from a dream, for the hum of the engine and the heat pouring through the window were enough to lull him to sleep, albeit a fitful one.

A cold, refreshing breeze woke him when Vrej rolled down the window.

"We're almost there," Vrej said. "You've been asleep for an hour."

"Can't I ask what the mission is about?"

Korvat pumped his right fist into his left palm. "Revenge!"

"I got that. But how? Are we going to shoot someone from a rooftop?"

Vrej laughed. "That's too quiet an act to match our demand for justice and redress. This will be big. You'll find out shortly."

Jonah quit probing further and his impatience gave way to more reflective thoughts. "Vrej, why did you join the ALA?"

"All the members of my family, in one way or another, have been victimized by the Turks. My ancestors are from Adana. Most of them were slaughtered during the genocide. I grew up with constant reminders of the hateful and heinous crimes committed by the Turks. I want to avenge the brutal murders of my family members and I want justice for my people."

"I feel that way too. But...at what point do we become just like them?"

"Revenge and justice are not synonymous with cold-blooded massacres. We will *never* be like the Turks!"

Confused and apprehensive, Jonah pondered the response silently.

"We're here," Vrej announced, as they drove along a potholed street littered with debris.

Garbage spilled out of bags that had split open on the sidewalks, and scrawny dogs and cats scavenged for tidbits in front of dilapidated homes.

"Where are we?" Jonah asked.

"Our command center," Vrej said casually.

Jonah's heart sank. *Just like Tarlabashi.*

They parked outside a small garage with a pull-up door, the metal siding of which was rusted and covered with mildew and mold. Vrej walked up to the side door, unlocked it, and pushed it aside to reveal a shiny Citroën sitting in the otherwise empty garage.

They followed Vrej through the garage into a small house, where they found two young men sitting at the kitchen table, sipping tea. They rose, greeted Jonah and Korvat with a nod, and then embraced Vrej.

"Punctual, as usual," one of the men said with a nervous smile.

"Let's not waste any time, then. Where is Tavit?"

The man pointed to a trap door leading to the basement. "Downstairs."

Vrej led them down an unlit stairway with wooden stairs that creaked with every step. Jonah ducked under the framed opening, but Korvat, who was following, didn't, and Jonah heard the thump of his head hitting the frame.

They entered a small, cramped room whose sole source of lighting was a single bulb swinging from a wire slung over a beam. The damp room was cluttered with all manner of electronic equipment and paraphernalia scattered haphazardly on old, sagging bookshelves. In the middle of the chaos, a man leaned over an old wooden table.

"This is Tavit. He's our explosives expert, as well as our driver. Tavit, this is Jonah and Korvat. They're the ones we've selected for the Orly project. I want you to fill them in on the details of the device. Tell them how to handle it and whatever else you think they need to know."

A man in his late forties with a receding hairline and a neck scarred with burn marks, Tavit pulled out a suitcase from beneath the table where he was working. He said nothing. Instead, he snapped the two buckles to open the suitcase, which seemed to contain nothing unusual—just a few sweaters, a pair of shoes, a pair of socks, and a tweed suit that reminded Jonah of the one Aghvesian wore.

Tavit gestured to them to approach him.

Jonah did so reluctantly, followed by Korvat.

"There's a latch here." He reached under the clothes and casually pulled out a small leather latch. "Tug gently. The device is in the false bottom."

Jonah and Korvat exchanged glances as they noted a sophisticated measuring device, some wiring, other electronic gear, and a package of what looked like Silly Putty.

"Is that a—"

"Yes. It's the explosive. This device is an altimeter. It's very sensitive—up to a point. It's set to go off at five thousand feet. But I wouldn't drop it if I were you. And whatever you do, don't disconnect the wires. If anyone—and I mean *anyone*—tampers with this device, it *will* explode."

Vrej patted Jonah on the back. "It will be your job to get the bomb onto the plane."

"This isn't a suicide mission, is it?" Jonah asked, trying to hide the tremor in his voice.

"Your assignment is to check the suitcase onto the plane. You're not going to get on it."

Jonah nodded and wiped the sweat off his brow.

Jerusalem, August 11

Mr. Aghvesian spotted her and ran to inform Sevantz, who hurriedly tried to intercept her. But the archbishop was too late.

She stormed into the patriarch's office. "You should be ashamed. I wouldn't put my dog in the hands of the Turks and you...you..."

Caught in the middle of lighting a cigar, the patriarch nearly burned his fingertips. He wasn't sure what shocked him more: seeing her after so many years or being the target of her blunt, belligerent rebuke. "Ms. Paravonian, I didn't know you were coming," he managed to say.

"I am not here on a courtesy call."

"That's rather obvious."

"How can you live with yourself? You have no scruples whatsoever!"

"Is this about Jonah?"

"Yes, it certainly is! And it's also about all the boys this Vank throws to the wolves."

"That is rather harsh."

"Harsh? What is happening is inhuman!"

"What?"

"Karnig."

"Are you holding me responsible for that?"

"No, but if it happens to any of the other boys, you bear sole responsibility."

"I pray every day that it doesn't happen to anyone else."

"It's good of you to pray, but it would be more prudent to protect the children in your care."

"I don't understand."

"Perhaps you don't *want* to understand. You banish Jonah to Turkey. What do you think will happen to him there?"

The patriarch bowed his head and studied the still unlit cigar in his hand.

"Why didn't you send him to me?"

"What? But...Sevantz said you were not interested."

"He said that? He's a liar! The only correspondence I've received from Sevantz was his reassurance that the paperwork for the adoption was in progress."

"Do you think he played the same game with Switzerland?"

"What?"

"Never mind."

"Why did you expel the boy?"

The charming, articulate, ever-confident patriarch, the expert at expression, the poet and famous author waited a moment to compose himself. "I never gave any orders to expel him," he finally replied, his eyes welling up. "He was like a son to me."

"Who did?"

"Sevantz."

"You allowed it."

"Not exactly. No, you are right. I'm responsible. Until I deal with Sevantz, my conscience will not be clear."

"You should be expelling *him*. He has defiled your name, robbed the Vank, and hurt the boys."

The patriarch reached for a matchstick and lit his cigar. After a few puffs, he leveled a determined gaze at the American. "Ms. Paravonian," he said calmly, "I give you my word. Before I die, I'll take care of this matter. I will not leave the Vank to him!"

Sevantz and Aghvesian nervously waited for her outside the patriarch's office, but Nora was in no mood for any of their machinations.

"Excuse mè. I must be on my way." She tried to brush past them, but Sevantz stepped in her way.

"You're very wrong about that boy. He's nothing but trouble. He's just an arrogant, ungrateful peasant."

"*You* are the arrogant, ungrateful peasants," she shot back. "You shame us all!" There was fire in her eyes as she glared at Sevantz.

He retreated and bumped against Aghvesian, who had slunk up behind him.

At the King David Hotel in the New City of Jerusalem, a still-seething Nora threw her clothes on the bed and reached for her suitcase. "Arrogant, ungrateful peasant!" she kept muttering.

The phone rang.

"Front desk," the clerk announced with an accent.

"Yes?"

"Madam, there are two gentlemen in the lobby asking for you."

"Tell them to go away. I have no time for them."

There was a brief pause, during which Nora could hear a muffled discussion.

"Madam, they say they are not here at the behest of the archbishop. It is about the boy you are looking for."

She rushed downstairs to find Father Djift and his inseparable colleague sitting stiffly on the lobby sofa. They rose as she approached.

"Ms. Paravonian," the pretentious priest said, "it is so nice to see you again."

She stared at him skeptically.

"I can help you locate Jonah," he said nonchalantly.

"That's very kind of you."

"Not at all. I know you want to help him." Djift cleared his throat awkwardly. "Even though he's not Armenian."

Nora's back stiffened. "You are all bas...I'm sure *you* can trace your Armenian lineage to the foothills of Ararat—all the way back to Noah!" She turned and stormed off to her room.

In his office, Sevantz was deep in thought and failed to notice Aghvesian's entry. The sneak fidgeted and then, when the archbishop still hadn't noticed him, coughed tentatively.

"Oh, it's you," Sevantz said in a tired voice.

"The patriarch is in a foul mood," Aghvesian stuttered.

"He's going senile," Sevantz said dismissively.

"He was cursing *you!*" Aghvesian dared to say, his voice barely audible, realizing he was on shaky ground.

Sevantz raised his head and squinted at the sly fox.

"May I offer an opinion?"

"Go on, you sleuth."

"How shall I put it..."

"Spit it out."

"It may be best to make oneself scarce for a while," Aghvesian ventured to say.

"What do you mean?"

"The patriarch was proclaiming to the clergy in his office that he will deal with your situation soon. I couldn't hear the whole conversation from my vantage point, but I heard the word *excommunication*."

CHAPTER 43

Lebanon, Tuesday, August 15, early evening

At the ALA compound just outside of Beirut, Musa and Petros sat at their desks in the small office and reviewed documents, including newspaper clippings of bombings and sniper attacks—the work of the ALA—to familiarize themselves with the group's operations. Inside one of the folders marked "Confidential" was a document entitled "Orly Mission." A printout listed Turkish Airlines departure schedules for flights from Orly, Paris, to Yesilkoy, Istanbul. One of the entries was highlighted. The date was set for August 18, three days later.

Musa turned his attention to an outline that accompanied the printout. The blueprint, labeled "Device," was highly technical and included sketches. But it clearly depicted an explosive device—a bomb, set to go off at five thousand feet.

The final document detailed the mission:

1. *Team members: 4.*
2. *The commander, a driver, a lookout/backup, and the bomb carrier/point man.*
3. *Target plane is Turkish Airlines Flight No. 1183, leaving Orly for Istanbul.*
4. *Point man to pass as a Turkish student returning home. He is to check in suitcase containing device at ticket counter and rejoin the group.*

5. *The driver will take group to another terminal where they will board plane to Marseille.*
6. *They are to stay in hiding in Marseille until contacted.*

Next to the document was a diagram of the airport, along with a detailed map of the international terminal. A second page showed an enlarged diagram of the area covering the Turkish Airlines ticket counter, the waiting lounge, and the restrooms nearby. The path from the terminal curbside to the Turkish Airlines ticket counter was highlighted. *A simple plan for maximum damage and impact,* Musa thought.

Also attached was a list of the partisans selected for the operation:

> *Commander: Vrej*
> *Driver: Tavit*
> *Lookout/backup: Korvat*
> *Point man: Jonah*

Musa shook his head. "And Vrej thought I would be proud of this mission."

Petros reached for the file. "Let me see it."

A paper fell out of the folder and Musa picked it up. It was a handwritten note from Vrej to his superior:

> *Dear Comrade AK;*
> *All is clear. Jonah's recruitment was successful. He is a quick study and very enthusiastic. He will be a great point man for the Orly mission. Musa Tchengo will be very proud of his great-nephew following in his footsteps.*
> *Vrej*

Great-nephew? Confused, Musa sat back to reread the note and as he did so, his hand began to tremble. "Let me see the list again."

He read the names aloud. "Jonah? Impossible. How can it be? It must be a mistake."

"What is it?" Petros asked.

Musa crossed himself several times in quick succession. "Good Lord! What have we gotten ourselves into?"

"What?"

"I need to get to Paris."

"Paris?"

"Orly."

"Musa, we're not *fedayees* anymore. I'm sure they can—"

Musa rose from his chair and headed for the door. "I must get there in time!"

Istanbul, Thursday, August 17

Colonel Kurt drummed his fingers on his desk. Then he stood up to pace, but didn't stay long on his feet. He plunked himself back down in his chair and stared at the phone sitting idly on his desk. *How can these imbeciles screw up so badly? They haven't caught even one damned terrorist! How many more assassinations do we have to face before the bureaucrats in Ankara lose confidence in me and the counter-insurgency program?*

"What?" he barked into the speaker when the phone finally rang.

"Colonel! Sir, there is news on one of the terror groups."

"Which one?"

"The ALA."

"Well? Go on."

"There is a perceptible increase in the level of activity in Paris. New recruits, frequent meetings."

"Anything specific?"

"An attack doesn't seem to be imminent. They aren't stalking any of our diplomats."

"You imbecile! Is this all you have to tell me? Why are you wasting my time?"

"Colonel, sir," the man on the other end of the line said hurriedly, "they have two new recruits that may interest you. The Paris apartment you instructed us to keep under occasional surveillance yielded this new data."

"Who are they?"

"Two former Jerusalem boys."

"What?"

"Two—"

"Shut up, you idiot! I heard you. Names? I want the names and every single detail about them."

"One is Korvat."

"It makes sense. Providing shelter for his bastard son."

"Whose son?"

"Never mind. Continue."

"The other one is Hanna—"

"Ibelin!" The colonel leapt from his seat and pumped his fist in the air. "Yes! This will confirm it. Bible orphanage, my ass! I always knew it was a cover. A training ground for the philistines."

"Do you want them snatched? Or we could rub them out."

"Don't be stupid! Just have them watched very closely. If you lose their trail, I need not tell you what will happen to you."

"We will not lose them."

"OK. Pick me up at Orly tomorrow morning at ten thirty."

CHAPTER 44

Friday, August 18, 12:30 p.m.

A Turkish couple sat in the Hotel Paris lobby, waiting for a taxi. Mr. Inonu, a short heavyset man, had dark skin, prominent cheekbones, thick eyebrows, and coarse black hair that had begun to gray. His wife's bleached-blond hair sat oddly with her swarthy complexion.

"Please, stop running around like that, darling!" she pleaded with her four-year-old. "You'll make your father mad."

The blond, blue-eyed boy ignored his mother and kept circling her.

"Stop it!" snapped the father who was seated nearby, next to the suitcases.

The boy sought his mother's arms for protection.

"You don't have to be that snippy," she told her husband. "He's only four."

"Then *you* discipline him! You know I don't like to attract attention to him."

"You're paranoid."

"If discovered, we'll be ruined."

"You mean your *image* will be ruined."

"Shut up!" Almost as though it were a reflex action, his hand rose to strike her. But then he thought better of it and dropped it quickly into his lap, looking around to make sure no one at the front desk had observed his threatening gesture. "You're getting so bold that very soon, you'll start showing me this kind of disrespect in public as well. I knew I shouldn't have brought you along."

His wife turned her head away from him and clutched the boy harder to her chest, hiding her face in his curls to shield her welling eyes from her husband.

In Istanbul, Mr. Inonu was a man of wealth, high standing, and political power. The discovery that he was sterile had been a severe blow to his self-esteem. Fortunately, only his doctors and his wife knew about his problem. When he had "sired" the baby boy, he had felt elevated in the eyes of his family, friends, and constituents. But now he was haunted by an irrational fear that someone would uncover the reality and the callous manner in which the boy had been acquired, and thereby expose his inadequacy. Thus, the boy was kept under constant supervision and away from public places.

This week, however, Mr. Inonu had acquiesced to his wife's demands and, despite his better judgment, taken the family with him to Paris. *Allaha shukur*, thank goodness, it had all passed without incident!

Mr. Inonu was relieved when their ride arrived and they were whisked away to Orly to catch a flight home.

Tavit drove while Vrej, seated in the front passenger seat, recapped once again the logistics of the mission.

Jonah sat next to Korvat and listened attentively, his anxiety rising.

"Tavit," Vrej said, "you'll be dropping us off at three separate locations. We all walk to the second entrance of the terminal in question and Tavit circles the airport a few times and then waits for everyone by the first entrance. Don't attract attention by waiting at the entrance too long, but at the same time, *don't be late for the pickup.* I estimate we'll be out of the terminal at three thirty."

Vrej turned to the back seat and eyed Jonah. "I'll keep the suitcase, your passport, and your ticket until it's time for you to approach the check-in counter. Remember: you're the son of a wealthy Turk. You're a student in Paris. Be polite, but assertive— someone who is used to getting his way."

Jonah felt the color draining from his face.

"You'll give yourself away with that morose look," Vrej warned. "Hey! Cheer up. It's not the end of the world."

Jonah forced a smile, straightened his back, and stuck out his chest. *It will be for the passengers,* he thought.

"You must approach the airline counter with confidence. Once the suitcase is checked in and put on the conveyor belt, take your passport and ticket and leave the counter area calmly, but *immediately.* Go down the hall to the restroom. Do you remember the map?"

Jonah nodded.

"Change into the clothing, hat, and sunglasses that Korvat will stash in the third stall, behind the toilet. You'll stay in the stall until Korvat comes to get you." Vrej turned his attention to Korvat. "Are you clear about where you're supposed to go and when to drop off the disguise outfit?"

Korvat blinked and nodded.

"Then we leave the international terminal," Vrej continued, "and Tavit drives us to the domestic terminal to board a plane for Marseille. During the drive, I will hand you another passport for the domestic flight. We'll board separately. There will be a pickup at the other end."

Jonah felt beads of sweat forming on his forehead.

"Timing is important," Vrej said. "Jonah, don't go to the counter until they announce the last call for boarding the Istanbul flight. There will be a last-minute rush and the officials will be less vigilant. I don't need to remind you to be careful with the suitcase, do I? There's enough Semtex in there to blow the plane apart. Understood?"

Jonah felt his hands begin to shake, but he clasped them together so no one would notice. "Is it going to kill...*everyone?*"

"A midair explosion? Instantly."

"I...I just don't like the idea of killing innocent—"

"Innocent?" Korvat snapped. "There are no innocent Turks!"

Vrej remained calm. "You have to keep your focus on the motive and the reward. Bear in mind our two million martyrs, our occupied homeland, and our destroyed heritage. Remember Musa Tchengo's missing arm. Remember the Turks and how they struck your mother down."

Jonah closed his eyes, terrified. "But these people had nothing to do with my mother's murder!"

"That's where you're wrong, my friend. These passengers have *everything* to do with her murder. They support the fascists in Ankara. They are *all* guilty of the crime. These very Turks, these passengers, wouldn't hesitate to massacre all our people, murder any one of us, at the next opportunity. History has shown that time and time again."

Jonah shifted his gaze from Vrej to Tavit and noticed the driver tightening his grip on the steering wheel. *Is it too late?* he wondered. *Am I committed? Should I jump out of the car?*

"Remember Karnig?" asked Vrej, perhaps sensing Jonah's growing doubt. "Kurt and the Turkish government have targeted you next. Why?"

"Because you are Armenian!" Korvat answered, before Jonah could respond. The irony of Korvat now affirming his heritage didn't attenuate the tension that gripped Jonah.

"What do you think they'll do to you if they capture you?" Vrej said softly.

Korvat placed his hand on Jonah's shoulder and gave him a cold, steely look. "It's time to pay them back for your mother's death, Jonah. *It's time.*"

Jonah nodded and grimaced, trying not to cry. He shut his eyes and remembered sending his mother to collect the farthest desert flower for a wreath, just minutes before the Turks cut her down.

Paris-Orly International Airport, 2:25 p.m.

The cab pulled up to the curbside of the international terminal at Paris-Orly, and Mr. Inonu got out and joined the driver, who was already hurriedly removing the luggage from the trunk.

Mr. Inonu's young wife hoisted the little boy up in her arms and gave him a tight hug. "We'll be home soon, my little one. Then we can go to the park, just you and Mama! OK?"

The boy sniffled and wiped his eyes. His father had just scolded him and slapped him across the face—a warning to ensure good behavior at the airport.

Mr. Inonu, for his part, was impatiently eyeing the growing crowds. They would have to hurry to the counter to check in their bags, he fretted to himself, but at least the child would come in handy for getting them good seats. Then again, all first-class seats were good. He looked forward to returning to Istanbul where he was revered. Here, people were indifferent to him, some even downright disrespectful. Such treatment was disconcerting, *emasculating*.

With his wife and son at his heels, Mr. Inonu started for the terminal, but had to halt abruptly when a young man almost slammed into him as he swung the door open.

"*Pezeveng herif!*" Mr. Inonu cursed through clenched teeth. *Yes,* he thought, *it will be good to get home and away from this Parisian grime.*

About to jump out of the red Citroën, Vrej turned to the anxious driver of the getaway car. "Tavit…"

He didn't have to say more. Tavit nodded to indicate he knew his part.

With that, Vrej got out and hurried to the terminal entrance, accidentally pushing a portly gentleman out of his way as he stepped inside. The man grumbled a bit, but Vrej ignored him.

The three of them met inside the busy concourse where streams of travelers were rushing in every direction: toward baggage claim conveyor belts and departure gates and into the arms of loved ones who had been awaiting their arrival. The public address system broadcasting announcements in multiple languages only added to the confusion.

"There." Vrej nodded toward the Turkish Airlines counter where a handsome young man and an attractive young woman in smart-looking uniforms were busily checking passports and tickets.

"I will be by the lockers to the right of this entrance," Vrej said, turning to Jonah. "I will have neither a view of the counter nor of you. I will hold on to the suitcase, your ticket, and your passport. When it is time, you will come and get them from me. Remember: your name is Turgut Erdogan. Place the luggage on the scale gently. Remain calm. Speak no more than you need to."

Jonah nodded, his gaze fixed on the Turkish Airlines ticket counter.

"Korvat, you take up position another hundred meters away. Jonah, *don't* make a move until it's closer to flight time: between

three ten and three twenty, depending on the length of the queue
at the counter. Any questions?"

Neither boy spoke up.

"OK, then. Let's do it!"

Jonah left without saying a word and positioned himself a
safe distance from the counter. From there, he could see the line
forming in front of the counter, the clock on the far wall, and
a pair of French policemen strolling by, each man wearing the
distinctive de Gaulle cap and swinging his baton casually. Would
he have the courage to implement this audacious plan? Would he
live up to Musa Tchengo's legacy?

He swallowed hard and tried to ignore the acrid taste of fear
in his mouth. He closed his eyes, tried to picture his mother, and
failed. Instead, successive waves of apocalyptic impulses overwhelmed his faculties...

3:10 p.m.

"Do you think he'll go through with it?" Petros asked, as their
taxi slowed to a stop outside the international flights terminal.

"I pray not," Musa said, his one good arm awkwardly reaching across his chest to open the passenger door.

Petros hurriedly handed the cab driver a handful of francs
and the two old men limped inside.

"He should be—"

"I know where he is," Musa said and led the way toward the
Turkish Airlines counter. He was still furious at Vrej for involving his great-nephew in his monstrous plan. His only hope was
to whisk Hanna—Jonah—away, before he could plant the bomb.

"There!" Petros said excitedly.

"I see him," Musa said tersely.

A young man had just picked himself up off the floor and was dusting himself off indignantly. He was twice as tall as Musa remembered him, but he had the same blue eyes and curly blond hair.

As Hanna turned to leave, Musa spotted an older man, a portly Turkish gentleman, standing nearby and glaring at the boy. But Musa had no time to settle whatever dispute had just erupted.

"Hanna!" he hollered to his great-nephew. "Hanna!"

Jonah felt his heart in his throat when he spotted the old man with one arm. Could it be...?

"Hanna!" Musa Tchengo said and hugged his great-nephew with his right arm.

Jonah felt his breath squeezed from him. "Uncle Musa?"

"Let's get you out of here. We have no time."

"But," Jonah stammered, "I have a job—"

"I know," Musa whispered.

Jonah's eyes lit up. "You know?"

"Yes. I can't let you do it. Let's go."

"But my friends..." Jonah looked in the direction of the lockers and then scanned the crowd for Korvat.

"There's no time." Musa seized the boy's arm and pulled him toward the exit.

"We must abort!" Jonah gasped, suddenly realizing the magnitude of what he was about to unleash.

"It's done."

"No. No. No, you *don't* understand! My friends..."

"I know! Petros will warn them. We must get out of here fast! Where is your getaway car?"

"There." Jonah motioned with his head toward the first entrance.

"Let's go!"

Musa and Petros sandwiched Jonah, practically lifting him off the ground as they each grabbed an arm, and took long strides toward the doors.

"You must alert them. Now!" he protested.

3:18 p.m.

"He's gone!" panted Korvat after returning from his hurried reconnaissance of the bathrooms and the area around the check-in counter.

"Where the hell did he go?"

"Should we abort?"

Vrej rubbed his face nervously. "No, we can't," he said, a hint of desperation in his voice. "I have strict orders." He rubbed his face more forcefully this time, as he pondered his options, but stopped when he felt sweat on his fingertips. "Backup plan. It's your game now."

"What?"

"Don't be a coward."

"But—"

"Prove that you are a better man than your father."

"You know about my father?"

Jittery with tension, Vrej ignored the question and rummaged, instead, through his satchel. There was only one passport—the one with Jonah's picture on it. "Where the hell is the one with your photo?"

Korvat drew a sigh of relief, but his relief was short-lived.

"Oh, yes, the suitcase. We put it there to check it through. In case the passport survived the explosion—for the authorities to think it was a suicide mission."

Vrej cracked the latches open and fumbled through the neatly folded stacks of clothing. "Here." He fished out the document and then slammed the lid shut and locked the latches. Neither man noticed the hem of a shirt poking out from under the lid.

"Take the passport and the ticket."

"Have you gone mad? The picture is awful. And the stamp is faded. It will raise suspicion."

"It's your picture. It's a little blurry, that's all."

"I can't—"

"Wait until the very last minute. In fact, wait until the final boarding call. Then run there and apologize profusely for the delay."

"This is madness!"

"I will run to the counter after you. Knowing there are more passengers waiting will pressure them even more. And they'll be careless."

"Are you sure?"

"Go! There is no time to waste."

Korvat frowned deeply. "This should certainly make up for my father's self-serving pursuits," he mumbled.

Vrej sensed he had pushed the right buttons.

Korvat jostled his way to the counter, with Vrej close behind.

"You're late!" snapped the airline representative.

"I...I..." Korvat was trembling.

"Please hurry!" Vrej called from behind Korvat, shifting his weight impatiently from one leg to the other. "I can't miss this flight!"

The agent at the ticket counter mumbled something unintelligible.

"I'm so sorry," Korvat said, his voice barely above a whisper. "I was taken to the wrong terminal."

"Let me have your passport. Put your valise on the scale."

Korvat placed the suitcase gingerly on the scale and handed over the document.

The airline official, though, didn't appear as harried as Vrej had hoped he would be. He studied Korvat and then the photograph in the passport. "Did your dog lick this passport or something? The page is hardly decipherable."

Korvat remained silent.

The agent leaned on his desk and scribbled the seat and departure-gate numbers on the boarding pass. Then he reached for the suitcase to tag it. It was then that he noticed the hem of the shirt sticking out. He stepped back and glanced at the passport photo and then at Korvat once more.

"Could you please hurry up?" Vrej said in an irritated tone.

The agent remained unruffled. He picked up the phone and whispered something into it.

Korvat was shaking noticeably.

"What seems to be the problem?" asked the approaching superior with a French policeman trailing him.

The attendant turned over the passport. "This man's valise should be inspected."

"Let's step aside. What's your name?"

"I may be at the wrong place," Korvat stuttered. He reached for the luggage, but the policeman grabbed him by the arm.

"Let's take a look and see what you have in there," the supervisor said, passing the suitcase to the policeman for inspection.

"The usual problem is hashish entering France from Turkey, not the other way around," the policeman remarked with a chuckle.

The officer grasped the suitcase by its handle, spun around, and with an exaggerated motion of his arm, lifted the suitcase high in the air before slamming it down on a nearby table.

Vrej cupped his ears and ducked, but the only sound he heard was the thump of the suitcase landing on the steel table.

With his back turned to Vrej and Korvat, the policeman snapped the latches open with pliers and began casually sifting through the contents.

3:25 p.m.

Colonel Kurt impatiently fingered his shoulder holster as they took the exit to Orly. His driver was a Paris-based MIT agent and he too was armed. Kurt's men had spotted Jonah and Korvat heading to the airport.

"Can't you get around these damn cars?" Kurt wanted to appear icy calm, but he was boiling inside. *I won't let these punks get away again!*

The large box in the car's central console crackled and Kurt flipped it open and picked up the handle.

It was the advance lookout on the phone. "I saw them skulking near the Turkish Airlines counter."

Kurt slammed the receiver down and turned to the driver. "If you don't step on the gas, I'll blow your brains out!" *Are they planning something against the airline? Am I too late?*

They approached the terminal drop-off area and Kurt spotted the Turkish Airlines sign up ahead. "Honk your horn, dammit! Why doesn't this vehicle have a siren?"

"You said no—"

"Never mind what I said! Just get me there!"

The car pulled to a screeching halt in front of the terminal entrance and Kurt jumped out, inadvertently crashing against two old men flanking a boy. He shoved aside the old man standing in his way and started toward the gate. But as one of the old men said something to the other, Kurt froze in midstride.

That's Armenian. Too much of a coincidence. He spun around to examine the speaker and instantly recognized Musa Tchengo from the Ibelin files he had sifted through so many times. *The one-armed* fedayee! Kurt drew his gun.

Musa had just sent Petros back toward the terminal and turned to say something to Hanna, when he heard his old friend hollering frantically behind him.

"Movses! Get in!"

Musa whirled in time to see Petros hurtling toward a man with slicked-back black hair. The man had a pistol leveled at them, but Petros was obstructing his view and fast closing in.

Musa forced Hanna into the waiting Citroën, just as a shot ricocheted off the roof of the car.

The driver covered his ears. "What the hell is going on?"

Another salvo rang out, followed by three more rounds, and Musa was splattered with bright red blood. He turned and saw Petros drop to his knees and then keel over, face-first, on the concrete.

The driver hit the accelerator, tires squealing, and Musa jumped in, grasped the door handle, and pulled it shut, just as a deafening explosion rocked the terminal, the impact so bone-jarring that it lifted the Citroën off the pavement for a fraction of a moment before they sped away.

Chapter 45

Colonel Kurt was thrown to the ground by the blast as shards of shattered glass and other debris flew in every direction. The concussion he suffered was a minor one, but the ringing in his ears would last for several hours. He got up and scanned the wreckage. *The bastards blew the damn place up!*

"Let's get out of here before the French police arrive!" Kurt yelled at his assistant who was still sitting on the ground with a dazed look on his face. "And get to the car so we can chase the bastards!"

They jumped into their car and took off, only to find the road blocked by crowds of panicking people trying to flee the terminal. Sirens blared in the distance. Kurt could still see the shiny red Citroën not too far ahead of them. He was determined to catch them. But at least half an hour went by before they could finally manage to emerge from the airport's chaotic loading zone. By then, the Citroën was nowhere in sight.

Kurt slammed his fist against the dashboard. "I'll get you!" he screamed. "I'll kill all of you!"

Jonah sat still in the back seat of the Citroën.

"Are you hurt?" Musa reached out and stroked the boy's forehead.

"Korvat. Vrej. The little boy?"

Musa didn't reply, but continued to rub Jonah's face and neck gently.

The boy slowly turned around to look behind them. Smoke and dust hid the terminal entrance from view. Sirens, screams, and confusion reigned supreme. "What happened to them?"

Musa hugged Jonah tightly and the boy began to cry softly, lowering his head onto his great-uncle's shoulder. They sat silently while Tavit skillfully maneuvered the car through the terrified crowd.

When they had finally exited the airport, Tavit turned and asked, "Who was the man shooting at us?"

"I don't know."

"Who are you?"

"I'm this boy's great-uncle. I'm with the ALA from headquarters. What do we do now?"

"I have my orders."

"Obviously, there will be a change in procedure."

"What do you suggest?"

"We must return to Beirut. But how?"

Silence followed. It was obvious Tavit was not pleased.

"No," Musa said as he mulled over their options, "we can't go there. Sweden! Yes, we will go to Sweden. His brother is there and we can hide until this whole affair dies down. Drive straight to Sweden."

"I need to speak to somebody from the command center."

"Sweden! Now!" Musa commanded. "You need to get away just as much as this boy does."

Tavit shook his head, mumbled a few words, and headed for the freeway.

Jonah was sitting silently when it hit him. "Azad's passport! My documents! Tavit, we need to stop by the apartment!"

"There's no time," Musa said emphatically.

"They'll sift through the apartment and find my belongings. I've got to go and remove my stuff. And I need the passport."

Tavit drove to the side of the building and Jonah jumped out and ran inside.

"You have three minutes!" Musa called after him.

No sooner had Jonah gone inside than Tavit slapped the steering wheel in frustration. "Oh, shit!" he said, pointing to a man approaching the building.

"Who is he?" Musa asked in fright.

"The archbishop."

"Who?"

"It's his apartment."

"Damn!" Musa wasn't sure who the man was, but he knew Jonah would need help. "Keep the engine running," he said and took off toward the back of the building.

Excommunication? How dare he!

Sevantz climbed the stairs to his apartment slowly, still obsessing over the patriarch's tirade against him. He reached for his key, but was surprised to see the door to his apartment thrown wide open. He instinctively reached under his robe and pulled out a small-caliber weapon. Hugging the wall, he approached the entrance and cautiously peeked around the corner.

Jonah stuffed his belongings into the small bag, zipped it shut, slung it over his shoulder, and hurried out of the bedroom, closing the door behind him. He scurried through the living room and turned down the hallway to leave.

"What's that?" he wondered aloud and darted back to the living room. *It wasn't there when we left this morning.*

On the coffee table, on a small pedestal sat a chalice.

Jonah picked it up to examine it, stroking the gold carving and the precious stones. "My chalice," he whispered with a smile.

"Put it down!"

Jonah's whole body seemed to lurch out of control in response to the screamed order. He looked up to see a man aiming a small revolver at him.

Jonah stared at the silver glint around the small, dark opening of the pistol and shuddered. He recalled his mother's splayed arms, the blooming dark stain below her breast, and her graceful crumple to the desert floor to join the millions of pieces of bone strewn just below the surface of the sand and rock.

"Put it down!" the man said in a more persuasive tone this time.

Jonah gently lowered the chalice.

"*You?*" the man bellowed in shock. "You!" he repeated in his familiar raspy baritone.

"It can't be!" Jonah stepped back with his hands clasped over his gaping mouth.

"You bastard! What are *you* doing in *my* apartment?"

"You stole my chalice! You're going to sell it, aren't you?"

"Who do you…?" Sevantz waved his revolver at the boy. "You scum, you peasant! You will be my ruination. The seminary's end. The Vank's—"

"*Khatchakogh!*" screeched Jonah, calling Sevantz a thief of the cross, the most insulting Armenian curse that can be aimed at a cleric who pilfers and usurps the belongings and holy relics of the church for personal gain.

"Shut up! You…"

Musa came up behind Sevantz, yanked his arm aside, slapped the firearm away, and pushed the terrified archbishop to the floor. He turned to Jonah. "Let's go."

Jonah remained motionless, staring at the chalice.

"Come on, my boy," Musa said firmly. "Get your bag and let's get out of here."

Jonah gathered his bag and hurried past Sevantz.

"Where is Korvat?" the archbishop stammered.

The question froze Jonah. He stared at Sevantz, unsure of how to respond.

"I said, *where is Korvat?*" Sevantz repeated, this time more boldly.

"Who are you?" Musa demanded.

"I am Archbishop Sevantz Aminian. I am the owner of this—"

"Aminian? Petros Aminian's son?"

A car came to a screeching halt outside.

Musa quickly searched the hallway, seized Jonah by the hand, and ran to the back stairwell. Once downstairs, they cautiously stepped out through the back door. They spotted Tavit nervously tapping the stick shift.

He too spotted them and motioned for them to hurry.

They ran the short distance to the car, with Jonah hopping into the backseat first, but before Musa could follow, a succession of popping sounds rang out. The boy turned in time to see his great-uncle crash against the car door and slump backward onto the pavement.

Tavit put the car in gear and slammed on the accelerator, almost choking the engine. The Citroën lurched forward.

Jonah could see Colonel Soluk Kurt through the back window, taking aim once more.

CHAPTER 46

Husqvarna, Sweden, the next morning

Tavit sat a listless Jonah down on the steps of Azad's apartment building and held him by the shoulders, shaking him vigorously.

Jonah was too numb to respond. Even a gentle slap from the driver elicited no response.

"No use," Tavit muttered. He rang the buzzer and waited just long enough for Azad to answer the call before getting into the Citroën and driving off.

It wasn't until his brother appeared in the entryway that Jonah seemed to stir, although he had no recollection of the immediate past, not even of the journey that had brought him to Azad's doorstep.

Later that night, the two brothers were sitting on the sofa when Azad picked up the newspaper lying on the coffee table, unfolded it, and handed it to Jonah. "Have you seen this?" he asked gently. "It happened at Orly."

"Orly?" Jonah stared at the newspaper impassively for a moment, trying to cling to the cloak of amnesia protecting him. But it was no use. The plan, the boy, the sight of his great-uncle crumbling to the pavement—it all came back to him in one sickening flash. He bowed his head and covered his face with his hands.

"Everybody's talking about it."

The cover page prominently displayed a picture of the shattered terminal entrance—or what was left of it—a soot-blackened wall with a cavernous fissure with jagged edges running down the middle. Jonah tentatively reached for the newspaper.

Bomb explodes at Orly. Six dead and a dozen injured. Terrorism suspected.

A bomb set up to detonate on a plane destined for Istanbul exploded prematurely at Paris-Orly International Airport. The target was Turkish Airlines Flight 1183, scheduled to leave for Istanbul on Friday at 3:45 p.m.

The bomb, which exploded near the Turkish Airlines ticket counter, killed two of the airline's agents, a French security guard, a passenger, and a suspected terrorist. The body of a second suspect, allegedly shot dead by an unknown assailant, was discovered outside the terminal.

No group has claimed responsibility, but officials, pointing to the recent wave of assassinations of Turkish diplomats, suspect the involvement of an Armenian terror group. French and Turkish security forces have launched an intensive investigation.

Reuters News Service, Paris

Jonah pointed to the paper. He opened his mouth to tell his brother he had been there, but couldn't speak.

Azad placed his hand on Jonah's shoulder. "What is it?"

Jonah started to shake uncontrollably and buried his face in the newspaper.

"There's nothing you can do about it now," Azad offered in a consoling voice. "It's all in the past."

It's not! Jonah thought. *It's still with me. Now and forever. And I'll never speak of it. If I do, that'll signal the end. Of the Vank, the students, Father Abram, my family, my own life—everything.*

Two weeks after his return, Jonah declared resolutely, "I'm going to apply for Swedish residency status."

"Once they see the German stamp in your passport, you'll be doomed." This time, it was Azad who was not willing to take the risk.

"We don't have to show them my passport. We don't have to tell them the truth. In fact, we should make up a story as fantastic as one of Father's tales."

They met with a social services employee first. That ensured, at the very least, a record as a political refugee without a country or nationality and a process that precluded immediate deportation.

"What is your name?" the social worker asked, once they were all seated in her office.

Jonah hesitated. The simplest of questions and he had not given it a thought. "David," he said tentatively. "Yes. David Danielian. That's my adoptive name."

Azad flinched, but Jonah remained composed and focused intently on the social worker.

"Date of birth?"

He hadn't thought of that question either. "June 14, 1960."

Azad was clearly puzzled, but said nothing until they had left the social services office. "Where did you conjure up those names from?" he asked excitedly.

"The Bible."

"Interesting. You are starting a new chapter by falling back on a very old book." Azad looked at Jonah quizzically. "And the date of birth?"

"My number in the seminary."

Jonah was assigned a translator to accompany him to the immigration office. He didn't need one, but gladly accepted the service. *The man could be a buffer during the interview,* he thought, *and perhaps a resource.*

The translator, an immigrant from Greece and a recent Jehovah's Witness convert, proselytized on the way to the immigration office.

Jonah listened politely, but his mind was on what he was about to tell the immigration officer. He crossed himself before entering.

"Please give me the details of your case," the man behind the desk said.

With precision and great clarity, Jonah explained to him that his parents had given him up for adoption at an early age to relatives in Lebanon. His adoptive parents, in turn, had shielded him from the dangers of the Lebanese civil war by sending him to an Armenian boarding school in Cyprus. Unfortunately, his adoptive parents had perished when a stray rocket landed on their house in the middle of the night. He had always kept in touch with his birth family and, with nowhere to turn, had decided to join his older brother Azad. He had bribed the captain of a fishing boat in Cyprus to take him to Greece. From there, he had boarded a train, bound for Sweden, as a stowaway.

The officer, clearly intrigued by the tale, took copious notes. At the end of the interview, he stamped a few documents and handed one to Jonah. "Temporary papers. You cannot become a burden on the state. Every Friday, you must report to the police station to register your whereabouts until the central office comes to a decision on your application. Otherwise, you are free to live like the rest of us."

In spite of his many years of seminary life, his religious upbringing, and the strong contempt he felt for anyone unable to tell the truth and face the consequences, Jonah left the government building with his head held high. Had the circumstances been different, he would have hurried to the nearest church and lighted a candle to ask for forgiveness. But today, he felt no guilt, for telling the truth was akin to asking for extradition to Turkey where the Gedikpasha Prison, the hellhole that had swallowed Father Karnig, awaited him.

Chapter 47

Husqvarna, Sweden

Jonah and Azad met her at the Husqvarna Airport. In the five years since Jonah had last seen her, the blond American had not changed. She was still the youthful, vivacious, and confident woman he remembered. Jonah could still picture her in the courtyard of his school in Jerusalem.

Nora gazed at him tenderly, as if she could probe straight into his heart and see all that he had endured.

"Thank you for visiting us," he said gratefully. "This must be quite an inconvenient detour from your business."

"My business takes me to the Far East twice a year," Nora explained. "Once I am done with my professional commitments, I take a few weeks off to travel around the world. This is my first visit to Husqvarna."

The brothers drove her around the city and showed her their grocery store.

"To buy and manage a successful business at your age is truly commendable," she observed. "I like your confidence and your determination."

They had dinner at the apartment, with Azad cooking chicken and pasta. He talked about the Swedish prime minister, Olof Palme, while Jonah asked about New York. It was clear to him that Ms. Nora had come on a mission. The American was here to see for herself whether he could live up to the hopes she nurtured for him.

"I can't stay in Sweden for more than a few days," she said abruptly and then broached the matter they all wanted to discuss. "Do you still aspire to become a doctor?"

Jonah's eyes widened and his heart skipped a few beats. "Yes," he replied trying not to betray his excitement. "It is still my dream."

"You clearly will not accomplish it if you stay in Europe. America is the land of opportunity. Are you willing to come to America and work hard to make your dream come true?"

Jonah knew this was his moment. His heartbeat quickened, moisture accumulated above his upper lip, and sweat beads formed in his armpits. In a quivering voice that belied the strength of his determination, he articulated the thoughts he had secretly harbored inside him for many, many years: "I want to come to America and I am ready to work very hard to achieve my goals."

Ms. Nora leaned back in her chair with a smile of deep satisfaction. "All right, then. Tomorrow we will go to Stockholm and visit the American Embassy."

Jonah was willing to allow Mardin to become a quixotic reminiscence, Jerusalem an ambivalent experience, Germany a byway, Paris a riddle, Sweden a fleeting refuge, and Istanbul and its perils an episode in his life that he needed to permanently efface from his memory—but he was not yet ready to discard his faith in the future, America.

"I will drive you there," Azad said protectively.

"We can fly," Nora offered. "You have the store to worry about."

"Are you sure you want to fly?" asked Jonah. He thought of Orly.

🍎 🍎 🍎

They did fly to Stockholm the next day. And despite his initial trepidation, Jonah enjoyed the flight and the aerial view from the window. That evening, seated in a cave-like basement restaurant, one of the city's finest eateries, the American quizzed Jonah about the recent past.

"Sevantz, Aghvesian, and one unscrupulous priest accuse you of arrogance," Nora informed him.

Jonah desperately wanted to go to America and did not want to jeopardize his future by dredging up the past. So he remained silent.

"They claim you betrayed the Vank," she continued, "that you're not Armenian."

"Do you believe them?" an offended Jonah asked.

"Before my arrival here, I went to Jerusalem and Istanbul. I spoke to the patriarch, Father Abram, and to your own father. I did confirm your Armenian roots."

Jonah sat back in his chair and held his head high.

"In any case," she continued, "your ethnicity is irrelevant. I want to help a fellow human being."

"Thank you."

"I feel you should know that the patriarch wept when I spoke to him about you. He never intended to have you expelled. He truly loved you."

It was comforting to hear it. "Why does he keep Sevantz?"

"He promised me that he would take care of that situation. He said he wouldn't leave the Vank in Sevantz's hands."

Would he do it in time to save the students and the Vank? Jonah wondered. He thought about his chalice, which, in his hurry to flee, he'd left behind at Sevantz's apartment in Paris.

"I want you to know that the patriarch was not the only one who asked me to take care of you. Mrs. Shakarian and practically all your teachers, along with the priests, told me that you were a very good, smart boy and that I should do my best to help you. Sevantz, Aghvesian, and their disciples are a minority. I told the patriarch I wouldn't rest until the rotten apple was cast off."

Sevantz has met his match, Jonah thought, feeling vindicated.

He slept soundly that night and for the first time in years, felt liberated from the fear that had haunted him since his ostracism at the Vank.

The next day, when they reached the main gate of the American Embassy, Nora removed from her handbag a large Armenian cross with a long chain and put it on, letting it dangle from her neck for all to see. "I wear it for these occasions."

"Is it to get divine help?" Jonah asked.

"No, for that purpose, it's enough to keep it in my handbag. I'm wearing it now to impress the consul."

"What if he's not religious?"

"America, the realm and the notion, *is* a religion."

They asked to see the vice-consul. These were special circumstances and they had a specific request.

A middle-aged man ushered them into an office and introduced himself as Mr. Hasker. He was a pleasant, considerate man, unlike the arrogant government officials Jonah was used to dealing with.

Nora had already confided to Jonah about her plan, which was to make a case for refugee status. She would argue that the boy was a political fugitive from Turkey.

She began with the Armenian genocide, moved on to Turkey's enduring state-sponsored persecution of minorities, especially Armenians, and finally reminded the vice-consul of the unlawful incarceration of Father Karnig and the brutal torture he had been subjected to.

As a dramatic finale to her account, she implored Mr. Hasker to save an innocent young boy from mortal danger.

"How can I help?"

"We can rescue him if you help me take him to America."

"I want to help, but political protection is out of the question."

"Why?"

"Ms. Paravonian, despite our government's condemnation of human rights abuse anywhere, we have to be particularly careful about not alienating a close ally."

"In this case, the close ally has committed genocide, Mr. Hasker."

"It's not part of official American policy to acknowledge the atrocities committed against Armenians during that era of Turkish history."

"Mr. Hasker, it was nothing short of genocide. And it's not simply history; it's a reality that must be faced every day by the survivors, like my father and their descendants."

"Yes, it was, indeed, the first genocide of the century. However, the fact remains that Turkey is a close ally." Mr. Hasker paused to make sure the gravity of his observation had sunk in. "Our government would not accept claims of Turkish persecution as a basis for asylum." He sounded embarrassed by his own assertion.

"Are you telling me, sir, that our government will not protect an innocent child from certain death?" Nora was indignant. "Are we willing to sacrifice our values and principles because *Turkey is an ally?*"

Nora's defiant tone in the presence of a government official shocked Jonah. How could she dare speak so freely and boldly to this figure of authority?

"My dear lady," the vice-consul replied, "I'm simply trying to make you aware of *official* policy."

"It's a seriously flawed policy if it conspires to deny a genocide and seal the fate of an innocent descendant of the victims. As a citizen, I will not hesitate to uphold the values of my country, even if its government betrays them for the sake of placating Turkey," Nora said proudly. "I am determined to save this young man. I will take him with me to New York. I will adopt him."

"I must caution you that the adoption process is very complex and takes years to complete."

Nora's plans seemed to be leading nowhere. Once again, Jonah began to experience that all-too-familiar sinking feeling. He expected Mr. Hasker to rise and usher them out in his polite, diplomatic manner, but the vice-consul remained seated and did not appear in a hurry to dismiss them.

"What would be your advice in this matter?" Nora asked in a more conciliatory tone.

The question brought a rare smile to Mr. Hasker's face. "My recommendation would be for the boy to apply for a student visa," he said in an undertone. "Once he's in America, you can pursue other options."

They both thanked him profusely.

As they were about to leave, Hasker added, "He needs a passport valid for at least six months to enable me to issue the student visa. Regulations, you know."

They walked out of the embassy with Nora smiling buoyantly.

Jonah tried hard to conceal the sense of devastation that overwhelmed him and didn't utter a word. What was there to say? A valid passport, with the date of expiry at least six months away, was a condition that he simply could not meet. His Turkish passport had expired.

"I will send a telegram to my father to handle the school documents," Nora said excitedly.

They went to the hotel concierge and Nora dictated:

> *To: Arkan Paravonian*
> *Dad. For student visa, boy needs school acceptance papers.*
> *Please mail him necessary documents.*
> *Nora*

Clearly satisfied with her work, she gave Jonah a peck on the cheek. "He'll mail you the package."

Jonah forced a grateful smile, but he knew better. He wanted to explain to her that her efforts were in vain, but he neither wanted to dampen her spirits nor shut this door of opportunity. *Am I doomed to spend my life on the run, with neither home to look forward to nor roots to return to, or will I, for a change, find a way out?*

Dejected, Jonah returned to Husqvarna the next day.

"It's not meant to be," he told Azad.

They considered phoning Father Abram for assistance, but ruled it out as far too dangerous. Now under constant surveillance, the priest had been taken in for questioning thrice already, following the Orly bombing, and his passport had been confiscated.

Just when they were deciding to drop the quest, the unimaginable occurred. A miracle. A package arrived in the mail from the Swedish Immigration Office. Inside was his approved application for permanent residency, complete with a temporary Swedish passport.

At last, he was rid of the Turkish yoke.

It was time for Jonah to make a covenant with his future. The discussion with Azad was brief.

"I'll always be grateful to Sweden," he told his brother, "and it will always be here for me. But the land of opportunity beckons."

The school acceptance forms from Mr. Arkan Paravonian arrived a couple of weeks later, and Jonah went to Stockholm on his own. With a sense of great pride, untrammeled by fear, he handed his Swedish document and the school-enrollment papers to the clerk and asked to see Mr. Hasker.

CHAPTER 48

Yesilkoy District, Istanbul

Colonel Kurt was lost in thought as he drove down the rural road on the way to the airport. If the tip from one of his many sources was reliable, Hanna Ibelin was now in Sweden.

In his obsession to arrest or eliminate the young terrorist, as he called him, Kurt had put his career on the line. An international incident would surely have threatened his standing in the MIT, and the French police had almost caught up with him following the shooting of the one-armed *gavour*. But he was still on the boy's trail and would not rest until he had returned him to Turkish soil where the law would make an example of him.

Kurt spotted five pure white doves gliding gracefully up ahead and watched as they landed softly on the shoulder of the road. He pressed on the accelerator, unable to resist the temptation As he bore down on them, he was surprised to see the doves stay put. Were they oblivious to the imminent danger? Did they assume they were safe on the side of the road?

At the split second the car was to pass the unsuspecting doves, Kurt veered slightly but decisively to the right and onto the shoulder, catching the birds off guard. The tires plowed through the flock.

Kurt felt the crushing of their fragile bones. He skidded to a halt and peered through the rearview mirror. A plume of feathers as white as snowflakes floated, as if suspended in midair. The collision had tossed the birds several feet up in the air. For a fraction of a second, their necks dangled, their wings flapping frenziedly. Finally, their bodies flopped down on the grass near the edge of the road. The doves continued to flutter and convulse briefly before becoming still.

The obscene act pleased Kurt. It was a sign, a portent of things to come.

Then he saw it in the rearview mirror. By the road, a lone dove, with its neck cocked high, jerked its head from side to side.

"Damn it!" Kurt banged his fist against the steering wheel so hard, it hurt. "I'll get you! I'll not rest until I get you!"

He threw the car in reverse and slammed his foot on the pedal, the tires spinning as the vehicle careened backward.

The white dove stretched its neck, thrust its chest forward, and homed in on the oncoming car. And before Kurt could reach it, the creature had spread its wings and soared into the boundless sky.

It was not easy leaving Azad, who had been Jonah's big brother, protector, father, friend, and partner since early childhood. There were times the two brothers clashed; yet through it all, they had remained close.

"I'll come and visit," Azad promised in an upbeat voice that sounded a little forced. "Remember how I ended up in Sweden? Don't be surprised if I show up in America—without warning."

Jonah walked in a leisurely manner toward the gangway to board the small commuter plane that would take him

to Copenhagen for the SAS flight to New York's Kennedy
Airport.

"Stop him!" a man's raspy voice shouted in English.

Jonah turned to see Colonel Kurt, his black hair still slicked
back like his hero's, his eyes still sparkling with intensity. He and
an associate were scuffling with a Swedish police officer trying to
block their path.

"Stop him! He is a *terrorist!*"

The word rang out in the small terminal, and several officers
and agents hastened to the scene with handguns drawn.

Jonah waited for the pop to end his life. *It's time to join my
mother and great-uncle.*

The security team surrounded him and Azad, and another
ring formed around Kurt and his subordinate.

"What's going on here?" asked one of the officers.

Kurt produced a document and handed it to the officer. "I'm
with the Turkish secret service. This boy is a fugitive from the law.
He's wanted by the Turkish police."

"*Pasaport!*" an officer demanded in a stern voice.

Kurt smiled broadly as he stared down Jonah.

His hands shaking, Jonah gave the officer the still-shiny light-
blue Swedish document of permanent residency.

"This Swedish document is authentic and valid," the officer
said calmly after examining it. He returned it to Jonah. "You can
go."

"What?" Kurt exploded. "He can't go anywhere! I demand
you arrest—"

"You have no authority here. You can't demand anything."

"Hanna Ibelin is a Turkish citizen. He is a fugitive. He is
suspected of complicity in a terrorist plot!"

The officer motioned for Jonah to hand him the document
again. "What name did you say?" he asked Kurt.

"Hanna Ibelin."

The stoic Swedish officer examined the document again, this time more carefully. He shrugged, handed it back to Jonah, and turned to Kurt. "You've made a mistake. His name is David Danielian. He's a Lebanese citizen."

"That's a lie!" Kurt growled.

"A Swedish document doesn't lie."

"He is a terrorist!"

"You have the wrong person."

"Damn it! I know who I have and I'm not letting him go!"

"He carries an official Swedish document. We respect laws in this country."

"Then we'll do it my way!" Kurt reached for his gun. But before he could pull it free, the guards had grasped both his arms and pinned him against the wall.

"Run!" Azad whispered in Armenian and shoved Jonah in the direction of the waiting plane.

Suddenly dizzy, the boy took a few tentative steps backward, certain that Kurt would riddle his body with bullets if he turned his back on him.

"Run!"

The second command galvanized Jonah into action. He picked up his bag and ran to the plane as fast as his wobbly legs could carry him.

"*No!*" Kurt called after him. "*Gavour pezeveng!* Infidel bastard!"

Jonah ran crosswise through the strong stream of air created by the jet's whirling propellers and bounded up the aircraft's ladder, waving the boarding pass high above his head.

Once inside the plane, he hurried to his seat, his heart pounding in his throat and his hands shaking violently as he gulped air in shallow breaths. He was frantic, terrified, yet elated by the promise of things to come. He felt giddy. *Is it possible. . .?* He was afraid to complete the thought.

The engine revved and the plane lurched forward. It raced down the runway with increasing velocity and rose skyward, leaving the earth behind.

For the first time in years, Jonah felt himself poised on the threshold of life.

ABOUT THE AUTHOR

John D. Balian, MD is a graduate of Columbia University and Tufts University School of Medicine. Dr. Balian currently works as a senior executive for a U.S.-based global corporation. Though his writing has been widely published in trade journals, *Gray Wolves and White Doves* is his first novel.

READING GROUP GUIDE

1. What are the distinctive features about the characters, setting, and plot of this book?

2. To what extent does Jonah's story remind you of yourself or someone you know or is this story unique to him?

3. How do characters change or evolve throughout the course of the story? What events trigger such changes? Can you relate to the characters' predicaments?

4. Is the mother irresponsible by straying away from the path and the group? Is the father's spirit broken? Does he fall victim to his own tales and delusions?

5. Why does Jonah seem to be guilt-ridden and what factors contribute to his guilt?

6. What do you think is the source of Sevantz's and Nersotz's hatred toward Jonah?

7. Why do you think the author chose the title *Gray Wolves and White Doves?*

8. What is the meaning (in Armenian, Turkish, or English) of the names of some of the characters? Could they be veiled

references to a character's role in the story, the author's own relationships and experiences as a youth, or Biblical figures or events?

9. What scenes are reminiscent of the New Testament or other Biblical events?

10. Why are photographs so significant to this story – the complete absence in certain cases, the predominance in some, and inferences in yet other scenes?

11. Why is the Armenian Genocide referred to as the "forgotten genocide"?

12. Who stated, "Who now remembers the extermination of the Armenians," and in what context?

13. What are the common elements of the first genocide of the 20th century, the holocaust, and the last genocide of the 20th century?

14. The Book "The Forty Days of Musa Dagh" is a 1933 novel by Austrian-Jewish author Franz Werfel based on the valiant self-defense at a mountain top (Musa Dagh—Mountain of Moses) by a small community of seven Armenian villages against the deportation orders of the Ottoman Empire in 1915 during the height of the Armenian Genocide. What is this rebellion's connection to Masada? Is the author trying to put the history of the genocide in context of "history repeating itself"? Is it an age-old problem that he is trying to help modern-day readers understand?

15. How do survivors of a national calamity such as genocide and victims of ethnic cleansing pick up the pieces, move on, and reconnect with their kin and re-enter human society? How do they overcome the all-consuming sense of shame and survivor's guilt? Should they succumb to the enticing notions of assimilation into the nationalities and peoples of their new host countries?

16. How do empires and dominant ethnicities/races/nations justify their sense of entitlement to the belongings (and in fact to the actual lives) of the weaker and docile subjects that are different than their own?

17. Throughout the Ottoman history the ruling Turkish tribes, governments, pashas, and sultans appropriated not only properties but also levied a "head tax" — took children from their non-Turkic subjects such as Armenians, Greeks, Assyrians, etc., at a young age and indoctrinated them to become Muslim Turks. Some were enlisted into the infamous and powerful Janissary ranks (private armies of the Sultan). Also, it is well documented that during the genocide, more than two hundred thousand young Armenian women and children were enslaved into Turkish and Kurdish homes as servants or concubines. Is the kidnapping of the aunt and later the half-brother a reference to the head tax and the stolen children during the genocide?

18. Why has the term "Young Turks" been distorted in the American lexicon from a genocidal, barbaric notion to one that is glorified as agents of change, especially in the context of sports, business, and politics?

19. Do you think the events of September 11, 2001 influenced how the author shaped the story?

20. The history of the Middle East is interwoven with persecution of many diverse ethnic groups. Early in the book Hanna (later Jonah) was told he should pretend to be Assyrian and not Armenian, then to hide all identities, yet later he is asked to affirm his Armenian heritage and hide his Assyrian upbringing, and ironically at one point in Europe when he claims to be an Armenian the official states categorically that it is irrelevant since his nationality is Turkish. Do you think the author is trying to help the reader understand the various levels of discrimination, bigotry and hatred that exist between various groups of people today and/or is he highlighting that bigotry is prevalent and indolent among all peoples, ready to be released at an opportune moment and against anybody?

21. Is the survival impulse in humans so powerful that even a young boy at a tender age is able to instinctively navigate through the Byzantine quagmires he faces?

22. This is a story of overcoming adversity. Do you think the author is attempting to illustrate the importance of adults helping young people coming from disadvantaged circumstances to realize their true potential?

23. A disclaimer in the book says that while the story is based on actual events, any similarity to real persons is coincidental. Is this story a recounting of the author's own early life experiences? How much of the book is historical and how much is autobiographical? Where does fact end and fiction begin?

24. What do you think is the author's main intent of writing this book? Is it simply a coming of age story, or do you think he additionally wants to educate readers about the consequences of policies of denial: pernicious bigotry, perils of revisionist history, cultural genocide, etc.?

25. Is this story an artifact or are its main themes a persisting challenge to powerful nations and people in authority positions? How has reading this book changed your opinion of human behavior or lead you to a new understanding or awareness of history and some aspect of your country, community, family, and your own life?

GRAY WOLVES AND WHITE DOVES
Reviews From Amazon.com

"**Inspiring for ages 8 to 80.** There are many books that we read, and forget. John Balian's Gray Wolves and White Doves is a book that remains etched in the minds and hearts of readers...read by my mother who is close to 80, husband, and other friends and family members...(we) were deeply moved and inspired with the turn of each page. After reading the book, our hearts yearn for a sequel which would continue to inspire readers like us. I would strongly encourage kids from 8 onwards to read this book in order to feel blessed about what is provided to them in life and how to make the best of every moment."
                          - Shobana, Prashanth and Mom Visweswaran

"Very intriguing and filled with great stories....This book was a great read and I would recommend it."
                          - Jade Brown - Age 11

"...An inspirational read...leaves you awestruck."
                          - Margaret Mary Seitter

"Gripping, page-turning novel that tugs at the hearts....I am looking forward to the movie premiere!"
                          - Anne Nguyen

"The author brilliantly creates all the scenes and the emotions of the characters...I consumed this novel!"

- John Loffredo

"This inspirational book is well-paced and quickly grabs hold of the reader - I read the final 300 pages in one sitting as I could not put it down...tie(s) all of the different threads together into the stunning conclusion."

- Jon Spector

"A captivating adventure story...increases the appreciation of the freedom and protection which we enjoy in the United States."

- Eric Lanzieri

"A heartwarming tale of a boy's struggle...filled with unsuspected plot twists and memorable characters. This beautifully told story...will hold your attention to the end."

- James Chen – Age 12

"One of the best books I have read!"

- Julie Thomas

"...(The) vivid writing style kept me entertained and guessing throughout...as if I was right there with the story's many intriguing characters."

- Sunil Kapadia

"A richness and depth that you will rarely find....BRILLIANT book!"

- Stuart Henderson

"Amazing, Inspiring Story a Must Read.... This book is for every person who "thought" they had a difficult childhood."

- Lory Greene

"I need a sequel!!!! The writing is so vivid I felt I was watching an epic movie. I didn't want this beautifully written and powerful story to end."

- Timothy Burnash

"I truly felt a part of the story and Jonah's journey....(An) uplifting ending. As a mom of three, I am always looking for books that provide an escape from my hectic life. I really looked forward to reading this book each evening and highly recommend it!!"

- Jennifer Pluciennik Healy

"Unbelievable, a truly incredible inspiring story of what can be accomplished when you never give up hope and faith...kept me on the edge of my seat."

- Scott Malatesta

"Compelling and bittersweet...left me breathless! When the threads of this exciting adventure are pulled together an amazing tapestry of intrigue, raw human emotion and drama is suddenly revealed! The pace is quick and the subject matter brilliantly filtered through the innocent and bewildered eyes of a growing boy who does not feel he truly belongs anywhere. The writing style is so unique I look forward to more books from this author!"

- Mary McGuire

"What sets this book apart is its "heart". And this gives the book a special power that makes reading it a real experience…. Hugely entertaining, strongly memorable, and highly educational…nothing short of a gem."

- Geoffrey Levitt

"John Balian's account…through the eyes of a young boy is descriptive, emotional, and inspiring."

- Linda Ducay

"This book is a tremendous drama/adventure. I haven't visited such locations as Armenia and Jerusalem but the author brings you there and makes it feel so real….The vivid descriptions, the sights and smells evoke visceral reactions. Every book has to end, but this one left me wanting to know more about the next phase…I hope this author doesn't stop at 1 novel."

- Brian Stewart

"Utterly enthralling page turner, Balian paces the story beautifully, lacing it with wit, compassion and even at the darkest moments, a ray of hope. This is a surprising and heartrending novel about…fight for survival. This is truly an unforgettable character that is ambitious, fearful and at the same time fearless. Brilliant job!!"

- Maria Bush

"A Must Read, "Gray Wolves and White Doves" is an adventure with suspense and intrigue taking the reader through an amazing and unexpected journey….I found myself experiencing sincere emotions throughout the book as I empathized with the characters, felt sadness in dire circumstances, laughed during the lighter moments, and felt uplifted when the main character experienced a long-awaited break. This is an excellent story with tremendous depth and substance."

- Chris Roberti

"John D. Balian has hit this one out of the park."

- Kris Fletcher

"...A riveting tale of adventure and discovery that is germane to any time, culture and age."

- Doina Lavoie-Gonci

Made in United States
North Haven, CT
03 September 2022